DESIRÉE

WHERE MEN TOOK WHAT THEY WANTED WITHOUT ASKING . . .

She was trembling like some fragile orchid in a high wind, tossed about like a flower before the hurricane. He kissed her brutally hard, her lips stung with the fury of his anger. He bent her neck back until she thought it would break. His hard body was pressed all down her slim length. He kissed her again, a long kiss, which went on and on, until she was limp and fragile and shaking in his grasp.

ISLAND OF DESIRE

A searing novel of wild, breathless innocence, heartless passion for power, and a love that binds beyond time.

Island of Desire

Janet Louise Roberts

BALLANTINE BOOKS • NEW YORK

 Published in the United States by Ballantine Books, a division of Random House, Inc., New York, and simultaneously in Canada by Ballantine Books of Canada, Ltd., Toronto, Canada.

Library of Congress Catalog Card Number: 77-1083

ISBN 0-345-25408-2

Manufactured in the United States of America

First Edition: October 1977

TO MARCY RUDO,

whose encouragement and enthusiasm helped create this novel

ISLAND OF DESIRE

Chapter 1

Silva floated on her back in the blue translucent waters of the lagoon. She liked best the early morning for swimming, when the pale pink of the eastern sky glimmered over the cream-colored sands. Usually her troubles seemed to float away like the soap bubbles from her golden tanned body.

Her twin, Tyrone, had been gone again all night. Maria Luisa said he had gone to Miami with the rumrunners. Silva frowned slightly, turned over and dived under the surface to scan the sandy bottom for shells, but she could not cleanse the worry from her thoughts.

Tyrone would get in bad trouble, Maria Luisa had said, and the old wisewoman was usually right. Even the toughest, most skeptical native would turn to her for help. On this beautiful Caribbean island of Desirée, Maria Luisa was the acknowledged and respected queen of voodoo. She had taught Silva the songs and dances, the natures of the all-powerful gods, and how to pray for curses and blessings.

Up on the green hills where mahogany and breadfruit trees, cedar and royal poincianas were tangled together with vines of bougainvillea, a horseman drew up to survey the half-moon bay. The pink-silvered lagoon seemed to have his attention. Silva saw him, ducked under the water in alarm. Then, as the horse started down through the thick foliage, she swam wildly to shore.

Once on the sand, she grabbed her flowered cotton

shift, yanked it down over her wet body to conceal the naked curves. She was kneeling on the white sand, wringing out her long straight silver-blonde hair, as the horse trotted out of the undergrowth into the light.

Silva gazed up at the man as he slid down from the powerful black stallion, drew the reins over the horse's head, then strode toward her. A warning chill went down her spine. No one else was so tall, so arrogant with his jet-black hair and steel-blue eyes. Brian Cameron had returned from his three-year absence.

She slid her sandals on, tied them carefully as he came up to her. Three feet from her he stopped, booted feet planted in the sand as though he had every right to be there. She glanced up, green eyes narrowed and shimmering through her pale brown lashes.

She was just in time to reach up, automatically, and catch the flower he threw at her with a gleam of a smile softening his bronzed face. It was a green orchid. She rose gracefully, looking at the flower.

"Silva Armitage," said the deep, well-remembered voice. "You're grown up, child. Still the same silver hair. I would have thought it would darken!"

"Why?" she asked bluntly.

His expression turned cynical. She could see him clearly now, in the sunlight. His mouth seemed carved into lines of disillusionment, the hard lines beside his lips deeper. "It does for most women, unless they turn to a bottle for aid. Never mind, don't puzzle your brow over it. Come and sit down. It has been a long time."

She sat down obediently, curling her bare legs under her. He lounged down at her side, still gazing at her, his blue eyes squinting against the rising sun.

"Seen Rodrigues Estavez this morning?" he asked.

She blinked. "No. Not for two days."

"He was supposed to meet me at dawn, to look over the sugar cane." He shrugged. "Lazy as usual, I suppose."

"He has worked hard for you these years, Mr. Cameron!" Silva fired. "Why should you care? You have not bothered to return in three years. He has done all the overseeing. Now you complain because he is late for an appointment with you! When did you return, last night?"

He laughed. "Still the spitfire! Put the flower behind your ear, little one. What does a slim wood nymph know of work in the cane fields?"

"I see things," she said sullenly. She was about to throw the flower away, then put it behind her ear instead, tucking it carelessly into the silver-blonde strands. Now that the surprise of seeing Brian Cameron had subsided and she could think, she was uneasy. Rodrigues Estavez had probably taken his motor launch and gone rumrunning with her brother, and maybe Pedro Ortega with them. On the mainland it was illegal to bring in rum, now that they had something called Prohibition. Lately, fast boats ran past the island, and once Silva had heard shots fired in the night.

It was bad work, Liane said, and Maria Luisa would mutter and frown. Silva did not understand it. It was 1924, a modern age. Could not people do as they pleased?

She did know Tyrone craved excitement, danger, money. He was no longer satisfied to put his feet over the side of the rowboat or a canoe and snooze until a fish tugged at his line.

"I returned yesterday, with a party of guests," Brian informed her after a little pause. He had stopped studying her face with his keen blue eyes, and was looking out over the lagoon. "I had forgotten how quiet it was here, how peaceful," he said, as though to himself. "Life is hectic on the mainland. It's noisy, and smells of gasoline fumes. Here I can smell the spices—the cinnamon and nutmeg, the cloves and vanilla and ginger. God, I had forgotten there was a paradise on earth, or perhaps I had stopped believing in it."

She waited patiently for him to return to the point. His mind was sharp; he was a shrewd businessman, and worth millions of dollars now, Rodrigues had said proudly. The overseer was torn between envy and pride: His boss was so important in the business worlds of Miami and New York City, in such demand that he could not return to Desirée, and Rodrigues had to make all decisions.

Silva and her brother and father had met Brian Cameron thirteen years ago, when they had first come to the island. Disheartened over the death from influenza of his beloved wife, Evadne, Valerian Armitage had bought a piece of property on a small Caribbean island, severed ties with his staid British family, and forgotten them. Brian had been kind to them in a casual way, seeing that they had food and medicines when they needed them, ordering his own servants to give them anything they wanted. But Valerian Armitage had wanted little but to be left alone to paint.

"How is Valerian?" asked Brian, his gaze still resting on the incredible blue-green of the waters beyond the lagoon. "Still painting well? I saw one of his exhibitions in Miami."

Silva made a choked sound, putting her hand to her slender, golden-tanned throat. The gesture brought Brian's attention to her. He sat up straight from the lounging posture.

"What is it?" he asked sharply. "Is he ill? He was always frail—"

"He's dead," she said flatly, still unable to believe in the fact of the dying, the burial in the ground, the cutting off forever of the close bond between children and father.

"When? Recently? No one said—"

"A year ago. It was September."

"God Almighty," he whispered. "Child, I am sorry.

Why didn't you send word? Damn that Rodrigues, he never notified me. What happened?"

She averted her face. Brian Cameron was easier to endure when he was brusque and hard. When he was tender and gentle, he made tears come to her eyes. "Why—he just went down and down, Mr. Cameron. He—he didn't want to—live—you know—after my mother—after she went—he didn't really care."

"I knew that. But, my God, you two children loose on the world," he said sharply. "Who looks after you? Did he appoint some guardian—?"

"Maria Luisa looks after us; she always has."

He was silent for a time, and she glanced at him. His face was tough, masklike, implacable. What was he thinking? That it was none of his concern? It was odd to talk to him, Silva thought. He was the first white man, other than her brother, with whom she had conversed in over a year, since her father's death. He spoke so differently from the natives, whose lazy drawl was a mixed patois of English, Afro, and Indian, with a smattering of French. Brian's speech was crisp, correct, according to the grammar books that had caused her such struggles in her early years.

"What will you do, then?" he asked quietly. "How old are you now?"

"We are eighteen," she said proudly, stiffening. "Why is it necessary to do anything? We have food, a house, clothes."

His glance flicked over her cotton shift, made by herself and Maria Luisa from the same pattern as all her other dresses. She flinched, and drew her slim feet further under her, her feet in the homemade sandals of fiber. She felt like a snail, wishing to draw into a little shell away from the hurts of the world. That look at her, as though she were nothing much!

"And Tyrone? Is he satisfied?"

She was silent. Tyrone was restless, feeling his young manhood, chasing after beautiful Oona, whom everyone knew was the girl of Rodrigues. There were no white girls on the island except Silva. Tyrone spent nights away from the house. Maria Luisa went about muttering dark threats, words in her native tongue which were words she had not taught to Silva.

"About time I came back. What is everyone thinking of? Don't you have family in England?"

"Father said he would never acknowledge them again, not after the way they treated Mother. She was a pianist, you know, and played in nightclubs. It was really because she could not get other work," Silva explained defensively. "She was very talented. But they thought it beneath an Armitage. Father's older brother had some title or other. And I think they didn't care for Father, either, because he could not serve in the war."

Silva and her twin had been only five years old when beautiful Evadne had taken influenza. She had gone down so quickly, and died within days, leaving Valerian and the children stunned.

With a vague notion of painting in the South Seas, Valerian had packed up himself and the children and set out on a ship. They had reached Florida when the money ran low. Valerian had happened to meet Brian Cameron's father in an art gallery in Miami. The American had admired his work, suggested they all come to his own island in the Caribbean. Valerian could work as well there as in the South Seas, Mr. Cameron had said, patting Silva's blonde head kindly.

War had swept Europe. Valerian ignored letters from home, urging him to return and fight for his country. He cared only for painting, now that Evadne was dead, and only spared a grave smile now and then for the two towheaded children who knew enough not to disturb him. The years melted into each other and Valerian stayed on, uncaring of the outside world, even his family in England. The letters ceased.

Now Mr. Cameron and Valerian Armitage were

both dead, and Brian Cameron had returned to Desirée.

"Ah, yes, that damn war," he muttered, leaning back on his elbow. Silva eyed him curiously. Brian Cameron had been in the war in Europe, driving something called an aeroplane, but he had never spoken of it to her. She knew only that when he had returned, he had been much more mature, hardened, tough. And when he went away, it was to make money—"piles of it," said Maria Luisa.

"So—what to do with you and that twin of yours," he mused, half to himself. "Ah, well, that will work out in time. Silva, I have brought some friends from New York, much older than you, but white people. It will do you and Tyrone no end of good to come around and meet them, have a chat. Why not come this evening?"

She stiffened. Meet his grand friends, and her wearing a cotton shift? And Tyrone ashamed of his rough drill trousers and cotton shirts like those the natives wore? Fat chance!

She changed the subject abruptly. "What have you been doing these three years, Mr. Cameron?" She sifted white sand between her slim fingers, poured some into a large conch shell she had found. He would probably laugh to see her put the shell to her ear, to catch the roar of the vast ocean she had once crossed.

"What have I been doing, little one? Ah, those tales are not for you, with your youth and innocence!" he said in that hard, mocking voice she detested. Then he softened as he noted her flinching. "Ah, child, I have been working much of the time. I began one company of sugar importers, then that led to another in molasses, and now I head a corporation which deals in many diverse imports. I am a mining engineer; perhaps you did not know that. I have traveled to Central and South America in search of minerals. To explain it all to one of your inexperience would strain my powers of description."

"And you think I am stupid," she said harshly, frowning over a handful of shells.

He reached out and tugged a strand of wet blonde hair. "No, only very young, in spite of your years," he teased. "Don't look so—it is best that way. You don't know how fortunate you are here, on this paradise island, away from the robbers of Wall Street and the thieves of Miami."

She scarcely knew what he said; no one she knew talked like this. Her books were few, and they said nothing of robbers on Wall Street. She sighed. Her father had taught her and Tyrone their arithmetic and grammar and spelling, and reading and such history as he thought they should know. But it all seemed rather dim and vague. The myths of heroes were more real to Silva. King Arthur was her idol, much finer than Queen Elizabeth or George Washington, and the *loa* of the island were closer to her than the God of the Church of England.

"And what have you been doing these years, Silva? You must confide in me in turn," he told her lightly, smiling up at her as he stretched out his muscular body lazily on the sands. He was very long—she thought he must be more than six feet tall—and very tanned and powerful. The natives were short and stocky, and Tyrone was just a little taller than herself. It was strange to be with a man like Brian Cameron. Perhaps that was why she felt butterflies in her stomach and a funny trembling in her limbs.

She was conscious of his gaze on her, lingering on her slim throat, on her slight, high breasts outlined by the clinging wet cotton. Rodrigues sometimes stared at her like this, and it made her feel like hiding somewhere in the thick liana-strewn trees. The blue gaze flicked over her, from her head to her heels, those bare legs under the short cotton dress. Just when she felt so nerve-shot that she would have jumped up and run away, the long lashes over his eyes closed. He seemed to lie in the sun like a great panther, basking in the sunshine and cool breeze.

"Oh—I used to study with Father. So did Tyrone," she said finally, not sure how interested he was. Sometimes adults, like the natives, would listen indulgently, not really hearing. "We have a garden, and Liane and I grow tomatoes and lettuce, corn and beans and yams. I take care of the chickens, and Tyrone does the pigs. And—we go fishing and swimming."

"Do you still play the piano?" he asked.

She closed her eyes tightly in remembered pain as she thought of her mother's body in a church graveyard somewhere in England in a town whose name she could not spell. She could recall little of her mother, except sometimes the evenings when Evadne would play for them on the piano which later they had brought with them from England along with some of the furniture. She remembered sitting cozily on her father's lap. The music flowed about them, there in the chintz-flowered room of their small cottage. Tyrone was on the floor playing absorbedly with his little train. Her mother was smiling in the lamplight, the silvery-blonde hair flowing about her shoulders, her green eyes dreamy. There was a scent, dimly remembered, of wood smoke, and lilac perfume, which her mother wore, and her father's pipe. . . . The peace and closeness of it was lost forever, as was the feeling of belonging and being cared for. Silva would remember that time in the quiet of the night, before she slept, and unbidden tears would fill her eyes as she thought of the long ago, when her father's arms were warm about her, and her mother's smile was sweet, and fragrant roses grew in clusters all around the cottage. All gone, all gone . . .

"The piano got mold in it, the keys don't play, and the strings are mostly broken," she said abruptly. "Pianos don't last long in the tropics."

"But you play something? A guitar?"

"Yes, and a flute, drums, and a lute." Silva sat quietly on her folded legs, looking out at the blue seas, the white foam lashing against the rocks at the end of the lagoon, the fish that played and leaped out of the waters. Sometimes she felt so sad and confused . . . and only music could soothe her.

"I'd like to hear you play one day," Brian said gently, as though feeling her pain. But how could he? He was a stranger, a man of millions, who lived on the mainland and made piles of money, and knew many women, so they said.

She said nothing for a time, gazing off into the distance with eyes half closed, as though the bright sunlight hurt them. When she stopped to think, she became frightened. What *would* become of her and Tyrone? Could they live on this island forever, just going on and on and on, the way the natives did?

Her father had spoken toward the last of taking them to Miami, but how could they go? They had no motor launch, and even if Rodrigues took them over, who would look after them? Silva did not know how to work there, nor did Tyrone. All they knew was gardening and fishing.

If it had not been for Maria Luisa and her daughter, Liane, how would they have managed? It was Maria Luisa who had raised them, taught them the earthy wisdom by which she lived. She had introduced them to native friends, scolded them, fished with them, kept the evil gods from harming them, besought the blessings of the kind gods, and kept them alive. Although she was a year younger, Liane had always been Silva's best friend, confiding in her, advising her, laughing with her over foolish jokes, holding her hand tightly when her father died.

"Did your father take you to Miami often?" Brian asked, interrupting her musings.

"No, never," she said absently.

"Never?" He stared at her. "Then—how did you manage? How did you buy clothes? How—? Oh, I see. God, child, what you have missed. Have you never left the island since you came?"

She shook her head. Her fine blonde hair, almost dry now, flew about her face, and she brushed it back impatiently. "Sometime I would like to see Miami," she confided, "and see my father's pictures. He did a portrait of me two years ago; he said it was one of his best."

"I saw it in Miami. It is sold now," he said. His blue eyes were narrowed and thoughtful, the lines about his eyes and the tanned cheeks were deep. "Perhaps we can manage—I could take you and Tyrone to the mainland—"

She jumped up, shaking out her drying dress. "No, you don't need to," she said with offended dignity. "I was not hinting! Tyrone and I can take care of each other, you see."

He stood up quickly, amazingly light for one so tall and sturdy. "Don't take offense, little one." The smile quirked his mouth. "I forgot what a pepperpot you are. Look here, why don't you come back with me for breakfast? We can eat at Cameron Hall, and talk matters over. You should think seriously about your future, yours and Tyrone's. Now that I'm here—"

Come to Cameron Hall, he said casually. In all her years on the island they had never set foot in it! Temper blazed in her. She had seen the plantation home from a distance only, shining white and red-tiled in the distance, as she stood on the range of hills overlooking the valley where it lay, on the windward side of Desirée. Her own home and lagoon were in the west, the native village in the south, the sacred mountain in the southeast, and the cane fields north of the mountain. The Camerons had owned the island since the days of James II of Scotland. Fighting for him, Brian Cameron's ancestor had been captured, and transported to the Caribbean islands as an indentured servant more than two hundred years ago. He had escaped from the island where he had served as a worker in the cane fields, and come to Desirée.

Over the years he and his descendants had built the Spanish-style Cameron Hall. Wide rooms and hallways, tall pillars, white stone and red tiles made it a truly imposing sight. There were patios with fountains and singing birds and black iron grillwork in lacy patterns. The extensive stables had the finest-bred horses. But not once had the Armitage family come to Cameron Hall on invitation.

Silva had longed to see the house, had dreamed of walking through the beautiful rooms, touching the splendid blue tiles imported from Portugal, listening to the birdsong, enjoying the coolness provided by thick stucco walls on the hottest days. But not like this—a charitable invitation from the condescending owner who had not bothered with them ever before but for the most casual speech.

"No, thank you," she said coldly. "I said we could manage, and we will. Hadn't you better get back yourself? Your guests will wonder where you are."

"My guests are abed, and will be until noon," he said, catching at her hand. "Come on, don't be silly. Maria Luisa won't mind if you breakfast with me."

She backed away from him warily, tugging her hand free. He eyed her as he would a nervous filly, she thought furiously—a half-smile on the wide sensual mouth, a cynical curve to his lips, his head cocked, the black curly hair shining in the sun like a blackbird's wing, the blue eyes coldly amused.

"I have to get home for breakfast," she said swiftly. "And Tyrone and I are going fishing for our lunch. Too bad I cannot accept your kind invitation. You should have asked Father when he was alive; he might have enjoyed it!"

"I did, but he would not come. It reminded him, I think, of his English relatives." Brian's smile had disappeared, and he spoke gravely, a little wearily. "I tried to be friends with Valerian, I assure you, Silva. But he would have little to do with any of us. He lived in the past, and did not want to be disturbed from his memories."

Silva looked at him uncertainly. That could be true; her father had resisted all efforts to draw him into the present. Even his paintings had been mostly of the past: pretty English scenes, Evadne at the piano, a fire on the hearth, a desolate moor, cattle coming home. The glorious island of the present had only been a dim setting for him. He had not seen the glorious flowers she loved, nor had he cared for the beautiful songs of the birds, the curious customs of the people, the enchanting stories of Maria Luisa.

"Come now," said Brian authoritatively, frowning at her. "Let the past bury its dead. Come along to the Hall, and let us eat in peace and talk of the future. You do have a future, you know. You are quite grown up and beautiful. Hasn't anyone told you so?"

She eyed him, backing away instinctively from his outstretched hand, like a nervous yellow jaguar from a stranger. She sensed danger from him, from the lean body, the whipcord strength, the lift of his head, the narrowing of his blue eyes.

Suddenly she darted past him and away into the undergrowth. He shouted after her, "Come back, you little devil! Silva, come now, don't go up there, you'll get lost!"

She made a laughing face to herself. Get lost, in the groves where she had played and run from young childhood? No, this was her home—the woods, the lagoon, the beach, the hill. She slipped away into the dense foliage and stood absolutely still while he pounded past her, heavy-booted, frustrated.

"Silva, damn the girl!" he raged. "Silva, where are you?"

She waited until he gave up the hunt and returned to his horse, furious, scowling. The black stallion was turned, and Brian rode back up the hill, crashing through the brush, back into the trees.

She waited. Silence flowed in his wake. The birds

were silent, and the little frightened animals hid. Then gradually the horse's hoofbeats were gone, and some small bird squeaked. A parrot mocked at it, and then the animals scurried about once more.

Shyly, like a frightened wild creature, Silva slipped out of her hiding place, and surefooted made her way up the hill to the north and west, toward home, finding a path where few would have found it.

Chapter 2

Brian, riding home on the powerful black stallion, was fuming with vexation. That slip of a girl, to disappear like that with her green eyes mocking him! Damn it!

How lovely she had been, all honey-gold against the blue waters of the lagoon. He had thought from up on the hill, as he looked down on the well-remembered beauty of the half-moon bay, that he had seen a mermaid in the waters.

Silver hair shining, golden arms glistening, her supple body waist-high in blue-green water—how glorious she had been! He had stared, thinking he dreamed. When she raised her arms, to flip back the wet silver hair with her hands, he saw the young breasts, rounded with rosy points. So young and lithe-limbed she was, flashing through the waters, cleaving them to the bottom, feet vigorously propelling her to the white sand bottom.

Then on the beach he had studied her. The lovely curves under the wet cotton shift. The wary turn of her smooth face. Pink blossoming on the creamy face when he embarrassed her. Green eyes sad, mocking, laughing, or dreamy, but always expressive. Long brown lashes with no flirtatious skills resting sadly against her peach-bloom cheeks as she spoke of her father.

A little brown dryad, a creamy gold sea nymph, innocent of the world—or was she? His dark blue eyes narrowed against the growing brightness of the sunlight. Perhaps growing up wild as she had, one of the long-limbed handsome native boys had initiated her. He had seen veiled innocence before, and all it ever veiled was a scheming heart and calculating mind. That girl in Paris, a gamine with her pixie face—stealing his wallet! And the beautiful English woman he had come close to marrying—until he had learned of her secret meetings with her aviator lover, the man she wanted to marry in spite of Brian's wealth and her family's poverty.

Women. They disgusted him. Silva was probably no different. The girl from Desirée—no, Silva Armitage had probably as many wiles as her mainland counterparts.

But she was alone in the world, she and her twin. Brian could not leave them to grow up wild. They were not natives, not like the Afro-Indian people of Desirée. He should have returned before, he thought, swinging down from the stallion in the stableyard. Those children needed a strong hand—his.

Brian looked about the stables as the groom ran to take his horse. He was proud of the horses; he had brought them here from Europe himself. They had not been ridden except by native stable boys for three years. I must look them over more carefully, he thought as he left the large stables, where a half dozen purebred mares and a silky colt frisked about the stableyard.

He wondered if Silva rode. Probably not. She could have been riding his horses these years—if he had only thought to command it. He frowned. Silva and Tyrone, a pair of rascals, probably.

Brian glanced toward the cane fields—good crop. Estavez was not doing a bad job of managing—except that damn little income had been made from the sugar cane. It was much less than it should have been, and seemed smaller each year. To check on the estate was one reason he had returned. But if all worked out, the cane could be forgotten.

He walked back to the huge plantation house, passing his small brick and clay laboratory where he kept his engineering equipment securely locked. He would go out this afternoon, he decided, while the natives took their siestas. He did not want to be watched.

Before entering the white arched doorway into the patio, he paused to stare to the southeast. There loomed the mountain, the Monte del Gato, the Mountain of the Cat. To the natives it was the sacred mountain, where many of their festivals were held, sacred to the small yellow jaguar that roamed there freely. Brian thought the animal must have been brought in by Indians from Central America long ago. He had shot one three years ago when they had been harassing the natives and his prize horses.

He thought of what else that mountain hid, and smiled a little to himself. He was supposed to have a golden touch where wealth was concerned. Well, they would really wonder now! A prize find, to add to his holdings.

Impatient now for his breakfast, he strode into the patio. It was past nine o'clock. He went to his rooms on the side of the patio, where he washed, took off his boots, and substituted soft native slippers like those the girl had worn. He wondered why he kept thinking of her. Maybe because she was a puzzle, and he always enjoyed a puzzle.

He left his large sombrero in the room and went out to the dining room, off another side of the patio. In the cool, yellow-walled room the chandelier set with candles glistened in the early sunlight. No lights were needed during most of the daytime. A precious rug from Persia was set on the highly polished parquet floor. He ran his hand over a graceful mahogany chair. He had forgotten how beautiful the rooms here were.

Even as he seated himself at the large round mahogany table, set with lace mats and fine crystal which rang at the flick of a finger, a plump maid padded in softly on her bare feet.

"Good morning. Coffee, if you will, hot and black. And eggs, bacon, mango."

"Ah, sí, señor," she murmured, and sidled out again.

Brian smiled. He never knew what language the servants were going to speak: French, Spanish, English, or Indian. As a boy it had never mattered—he spoke them all, and answered as they spoke. As a man, it was a curiosity.

He was drinking his coffee, idly leaning back and surveying the sunlight on the fountains in the patio, the creamy hibiscus, the golden allamanda, the blue petrea, the pink frangipani, when he heard the click of high heels. He raised his eyebrows, then stood up as the woman came in.

Astrid Larsen entered the room, beautiful in an impossibly intricate lace dress of cream with green ribbons. She was a full-blown and voluptuous woman, and in New York she had looked sophisticated, wealthy, magnificent. Here, she was slightly out of place, Brian thought, unusually critical this morning. She gave him a warm smile, touched her red lips with her fingers, and put her fingers on his lips casually as she went past him to her chair. He held the chair for her.

"I didn't expect to see you until noon, Astrid." He sat down after she had seated herself.

She yawned, stretching seductively. "I know. It is quite out of character for me. But that sunlight was positively glaring into my room! And the servants slipping in with trays of tea and making a racket."

"I'll order them to stop," he said easily.

The maid returned, took the woman's order for coffee and juice in silence. With a graceful hand Astrid flicked back the lace of her sleeve, which drooped over the long fingers. A diamond shone in the light, glinting like a dewdrop, and an emerald sparkled at her breast. Her husband had been generous on their divorce, she had said. Or had he been glad to be rid of her and her extravagant ways? Brian had wondered lately. She made no secret of the fact that she expected Brian to be her next husband, but Brian was not so sure. He admired her beauty; he liked to have her on his arm for the opera in New York, the horse races in Miami. But permanently? He liked no woman well enough to make their association permanent. Perhaps he never would. He could see through them too easily, to their greedy little hearts. He had made her his mistress, but not his wife.

Donald Keller came in, yawning, blinking at them with his clear brown eyes. He was a stockbroker in New York, and when he had learned that Brian was coming to Desirée, he had begged to be allowed to come along on his vacation. He was bored to pieces in New York, worn out with late nights, he had confessed, and a paradise island would be just the thing.

He gazed admiringly at Astrid as he seated himself. His breakfast was more hearty than hers; he seemed to enjoy the papaya and lemon juice, the ham and eggs she scorned. "Well, what's for today?" he asked over coffee as the other two talked idly of the beauty of the flowers. "Going riding this morning, Brian?"

"Just got back a while ago," Brian told him, smiling at their amazement. "When I come down here, I'm up early. Old habits are hard to break."

"Darling, you must have gotten up before the birds!" Astrid exclaimed with a pout. "I was looking forward to riding, or at least driving about in one of your darling carriages. Such a change after the noisy automobiles in New York. You will take me out later, won't you?"

"Donald can. I have work to do," he said deliberately.

Her mouth tightened, her eyes flashed ominously. She was about to have a tantrum, he observed with detached interest. She had never become furious at him, though he had seen her throw a glass at a maid, slap a man, scream at a waiter. Her unlovely side, he thought. She calmed herself with an effort, and turned to coaxing.

"But, darling, I came especially to see your adorable island! I love your gorgeous flowers and rolling hills. We are going to bathe in the sea, aren't we?"

"Oh, yes, of course, Astrid, whenever the sharks aren't around," he replied coolly, watching her reaction with amusement. It was true enough about the sharks. "Other times, you can use the pool."

"Sharks!" she gasped, her cheeks paling even under her rouge. "God, Brian, tell me you're joking!"

He sobered at once. "No, I'm not. You listen to me, Astrid—you also, Don. There are sharks in the waters, and you don't ever go swimming alone. Also there are jaguars in the hills, so don't go walking or riding by yourself. Understand?"

Astrid was gazing at him with incredulous blue eyes. Donald managed a little stiff grin, but he was visibly shaken.

"Well, you've convinced me," said Donald. "I go with white chief or many bearers on safari, right? Otherwise I'll stick around this palatial residence and gather me a suntan which will be the envy of Wall Street."

"I think you're joking," muttered Astrid.

"I'm not," he said curtly. "Sorry to frighten you, but you might as well get things straight right from the first."

"*You* go out alone," said Astrid, not quite convinced. "Why you? Why don't you take that manager of yours?"

"I do sometimes. But I also carry a pistol, loaded at all times," said Brian crisply. He shoved back his chair. "Sorry to leave you, but I have some paperwork to do this morning."

He went off to his own rooms, aware of Astrid's

repressed rage at not being entertained by him. She would have to learn the hard way that he had not come here on vacation, he thought.

In his study he stretched back in the swivel chair, picked up the first record book, and began to study it. Yes, he had been right in his recollections. The years when he had first taken over the plantation from his father, after the older Cameron's death, the plantation had made money from cane and molasses. The past four years the income had gone steadily downward. Yet the cane looked good, the weather had been great, and there had been no hurricanes to damage the cane in the critical seasons.

He set down the book, got to work on some papers he had brought over from the mainland. His managers in the New York and Miami offices were efficient; they knew what he wanted and got results. He studied their recent reports, writing comments in the margins that would be sent out on the boat when it came with supplies.

About twelve-thirty he leaned back, stretched, and shut his eyes to think. The trouble was, the reports were not floating through his mind. Instead the image of a green-eyed girl with slim golden limbs kept recurring. The way she had looked in the water, so alone and beautiful and slim, a fitting part of the scenery, a nymph sunning her lovely body undisturbed by mortals—until he had ridden down the hill.

Impatiently he rose and went to his bedroom next door. He was glad he had kept the suite of rooms to himself. He had a hunch the villa had been used during his absence, probably by Estavez playing big shot in the boss's years away. But these rooms had remained untouched. The maids had hastily cleaned as soon as he had arrived, and layers of dust had flown through the air, white feathery dust and black flecks of lava rock.

In the huge bedroom with the massive four-poster mahogany bed, he undressed, and went to his bathroom to take a shower. At least the modern conveniences were installed, and usually worked. The island rested on lava rock, and it trapped fresh water, or only lightly salted water, according to the tides. The hot water heater and electricity from the power plant made it all easy. Brian idly wondered how the twins managed. Lived like the natives, probably. That half-moon bay must be Silva's private bathing tub. He gave a slashing grin at the thought. He would try to keep Astrid away from that. Somehow it would spoil it, to have Astrid and his other sophisticated guests squealing about and dipping their toes in Silva's pretty tub.

He dressed in a cream tropic suit of cool linen, added a flowing cream tie to his frilled lawn shirt, and went out to luncheon. The Leoni couple had joined the others, and he looked with interest from one to the other. They were an odd lot, and he wondered vaguely why he had invited them all—or had they invited themselves, like Astrid?

Giovanni Leoni was his favorite rumrunner in New York City. He could produce the best brandy at a moment's notice, genuine Scotch at a day's notice, and any wines Brian required. He was a heavyset man in his late forties, swarthy with dark curly hair and gesturing hands. Only the sadness of his olive face was out of place. He used to be a jolly man. Brian wondered briefly if business had gone sour.

Mrs. Leoni—or Flora, as she wanted to be called—was a little younger than her husband, plump, anxious, motherly in spite of her sophistication. She usually dressed in black or gray. Her black eyes, straight black hair tied back in a smooth chignon, the gold earrings in her pierced ears, added up to a smart woman, in Brian's book. Yet she too, in spite of her huge family, had dropped everything to come with her husband to Desirée. What did they want? Or were they really tired of the rat race, as Giovanni claimed, and wanted a real vacation?

Donald Keller was pouring drinks. He gave Brian an apologetic smile. "Didn't mean to usurp your role as host, Brian. Giovanni wanted a drink; so did Astrid."

Brian noticed he had poured nothing for himself. "No problem. Carry on. I'll be lazy after my morning of work." He accepted a straight Scotch and observed that Mrs. Leoni was drinking only some lime juice. Giovanni had already had a couple whiskeys, Brian judged from the flushed face and glazed eyes.

He thought Giovanni would be in no condition to go for a ride in a carriage on such a warm day. He kept quiet, letting the conversation drone on during the drinks and luncheon. Mrs. Leoni enjoyed the rice in the Spanish style, with tomatoes and peppers and spices, the fried chicken and yams, the fresh green salad. Astrid nibbled daintily at chicken and salad, having refused the rest. Her figure must be getting out of hand, thought Brian. Somehow after Silva she seemed too—too much of everything. Too painted, too voluptuous, too daring, too flirtatious—

She brought up the ride again, impatient with his silence.

"Not today, Astrid. Let the others relax. Why don't you swim this afternoon in the pool? Donald, you keep an eye on her, right?"

Donald flushed. "Too easy a job," he said ruefully, which softened Astrid. She lived on admiration.

Astrid patted Donald's hand, gave him a sidelong look. "You haven't given me any stockmarket tips yet," she remarked. "All boy friends of mine in the stockmarket are giving me hot tips. How come you don't?"

Brian gave Donald a lazy look, made thoughtful by the man's flush. "I came for a vacation," he said quickly. "The office will struggle along without me for a few weeks. We can discuss it after we get back home."

"You know, I think I like you very much," murmured Astrid, loudly enough for Brian to overhear, and she gave Donald's hand a squeeze with her slim ring-laden fingers. Brian gazed into his wineglass, inwardly amused. She was trying the jealousy bit.

Giovanni finished the bottle of wine. Mrs. Leoni refused the custard dessert, and murmured she would sit in the shade of the patio for a time. She managed to get Giovanni to come with her. Brian went back to change to riding clothes.

As he rode out later he heard sounds of laughter near the round swimming pool, glazed with blue-green tiles from Portugal, and caught a glimpse of Astrid in a daringly low-cut beige suit. It was difficult to see where the suit stopped and Astrid began. Poor Donald, Brian thought, and went on.

He rode south, along the cane fields, eyeing them critically. They seemed in good shape, about ready for harvest. The report from Rodrigues Estavez was that harvest would take place in a few weeks. The cane looked ready right now to Brian. He wondered if the man was truly lazy and would have to be pushed. Maybe that was why they had had poor harvests lately. He would look more closely at the fields on his way home. He had checked the sugar mill, and it looked in good shape, though it had been built of limestone more than two hundred years ago. Open to the sky, with arched entrances, the blackened interior told of many years of burning pressed cane.

He rode steadily south, past the boiling house, past more cane fields. The sugar mill stood out gauntly against the vivid blue sky, on a rise of the hills, rugged and sturdy. About four miles farther, through the waist-high grasses and rice patches, he came to the foot of the mountain, the Mountain of the Cat.

He paused, to let his horse rest, swung down, and walked about lightly. This was the lair of the jungle cat. He took his revolver from the holster, checked the loads, replaced it lightly. The jaguars were nothing to fool with; they would spring out, lashing their yellow tails, green eyes agleam, ready to kill—even a man, if he should bother their rest or the prey they were after. He mused, thinking of the old days when his father had taken him hunting. "Have to clean out those pesky varmints," Cameron had growled, and shot two of them.

But the natives had come running, begging him not to kill their sacred cats. Cameron had reluctantly agreed to leave them, so long as they left him alone. "Something to do with their voodoo, shouldn't wonder," he had told Brian. "I never mess with their religion. You take away a man's religion, you're in trouble. You mess with a woman's religion, you're in more hot water than if you take away her virginity, around these islands."

He always talked that way to Brian—frank, blunt, to the point. Brian had missed that later, after his father's death. The rest of the world seemed to deal in evasions, half-truths, and euphemisms.

When Brian's father lay dying of cancer, he had called the young man to him. "I'm dying, boy, and there are things you need to know." And he had laid them on the line. No pretty talk, no dressing-up how he operated.

He had wanted Brian to carry on the same way. Brian wondered sometimes if the world had changed much since his father had done his rather ruthless dealings and managings in the world of commerce. Nowadays one wooed the customer, slipped money under the table to government officials, flattered and paid off the politicians of Latin American countries, anything to get the mines working, the men turning out the minerals, digging at the precious ores, selling them to the businesses that needed them.

A business journal had called Brian one of the new breed of wealthy tycoons: soft-spoken, but hard as nails. That had amused him, until he had realized there was some truth in it. He did get on the track of something, and no man in the world was able to stop him. No woman, either. He had had his share of lovely women, and paid for the privilege of their company in jewels, money, or stocks—whichever they preferred. The deal was fair on both sides, he thought, but he married no woman. He was married, he said sometimes, to his work.

And it had taken him to Europe, Asia, South America, and the Caribbean; to New York's Wall Street, to Miami, Washington, London, and Paris. Now, at thirty-two, he owned four houses, two apartments, a fleet of ships, more clothes than he could wear in each place, more money than he could count—and a restless hunger for something he could not name.

He stroked the neck of the black stallion, then swung back into the saddle. He rode steadily up the side of the mountain, following a path he remembered, beside a small stream. Every now and then he would pause, swing down, get out his small cloth bag, dig in the earth, and put something in the bag. Then he would get up and go on.

Twice he came across crude huts with sides and no roof. He frowned. Voodoo ceremonial places on the side of the mountain, he realized. There were signs of fires, grass trampled smooth by dancing feet. He went on.

He paused near the top of the mountain, dismounted, and took out some instruments. He measured, recorded the measurements, then strode about, searching. He found what he was looking for, and bent over to study it. He scratched with the instruments, took more samples and put them in his cloth bag. It was just as he thought: copper. The most precious of the metals he worked with. Copper for wire, for cables, for electric lines, for fine instruments, as well as the pans and kettles of the world. Precious copper, and the mountain they called the Mountain of the Cat had a vein of copper a mile wide.

He scratched at one sample. High-grade ore if he was any judge, and he ought to be. It was as he had remembered it. Satisfied, he measured some more, and planned where the mine would be started, where the shaft would be set. He had already arranged for equipment for the mine and a smelter to come by ship, along with a cunning engineer friend of his, an old buddy, Mickey McCoy.

Below him on the mountain, though he was unaware of being observed, a dark face peered out from the thick vines. Pedro Ortega was puzzled. He had been following Brian Cameron all across the cane fields, to the foothills of the mountain, and partway up to where the man had stopped and begun digging and measuring.

"What is that man going after?" he muttered to himself in his gruff deep voice. He was tall and thin and bronzed, with a slash on his left cheek. He had an ugly irregular face, and women on the streets of Miami or Havana sometimes laughed at him—once. They never laughed a second time; Pedro Ortega had a reputation.

He was twenty-eight, and had been thrown off several islands for making trouble, as they called it. He was part Spanish, part Indian, and all cunning. He could creep like a jaguar through the bush, he could command men and hold their lives in his palms. But he craved more power. And money was power.

What did the white man want up here? Why had he returned? What was he doing, digging up the dirty earth that grew nothing of value on this island? He must find out. Later on was time enough to kill the man and claim the island for himself, and throw out all the white people. This was the island he had decided to rule. Here he would be king. Why should a white man rule, when he did not even care enough to live here? Why should he claim the sugar cane, the labor of the natives? It was their island, and Pedro would rule them.

The white man swung on his black horse and rode down the mountain, pausing to bend and look at the ground. He passed within five yards of Pedro, but did not see him. The stallion smelled him, and shied nervously, and Brian rebuked him.

Pedro's mouth curled in contempt. The white man was stupid; he could not live long here, Pedro thought with satisfaction.

He watched the man go, then followed the path that led more quickly to the cane fields. There he found Rodrigues Estavez standing and watching the workers as they cut near the mill.

Rodrigues raised his hand in welcome. Pedro did not. He came close, spat deliberately at his friend's feet. Rodrigues went red with anger, but dared do nothing. Pedro had bested him in fights before.

"Why that man come back?" Pedro demanded ominously. "I thought you said he stay away."

"He stayed away three year. Why come back? I don't know." Rodrigues was nervous, his eyes shifting away.

"You find out why. Tell me soon. He takes earth and puts it in bag. What is he doing?"

Rodrigues looked puzzled and gave a massive shrug, hands up and palms out. "He is crazy, maybe."

"Crazy like a fox, make all that money." Pedro paused, looked at the sky. "He won't come near here. We take rum to boat."

"Right, man." Rodrigues motioned to three of the native workers. They got the cart, hooked up one of the horses to it, and started loading the jugs of rum from the sugar mill.

"He come see mill?" asked Pedro.

"Not yet."

"We get rum away now."

They had been turning much of Brian Cameron's sugar cane into molasses and then rum, taking it to the mainland, where the stupid white men met them and paid enormous sums of money for the eagerly sought Caribbean rum. The money was piling up, in spite of Rodrigues and his stupid purchases for that girl Oona.

They started the cart and two of the men toward the boat. Pedro jerked his head at Rodrigues and the two men walked a little way apart into the cane, watching the horse and cart on its way.

"You watch the white man. Tell me what he does," ordered Pedro. "You bring me stuff from his cloth bag."

Rodrigues swallowed. With curious contempt Pedro saw the Adam's apple go up and down. Rodrigues was a coward; he was afraid of his shadow, especially if the shadow contained a white man. White men were no different from native men—they just were more stupid.

"I—I cannot do that," Rodrigues blurted. "He is watching me now. His eyes watch me always. He want to know why no much money for cane."

"You tell him poor crop," said Pedro.

"He—he not believe. He say sugar cane look good. We harvest soon, he say."

Pedro moved lithely on his sandaled feet closer to Rodrigues. With the speed of a black snake he struck out with both hands, clutching the throat of the shorter, stockier man. Remorselessly he choked him until Rodrigues fell to his knees.

Rodrigues caught at the wrists that held him, but could not move them. They were like liana, clinging and hard and impossible to chop through—like death, with red blood before his eyes . . .

Pedro let him go and Rodrigues fell at his feet, holding himself and choking, crying silently with great tears of pain and humiliation.

"You do what I say, huh?" drawled Pedro in a deadly tone.

Rodrigues tried to speak, but failed. When Pedro kicked him, he nodded hastily.

"You'll go back to house. Tell white boss the cane not ready to harvest. Go."

Pedro watched the man stumble away. His mouth was straight with fury. Stupid Indian! Why did he always work with stupid men! They could not see farther than their noses, not into the glorious future where they would all be free of the white man.

Pedro hated all whites, and with reason. As a boy he had stood outside his mother's hut, banished like a child, while white men entered and possessed her body with piggish grunts. Then they had departed, contemptuously flinging coins at her naked body. Pedro never forgot or forgave their contempt.

As a man he hated them more. A white policeman had discovered Pedro's profitable gambling enterprise on one island. When Pedro refused to let him have a share of the profits, police had swarmed in, and Pedro had been forced to escape from the island.

Everywhere was the same story. If one was not white, he could not operate a business without paying high for protection. The white man who took Pedro's girl, used and discarded her, had been stunned by Pedro's revenge. The fight that followed was bloody and final. The white man died over the body of the mistress, whom Pedro's fury had killed. The white man died—and Pedro was scarred for life. He had run again, this time to Desirée. He was determined to remain here. No white men could stay; he would drive them all out. Pedro would own all: the sugar cane, the rum, the loyalty of the hundred or so natives in the valley, in the village at the south of Desirée.

He would be boss, he alone. He would rule some green piece of earth, and men would bow down to him!

He followed Rodrigues slowly, to make sure the man went to the plantation house. In the distance he could see the house shining. He had visited that house while Rodrigues lived there, walking on bare feet along the blue-green tiles, staring with envious fury at the beautiful furniture, the rare carpets, the locked-up silver in white cloths, and the crystal in glass-front cupboards. All that wealth, and the white man did not even bother to come and count it!

Satisfied Rodrigues had done his bidding, he turned off and went back through the cane fields, watching cautiously for the deadly snakes that dwelt there. Back farther in the cane, near the ocean, he found the place he wanted, where the cane was stunted and white from the salt of the sea. He squatted, took out flint, and worked patiently. When he rose, the cane was on fire.

He left, casually, through the tall cane, toward the hills, and south to the village. When the fire was discovered, he would be resting in his hut, quite unaware of any fire in the cane fields. When the cane burned, and no profit came of it, the white man might leave. It was worth the try. If that failed, there were other methods he could use.

Brian had paused several times on the way home. He had remembered a brook where he had drunk sweet water, and he found it again. He sat for a time beside the purling waters and gazed along the banks to the wild flowers of crimson, white, shy blue. He had things to think about.

It was late afternoon when he started for the last stretch to the plantation house. He was riding along lazily, jogging, the black stallion weary, its head down. It had been a long day. Brian mused about his plans for the smelter. Mickey would soon have it set up, and Brian would have copper out of the mine and on his fleet of ships, moving regularly to the mainland, before many weeks had gone past.

Lost in thought, it was the smell he noticed first. Into the sweet smell of the evening, the fragrance of frangipani along the narrow path, the salt of the sea air, came a strange sweet odor, sickly sweet. Burning cane—sweet, smoky!

He glanced quickly about, saw the plumes of

black smoke going up. At first he thought the natives were burning in the mill, but realized the smoke did not come from there. He touched his heel to the stallion's flanks, and the gallant horse started up.

Brian arrived at the stables at a gallop. A breathless groom met him.

"Fire in the cane, the east fields near the ocean," he said crisply. The groom stared at him. He lifted his voice. "Fire in the cane! Get the wagons and sacks!"

He soon had them pushed and prodded on the way. He himself started out again on a fresh horse, and Donald Keller came out and joined him, excitement reddening his cheeks.

"Say, did you yell fire?" cried Keller, running to the stableyard. "Let me come. I can help—"

"Right—come along—" Brian did not wait for him, but galloped out of the yard and down the path where the water cart was rattling along. Natives appeared out of the semidarkness, running from their huts, carrying shovels, picks, axes. He yelled at them, "Fire in the cane—come along!"

In the east field the fire had a good start, but it was still confined to a few acres. Brian directed them to dig a wide trench through the cane as a firebreak, in the direction of the wind. When that was contained, they soaked the sacks in water and began beating at the burning cane. Wind picked up the burning stalks and hurled them through the air. Brian plucked one from his shirt as it burned through to his flesh, scarcely noticing it as he continued to beat out the fire.

Where was that damn Rodrigues? He should be here, helping, directing. What was going on? Was that why the cane never produced much money any longer? Fires starting, no one to stop them? Damn him anyway. Brian was fuming as he got down and beat at some cane that had jumped the trench and started to fire the next patch.

It took more than two hours, but finally the fire

was out. Brian stationed two men to guard, warning them sternly to watch and notify him at once if it flared up again, then he and Donald Keller started back. The natives were chattering, casting wary looks up at him. He caught some of the words but kept his face impassive. They did not realize he knew their *lingua,* had spoken it from boyhood. If they knew, they had forgotten, but he hadn't.

The fire had been set, he had caught that much. Someone didn't want Brian Cameron to come back, to come messing around the cane. Why? He would find out.

He glanced at Donald, at the burned shirt, the blackened arms, the reddened face. "I owe you a new shirt," he said dryly.

The white teeth gleamed in the darkened face. "I'll charge it off in your wine," he said lightly. "I could do with a long cool glass of lime and whiskey."

"It's yours, as soon as we get home." Brian hesitated. "Thanks a lot for your help. It wasn't your fight." He was curious about the man's motives.

Donald Keller shrugged. "I like excitement," he said simply, eyes gleaming. "You couldn't keep me away."

"Funny statement for a stockbroker," said Brian dryly, remembering what Astrid had said about him, that he had not tried to sell her some stock.

"Why so? Dangerous a place as any!" laughed Keller.

They swung down from the horses in the yard. Astrid came out of the patio, looking cool and charming in white lace, her hair tied back in a silver swath.

"What happened? Are you all right, Brian?" There was real anxiety in her voice.

"Right as rain. Just a fire in the cane and that Rodrigues wasn't around," he said calmly. "Anyone seen him?"

The grooms looked at each other, and Astrid seemed puzzled. "No, boss, haven't seen him—no, haven't seen that man," the natives chorused.

"Well, I'll see him tomorrow," said Brian and walked in. Astrid touched his reddened arm lightly, her beautiful face concerned. "I'm all right, just very dirty, Astrid. If you'll excuse me, I'll indulge in a shower before I join you."

"I'm not so proud; I'll take a drink first," said Donald. "Fix it for me, will you, angel?"

She went with Keller, but looked back over her slim shoulder at Brian, giving him one of her sultry looks. He was grinning to himself as he went to shower. But the smile faded as the cool water washed down over his sooty hair and burned shoulder. That fire had been set. In the morning he would have more than a few words with Rodrigues.

Chapter 3

Up on a hill overlooking the blue sea, Valerian Armitage and some natives had built a large shack of a house with half a dozen rooms, a roof of thatch and wood, and a hut in back. The chicken pens were farther back, with the pig pen. No big house like that of Brian Cameron, but it was home, thought Silva with satisfaction. He could rattle around in his huge Spanish mansion like a lord, but she was happy, and he had lines of dissatisfaction about his face.

She ran lightly around the house and back to the open kitchen. Maria Luisa looked up from stirring the fire, and her wrinkled face was keen.

"Where you been, girl? I thought you back one hour ago."

"Swimming, Maria Luisa," said Silva with a flush, turning away her face. Maria Luisa saw too much. "Is breakfast ready? I'm hungry."

"Where your shells? Thought you went to get more shells for your table."

"I forgot them," she said, and sat down at the rugged wooden table behind the house. Maria Luisa grunted, filled a plate with beans and rice, and put a plate of corn cakes near Silva's hand. She filled a cup with coffee and added thick cream to it.

"Tyrone, he come back this morning," said Maria Luisa, squatting again beside the fire. Her graying head was bent with weariness or worry.

Silva glanced over at her, busily spooning up the beans and rice. "Tired? He went out with Rodrigues?"

"Yes, and that man, he no good. I talk to him, he just laugh. We talk to your twin—he got to listen to us."

But there was little hope in the woman's voice. Tyrone laughed also at their fears that he might be caught, that he might be shot.

"We'll talk to him," said Silva firmly. "We don't need that money. We can manage. One day I'll send my paintings to Miami, and they will sell too. Daddy said I was becoming good."

"Sure, my baby, sure."

Liane strolled around the house, paused to hug Silva with absent affection. Her glowing dark eyes told Silva that Liane had been with her lover, Nathaniel. They would marry one day, when the signs were right.

"Where yo' man?" asked Maria Luisa.

"He went fishing for us, said he knew where to get a turtle."

"Good. He good man," said Maria Luisa with satisfaction. "One day we get good man for Silva here. You two marry good. I watch the signs, I ask the gods."

Liane smiled happily, her beautiful oval face glowing with the serenity of love. Silva bent her pale head over her coffee cup. Marriage? For her? She flinched from the thought. Rodrigues tried to paw her sometimes, and it made her sick. She had bit him once, and run away. There was no one for her to marry, and she did not want that anyway. Love made people sick and strange, like her father.

"Mr. Cameron, he come back," said Liane in a pause while she drank her coffee dreamily. "Nathaniel, he told me that man come back last night, and he have rich guests, oh, so fine, and clothes, like oh my."

"Mr. Cameron, yes, he come back," said her mother, showing no surprise. "I think he come back for some time now. I see where he stay for some time; he mix up with us folks. I dream about that."

Silva glanced at her sharply, but asked no questions. Maria Luisa would tell her what she wanted her to know in good time.

"I think Rodrigues will be mad that Mr. Cameron come," Liane mused. "Nathaniel, he said Rodrigues be damn mad. Maybe he keeping money from Mr. Cameron. I think so. He tell Mr. Cameron in letters that the sugar cane, she not good. But he tell Nathaniel we got good crop, make much money."

Maria Luisa nodded placidly. "Mr. Cameron, he sharp man. He find out soon, I betcha!"

"You mean," asked Silva slowly, puzzled, "that Rodrigues is keeping the money he should be sending to Mr. Cameron? That he has been cheating Mr. Cameron, who employs him?"

"Sure," said Maria Luisa. "Mr. Cameron, he go three years. Not come and watch. Rodrigues, he wants motor launch, he wants trips to Miami, he make big money, buy a watch. He wants jewelry for that Oona girl, too, I betcha. She no good."

The talk troubled Silva. Their father had not taught them much of the world, yet he had emphasized honor, honesty, trust, the virtues by which men lived. Sometimes they conflicted with what Maria Luisa said. Yet the old woman was honest also, viewing the dishonesties of some natives with open contempt. Her father had not known that Maria Luisa had taken the twins she adored to many a voodoo ceremony.

Maria Luisa had come to them as soon as they had arrived on the island of Desirée. She had stared narrowly at the towheaded twins, and at once offered to come and live with them, she and her Liane, and take care of them. Surprised, Valerian had agreed. Only later did Silva and her twin find that twins were highly respected in voodoo, that they were special, and Maria Luisa became more highly regarded because she had the twins in her care.

Because of Maria Luisa, the natives had worked willingly for them. They had helped build a house and a hut, told them how to till the soil, sheltered them in hurricane time, brought them pigs and chickens, brought back goods from the mainland in their launches.

After breakfast Silva and Liane hoed the garden, pulled out weeds, picked some beans for lunch, then fed the chickens and the pigs because Tyrone would sleep until evening. When the chores were done, the sun was higher overhead and a langorous heat was stealing over the green island.

Silva retreated to the living room of their crude home. Liane would sleep for an hour until her lover returned with his fish or a turtle. They would prepare lunch, make love, giggle, and talk in their native language.

Silva had other things to do. In the living room she had set up her easel which had been her father's, and there she worked. She was working on a new painting, and she thought it might be the best thing she had done yet.

On the walls of the voodoo temple she had seen paintings she had admired. Pictures of flowers larger than life, of animals and birds of strange shapes, of gods dark and beautiful. She had longed to translate that into her own talents, in her own way.

So she had sketched out a large canvas, the last one left from her father's possessions. And now she was painting it carefully. The only trouble was that most of the tubes of paint were empty. She had had to stop to grind some nutmeg and ginger, and experiments with plants had yielded some reds and yellows and browns. But it was slow, painstaking work to paint like this.

In the center of the painting was a woman, crouched and bent, her face young and eager, belying her gray hair. That was Maria Luisa, idealized, as Silva saw her when she was in a trance. About her were huge flowers of glorious hues—crimson, yellow, the green orchids, the purple and red of bougainvillea. The flowers drifted about the woman, spilling colors on her, as in a dream. In her withered palms lay a little spirit, like a doll, struggling and thrusting with life, eyes opening, a baby-child beginning to live. In the background loomed the sacred mountain, and peering from underbrush glowed the green eyes and the yellow glistening hide of a jaguar.

Silva forgot herself for hours with her painting. She worked slowly, lost in the art, creating what she saw in fantasy.

She started when she heard voices from the kitchen, raised and laughing. Sighing, she put down her brush. Once roused from her fantasies, she could not easily return to them. She rinsed her brushes, laid them to dry, and went out to the open kitchen.

Nathaniel had returned with a huge snapping turtle he had caught. Now respectfully he and Liane were standing aside while Maria Luisa mumbled a prayer over it, and asked the approval of the gods to kill this fine being for their nourishment. Silva also stood silently, her head bent, observing the turtle lying on its back helplessly, paws waving, head ducking in and out of the shell.

A kettle of steaming-hot water was set on the fire, hanging from an iron rod. Maria Luisa said cheerfully, "It is good," and she and Nathaniel popped the turtle into the water. Silva and Liane began to prepare the yams in leaves to thrust under the glowing coals.

She wished Tyrone were awake. But if she awakened him he would be cross and sleepy, and would not enjoy the feast. And it would certainly be a feast, a change from fish and the occasional chicken they allowed themselves.

Presently they sat down to eat, talking and laughing, enjoying the fresh meat of the turtle, the deli-ious soup which Maria Luisa made so well. It would last a couple of days, for the turtle was huge.

Liane was showering approval on Nathaniel, and he beamed under it. He was a good man, Silva thought. He was lean, tall for a native, strong with dark skin and dark eyes. Usually he was serious, but today he laughed and sparkled at his loved one, for he had proved himself a provider. Liane was a year younger than Silva, but she had been Nathaniel's girl for more than a year. It made Silva feel rather lonely, for Liane had always been her best friend until she had turned in her maturing to Nathaniel.

After their fine luncheon they washed the dishes and prepared the turtle meat for dinner and tomorrow. Then Liane and Nathaniel wandered off hand in hand to take their siesta together under some tree. Maria Luisa, happy and stuffed full, lay down on the ground under her favorite tree and was asleep immediately.

Silva went to her room and lay down on the cot. She usually slept, but today, in the heat and closeness, she could not. Her mind bothered her. When she closed her eyes, she could see the blue gaze of Brian Cameron flicking over her cotton shift, her bare legs. What did she care? Only, those women of his, those guests, were probably dressed in the current mainland style, and she looked like a native. It hurt, somehow.

Those questions he had asked—as though he cared! No, no, she and Tyrone could take care of themselves, with Maria Luisa's help. She had raised the twins; she knew everything they needed to know. Except—except—

Silva shifted restlessly on the cot. Her dress felt hot and sticky on her, and her body was salty from the brine of the lagoon. She longed to be lying there once more, relaxing in the cool blue waters. Yet this afternoon it would be warm and sultry.

Her hands went slowly over her body. Her breasts

had grown so the past year. Now she was as big there as Liane, and Rodrigues was always trying to touch her there. Why did he want to? What was there about breasts that made a man want to touch a girl? Nathaniel was always looking at Liane, his gaze going from her head to her feet. What did they do when they wandered off together? Why did they want to sleep together under a tree? Did they talk and laugh—or did he touch her?

She wanted to ask Maria Luisa, but somehow she did not want to know the answers. She had promised Maria Luisa that when she married, Maria Luisa would be there, and the woman had nodded, satisfied. "Then, that time, I tell you things you need to know," the woman had said.

"But what things?" Silva had persisted.

"Woman things," said her mentor compassionately. "You don't need them yet. You wait. Liane older than you, not in years, but in body. You wait."

It was something, Silva decided, about there being no white men about that made Maria Luisa want to wait. Time enough, when Silva met a white man and marriage was talked and arranged with the approval of the right gods and at the right time.

But Silva knew no white men—except Brian Cameron. A flush burned her tanned cheeks, and she turned her face to the pillow and pushed back her long straight hair.

She slept finally, tossing on the narrow cot. In her dreams, someone was bending over her, caressing her breasts. She lay still, trying to see his face in the darkness. The touch of his hands was sweet and exciting. It was not evil; she wanted this.

Silva writhed and twisted as the man kissed her breasts and throat. In her dream she felt the heat of his body against hers. She moaned, and wakened herself.

Flushed and hot, she got up and drank from the dipper. All was quiet; Maria still slept. Silva lay down again and closed her eyes. Why had she dreamed such a crazy thing? She hated for a man to touch her. Yet, in her sleep she had wanted it.

What was it like, when a man lay with a girl? She looked down at her slim body, the soft rounded curves. Brian Cameron had looked at her as though he wanted to see what was under her dress.

She sighed, trying to relax. It was so hot, she felt very hot and sticky-damp.

Finally Silva slept again, a troubled sleep in which dreams invaded her mind—dreams of a dark man and vines of twisting green looping her and the man together, dreams of green orchids and fragrant spices. She dreamed she was running along the beach and someone was running after her, coming closer and closer—

She wakened with a cry as the thing was about to touch her shoulder and pull her down. She had been about to be thrown into hot water like the turtle, and boiled alive. She was shaking, and her cotton dress was twisted up about her thighs.

She sat up and wiped her face with a piece of cotton. It was early yet; the sun was streaming through the gaps in the torn curtains. She lay back down and gazed at the walls, whose whitewash she had covered over with her youthful paintings. Fish swam in blue waters, pink corals crested against white sands, and exotic flowers bloomed over the ceiling. Her dressing table was of cedar. Tyrone had made it when he was twelve, and her father had sent to the mainland for a fine mirror which had arrived cracked. However, she could see her face in it, and brush her hair properly. In the corner were hooks on which she hung her half-dozen cotton shifts and her nightgown of white cotton.

Presently she heard Tyrone groaning and stumbling about. He must have drunk some of his own rum on the return, thought Silva, her mouth tightening. His head would be large and woolly, as he said.

Damn, why did he have to hang out with that filthy Rodrigues?

She got up, and washed when Tyrone had left the small room that served as their bathroom. A fresh-water stream outside ran nearby, and her father had managed to set up a pipeline with valves to run inside. There was no tub such as she remembered from England. They used huge basins and stood on straw mats to wash.

Then she put on a fresh cotton dress, one of lime-green with darker green orchids on it. Rodrigues had brought the material from the mainland, and she had not been able to resist the pretty fabric, though Maria Luisa had scowled and said he need not expect to be paid for it. Rodrigues had only laughed and said his payment would be to see Silva pretty in the dress.

Silva sighed. Oh, what was the matter with her? She questioned everything, especially since her father's death. All had changed. There was no tall, sober father to run to with childish hurts and maturing questions. There was no absentminded criticism of her paintings, occasionally a shrewd remark that she would store in her mind to treasure.

She went out to the back. Dusk had fallen quickly over the Caribbean island, and the sky was a lilac-purple in the west. From their house they could see out over the sea, and the stars were pricking the skies and reflecting in the shining waters as they boiled around the rocks and drifted into the lagoons. A thin crescent of a new moon was rising, and Silva stood to watch it happily. Good things happened in the new moon, sometimes.

Tyrone came out, gave her a hug. "'Guess what I brought from mainland," he said carelessly.

She hugged him back. "A headache," she retorted.

"Wicked sister!" He laughed and pushed her affectionately. "Look at this." He opened his palm and showed a pair of fine golden earrings. "Topaz," he said proudly. They were wired for pierced ears, so Silva knew they were not for her.

Maria Luisa came to look. "Huh, for that no-good Oona," she sniffed.

"Right you are. Her eyes will sparkle when I give them to her." And Tyrone laughed, his face flushed, his eyes shining green in the firelight.

"What you bring your own twin sister?" asked Maria Luisa bluntly. "Something pretty, huh?"

"Sure, I brought her some material for a dress. Rodrigues picked it out. It's blue and pink," he said.

He brought the material, and Silva thanked him, fingering it curiously. It was a fine pretty material, softer than cotton.

"It has some silk in it," he said proudly. The fabric shimmered in the lamplight. Maria Luisa studied it critically.

"We make it up long dress, for your sister. She getting older, want new clothes," said Maria Luisa.

Tyrone stared at his sister, but Silva thought he did not really see her. His fingers were playing with the earrings, and his thoughts were with voluptuous Oona, only sixteen but fine and big now, with large dark eyes and long lashes that fluttered at Rodrigues, at Tyrone, at Pedro Ortega.

"You fool going on them trips with Rodrigues," said Maria Luisa. "Don't I tell you not to go? He get you in trouble, him."

"He gets me in money." Tyrone shrugged. "Is that bad? No way to make money on this damn island."

He was beginning to talk like Rodrigues also, Silva sighed to herself. She said seriously, "Tyrone, he *will* get you in trouble. He won't care. He'll let you take the blame, and maybe go to jail, and he'll slip away. He is as slick as a fish."

"So am I," said Tyrone confidently. "We haven't ever been caught, not even close. Pedro teaches us all the tricks."

"That Pedro, he no damn good," snorted Maria

Luisa. "Don't I tell you, don't mess with that native? He no good at all. He make big trouble wherever he go, one island and another."

"Oona says he is the smartest man around, Pedro Ortega," Tyrone told her defiantly, standing with his legs apart, his head high, the blond hair shining. His green eyes flashed. "He is smart; he knows all the ways of running that launch so no one can hear us get into harbor. No one hears us, no one."

"One day you get caught," said Maria Luisa, sighing. "And all for that no-good Oona, who will marry with Rodrigues one day. She not for you, that one."

Tyrone smiled secretively. Silva, watching him, thought how her brother had changed. He had been gay, happy, always singing and playing his guitar, or going fishing or swimming with her. But the past year he had changed as much as Liane.

"She likes me best, she says so," he said.

Liane and Nathaniel approached, hands swinging, heads close together as they murmured. They fell silent as they heard Maria Luisa arguing with Tyrone. Nathaniel turned serious, his dark face intent, listening to the quarrel.

"Oona is crazy for me," said Tyrone, and swung away impatiently. "You going to fix dinner for me, or shall I go away hungry?"

Maria Luisa had her hands on her hips. Silva caught her dark gaze and shook her head decidedly. Tyrone was turning stubborn now, and there would be no talking to him.

"Let's eat," said Silva. "We have turtle, Tyrone. Nathaniel caught us a turtle."

"Oh, great!" cried Tyrone, a boy again. "How did you get him, Nathaniel? Why didn't you call me?"

"You sleeping like the dead with a *loa* on you," said Nathaniel dryly.

Maybe that was it, Silva decided. A *loa* named Oona, a beautiful, cold, calculating female who wanted jewels, clothes, and admiration from her men.

She might marry Rodrigues as Maria Luisa and others thought. Maybe not. Maybe she would keep them all dangling after her, giving her presents.

But they put the topic from them and made merry over the turtle soup, the rice and beans, and the sweet honey cakes Silva had made the day before. It was a good meal, with music and laughter to follow.

Tyrone brought out his guitar, Silva took her lute, Liane her smaller guitar, and Nathaniel a small drum. Maria Luisa listened and clapped her hands and sang the old songs, chanting and singing and urging them on.

The music drove away the bad spirits which had made them quarrel, and they laughed and were merry together. Liane crept closer to Nathaniel and he grinned down at her, and they sang a love song together while Maria Luisa watched them shrewdly.

It was a good ending to a poor restless day, and Silva went to bed happily as the moon drifted over the hills and lit up the lagoon with white light.

A good sleep made Silva feel better. However, the next morning as she was painting, she heard voices and went outside.

Tyrone was standing, hands on hips, talking to Rodrigues, Pedro, and Oona. Maria Luisa was bent over the fire, muttering gloomily to herself. Liane and Nathaniel had disappeared, off by themselves.

Rodrigues swung about when Silva came out to them. His sharp black eyes went over her, and his easy smile came with a flash of white teeth. He was over thirty, she knew, but he seemed younger and merrier than Pedro Ortega.

"Hey there, Silva, not see you two, three days. How you like the present, hey?" said Rodrigues, coming over to touch her arm. Maria Luisa straightened herself to watch them sharply.

Silva slid easily away from him, making the movement leisurely so he would not be offended. "I like it, Rodrigues. It was good of you to help Tyrone choose it."

"You make pretty dress, hey? Maybe go to dance with Rodrigues sometime soon, hey?" He had been persistently asking her to go to dances with him for a time now, but she avoided them. Tyrone went, but Silva felt uneasy about that.

"How about some coffee for everybody?" said Silva, not answering him.

Oona gave a little cooing laugh. Silva looked at her. The brilliant dark eyes looked at her contemptuously, the full hips swung as she turned from Silva to Tyrone. "Your sister, she don't like our dances, huh?"

"Oh, sure, she's just busy now, plenty busy with her pictures," he said easily.

Silva compressed her lips. She set out cups and poured hot black coffee into them. It was the ritual, the gesture to guests that must be made. But she wished they would all go away. They made her unhappy, staring at her.

Pedro Ortega said slowly in his gruff voice, "She white girl, not native. She don't belong here—don't like our dances, don't like our ways."

Maria Luisa said quickly, "She goes with me to voodoo. She dance before the gods, she good girl. You know that, Pedro Ortega."

The man shrugged. His left cheek was marred by a deep slash that had turned red against his heavy brown cheek. It pulled down his left eye in a peculiar way.

They drank the coffee and talked easily. Tyrone kept his gaze on Oona, and his hand in his pocket fiddled with the earrings. He longed to be alone with her, Silva realized, with some new wisdom.

Rodrigues held out his cup to Silva to be refilled. She held the huge pot steadily, her gaze intent on the cup, aware of the masculine smell of him, the hot pungent odor that came from him sometimes. He put his hand on her wrist as she would have drawn back. His touch was gentle, but commanding.

"Why don't you come to dance with me Saturday night?" he murmured urgently. "You like me, I know you like dance. Come on, Silva. You be the prettiest gal there."

"You take Oona to the dance, don't you?" she replied coolly, her eyes narrowed like a cat's. "She would be angry with you if I came."

"Not this time. I take you with me."

"No, thank you. Maria Luisa says no," she said definitely.

A shadow crossed his face, and he gave an ugly look at Maria Luisa. "Don't listen to that old one. She is sour. You are sweet and pretty. You grow up now."

A shiver of premonition went through her. Sure, she was eighteen, and many island girls took their men earlier than this. But she didn't want to—she didn't want to. And why should she? She didn't like Rodrigues the way Liane liked Nathaniel. She had no respect for him or faith in him.

"We going to a cockfight," Pedro Ortega was saying to Tyrone. "You come, bet. Maybe you win this time."

Silva opened her mouth to warn him against betting with Pedro, but she caught Maria Luisa's gaze and shut her mouth again. Tyrone was getting to be a man; he would have to learn in his own way. Pedro was tough, cunning. If there were only some nice white men for Tyrone to associate with! But he and she knew only the islanders. And Nathaniel did not bet much; he was saving his money for marriage to Liane.

"That Mr. Cameron, he come back," said Maria Luisa suddenly. "Why you not work today, Rodrigues? He let you go?"

The strong brown chest swelled under the loose shirt. "Let me go? Huh! He need me—he says so.

He knows I best damn boss he ever got! No, the folks, they work—I come away, they do fine. If they let up behind my back, I give them hell, I do."

"That Mr. Cameron, he should not own our island," said Pedro Ortega, scowling. "He not live here. It is our island."

Again Silva felt a little shiver run down her spine. Maria Luisa was listening with her graying head bent, and Silva caught the flash of her black eyes.

She did not try to answer Ortega. She feared him a little. He was strong and bullying, and he had killed men, she heard, on other islands. He had a fierce temper when he was roused.

"You bring me something from Miami, huh?" Oona asked Tyrone softly, coaxingly. Her voluptuous body, outlined by the tight-fitting cotton sheath, leaned against his briefly. She gazed up at him with lustrous eyes. "Hey—you did bring me something pretty? Where is it?"

Tyrone laughed, his face flushed. "Oh, if you go to the dance with me come Saturday I'll give you something, maybe," he said easily.

"She goes with Rodrigues," said Maria Luisa sharply.

"Maybe I go with Tyrone; he got something for Oona," said the red-lipped girl, pouting. Tyrone seemed unable to keep his look from going over her in a way that made Silva flush and turn from them.

"You go with Oona this time. I go with your sister, Silva," said Rodrigues, lounging against the back of a chair.

Tyrone looked away from Oona and stared at his sister. She shook her head, the blonde hair flying about her shoulders.

"She won't go," he said sharply, protectively. "If Oona wants to go with me, that is it. No bargains. Just Oona makes up her mind."

"Why don't you make up your mind, or we miss all the cockfights," said Pedro Ortega, standing erect from lounging against the side of the house. His black eyes were sharp.

Tyrone shrugged, and went with them. Silva could hear their easy talk, their laughter, with Oona's sensuous tones weaving about the men's deeper voices.

They left a bad smell. Silva brought some branches of frangipani, red blossomed and fragrant, and waved them about the fire and across the dirt floor of the crude patio. Maria Luisa watched her seriously.

"You no mess with them men," she said finally.

Silva nodded. "I know, Maria Luisa. They are no good. I wish Tyrone would stay away from them, but what else is there for him on the island? He likes to sing, play his guitar, laugh, make man talk. Who can he do it with but them?"

Maria Luisa nodded, muttered to herself for a time. Silva felt too unhappy to return to her painting. She sat for a time on the crude chair, but it was uncomfortable. Presently she moved to a straw mat and sat with her legs crossed before her, brooding at the fire.

They heard the horse's hooves before they saw anyone. Silva looked down the hill, toward the west, and saw the black stallion weaving in and out of the trees, coming closer. Seated erect, the tall man was looking up at them. She did not wave.

"Mr. Cameron is coming," she said to Maria Luisa, who was peering intently. Silva thought her eyes were not so good as they used to be.

The horse trotted around the house. Brian pulled him up and slipped down. Silva did not get up, but sat gazing at him from under her lashes.

"Hello, Silva. Hello, Maria Luisa. Long time since I saw you," he said casually, his blue gaze on them.

"Come and sit," said Maria Luisa. She poured a cup of black coffee for him. He accepted it and drank it as though he didn't care much for their strong brew.

In one hand he carried a pink hibiscus. When he

saw Silva was looking at him, he tossed the flower to her. She accepted it, studying the pretty veined leaves and the delicate color. Then she stuck it into her blonde hair behind her ear.

"She has grown up, Maria Luisa," said Brian, his coffee finished. He sat down easily on a mat, disdaining the chair. It would have been too small for him anyway, thought the girl. "All grown up and beautiful."

"Yes, my girl beautiful," said Maria Luisa. "You come back, stay a long time," she added.

"Maybe stay for a while. I brought guests with me, some people from New York City. We may not stay long."

"You stay long time," she repeated dully, gazing into the fire.

Brian Cameron frowned at her, his tanned face showing lines he didn't used to have. "What do you mean?" he asked sharply. "Are you reading the future for me?"

Silva stirred angrily. "Don't talk to Maria Luisa like that," she told him. "Maria Luisa can see the future. She doesn't have to tell you what it is."

He looked her over thoughtfully, eyes narrowed against the sun. He was so big and tanned, so lean and different from the natives, that he made her uneasy. And he wore a silk suit, with a beautiful ruffled shirt that would have made Rodrigues green with envy. On his tie he had a stud of ruby, glittering in the sunshine. He wore a thick leather belt with a holster, and a pearl-handled revolver stuck in it. Again he made her conscious of her faded cotton shift, her bare legs, and her bare feet, for she had left her sandals in her bedroom.

"All right, Maria Luisa, what is my future?" he asked, and laughed a little. "Am I going to marry and have fine sons?"

Maria Luisa was not disturbed by his laughter, but Silva smoldered inwardly.

"You marry one day soon, you have fine sons," said Maria Luisa calmly. "But first you go through much trouble."

"And have a long journey, I suppose."

He was laughing at Maria Luisa. Silva said tautly, "Why don't you go away, go back to your white folks, and laugh with them. We don't want you here."

Maria Luisa said mildly, "You don't send guests away, honey. He not bad man. Just foolish sometimes."

Now he lost his smile, and his tanned face flushed red. "Foolish? Why?" he snapped.

"You don't see under your nose, man," she said placidly. "You look around, see what there. Might surprise you, huh?"

"What do you mean by that?"

He looked from Maria Luisa to Silva. Silva kept her eyes lowered. Maria Luisa was warning him, couldn't he tell? She didn't bother to warn people if she didn't like them. But he was obtuse, like many whites who lived on the mainland. She had heard of them from her father. Callous, hard, seeing only the surface.

Maria Luisa was smiling to herself, and she began muttering to the fire. Brian turned from her impatiently, to Silva.

"Listen, child. I came to ask you to come meet my guests. Come with me now, for luncheon. Where is your brother?"

"At a cockfight," she said sullenly, her mouth tight. "I am not coming." Was he stupid? Couldn't he see she would not fit in with his fine white visitors?

"Don't be sulky, child. I can promise you, you will be safe. Our guests want to meet you and Tyrone. I told them about you."

"What did you tell them?" she blazed, jumping up. "That we are wild, native-grown little savages?"

He stood too, his blue eyes flashing into hers. "Don't be a little idiot." She got the distinct impression that crossing his plans put him out of temper. He was too accustomed to having his own way. The big tycoon, the big storm on the mainland. He isn't even a little breeze here on the island, she thought. He couldn't even see that Rodrigues was cheating him, even though Maria Luisa was warning him to look about.

"She come some other time," said Maria Luisa. "You want more coffee, Mr. Cameron?"

"No. I want Silva to come over to Cameron Hall, meet my guests. You can have fifteen minutes to change your dress," he added, his square jaw set ominously.

She stared at him. Change to what? she wondered. To another faded cotton shift? Didn't he know, couldn't he see, didn't he realize she was just a poor girl, in a crude home, with few clothes?

All at once she was unbearably aware of what she was. Pretty, sure—attractive to the native men. But as crude as they were. Little education. Her house a jumble of homemade furniture and broken-down stuff from England. Herself, straining out of her old cotton clothes. All these things, which had mattered little in the old days, were suddenly painful and close and terrible.

"I'm not coming."

He started at her quiet, definite tone, and glared down at her. He seemed shocked, as though unable to believe someone would refuse him. Great big chief, she thought.

"Of course you are. Why not? Tyrone can come next time. I am anxious to see him again, see how he has grown up." His voice was softening as though to soften her.

She was shaking her head. "No. You go away. We don't want you here."

Maria Luisa put her dark hand on Silva's tanned one. "Not today, Mr. Cameron," she said softly, in a sibilant whisper. "Another day, not today. She not ready to come today."

"Well, get some manners shaken into the girl and get her ready to come another day." Now he was angry, a clear hot anger that flamed in the big tanned body. "You're a little witch of a girl, Silva, but you can't go wild indefinitely. It's time you met your own kind, and got civilized. I mean to take you to the mainland, you and Tyrone, and see you get some proper education. Valerian would want that, I know."

Her chin was thrust out with youthful stubbornness, though her slim body was vulnerable, aching. Go to the mainland, see the world—not just this beloved green island—see the beauties of painting, hear the great music—just as her father had told them. Could that be for her? Could it ever?

"If Father had wanted us to visit the mainland, he would have taken us."

A half-smile touched his lips though his eyes still shone with fury. "Did he have a motor launch, or just a rowboat?" he mocked.

Her mouth tightened and she glared at him.

Maria Luisa interposed. "You go now. Maybe sometime soon she come, Mr. Cameron."

"I'm not coming, ever," Silva flung at him defiantly.

He bowed to her mockingly. He got on his horse, and rode away with an angry clatter of hooves on the dirt, dust flying up behind him.

"He is hatefully, horribly sure of himself, but he is wrong, Maria Luisa!"

"You come sometime to his house, child," said Maria Luisa gently, patting her arm. "Don't never say *never,* for you has to eat your words. He good man, just blind now. But one day he open up his eyes. You wait."

Silva did not understand. She turned away. "I need some blue paints," she said forlornly. "I'm going out. I will be back for lunch, by and by."

Maria Luisa nodded and watched her go, love and

wistfulness in her eyes for the child she had raised and adored. She was a special child, she had often told Silva, a very special twin-child, with silver in her hair and emeralds in her eyes.

Silva roamed the woods for a time, working her way up the hill behind the house, looking for blue flowers she could crush and grind for paints. She knew one variety and had seen a second that might do better. She did not know their names, only their beautiful blue fragility. Wistfully she thought of how much in the world she did not know, might never know or learn.

If her father had lived, would he have taken them to the mainland, given them more education, taught them of the world? Perhaps not. He had hated the outside world; he had said the island of Desirée was a paradise—except that his wife was not there.

Silva grew cooler in the woods, and more calm and content. There was something in the green dimness that called to her to come and rest, to be at peace. On the forest floor grew great green ferns, larger than she was, and lianas wound their great stems lovingly about the cedars and mahogany and breadfruit trees. She came to a waterfall and paused for a time, searching in its cool banks for the blue flower and finally finding it, hidden shyly in lacy ferns near the water.

She plucked a dozen or so, carefully, taking only the fullest blooms and leaving the new buds and little flowers. These would be enough for her painting, if she could crush and mix them properly.

Silva sat quietly for a time beside the waterfall, gazing at the massive height of the rocks, the rush of the white waters, the pool of green foaming with bubbles. She dipped her hands in, tickled a daring pink fish that came close to her fingers. It flicked away from her, hiding under the rocks. A monkey, lured by the quiet, chattered away in the tree above her head. A vivid green parrot answered him crossly, mimicking him, until Silva's laugh rang out softly and silenced them both.

She climbed higher, then crested the hill, driven and drawn to look once more at the great white Spanish house of the lordly Brian Cameron. Up on the heights the wind whipped more coldly, even in the green heat of noon. She was sitting under a tree, gazing out over the valley toward the red-tiled roof of Cameron Hall, when she heard the horses and the creak of carriages.

Swift as a frightened bird, she rose and fled to the sanctuary of a thick frond of fern. From there, hovering like a hummingbird, ready to dart away, she watched. The carriages advanced toward her, up the hill, on the narrow path that led up and then down again across the valley toward the cane fields.

They came within fifty feet of her. Brian Cameron drove the fine matched grays of the first carriage. By his side, holding a beautiful white parasol over her head, was a lady with blonde hair. She was beautiful, full-blown and voluptuous like Oona, yet not like her. Older, her face painted skillfully, like Carnival, yet gorgeous, thought Silva.

And her dress! It was of some fine creamy fabric that blew in the wind, and the edgings were fine-spun lace, and all about her slim, tall neck was a collar of lace a foot deep. Lace sleeves reached the long, delicate white hands. And with her red mouth she was laughing up at Brian Cameron.

Silva swallowed, gazing wide-eyed. She had never seen such a lady, such a gown, such a hat of lace and feathers.

Behind them was a man, young, leaning forward, face eager. Ordinary, but a white man, with brown hair and eyes. Listening, speaking a little, smiling. Then she looked at the next carriage.

One of the natives drove it. In the back seat was an older couple. Silva merely glanced at the swarthy red-faced man, the curly hair, the hat that fanned him. Her look went with hungry curiosity to the woman.

She was middle-aged, painted also, plump like Oona's mother, who was a favorite of the men. She was not blonde. She had black eyes, long lashes, and straight black hair drawn in a beautiful shining chignon under a white hat. Her dress was white lace threaded with crimson ribbons, and a crimson ribbon encircled her plump waist. Her hat was drooping with more lace.

The carriages went on. Silva sank back, breathless, with such a pounding feeling in her heart that her slim hand went to her chest and pressed in alarm. Oh, how beautiful they were, those ladies! Did all the mainland ladies look like that? She had sought to see something different—and caught a glimpse of slim white shoes, white stockings under the lace hems. So beautiful, and expensive, with jewels glittering in their ears and flicking rainbows into the air so that glory seemed to ride in the carriages, spilling beauty into the breeze.

Brian Cameron wanted her to come and meet those ladies, wearing her faded shift! Her mouth curled with self-contempt, then trembled with a sudden desire to weep. How crude she would seem compared to them! Even if Maria Luisa made up the new blue and pink silk and cotton fabric into a lovely long dress, Silva would never look like that!

She returned home slowly, reluctantly. She went to the bedroom, but the sight of her half a dozen dresses mocked her. Fiercely she turned to painting. She ground the blue flowers, added fixative and a little alcohol, and painted for a time. She managed to put in the blue sky, the blue flower, before the mixture dried.

But her heart was not in it. She kept thinking of those two smart painted carriages, and Brian Cameron smiling down indulgently at the pretty lady beside him, all pink and cream and smiles, all lace and elegance. She wished Brian Cameron had never returned to Desirée—she wondered if he had returned especially to taunt her.

Chapter 4

Brian drove his guests about the plantation in the two carriages, sensing the interest of the men and the boredom of the two ladies. When the heat grew more intense, they returned with relief to the house, and took shelter in a patio.

The houseboy brought tall glasses of lime juice and ice, pleasantly clinking, with mint leaves on the top. Astrid took a sip and grimaced.

"Darling," she drawled. "I didn't think you carried Prohibition this far!" She held out the glass to Brian.

He shrugged, went to the locked whiskey chest, and brought out a bottle of Scotch. He added some to her glass and to that of Giovanni Leoni. He sat down again, with his own lime drink.

"Ah, that's much better," she said with satisfaction, licking her full red lips. She glanced at him like a cat, from under her long lashes. "Darling, you're different here. What is the difference? Let me analyze it."

Astrid adored analyzing things. Brian leaned back and let her rattle on. He smiled occasionally and managed to answer her from the top of his mind. Underneath, he was thinking.

Why was Silva so distant and aloof, then so furiously angry? How did he offend her? He thought of her, shy as a child, her bare feet tucked under herself, the grave look of her green eyes. The long silver hair flowing about her shoulders, the fey look of her when he tried to approach her. Beautiful, unaware of her beauty, unawakened—how different from brazen Astrid who boasted that she always knew what she wanted and how to go about achieving what she desired.

They had luncheon on the patio, served from plates and cups of white china with rims of blue and gold, set off by glasses of cut crystal. The fare was island food: roast pork sliced thin and layered with yams, stuffed mushrooms with herbs and spices, crisp green salad, then a compote of passion fruit, papaya, pineapple brought in from Central America, and crisp little pieces of coconut. With it was served rosé wine, then white wine with the dessert of honey cake.

The Leonis retired to their room afterward to sleep in the hot afternoon hours. Donald Keller stuck it out for half an hour, but after a dozen yawns he apologized and left with a grin. "Can't stay awake—sorry. I'll perk up when the evening turns cool."

Only Astrid and Brian remained on the patio, stretched out in long chairs beside the pool, watching the butterflies fluttering above the frangipani, the bees buzzing in the honeysuckle.

It was odd, he thought idly, that he had brought such an assorted lot to the island this time. He had been ordering wines from Leoni when Mrs. Leoni had come in, her face weary and drawn. On impulse he had said he was coming to a beautiful island paradise, and would they join him?

To his surprise, they had dropped all and come with him. They had never been close friends, though he had dutifully taken presents to their children, exchanged greetings at Christmas, and given rides to their older boys whenever he drove around to see them in his latest-model Pierce-Arrow. Something about them puzzled him. Formerly they had been jocular and Mrs. Leoni rarely was sad. She would beam at him over the head of her newest baby, invariably a black-haired plump brown child, and make him welcome. Now there was something deeply sad about her. Were they in trouble with the rum-running? Or was the organization mad at Leoni for some reason?

Brian Cameron kept warily away from discussion of the Italian organizations to which Leoni belonged. They dealt in violence at times, and he wanted no part of it.

Well, perhaps being here in the Caribbean would get them away from their troubles for a time, and give them some ease. He hoped so.

Donald Keller seemed to have no trouble adapting to taking a holiday. He was frankly overjoyed at the sunshine, the beautiful home, Astrid's presence, the delicious food and wines. He had thanked Brian gratefully several times, for giving him the chance to get away from "the heat of Wall Street," as he put it.

Astrid Larsen—well, he would have been a fool if he had not seen through her motives. If he were poor, she would not even see him passing her on the street, he thought cynically. She might cast admiring looks at handsome men—as he had seen her do—when they were out, but marriage—no, she would look for a wealthy man.

He might do worse than to marry her, he thought, but flinched from it. She was like other greedy, voracious women he knew, thinking of little but their clothes, their jewels, their lovers, their marvelous trips to Europe, the latest dance music, where they might be seen. The height of their ambitions was to appear in a glossy magazine in the fashions of next year, with a suitably flattering paragraph beneath their pictures.

"Darling . . ." He became aware of her softly insistent petulant voice. "You haven't heard a word I said!"

"Sorry, I must be sleepy as well," he murmured, knowing he was not. He rarely slept in the daytime;

he was one of those men who needed less than six hours of sleep a night. His brain worked constantly; he enjoyed his work and was always thinking of fresh ideas. Social life bored him because it was repetitious, and he would not endure boredom. Work was the breath of life to him, for there was constant challenge in it. He had made enemies, and laughed about it. There was an excitement in having enemies, in defeating a smart company, in racing someone to a mining find and getting his claim in first. The pleasure in finding a rare high-grade ore was a hundred times that of escorting a beautiful woman to a social function where his picture might be taken with her.

If Astrid knew his thoughts, she would slap him with her long slim hand, he thought, drawing on his thin Havana cigar. She disliked thinking that any man could concentrate on his work when he was in her fragrant perfumed presence.

"Darling, are you really sleepy?" she murmured throatily and laid her hand on his knee.

He looked at the hand, at the red-painted nails, the sharp fingers. Suddenly he was remembering a sensitive golden-tanned hand, trembling in his grip, fingers pressed against a mouth like a hibiscus flower, pink and slightly open. Wide, puzzled green eyes, an averted face, with high cheekbones and masses of silvery hair falling about her shoulders.

New York would rave about her beauty, if she were dressed properly, he thought. Paris would go mad. Her slimness, her youth, her innocence and fey charm. Dressed in some pale green foamy material, or a cream lace that set off her golden skin, or a black chiffon that contrasted with her unreal silvery hair—

"Darling, you are not hearing one word!" Astrid's hand clenched more tightly on his knee, and annoyance sharpened her silky voice. "Wake up!" She snapped the fingers of her other hand in his face.

So might she snap her fingers at her pet dog, to get

him to come. Brian found himself stiffening with aversion.

"What is it, Astrid? Afraid I was thinking of other matters," he said with cool precision. "Another drink?"

He got up, and her hand fell away.

"No, thanks. I think I'll go lie down, since you aren't awake either. Darling—why don't you come along?" she murmured, rising to her feet in a lithe, sensuous movement of her long slim body. She pressed up against him, the lace of her dress against his shoulder, her half-closed eyes an invitation.

"Work to do, Astrid. Thanks, anyway."

She bit her mouth, and she would have sworn if she dared. With secret mockery he watched her struggling with herself. No, she would not swear. She was angling for him, and her bait was sweet, womanly understanding.

"Of course, love. Don't work too hard. See you at —cocktails?" She was an artist at the over-the-shoulder look, rounded chin turned, eyes flirtatious.

He smiled and nodded, then strode off in the other direction. He was vaguely amused at himself. He had accepted other such invitations. Perhaps she was just too blatant today with her motives, her gestures. Perhaps he just wanted to do the pursuing.

He went over to his small laboratory and unlocked the door. It was a sultry afternoon and the brick lab was hot. He left the door open and propped open a couple of windows. He was soon absorbed in his testing, working with the copper samples he had brought in the day before.

He worked for several hours, and finally stood back, thinking. He figured rapidly on some paper, nodding. Yes, it could bring in a couple of million, even after expenses. And what expenses would he have on this island? The natives would be glad of the work. He could soon teach them how to mine the copper, how to work in the blast-furnace building. And what he didn't have time to do he could trust to Mickey McCoy.

He became aware suddenly of another presence, a shadow between him and the door. He looked up sharply, to find Rodrigues Estavez standing in the doorway, holding his huge straw hat in both hands, peering at him curiously. As he looked, the foreman came farther in, boldly walking over to the lab table, gazing curiously at the experiments.

"You wish to see me, *señor?*" asked Estavez. "You send for me?"

"Two days ago," said Brian dryly. He stood up. "We'll go outside and talk. It's hot in here."

"I don't mind the heat, *señor.*" Estavez smiled, showing most of his white teeth. "The natives, we used to the heat. It is the white men who are not used to the hot sun of our island."

"Was that a warning?" asked Brian, then as the man looked puzzled he shook his head. "Never mind. Go outside and wait. I'll lock up here."

Estavez picked up a piece of rock sample, studied it curiously. "What you do, *señor?*" he asked, as though a child.

"Never mind," said Brian, taking the rock from him and replacing it on the table. He smiled a little grimly. They would learn soon enough.

Estavez left reluctantly. Brian shut the windows, made sure the Bunsen burners were turned off, then left also, locking the door and putting the key in his pocket.

"You mad with me?" asked Rodrigues guilelessly, his brown eyes troubled, seeking his worn sandals.

"I could have used you when the fire started in the cane, and you weren't around. Where have you been for two days?" Brian asked mildly.

"I work in the cane, to the south, near the village. The men there, they new, they young. I need watch."

It could have been true. Brian walked slowly toward the gardens, Rodrigues a respectful pace or two behind him. He stopped at the yellow allamanda; it reminded him somehow of the softness of Silva's face and her arms.

"How many men work in the cane, Rodrigues?"

"How many?" Rodrigues hesitated, obviously puzzled. "But you see, sir, many of the men, they are women, and the children, they work also."

"Just the men. How many?" Brian repeated patiently.

Rodrigues counted, his lips moving. "Maybe forty, maybe fifty sometimes. Maybe they go to Miami, come back to work. Maybe fifty. But the women, they work in the cane. They don't mind the work, they sing, *señor—*"

Forty or fifty men. That would be enough to work the mine, and run the smelter, and have enough to work on the two freighters running back and forth between the island and the mainland. Brian picked a golden allamanda and twirled it in his strong brown fingers.

"You want me to work them harder, *señor?* You mad because the cane is not good? We don't make much money these years."

The man was almost humble, biting his lips, looking anxious.

"No, don't work them harder. It won't matter, Rodrigues."

Rodrigues looked shocked. "It no matter, *señor?* Why not, it don't matter? You want to make the more money, no?"

He was getting excited. Brian smiled faintly. It wouldn't hurt to let him wonder for a while. "The cane is not enough income, Rodrigues," he said. "I may let it drop. Not grow cane any longer. But there will be work for the people—tell them that. They are not to worry about having good work and good wages."

"What do you mean, *señor?* I do not see what you mean. You mad with me? You wish me to come with you when you ride? There be bad men in the hills sometimes. More better I ride with you, *señor.*"

Brian stopped his slow pacing and turned about to face the stocky native. The man's gaze flickered, looked away, then faced him boldly. So someone had been following him. Rodrigues? No, he would have run to help in the cane, probably. Then who?

But Rodrigues knew he had been followed. Perhaps he had been followed to the lagoon—God, he hoped not! He didn't want any of them to see Silva the way he had seen her.

"Bad men? What bad men? On this island? Are there strangers?"

"Oh, no, no, *señor*, of course not! Only some of the men, they get drunk sometimes, and they bad. They follow you in the hills, maybe, they not see the jaguar which roams alone in the hills—"

Those hills of the jaguars—he could only mean the Mountain of the Cat. Brian's gaze sharpened, and he stared at Rodrigues. So someone had followed him up to the sacred mountain, watched as he had taken his core samples.

"What do the men get drunk on?" he asked softly.

"Why, the rum, *señor*. What else is there on Desirée?"

What else indeed? And the rum was potent. Were they making rum here? Was that what had been going on in the blackened sugar mill of his ancestors?

"You mad they drink, *señor?* Cannot keep the men from the rum, when the fiesta is held, and men make merry!" Rodrigues gave a vast shrug, and a big grin.

"No, not mad. Well, tomorrow I'll go down to the docks, Rodrigues. You meet me there, about noon. I have a ship coming in, and I'll need a dozen husky men to help unload."

The dark eyes flickered warily. "The docks, *señor?*"

"Yes, the docks. I have a freighter coming in." And what a surprise for them all on that ship, he thought, with Mickey McCoy roaring ashore, and the hold full of mining equipment, rail lines, a disassembled smelter they would put together.

He walked easily away, leaving Rodrigues to stare after him in a puzzled, worried way. Brian went to the house, avoiding the pool, where he could hear splashing and laughter. He went to his own quiet suite in the wing he kept to himself, and took a cool shower, then changed for the evening. He put on a fresh gray silk suit, a loose shirt of cotton weave, a blue silk scarf about his throat. Then he went out to the patio and sat down to watch the antics in the pool.

Mrs. Leoni was sitting there also, and gave him a happy smile. She was looking better, less sallow, he thought. "Ah, Mr. Cameron, how nice to see you. You work too hard, like Giovanni. You rested, didn't you?"

"I'm fine," he said, giving nothing away. "You're looking radiant in your beautiful green. The color is most becoming. No wonder Giovanni gets jealous of you still."

Pleased color tinted her plump cheeks. She giggled like a girl. "Ah, you tease me! But indeed, my dear Giovanni does become jealous of me, old as I am! We were married twenty-one years ago, would you believe it?"

"No, I would not," he said promptly, bringing fresh giggles to her. She bubbled over with them, and Giovanni hauled himself out of the pool, grunting, to look them over suspiciously.

"You see? Jealous?" murmured Brian, and her heavy form shook with laughter. Giovanni got up, dripping water, and came over to them.

"You finish with the work, eh?" he said. "I should be home working. What am I doing, lazing away like this? I ask myself."

"And I tell you, you need the vacation," retorted his wife, with spirit. "You work yourself to the bone, and for what? We have more money than we can spend, your sons are in the best schools, and your daughter is to marry this autumn to a fine young man. Why do you scowl with worry?"

"I will go get myself dressed. When my wife starts attacking me, she is hungry," he grumbled, and laughed when his wife threatened to kick him with her pretty green shoe.

Donald Keller hauled himself out of the pool, a slim young man with a muscular body unusual for a stockbroker, Brian noted idly. Astrid followed him, poised for a long moment on the edge of the pool, silhouetted against the flowery hedges that rimmed it, so one could study the curves of her rounded figure snugly encased in a tight suit of silver that left little to the imagination.

Brian ordered drinks, taking a long, cool lime for himself and requesting a special for Astrid. She seemed over her mood, but her large blue eyes studied him speculatively as she sipped her drink. The evening passed pleasantly, culminating with dinner of roast chicken, boiled greens and ham, fresh strawberries and white wine.

Brian found himself wondering what Silva ate for lunch and dinner. She certainly did not have a chef brought over from Miami, and two assistant cooks, with a houseboy to serve on the finest linen and china and crystal. She did not drink white wines and champagne. Did she drink rum? He frowned slightly. Surely Maria Luisa was too smart to let her do that. But he hated to think of the young girl left to the uncertain mercies of a native woman. Who knew what odd fancies the woman might take? She was known to be involved in voodoo; everyone on the island was.

Astrid's hand touched his lightly. "Business again, darling, to make you scowl? I am determined to make you forget it! Surely you can relax on this darling island!"

"'I rarely relax," he said with a smile, and gave

her fingers a quick squeeze. "If I did, a competitor would cut my throat! You wouldn't want that to happen, would you?"

Donald leaned forward. "Tell me about it—I love stories of big dangerous business!"

Brian laughed at the bright-eyed young man. He was so young and eager; Brian felt years older, though they were practically the same age.

"I am no good at telling stories," he evaded. He thought of the angry red-faced tycoon who had threatened to shoot him if he ever again took a mine out from under his nose. He might do it, too—not himself, of course, but a hired gun. Business was not a game for gentlemen these days. Perhaps it would bore him if it were.

"Is it true someone tried to shoot you in a nightclub just before we came down here?" persisted Keller.

Brian frowned. Astrid squealed. "Shoot you! Oh, darling, no!"

"Oh, just a drunk," said Brian. "You know how it is in nightclubs. Someone had a bit too much. They just took the gun from him."

"I heard it was someone from Lamotte's outfit, the one who has the coal mines sewed up in Pennsylvania. Didn't you beat him out of something in Brazil?" Keller asked again eagerly. "Oh, excuse my impertinence! But stockmarkets get pretty dull stuff, you know! And I enjoy reading about you big tycoons and your daring exploits on the Amazon." He laughed at himself, flushing a little.

"The story was much exaggerated. I expect the newspapers were desperate for news that day." Brian smiled, calmly lighting a long brown Havana cigar from a taper held to a candle at the table. "But if you want a story, I'll tell you one."

They all urged him on, even Mrs. Leoni. He began a story of a dangerous expedition into the Amazon jungles, where he had met with Indians who had rarely seen a white man, who shot poisoned arrows, and were probably descended from the Incas of long ago. He had seen some strange statues, an altar stained with blood, and figured he himself would be a human sacrifice unless he could persuade them he was just a poor innocent wanderer who stumbled into their territory.

"Fortunately one of them spoke a little Spanish. I contented myself with collecting some odd flowers and some herbs, and got out. I decided if there was ore there, it could wait for someone more foolhardy than I am, really a coward at heart." He smiled, knowing they did not believe him.

"Oh, darling, I hate stories like that," pouted Astrid. "I hate to think of you in danger—"

"I warned you I am no good at telling stories." He glanced about the table, saw that they were all finished, and rose. They followed. "Let's go out to the patio where it is cooler. Does anyone know the constellations and the stars?"

He managed to change the conversation completely, and they talked about astrology. Mrs. Leoni believed in it, and eagerly told them stories of people she knew who had followed advice and become wealthy or lucky in love.

The evening passed pleasantly enough, and they retired early.

Brian rose early the next day and went for a ride. But Silva was not at the lagoon. He was conscious of disappointment as he returned from his ride. He would not risk again so soon a rebuff from her at the house. He would let her cool down for a few days. From years of experience, he knew enough about women to let them cool down from their angers, and think about him for a time, before venturing again. Nothing piqued a woman's curiosity like a little spell of silence.

Yet she was scarcely a woman. More a girl-child, budding, about to blossom.

At noon he rode down to the docks. Rodrigues Estavez and a group of natives were on hand. The word had gone out, as he had expected. He noticed the man with the sullen expression, the slash mark on his face, the dark one who stared at him insolently.

The freighter came in, tied up, and the first man down the gangplank was short, red-haired Mickey McCoy. He came up to Brian, grinning.

"Here I am, me darling, and with your stuff all safe and sound, like you asks me."

Brian shook his hand heartily, grinning back. They had gone through some adventures together, and Brian knew he liked having Mickey McCoy at his side or his back in a fight. He could count on him as he rarely counted on anyone.

"And who'll be unloading this precious stuff?" demanded Mickey, looking about keenly, eyeing the openmouthed but wary natives. He glanced at the scarred man. "Not him, huh?" His tone lowered. "Looks like a man in trouble, to me. Who's the beaut?"

"Don't know him yet. We probably will." Brian had noted how the man had leaned against some packing cases, staring with arms folded as others came up and crowded about curiously. Not about to put himself out by working. He beckoned to Rodrigues, who came over importantly.

"Yes, *señor?*"

"Rodrigues Estavez, my manager. This is Mickey McCoy, who is a mining engineer. You have some men ready to unload the ship, I see."

"Mining engineer?" Rodrigues stared at McCoy, who frankly stared back, his pugnacious lips pursed. "What would the good Señor McCoy do here on this peaceful island?"

"You'll soon be seeing, me love," said Mickey jovially. "All right, all right, you men, you'll be coming with me—you—and you—" He pointed to the men he wanted, surveying them with the keen eyes of experience. Brian went up the gangplank to greet the captain and chat with him about the work ahead.

On the dock Pedro Ortega watched and waited, feeling alarm and worry curling inside him like a snake. Something was going on, something he had not anticipated. He must find out what it was, and handle the matter—and quickly.

Chapter 5

Pedro Ortega leaned against the cases in the shade, chewing on a plug of tobacco, occasionally spitting contemptuously on the hard ground as the men grunted and sweated in the sun.

Damn fools, to unload a ship in full noon, the sun beating down on them. All because a white man was in a hurry, as usual! He scowled at the face of Brian Cameron as the man leaned casually at the rail, in his tan suit and white shirt, the vivid blue eyes watching alertly as the men trod down the gangplank carrying load after load of packing cases, boxes, long pipes, long rails.

What the devil were they up to? Pedro watched, fuming, as the ship was unloaded. It seemed full of metal equipment, the hold giving up countless boxes and crates, more metal rails . . .

That was it! They looked like rail lines. But why a railroad on a small island like Desirée? Where would one go on a rail line? On Desirée, everyone walked, or rode on horseback like the grand white man who thought he owned all the island.

Something odd was going on. Pedro gave one last stare at Rodrigues, directing the arrangements of the packing cases and fussing over the carriages to haul the rail lines, and promised himself an early conversation with the foreman.

Then Pedro quietly slid away. One moment he was leaning as though glued to a packing case. The next moment he was in the shadows of the trees beyond the docks, moving like a panther—or a black jaguar—through the trees toward the native village to the south.

He walked slowly in the heat of midday, puzzling, turning over and over in his mind what he had seen. He was feeling depressed, savage, wishing he could take out on someone with a whip the feelings that he had. He had come to the island two years ago, and it had been good. He had soon obtained the upper hand over Rodrigues, and that meant over the other natives as well.

He had organized well. He had persuaded them to take the cane of the white man who never came to the island, to press it into molasses, and then distill it into the golden rum the white men in Florida so desired. He had stolen a motor launch, stolen gasoline for it, and made the first few runs with only Rodrigues for company on the boat. Now he had an organization, with three launches, boats often going to the mainland, and money hidden away. They all worked for him now—or did until Brian Cameron had suddenly returned to his island.

Pedro rarely looked back to the other islands he had lived on in the blue Caribbean. The past was dead, as dead as some men he had killed. They had caught him finally, and been unable to prove anything. But they had forbidden him to return. Desirée was the latest of many islands where he had lived, and so far the most successful. It was small, and the natives were stupid and uneducated. Only Maria Luisa resisted his efforts to organize them all. And that white girl and her brother. Well, he had her brother in hand, and he could go the way of other men in time, when Pedro was done with him.

He approached the village silently. It was somnolent in the midafternoon heat, the blue sky blazing with shimmering heat waves. He came to the hut where Oona slept, her dress above her knees. He bent over her, touched her shoulder.

She wakened slowly, gave him a sloe-eyed look, her full red mouth sensuous with her dreams. She started up when she realized who it was.

"Pedro. What you do here?" she breathed, giving the next hut a worried look. Her mother had been scolding her lately. Was she never going to settle down to one man? Her behavior was a scandal, for an unmarried girl. She must wait until she had married and borne children before she acted like this. For a girl of sixteen she was a disgrace, and so on and on her mother had raged.

He beckoned her with one imperious finger, and turned to go. She pouted, sleepy-eyed, lazy, but finally got up, smoothed down the dress to her knees, and followed him.

He led the way silently to the beach below the village. Parts of it were shaded, and he flung himself down under the palms, on the sandy beach. She stood above him, her full lips pursed.

"What you want, huh?"

"Talk, girl," he said lazily. He peered up at her from under his broad-brimmed hat, the scar flaring redly on his cheek.

"Talk! I might as well sleep!" She turned to go away. He caught at one ankle with his hand and jerked cruelly. She fell down across him.

"Hey—you come when I say," he ordered.

She struggled over him, her full body pressed to his. He felt amused at her feeble efforts, and one arm went about her, and pulled her closer to him.

"You let me go! I belong to Rodrigues," she said.

"Hunh. Does he know it? Does Tyrone?" he mocked.

She slapped at his chest, then giggled. This was more what she understood.

He could rule her easily. One day he would rule all this island, and everyone on it. He would drive out the whites, and he, Pedro Ortega, driven from other islands, would rule this one—he himself, and no one else.

She struggled a little, which only suggested to him that she was ripe and eager for a little fun. He pulled her to him, caressed her with his free hand, his fingers going over the full breasts that strained against her cotton dress. She stopped struggling, and a dreamy look came into her black eyes. She snuggled against him.

"You want Oona," she whispered with satisfaction.

"I been looking at you, girl," he murmured, and pressed his face against her soft throat. She was round and fleshy, with a thick musky perfume that excited him. He bit gently at her throat, and laughed at her protest. He rolled her under him and pressed himself at her.

"No, you don't do that," she murmured, closing her legs against him. He only grinned to himself. His hand went up and down her brown arm, and he watched her face change to sensuous need. He fondled her breasts, slid his arm under her. She wriggled. "I could scream," she warned.

Yes, she could.

He murmured in her ear, "You ask Tyrone what he bring you from Miami. You don't ask me. Why not?"

She stiffened, went silent. He could practically see the greed of her little heart.

"You mock me," she murmured, her eyes half closed, watching him sharply.

He ran his fingers slowly over her throat, then down over her breasts. She was a bitch, but a beautiful one, with her black straight hair, her sloe eyes, her long lashes, and her full figure. A brazen girl, for anyone's taking. She would not be his queen, not her, but she would do for now.

"You ask me," he said as he nuzzled her throat.

She wriggled. Finally she asked him, "Pedro, you bring me something pretty? Huh?"

He reached into his hip pocket, slowly brought out a golden bracelet, and fastened the hard, cool object on her wrist. She squealed and held up her arm, fascinated. Her eyes shone.

"Real gold? Real?" she demanded.

"I get only real gold," he said with contempt. She was still holding her arm up, admiring her new possession, as he quickly raised her dress and came astride her.

She gasped, then held to him with frantic hands as he took her, there in the warm shade of the palms, with the sea beating in their ears and the blood pounding hotly in their veins. She was a vixen, but she knew what a man liked, he thought, when he finally had his satisfaction. He drew off and lay back, breathing hard.

She breathed with her mouth open, turning her head from side to side, the black hair glistening, her face wet with sweat. A hot fragrance came from her. He caressed her legs possessively with his hand, then lay back again.

"Pedro, you a devil," she said, when she could talk, her voice husky with appreciation.

"Devil you like, huh?" he muttered. "You my girl now, huh? Say it, woman!"

She came over to lie with her breasts pushed against his bare arm, her arm across him, the golden bracelet glistening in the sunshine. "I your woman now," she said fervently.

Yeah, till another man come with another present, he thought with cold contempt. But she was good on her back, real good.

"How come you go with Rodrigues? He not man enough for you. You all woman," he said.

She swelled with pride, rubbed her cheek gently against his bare brown chest. "Oh, he only man big enough around here—till you come," she murmured.

"He work for white man. Is that why? You like man to work for white man?"

"No, no, I don't care. Rodrigues do anything I say—that's what I like."

"You'll do what *I* like, woman," he growled, tightening his arm about her and squeezing her buttocks roughly. She gave a murmur of pleasure.

He questioned her more about Rodrigues, managing to find out all she knew of him. Then he asked her about Tyrone.

"Why you go with white boy like that?"

She giggled. "Oh, he give me presents. I was his first girl, you know? He thinks he is a man!"

"When they come here? They belong to Brian Cameron?"

He questioned and questioned, puzzling over her answers. The white children had come with their father, she said. The father had been a painter; he had died. Pedro vaguely remembered the tall, gaunt man who wandered off by himself with sketch pad in hand. Maria Luisa took care of the children. No, Brian Cameron did not own them, she thought.

He played with her, teased her, until she had told him all he wanted to know that she could tell. But still there was a puzzle. Why had Brian Cameron returned to the island? She did not know. What was the man searching for on the Mountain of the Cat? She did not know that he searched for anything. She knew nothing of the arrival of the freighter, except that her friends had gone down to earn some money by helping unload.

He was dissatisfied with her vague answers, but she told him all she knew. He drew her to him, and they slept easily in the waning afternoon sun.

Brian saw to the unloading of all the equipment. It was coming to dusk when the work was completed, the natives paid, and he and Mickey could have a long chat over a cool tall drink.

He took Mickey back to Cameron Hall. Mickey gave a long whistle at sight of the white buildings, the red-tiled roofs, the wide expanse of gardens and fountains, the pastures and stables. The sugar cane earned more than one keen look from the Irishman.

"Got yourself quite a spread, me boy."

"The cane isn't earning enough to worry with," said Brian.

"And why not?"

Brian shrugged. "From all I can figure I think the natives are making rum on the side. The cane looks good. But even with their appetite for rum, I can't figure out how they drink it all."

Mickey gave him a shrewd green gaze. "Wouldn't be taking it to the mainland, would they?"

"They might. But it will soon stop. I'm going to put them all to work on the mine and smelter, soon as we get them up."

"Anybody know about the copper?"

"Not yet. They soon will. But it's my island. Nobody else gets a look-in," said Brian grimly. He was thinking of a mountain in Peru where he had had to fight for his rights.

His other guests showed obvious curiosity when the spirited Irishman was introduced. "A friend of mine from the old days," Brian explained briefly.

Astrid flicked a look over the banty-legged middle-aged man with the sharp green eyes, and dismissed him as not worthy of her attentions. Donald Keller showed more interest. "What's your line of work?"

Mickey gave him a tight grin. "Engineering, same as me friend Brian, here," he said cheerfully. "Anybody have a poteen of the good stuff?" he added hopefully, looking at his tall glass of lime.

Brian topped it with Scotch. The next drink was straight Scotch, undiluted with any lime. Mickey always liked the straight goods: in talk, in whiskey, in living.

They retired early, Brian because the unaccustomed hours in the hot sun had made him unusually weary, the others because they were bored without their host, especially the peeved Astrid.

Brian and Mickey were up and about early the next morning. They went out to the docks, saw to the loading of the first lines of rail in the carriages, and sent natives up toward the mountain with the orders to unload them along the trail. Puzzled, they looked at each other, hesitated, muttered among themselves.

Finally Rodrigues came forward. *"Señor,* we wish to ask the question, if you please." He was obviously nervous, twisting his big sombrero in his hands.

"Yes, what is it?"

Brian stood with feet apart, his boots solidly planted on the dusty docks. The freighter had sailed at dawn, gone to pick up the little engine and coal cars he had ordered to carry the copper ore from the mine to the smelter, then on to the docks.

"To where do you wish this rails to go, *señor?* Please?"

"Why, up the mountain," he said casually, a gleam in his blue eyes.

"The sacred mountain, *señor?"* Rodrigues looked appalled. "Why, but—but there be jaguars there. They are dangerous, you know this?"

"Yes, I know. I'll go ahead with a rifle," Brian said.

Mickey, listening carefully, spat at his feet reflectively. He had had a feeling in his Irish bones that all was not well. The stocky natives stood closer to listen attentively, eyes going from the six-foot white man to the leader of the natives, Rodrigues Estavez.

"But why for do you have the rails to the sacred mountain, *señor?"* Rodrigues was flushed, his tone a wail. "We do not go there except for the voodoo, you see this?"

Brian, his eyes narrowed, said, "Why, the roads on the island are but paths. We need good roads, railroads. Why not build one to the mountain?"

The men quickly consulted one another in whispered tones, and, finally nodded, bewildered. Brian set up a tripod and measured, Mickey paced off the way, and they began by cutting down palm trees and making railroad ties. All day the ring of the hammers and the whine of the saws echoed through the usually quiet southern part of the island.

Some of the women came to see what was going on. Mostly they were older women with lined faces, but one voluptuous young one with a pouting red mouth stared curiously from Brian to Mickey to Rodrigues. Brian ignored her. Mickey gave her a stare and a grin. She fled in fright.

"Bet she never saw a red-haired mick before," he said to Brian jovially.

"Enough to scare her to death," agreed Brian gravely, and dodged the punch from Mickey's friendly fist. Their laughter rang across the cane fields, much to the wonderment of the stocky brown men who worked on the rail lines.

That evening they assessed the work. "About three miles of track, I figure," said Mickey to Brian, in Brian's study. They sat with their booted feet up, hats flung to the floor, as they studied the problems before them. Mickey had drawn a rough map of the area. "Is it true there be jaguars in the mountain area?"

"Used to be. I reckon there still are. Big beasts, some of them; others are smaller, about two hundred pounds."

Mickey whistled. "That's no mean cat. I best keep my rifle with me."

"And a pistol, loaded at all times," agreed Brian. "I do. Not just for the cats, either."

Mickey's gaze met Brian's. "That way, is it? That surly foreman of yours? Making off with rum?"

"I think I interrupted a profitable venture of his. That scarred fellow knows him, too; they avoided each other a little too carefully."

"Um." Mickey tipped the last of the Scotch down his throat with a graceful gulp. "Ah, man, the scrapes you do get in. You love the adventure, do ye not? You should have been an Irishman instead of a Scots."

"Scots is bad enough," grinned Brian, and refilled their glasses. A tap came at the door. "Come in," he called, without putting his feet down.

Rodrigues entered, pushing a tall brown fellow before him. *"Señor,* I disturb you," he said, with a beaming grin. "I bring one friend, Nathaniel. Be good houseboy, you betcha."

Brian looked over the flushed-faced lad. He was a nice-looking boy, about twenty or so, serious, his hat in his hands.

"Nathaniel, have you been a houseboy before?" he asked.

Rodrigues gave the boy a punch in the ribs. The boy gulped.

"No, sir, not Nathaniel," he said in a soft shy voice. "But I can fish—cook, maybe. I learn fast—Maria Luisa, she say."

"You know Maria Luisa?"

The boy's chest swelled and his face glowed with pride. "I marry with her girl, Liane, someday—soon, I think. When I prove to Maria Luisa I good mate for Liane. I wish to earn money for her."

Brian thought about that, sipping his drink, his eyes shuttered. The boy could be a spy for Rodrigues. Or he could be honest. But the boy was involved with Maria Luisa, and Brian himself could use a lever in that direction.

"All right, Nathaniel. Report in the morning to the cook. He'll show you how to set the table, wait table."

The lad beamed. Rodrigues blazed with happiness, his eyes sparkling.

"You want I bring fish, sir? I cook fish good. I know where there is turtles, too."

The boy was eager, that was sure. Brian shook his head. "Not tomorrow—maybe later. First you learn this job. You come for meals, about eight o'clock, then at twelve, and maybe in the evening if you learn fast. Okay?"

"Yes, sir. I come when you want."

Rodrigues gave the boy a shove in the direction of the door, as he seemed unable to remove himself gracefully. "I see you tomorrow, boss," said Rodrigues importantly. "We make more road, yes?"

After the door had closed behind the two natives, Mickey said, "Who is Maria Luisa? Some big shot?"

"Voodoo lady, a power on the island," said Brian absently.

Mickey whistled, and crossed himself while reaching for the bottle, no mean trick. "Whoo-wooooo. Voodoo, yet? Boss-man, you could be in trouble. Isn't that mountain sacred?"

"Sacred to the jaguar. That's all. They can do their voodoo elsewhere," said Brian impatiently, his mind elsewhere. In a couple of days he would see Silva again, see if her quick young temper had cooled. He would make plans for that girl. She needed civilizing!

He set down his glass with a frown and drew the plans toward him. "I thought we would build the smelter near the docks. No point in dragging the ore any farther then necessary. We'll build the rail line from the docks to the mine up the mountain, and another track of dirt beside it for the horses."

Mickey leaned forward and they discussed the matter intently, as they had talked over projects from Canada to Argentina, in the mountains and valleys of mining camps all over the hemisphere. Mickey suggested a pulley system, and they talked about that. He wanted to see the ore samples, so presently they left the maps, Brian locked his study, and they went out to the laboratory, oblivious to the man with the scarred face who watched them—and waited.

Chapter 6

August slipped into September. Men watched the sky for any signs of the dreaded high winds, the hurricanes that could destroy the cane in a few minutes, or knock down the huts, carry roofs out to sea, swamp a boat.

Silva finally went again to her lagoon, cautiously. She went very early in the morning now, washing quickly, swimming, keeping her eye on the hills above the lagoon in case a large black stallion appeared.

But none came. She swam with more ease then, in a more leisurely way. Brian Cameron had forgotten them.

She had heard the talk about the rail lines. Nathaniel had gone to the big house, Cameron Hall, and gotten himself a job as houseboy. Soon he would earn enough money to marry Liane, he said proudly. He still had enough time of his own to come over mornings and afternoons, spending hours fishing or with Liane.

What did the big man want rail lines for? That was all the talk. The small red-haired man worked them hard, even in the heat of the day. He had little patience, and worked himself just as hard. Brian Cameron paid no attention at all to the cane. The workers had been removed from the fields, just when the cane was ripe and ready to cut.

Silva went back slowly to the house on the hill. She had completed her last painting, and she had no more canvases. Tyrone had sweetly agreed to her whitewashing his room and then painting his walls. But otherwise she had no outlet for her painting.

More and more the thought crossed her mind: What would become of them?

Tyrone was complaining because there were no men to make rum. If he could not make runs to the mainland with rum, he could earn no money. Rodrigues would sit and frown over the problem. Pedro Ortega was seen with Oona at dances.

The world seemed of a sudden topsy-turvy. Silva wondered that one man, Brian Cameron, had made all these changes in her life, and the lives on the island. It did not seem fair at all.

When she returned to the house, she sat on the straw mat and ate her beans and corn and drank fresh-ground coffee. There was nothing to hurry for. She had to wait until the whitewashed walls were completely dry before she painted them. She mused that she might grind more paint from nutmeg and cinnamon; perhaps she could use the bark of a tree to paint on. But she felt dispirited and blue-deviled. Maria Luisa kept giving her sharp, shrewd looks. She knew how Silva felt.

Rodrigues came in with Tyrone. They had gone out early to fish, because there was no rum to carry to the mainland. They had to eat. Rodrigues carried a string of fish, and Tyrone had a few more.

Rodrigues grinned when he saw Silva. His brown face lit up, his dark eyes twinkled. "Ah, there, Silva, I bring you food to eat," he said meaningfully.

He had been coming around more lately, bringing a turtle, a few chickens, some eggs. She eyed him warily.

Maria Luisa said calmly, "You good to us all, Rodrigues. We thank you. You stay for lunch, hm?"

"Sure, I stay." He carefully set down the fish on some leaves and rubbed his hands together, still staring at Silva.

She remembered her manners. "Thank you, Rodrigues, and you, Tyrone. Would you like some coffee?" She unfolded her slim brown legs and stood up to get the pot that stood over the fire on sticks.

She was conscious of Rodrigues watching her legs, her hips as she bent. Darn him, she thought. She didn't want him around.

"You go dance with me tonight?" he asked as she brought him coffee.

She shook her head. "Too hot to dance." The weather had been humid and still, the way it was sometimes before a storm.

"We have thunder tonight, you betcha," said Maria Luisa. "Big storm soon."

"We still have dance. Don't matter about a little rain," said Rodrigues.

"Ask Oona. She loves to dance," said Silva, with some hidden malice.

Dark color rose in his bronze cheeks and his eyes flashed, but he said calmly, "I tired of Oona girl. That girl, she no think of anything but herself. Giggle, giggle long time."

Tyrone flushed also, looking distressed and sour. He sulked for a time, then roused himself to go off. When he returned, he looked more cheerful. In his hands he carried two good-sized slices of bark.

"Brought you something to paint on, Silva," he said happily. He held them out. "Look, I smoothed them. What do you think?"

She stroked them happily. He had cut two long, wide strips about one foot by two feet each. She could paint something on each, as soon as they dried out. "That's good, Tyrone, thank you. I'll gather some nuts and grind paint for them."

"Next time I go to Miami I'll buy you some canvas and paints," he promised, his arm about her waist. He gave her a swift hug, and pressed a kiss to the top of her head. A silent apology, for spending so much on Oona and so little on his sister, she thought.

Rodrigues watched them, dissatisfied, even when Silva turned to cleaning his fish.

"I'll stuff them with corn and spices," she said. "That will make them extra good. These are fine big fish."

Rodrigues looked appeased, but kept hanging around Silva. Maria Luisa watched him without expression.

Liane returned early with Nathaniel. They ate early these days, because Nathaniel had to be at the big house by twelve to help set the tables and serve dinner. He returned often with grand, unbelievable tales of all they ate and drank, the magnificent kitchens, the chef with his strange dishes. The dresses the ladies wore, he described breathlessly. The young blonde lady was always grandly dressed except when she swam in the pool, and then—"Oh, my," he said. She wore only a small piece of clothing about her body which showed all her legs.

Liane prepared the yams while Silva stuffed the fish, and then they hoed the garden while the men rested. By eleven the sun was climbing high in the sky, the fish was cooked, and they all sat down to eat, the food on broad leaves, the coffee hot and fragrant.

Nathaniel said, "You should see the grand plates we use. Light as leaves, but precious china, they call it. White with blue and gold around the edges. And the glasses—oh, my. You see right through them, and they drink the red wine and the white, and it must be chilled, just the right, says the big man."

"I tired of that big man," said Rodrigues sullenly. "He spoil all. When I get workers for the cane? I ask him, he shrug, smile, say the cane no matter. It spoil in the fields. He take the workers away to build a railroad to nowhere!"

"Not right to let the cane spoil in the field," said Maria Luisa, unexpectedly on his side. "The work of the gods is spoiled. It's not right. You tell him the gods be angry with him; he must cut the cane, not spoil the food for the gods."

"You tell him—he not listen to me," snarled Rodrigues, spitting out a small bone from the side of his mouth.

"Maybe I tell him, yes," agreed Maria Luisa placidly.

They ate in silence. Then Nathaniel regretfully left to go to his work. Liane looked after him wistfully. "Sometimes I get the feeling all is bad," she said to Silva in a low tone. "He go off, his face happy at leaving me. It was not this way before."

"He likes the excitement of working at the big house," said Silva, troubled for her closest friend. "That is all. It is the excitement."

"No, it is more. He talk about the pretty woman there. She has the beautiful hair like the sun, she has the eyes like the sea at its most peaceful. She smile at him, he say."

Silva was silent. Liane walked away restlessly, her slim body drooping. How lovely she was, much more so than the painted woman at the big house. How could Nathaniel brag about her to Liane, whom he loved? No, it was not all right. She glanced up at the sky and was surprised to find it blue and quiet. To her it felt as though storms hung heavy in the air, and her heart pounded sometimes in fear.

Tyrone lay down in the shade to sleep, his sunburned face peaceful. Maria Luisa was gathering up the broad leaves to burn in the fire, and Silva went to help her, aware of Rodrigues watching her every move. It made her self-conscious.

She went later into the house to look at the whitewashed walls of Tyrone's bedroom. She tested the white, but it was not yet dry. It would not dry for a time; the air was heavy with moisture. Maria Luisa was right: A storm would come soon.

She started as a hand touched her shoulder, and

whirled about. She had not heard Rodrigues enter on his bare broad feet. He grinned at her.

"You come to dance with me tonight, Silva?" he asked softly. "I treat you right. You good girl, Maria Luisa say. You white, but you like native girl. You come with me."

His arm went about her waist. She stiffened. He had never before dared to come into the house uninvited.

"Rodrigues, you let me go!"

The smile left his face. He narrowed his eyes, and put his other hand on her slight breast. "You—come with me—" he breathed. "I bring you food—you need me. You need your man!"

"No!" She fought him, pressing her small hands fiercely against his chest, flinching from the heat of him. He was like a fire—she would burn herself there.

Her strength was as slight as that of a bougainvillea vine twined about a sturdy tree. He pulled her closer to him and she smelled the hard smell of him, the aroused smell of a man. She fought with her fists, but only made him laugh soundlessly. He pulled her closer, his nostrils flaring, his black eyes blazing.

She lifted her fist, but she could make no imprint on him that way. Never in her life had she clawed a man, but instinctively her fingers drew into claws and she scratched at his face hard, reaching for his eyes.

He yelped and drew back, striking her heavily with his fist. She fell across Tyrone's cot, and Rodrigues came after her.

"Rodrigues!" roared Maria Luisa from the doorway. She came into the room like a fighting lioness, yanking at him, pulling him from Silva. She cursed him. "Damn your hide, you touch my girl I'll kill you—bastard, devil! I bring down fire from heaven on you! I call the shark god to rip you to pieces! You die in agony, you touch my girl again!" With the flat of her hand she slapped him and cursed him from the room.

Silva managed to sit up, breathing hard, half crying

with rage and shock. She heard Maria Luisa screaming at Rodrigues to get out, to get away, to leave them.

"I bring you no more fish!" he threatened. "I bring no food. You starve! You witch woman, nobody listen to you no more!"

"You fool," said Maria Luisa contemptuously. "All you think is woman, woman, woman. You get away from us! Anybody die, you die! Get away from here —scat!"

Tyrone came in as the voices died away. He came over to Silva, who huddled on his cot, her face streaked with tears. "Hey, Silva, honey, what happened? Why did Rodrigues come in here? Did he hurt you?"

His arms were comforting, almost like her father's. She pressed her wet face to his shirt as he crooned over her, stroking her blonde hair gently.

"He's no good," she said wearily, against his chest. "He tried to grab me."

"He is mad about Oona. Pedro Ortega took her as his woman." Pain was in Tyrone's voice. He rocked Silva gently back and forth. "But he can't touch you. I told him he can't have you. You're much better than he. Someday you'll find a fine man, and marry him."

On this island? she thought. On this island? Bitterness like gall swept through her. She wanted no one on this island! She wanted to be left alone by those greedy men with their hands on her, and their eyes looking right through her dress. She shivered and sat up straight. "I'm all right, Tyrone," she tried to reassure him. "I just have to keep away from him."

"Sure, Silva. You stay away from him," Tyrone repeated. Gently he stroked her hair. "Trouble is, you are getting too beautiful," he tried to tease her and make her smile.

Silva turned to her twin and pressed her cheek to his shoulder. Oh, for the comfort and protection of a strong man! She remembered weeping on her father's shoulder once when she had fallen and hurt her leg.

He had felt so big, so hard, all protection and gentleness. But he was gone.

"Oh, Tyrone, sometimes I am afraid," she whispered.

He knew how she felt. They had always been close. He rocked her back and forth, patting her back, and she felt better. She had Tyrone, and Maria Luisa, and Liane. They would not allow her to be hurt.

Tyrone wiped her eyes with his frayed handkerchief and kissed her cheek. "All right now, Silva?" he asked anxiously.

"All right." She nodded, sniffed once more.

"I'll tell him to leave you alone. You're not interested in him."

She shuddered. "No. I don't want him, not even near me."

Maria Luisa came back, grumbling. "I put bug in that man's ear," she said, looking keenly at Silva. "He no touch you again or I call down all the gods on him to strike him dead! He know I do this. He stay away some time."

Silva stayed around the hut all afternoon, hot as it was. She helped cook a pig for supper, since Maria Luisa wanted a pig for something. Silva thought she was going to make offerings to the gods of some vital parts of the pig, for she was muttering and arranging leaves and vines into platters, adding flowers and fresh corn and yams.

Liane and Nathaniel came back about four o'clock, and heard about Rodrigues. Nathaniel looked worried, and so did Liane. "You stay away from that man," said Nathaniel to Silva. "I think he mad about Oona, brag he can have any girl he want. Liane, you stay away from him, too. You my girl, hear?"

Liane patted the hand on her knee. "I hear," she said softly, her brown eyes gentle with love.

"Silva stay away from him. We no need his fish. I fish for you, and Tyrone fish for you," said Nathaniel importantly. "We no need Rodrigues. He get himself another woman in the village, he want woman so bad."

"He hungry for woman and for pride," said Liane wisely, her eyes half shut as she watched her mother in the small hut open to the wind. Maria Luisa was crooning over her offerings, and small flames and smoke rose from the plates.

Presently Liane rose and left Nathaniel's side. He watched her with a puzzled but respectful gaze as she went to Maria Luisa, stood beside her, and arranged more flowers on the plates. Both women bent their heads before the offerings, and the murmur of their voices was like music.

Tyrone had joined them and was watching also. Silva knew they were making magic, and she remained silent, motioning to Tyrone to be silent also. Liane seemed more and more like her mother at times, her slim body bent at the same reverent angle, her long black hair sweeping behind her, her face set with an emotion and intentness like her mother's.

The late-afternoon sun had sent its last rays across the clearing before the smoke ceased and Maria Luisa came back to them. She was weary; she sat down heavily on a stump, her head in her brown hands. Liane followed her mother, her beautiful face grave and distant.

Nathaniel finally asked the question that wanted to burst from Silva. "What's the matter, Liane? What go wrong?"

"The gods not take the offerings," said Liane in a murmur. "Something will be bad; Maria Luisa knows, I know. Trouble comes like the hurricane, and sweeps the island clean. The gods are angry, and will not tell us why they are angry."

Silva was puzzled, and so were the others. Maria Luisa rocked back and forth in grief, muttering to herself. Silva finished the yams and beans for their dinner, serving the roast pork. Maria Luisa ate little, drinking only her hot coffee and chewing a little bread.

Nathaniel left soon afterward to serve dinner at the big house. He was troubled for them, but not enough to forget his fascinating new job. And it paid him good money; he showed them proudly the coins the big boss gave him. The big boss said he did good, and could work seven days a week if he wanted. Or he could take off one day if he wanted, he did so good.

Liane sat alone, her brooding gaze on the dying fire. Maria Luisa rocked back and forth on the stump. Silva and Tyrone sat closer together, so close they could touch. For once Silva felt uneasy and alien. Always before she had felt at home with Maria Luisa. Tonight was strange. She felt like a white person, nervous and forlorn among strangers, natives she did not understand. Maria Luisa was her good foster mother, but tonight she was apart, and Silva could not reach her.

Tyrone whispered, "Shall I bring out the guitars and flute? Maybe music would help."

Silva nodded, not surprised that he, too, felt their separateness. He padded silently into the house and brought out a guitar for himself, one for Liane, and a flute for Silva. He offered the smaller guitar to Liane, but she shook her head, not looking up.

Silva started the music, the plaintive whisper of the flute breaking the ominous stillness. The musical theme wove in and out, and Tyrone picked it up on his guitar. It was a song of the wine and the gods, the hurricane and the stillness, the island and the fragrant frangipani which made their lives beautiful. Silva went on to the song of the god of the mountain, and Maria Luisa lifted her head. Tyrone plunked the tones of the jaguar, the grunting *ha, ha, ha, huh, huh, huh,* the rough cough of the jaguar. The flute wove in and out of the sounds, soothing the jaguar, offering the music to pacify it.

Maria Luisa lifted her dark head and began to sing in her husky, tear-roughed voice. "Oh, god of the jaguar, god of the sacred mountain, hear us, hear us," she sang in her Indian tongue. "What have we done to you, that you are angry with us? You will not visit your wrath upon us. We strive only to please you. Why do you not accept our offerings? Ask what you will; sacrifices we will make in plenty—"

The voice went on and on, jangling Silva's nerves. Presently the voice stopped, and Maria Luisa leaned back and sighed. Liane picked up her small guitar and strummed out a happier tune. The twins picked it up and wove melodies with it, with relief. Soothing music filled the dusk of the night, the purple-blue of the skies, the fragrance in the wind from the night-folding flowers. Finally there was peace, and they finally went to their mats and slept.

Silva went early to the lagoon the next day. She had much to think about. Trouble hung about them; Maria Luisa's face showed she had not slept much.

She lay on her back, floating in the flower-strewn blue waters of the lagoon, lazily thinking, thinking. The water soothed away the weariness of the night-mares that had plagued her. The early-morning wind blew caressingly, with promise of a clear day. Maybe the storms had passed over.

A voice hailed her from the bank where the small river tumbled down into the lagoon from the hills. She started, then plunged down into the water. Had Rodrigues dared—? But it had not been his voice.

"Silva," came the clear, ringing voice. "Silva, I want to talk to you!"

It was Brian Cameron. She trod bottom, brushed the silvery hair from her face, and peered at him cautiously. He stood with his booted feet apart, look-ing sturdy and impassive in his gray corded trousers, gray shirt, the large hat tipped back on his dark curly hair. "Silva!" he called again, imperiously.

"Go away!" she cried at him angrily. "This is private property!"

She saw his grin slashing the dark face even at that distance.

"I came visiting!" he called back. "Come on out—don't be a stubborn little donkey! I want to talk to you!"

"I can't come out. I—I—I don't have anything on!" Humiliation washed pink into her cheeks.

"I'll turn my back—I promise!" The sturdy broad back was turned deliberately to her.

She eyed him with distrust, her slim arms waving in the blue waters to keep her afloat. Finally she came cautiously closer, up to her waist in water, still watching him with big eyes. She came onto the sand, snatched up her cotton shift, pulled it over her head, and down over her slim hips.

Her wet head came out of the opening and she pulled out the dripping strands of her silvery hair. "I'm dressed," she said in a muffled voice.

He turned around slowly, scarcely glancing at her. "Beautiful day," he said amiably.

"It *was*."

Again he grinned. He seemed in a lighter mood today. He sat down on the beach about five feet from her. Cautiously she sat down also, curling her bare legs under her, pulling the dress down about her knees.

"Well, what have you been up to these days?" he asked, still in that friendly way. He picked up some sand and trickled it through his strong brown fingers.

"Same. Fishing, cooking," she said.

"And that fills your days?"

He was not looking at her. She dared to study his face more freely. It was a strong face, with hard lines carved in the forehead and beside the mouth and nose. Vivid blue eyes danced amid a web of lines where he had crinkled the eyelids against bright tropical suns. His hat was pushed back, and a red line marked his forehead where the brim had lain.

She shrugged, her slim wet shoulders rising in the tight-fitting cotton sheath. "We play music," she said. "And I made a new dress," she added proudly, eyeing him from under her dark lashes.

"What color?" he wanted to know, as though he cared.

"Pink and blue, silk and cotton. Tyrone brought it to me from—" She stopped. She had almost said it!

He looked across the lagoon, eyes shuttered against the brightening day. "Long dress or short?"

"Long," she said. "To my ankles. Maria Luisa helps me."

"Must be pretty. You'll wear it to my house one day soon, Silva?"

Today he was not demanding. He seemed casual, friendly. Yet she distrusted him. He was clever, Maria Luisa said.

"Maybe," she said shortly. She had not worn the new dress yet. It was special. Maybe—maybe she would wear it to Cameron Hall, sweep through the patios she had heard about, sit down to the grand table Nathaniel had described . . . She drew a deep sigh. Why did she dream of this? She had no wish to come to his house! She did not want to know his grand friends, who would turn up their noses at the little blonde native girl.

"I used to dream of this place," he said abruptly, leaning back on his hands, his strong arms supporting him. "When I went overseas to Europe, in the war. Nights when I couldn't sleep I thought about the peace of this place, the silence, the fragrance of the mint and cinnamon and coffee, the flowers hanging from the vines—it was unreal to me."

She was silent for a little space, searching idly for shells in the sand with one hand. Finally she asked, "Was it bad, that war? What did you do?"

His gaze came back to her briefly, then shifted away again. "I was a pilot in an aeroplane. We went up in the planes. They float through the air like—like a bird on wing, Silva. It is a grand, glorious feeling, an incredible feeling. To be a bird, up there, moving through a white cloud, then out again into the clear blue of the sky. The earth seems far away, small and brown and wrinkled. Then—then the enemy would pounce—out of the sky above one—and then the battle began."

Her forehead crinkled with concentration, trying to follow his thoughts. "An enemy? One of the gods?" she said gently.

"No—no gods, Silva. Only mortal men, like us. Trying with all the skill and daring at their command to kill us, as we tried to kill them, in an idiocy named war. Shooting them down, one plane bursting into flames as the bullets traced—" He paused, wiped his hand across his forehead. It came away wet.

They were both silent. His face had gone grim. Finally he lifted his hand and tossed a flower at Silva. It was a cream hibiscus with a golden heart. She looked at it, twirled it in her fingers, then set it behind her ear in her drying hair. He watched every move, as though it mattered.

"You can be glad your father did not go to that war, Silva," he said. "It would have been agony for a sensitive man like him. It was bad enough for us. We longed for adventure, excitement. We got it, and to spare."

She nodded. "He would not go. He left England and came to the island because of it, partly. Partly because he could not live with the memory of—my mother—in the cottage. Everything reminded him of her. Here he was able to find some peace."

"I am glad of that. And you—do you search for peace?" The question was light, but his voice was grave.

She shifted more sand, found a small shell, studied

it intently without seeing it. Peace? Was that what she craved? Then why was she so restless these days? Why did she dream of herself in a white lace dress languidly holding a fan in her slim hands?

"No, it is peaceful here. I do not have to search," she told him abruptly.

"A young girl should not want peace," he agreed. "She should want excitement, a young man to court her, pretty dresses to wear, dances to attend where she will be much sought after—" He broke off as the wide eyes studied his frankly. "Do you know what I am talking about?"

"Some," she said, drawing back. "But I do not want men to seek after me." She thought of Rodrigues following her to the bedroom, and shuddered, her teeth clenched tight.

She thought also of Maria Luisa and the offerings to the gods which were not accepted. Abruptly she said, "May I ask you a question, Mr. Cameron?"

"Yes, Silva, and you may call me Brian."

She hesitated, ignoring the remark. "I wish to ask—" She shifted nervously. "I ask why you do not let them cut the cane. It will rot, you know."

"The cane?" He was clearly surprised. His dark blue eyes narrowed. "Why are you concerned about the cane?"

"Maria Luisa says it offends the gods when the cane is not cut," she told him simply. "You see, the food is grown, and when it is finished, some is given to the gods, in gratitude for their goodness in sending the rain, in shining the sun. If the cane is not cut, then the gods do not receive their offering. They are offended—"

"That is superstitious nonsense!" he burst out angrily. "I am amazed at you. Did your father let Maria Luisa teach you that voodoo? He should be shaken—I mean, you should now! Don't believe that stuff!"

"You do not believe in the gods?" she inquired. Perhaps that was the answer. She stared at him, her green eyes searching. Was he such a pagan he did not believe in the gods?

"Not in the gods of the rain and the sun," he said sarcastically.

She paled. Her hands clenched. Above them thunder rumbled audibly. "You have offended them," she whispered, in awe.

Brian looked slightly shaken, but shrugged. "Nonsense! It's coming on to storm, that's all. Look, let's forget all this. I want you to shunt that pride of yours and come on over to Cameron Hall, you and Tyrone. The folks there are anxious to meet you. Not just the ladies, but I have a friend from old days visiting me, Mickey McCoy—you'll enjoy him. He's an engineer also—"

Her face closed up. "We do not come," she said finally.

He took a hard, exasperated breath. "Silva, I am losing my patience! This is stupid. You are the only two white children here. You should get out, get off the island, meet other whites your own age. Do you think Tyrone will be satisfied forever with native girls? Do you think you'll find a husband among them? Your pride is a silly millstone about your neck! Forget it—"

She moved to stand up. He leaned forward, caught her arm, and forced her down again. His voice gentled.

"I'm not trying to make you angry, Silva. Listen to me. Your father would have wanted you brought up right. He was sick and grief-stricken or he would have taken care of you himself. I want to offer you and Tyrone a home, take care of you, until you are well launched in the world. This island is no place for you. What will you do with the rest of your beautiful life?"

His strong, forceful voice seemed a living expression of her own uneasy thoughts. She stared down at her hands. She could manage—or could she? What would become of her and Tyrone? Would Tyrone get restless and leave the island? If he did, what would she do? Marry Rodrigues? The thought made her shiver with disgust and fear.

Brian watched her shrewdly, as though knowing the conflict that was tearing her apart. She wanted nothing to do with him; she feared him as she feared the strong forces of nature—the hurricanes that swept the islands, the sea that lunged up on the beach and carried all before it, the fire that crackled through the cane and left all black and desolate, the volcano that belched fire from the top of the sacred mountain and sent red fire into the air and burning black rocks down the sides.

He was like this—yet he was temptation also, the devil whispering in her ears. You could wear a white lace dress, you could wear one of those flopping lace hats, you could wear silver slippers, and hold a tall green drink in your hands, and laugh with his guests. Or be laughed *at,* she thought bitterly, thinking of her bare brown legs, her native sandals, the dresses that all too soon were faded and shrunken.

What did he want of her? No man did anything without wishing a reward, she thought, with the wisdom of her young life. Nathaniel went fishing for Liane, for her kisses and the glow of her approval. Rodrigues had brought them fish, for the chance to grab Silva and hug her. Tyrone went into danger to bring back earrings for Oona, so he might take her to the dance and linger all night at her side instead of coming home.

What did this man want of her? To make a mistress of her for the short time he was on the island? Did he want to make love to her on the beach or under the palms, the way Rodrigues wanted her? She shuddered. Men were so—so strong and brutal. She wanted none of them.

"Tyrone and I—we take care of ourselves," she said shortly, stirring. She rose to her feet. "We do not need you—we take care of ourselves. We do not come to Cameron Hall. Father never went there."

He had jumped up also, and stood scowling down at her again. "You are crazy," he said forcefully. "What do you think I would do to you? Force you to leave the island? Yes, I would. You need civilizing, you and Tyrone. You've lived on paradise island too long, you've gone native. I'll bring you back to civilization if it's the last thing I do!"

Her chin tilted. "Take me to civilization?" she queried bluntly. "You would make a mistress of me? Then discard me when you return to Miami? I think so. That is what men do with the native girls!"

He glared at her, his blue eyes aflame. "Why, you little idiot—and you are just a child. I don't rob the cradle—of all the stinking things to say—"

She faced him defiantly. "Do you deny it? You grab me, try to kiss. You are all alike, you men!"

His face blazed with fury, and his whole body seemed vibrantly alive with anger. She stepped back fearfully.

"Why, do other men grab and kiss you?" he raged. "Well—you aren't such an innocent, then!"

He stepped forward; she dodged, tried to dart around him. His long arms were swift as the bills of water birds, seeking their prey in the cool, clear lagoon. He grabbed her, caught her wet body to his. She twisted, writhed, beat her fists against his gray cloth chest, to no avail. Then she remembered what she had done to Rodrigues. As his face came down, she made one fist a claw and went for his face. His fingers gripped her wrist and held it high in the air as he drew her to him.

His hard body was warm against hers. He did not smell like Rodrigues, though. He smelled clean, of some astringent cologne, of something nice. He pulled her to him and pressed his face against her cheeks. His mouth went to her smooth throat and he kissed her neck, all over to the ear, and over her cheek to her mouth. Then his lips closed hard on hers.

She was trembling like some fragile orchid in a high wind, tossed about like a flower before the hurricane. He kissed her brutally hard; her lips stung with the fury of his anger. He bent her neck back until she thought it would break. His hard body was pressed to her, all down her slim length. He kissed her again, a long kiss, which went on and on, until she was limp and fragile and shaking in his grasp.

Finally, slowly, he released her, holding only one wrist, holding her back from him, his gaze going appraisingly over her flushed face, her bruised throat, down to the wet cloth clinging to her rounded breasts. With her other arm she swung her fist up and struck him on the cheek. It hit the hardness, the scratchiness of his tanned face.

He ducked, shook his head hard. He pushed her away from him, as though he had a sudden distaste for her. "Grow up," he growled. "You asked for that. My mistress—you, a child! Grow up! And your brother, playing his dangerous games. Tell him I want you both to come to Cameron Hall. I'll take you to the mainland, put you both in school! You both need to learn some manners."

"So do you," she retorted as he strode away from her. He paused, turned, and glared at her as she stood there, slim, defiant, her chin up, her fists clenched at her breasts. "So do you, Mr. Cameron!"

For a moment, as he paused and glared at her, she was afraid he would come back to her and do it all over again. Then his face softened, and he almost seemed amused. His blue eyes sparkled.

"Maybe you're right, child! You bring out the savage in me. Or maybe it's this island." He turned, and strode up the hill to where he had tethered his black stallion, coming down on foot so she had not seen or heard his approach. She watched him go, fiercely angry, desolate, and wiped her mouth with her fist. He was no different from other men. He was a beast!

But even Rodrigues had not made her want to weep like this.

Chapter 7

Tyrone sat moodily about, his face gloomy and shut. Sometimes he went fishing with Nathaniel, catching enough for their meals. Other times he just sat and stared at the fire, or picked out mournful little melodies on his guitar.

All the island knew that Oona had become Pedro Ortega's girl. She had a new shiny golden bracelet on her wrist. Rodrigues glowered, but said little. Maria Luisa thought Rodrigues was afraid of Pedro. Silva knew that she was. That scarred, quiet man was dangerous, she thought.

The rail crept slowly up to the sacred mountain. What did it do there? The freighter had gone away and returned with a funny little engine and several open cars not suitable for people to ride. Everyone was whispering and wondering what was going on.

One evening Maria Luisa said she was going to a ceremony. She had her white dress on, and an elaborate headscarf. Silva went to put on her white cotton dress. She always wore white, because Maria Luisa told her to. White was pleasing to the special *loa* of Maria Luisa, Erzulie. Erzulie had much power, and she listened kindly to appeals for help.

Maria Luisa went out to the chickens, looked carefully among them, picked up a large white one, and tucked it into her basket. She had herbs, bottles, and cloths.

Tyrone looked up. "All right if I come, too?" he asked without much interest.

Maria Luisa studied him thoughtfully. "If you want to come, you come. Or you stay and keep fire going. We come back late maybe."

"I'll look after the fire," decided Tyrone without rising from the mat where he sat cradling his guitar.

Silva started out with Maria Luisa, carrying her own humble offerings of herbs and yams. She was not allowed yet to participate in the full ceremonies, but she did much under the guidance of her mentor. "Where is it tonight?" she asked.

Maria Luisa said, "At the place of Papa Henri."

Silva was thoughtful, keeping silent, a respectful distance behind Maria Luisa. She could tell by the look on the woman's face that she was already deep in thought. Papa Henri was a powerful *houngan,* a wizened old native highly regarded on the island. He had come here to die, they said, from Haiti, where he had lived many years.

It was about two miles along the trails through the hills, along the leeward side of the island. They walked alone for a time, then were joined by others from native huts. They greeted Maria Luisa respectfully, and she bent her head in acknowledgment. They were more informal with Silva, having known her many years, watching her grow up.

When they arrived at the *hounfor* of Papa Henri, they found Liane and Nathaniel already there, and also Auguste, a young *houngan* who worked under Papa Henri. Thérèse, the wife of Auguste, was working in the open near the blazing fire. She had a large pot of water prepared, and a pig slowly turning on a spit directly over the fire. She bent to greet Maria Luisa with a bow, kissing her hand.

Maria Luisa acknowledged Thérèse's greeting and went into the *hounfor*. It was a building of thatch about four feet high, and over it was a thatch roof with an open space in its center. Down the center was a pole on which the spirits might enter. One wall was of plasterboard, covered with large crude drawings of flowers, serpents, water, trees, and vines. A chair was placed for Maria Luisa, and she sank wearily into it. Auguste took charge of her basket.

Silva sat down on a mat near the doorway, watching soberly as the preparations were begun. Two of the three drummers were there already, testing the drums, beating softly on the stretched hides. There were three sizes: a large conga of mahogany with a pigskin drawn taut across it, held by pegs; a middle-sized drum of cedar; and the smallest, made of shining satinwood, a handsome instrument and the pride of its *hounfor*. Soon after Silva sat down the third drummer arrived.

Papa Henri shuffled in on his small brown feet, and Auguste helped him to his chair. He and Maria Luisa bowed to each other, and spoke softly together for a time. The round brown face of the woman looked young compared with the lined, wizened, walnut-brown face of the old man, who had a little fringe of white hair about his bald pate.

Someone glanced toward Silva, and beyond. She froze as she realized that the man who had come inside the *hounfor* and leaned near the wall against the back of a chair was Pedro Ortega. Oona slipped in, her sensuous mouth smug and bright red, her dress of scarlet. Pedro wore a scarlet shirt, and a scarlet scarf about his black head. Red, the color of the *loa* Ogun, the god of war! The god of the warriors!

Silva drew a deep breath. Maria Luisa's brown eyes saw the pair, flicked at them, then the heavy lids went down and she brooded there, a massive woman crouched in her place of honor.

Auguste bent and began drawing lines of grain and rice on the ground. Occasionally Papa Henri would direct him or draw the lines himself. The drummers beat a sharper tempo on their drums. The big drum went *ump, ump, ump,* with a hard beat that dwelt in their nerves. The smaller drums kept a steady patter, intensifying the beat subtly.

They waited. Sometimes the waiting seemed long. Tonight, with Silva's nerves stretched taut, it seemed hours before Liane rose and ran into the circle. She began to jump up and down quickly, then slowed to a graceful dance as she wove around and around the sacred pole. Nathaniel soon rose and followed her, then Auguste too, rose. They danced separately, aware of each other, following each other, but not touching. One did not touch another dancer unless someone was in danger of colliding with the pole or falling to the ground.

Maria Luisa got up slowly and went to the pole, her head down, her graceful bearing marred by her apparent grief and lamenting. She began to chant softly, and the others fell back, silently waiting.

Her chanting grew increasingly louder, though few understood the words. Papa Henri understood, for he would call out encouragingly from time to time. Auguste waited, his bare broad feet spread out, holding a jug of water in his hand.

Maria Luisa finished on a wail, and the drums took it up and beat faster, faster. Silva felt the blood pounding in her head, in her pulses, forcing her up. She leaped to her feet and dashed out into the circle. Liane was there again, and Nathaniel, and Auguste joined them, and several others. They danced round and round, and the shadow of slim bodies could be seen in the dim light from the fire outside.

One of the girls cried out and began to writhe convulsively. Liane turned and held her, and Silva helped restrain her arms. She felt the girl lurching against her, straining, as the *loa* possessed her. Her head fell back, mouth open, eyes staring, and she cried out wild, strange words.

Then she went limp. Liane took her to the side of the *hounfor,* where she lay down on a mat. Maria Luisa bent over the girl, wiped her forehead, then reverently wiped the cloth around the earth at the bottom of the pole. The small *hounfor* was silent but for the insistent drumming. Sweat gleamed on the dark faces of the drummers as they watched the ceremonies.

The drums picked up a faster beat. Silva felt an urgent need to dance, and she jumped up and down, landed on her bare feet again and again, and whirled about.

In the corner, Pedro Ortega watched her, his scarred face gleaming, his hand on Oona's shoulder. Then abruptly he left the girl and jumped out into the circle. Maria Luisa, now resting in her chair, watched, her eyes narrowed. Papa Henri's wise old face seemed to crumple up further.

The drums hesitated, then beat a faster tempo again. Silva was distracted by the presence of the man in the scarlet shirt weaving about the pole just behind her. They moved faster, bare feet flashing on the earth. Then behind her came a hand. It touched her waist. Startled from the rhythm, she whirled about and stared into the scarred, sinister face of Pedro Ortega. His hand was on her waist, the scarlet of his shirt against the white of her dress. She shrank from him, bumped up against the pole. She had touched the sacred pole.

Maria Luisa waved her hand. The drums halted abruptly. There was a deadly silence. Papa Henri came down from his chair.

Silva trembled there against the pole. She was suddenly very afraid.

Pedro Ortega stared down at her. Not a sound broke the stillness.

Then Maria Luisa said, "We go. It is not good. The gods are angry." She took Silva's arm and drew her away with her.

Behind them, the people muttered and questioned, and gave Pedro Ortega questioning looks and frowns. Papa Henri went wearily back into his hut and closed the door of it firmly on them. It was bad, very bad.

Maria Luisa was urging Silva along the trail in the

utter darkness. Scarcely a star shone. The sky was clouded over; the moon had covered her face.

Silva was shivering in spite of the warmth of the tropical night. She had felt no *loa* possessing her; there were no answers to her puzzling questions. She could think of nothing but the fear she had felt as Pedro Ortega touched her waist. It was as though he had said to her that he craved her. At a ceremony invoking the gods! They would be so angry!

Maria Luisa, hurrying along the trail, was muttering to herself. Her head jerked from time to time. The basket seemed too heavy for her arm, and Silva gently took it from her and carried it with her own. The empty basket swung from her young hands. She kept looking worriedly at Maria Luisa. Everything was going wrong, and the woman was very upset.

Silva herself felt the heaviness of her heart like a throbbing curtain holding her down, the violence of the atmosphere like that before a fierce tropical storm. The winds could blow, whipping the palms like a giant hand sweeping over them. The volcano itself could rumble and burst into flame.

Yet all was intensely still. The hillside was dark, the path only clear to one familiar with it, as they were.

About a mile along the path, they came to a clearing on the top of the hill overlooking the lagoon. Far below, Silva could see a little trace of moonlight glinting on the waters. Maria Luisa hesitated, then leaned with a groan against a tall mahogany tree.

Silva set down the baskets and waited. She dared not touch the woman until she was sure Maria Luisa was not in the power of the gods.

Even the birds were silent.

Maria Luisa flung out her arms, gazing up at the heaven. She uttered strange words, then began whirling about the clearing with the energy and frenzy of a woman half her years. Words burst from her, and she held up her arms, palms out, as though begging.

Silva knelt fearfully beside the baskets. She could feel the tension in the small clearing. The gods were there, she knew it. Were they angry with Maria Luisa —or with her, for touching the pole?

"I could not help it," she whispered appealingly. "I could not endure his touch. Oh, forgive me, Erzulie; forgive me, Papa Legba. I did not mean to defile the sacred pole."

Strangely then she felt a peace come over her. It was not her the gods were angry with. She lifted her silvery head and gazed up at Maria Luisa.

Her dear Mamacita, who had raised her, protected her, was radiant-faced in the dim light. She was nodding, as though listening; she pressed her hand to her lips, then held it up to the faint wind. She came over on her bare feet to Silva. She raised up the girl.

"You must hear my words," she said in a monotone, gazing lovingly at the girl. "You must hear and listen, and believe. Erzulie talks to me. She tells me of you, of my dear daughter."

"I listen, Mamacita," Silva whispered.

Maria Luisa's warm palms gently enclosed Silva's face. She held her, gazing into her eyes deeply. "Erzulie tell me of you. You will be possessed by a dark man. He will take care of you—oh, better than Maria Luisa, better than your daddy. Dark things will come, but you will live and rejoice in the possession of the dark man. Violence will pass near you, but you will not be harmed. Oh, praise to the *loa,* praise to Erzulie, for you are under her protection now—she has promised it to Maria. Erzulie will take care of my Silva."

She began to babble then, her form shaking as the words became unintelligible. Silva closed her eyes in a sort of happy terror. She had felt before a little of the power of the gods, but never had that power come so close to her. She felt in their possession, as Maria Luisa had said. They enclosed her with their powers

—their cloak was over her shoulders, their hands on her face like those of Maria Luisa, their agent.

They stood there for a little time, rocking back and forth with the dominance of the spirits, hearing nothing, feeling nothing but the power of the gods that were in the clearing. And finally the gods went away, and there was but the wind blowing gently in the trees, and the fragrance of the frangipani, and the sharper scents of the cinnamon and clove.

Maria Luisa relaxed, and seemed to crumple. Silva held her up, comforted her, wiped her wet face. She seemed so weary, so exhausted.

They walked slowly homeward, to find Liane, Nathaniel, and Tyrone anxiously waiting. "Where have you been, Mamacita?" cried Liane, jumping up and coming to hug her mother. "We have been so worried."

"We walk slowly, my child," said Maria Luisa gently, giving Silva a warning look. She did not want the matter discussed, even with her daughter, that look said. Silva nodded, a brief inclination of her head. She still felt dazed, weary, rocked by the demonstration of the power of the gods.

Tyrone scolded them mildly for going off without a man. He seemed serious and gloomy tonight. It was very late when finally they all went off to bed.

Silva was late awakening the next day. She ate little, slipping away to the lagoon after drinking some coffee and eating a piece of bread. She undressed, and with relief eased her warm, sweaty body into the lagoon. It had been so hot again last night; the sultriness seemed to have increased.

She bathed, swam, felt the tensions easing away. Finally she came out, pulled on her shift, and sat gazing out over the lagoon. What had happened to her last night? It all seemed unreal, except that now she felt strangely comforted that her future would not be bad. Erzulie had promised that it would be good, that she would be protected.

"Silva?" The voice—so deep, so near her—made her start violently. She whirled her head about to stare up at the man standing over her, booted legs apart, gazing at her gravely with vivid blue eyes. He seemed so dark, so godlike, standing over her. She wondered suddenly, inexplicably, if he were the dark man who would possess her. Surely not Rodrigues, not Pedro! Either of those men—it would be horrible—but Brian Cameron . . .

"Silva?" he repeated impatiently. "Did I startle you?"

She nodded dumbly.

He sat down at a polite distance, about four feet from her, stretching out his legs and crossing his booted feet. He looked out over the lagoon. "You are late today and there are shadows under your eyes. Didn't you sleep last night?"

"I slept. But it was hot."

"Did you hear the drums?"

She hesitated. "Yes—I— Yes, I heard the drums." They still seemed to echo in her ears, throbbing, like a part of her being—calling, demanding, enticing, forcing her to enter into the dark passions of the voodoo.

"Were they having a ceremony last night, the voodoo?" he asked as though casual about it, but he was frowning.

She shrugged her slim shoulders under the wet shift. "Maybe."

She was afraid he would pursue the question, demand to know if she had gone. Instead he changed the subject abruptly.

"I lay awake listening to the drums for a while," he said. "They have a strange rhythm. I wish you could hear a good symphony orchestra, Silva. I think you would enjoy it immensely."

She studied him from the corners of her eyes, her

silver hair swept forward over one shoulder as she shook it to free it from the drops of lagoon water. Was he being sarcastic? Or was he going to make his demands again, that she and Tyrone come to Cameron Hall?

"You always liked music. Your mother was a pianist," he went on, lying back lazily on one elbow. The free hand picked up small scoops of sand and let it trickle through his fingers. He did not look at her. "If you were in England, she would have taken you to some of the great concert halls, to hear the finest music. Once I heard a great concert in London. It was in a beautiful hall with crimson velvet seats and golden decorations. The chandeliers were of crystal, glittering and shining over the audience. Everyone was dressed in their best, the ladies in sweeping dresses of mauve and crimson, purple and blue and green. The men wore black formal suits, with white ruffled shirts . . ."

He went on like that, in a lazy, dreamy fashion, almost as though he had forgotten she was there. Silva listened, enthralled, her gaze hungrily intent on his dark face, seeing a part of him she hadn't known was there. He knew so much, and he had been so many places. He had seen the most beautiful art, heard the loveliest music—

"A princess was there, a real live princess," he was saying. "She wore a gown of white lace, and diamonds at her neck and on her wrist. She waved a fan of white ostrich feathers. And with her was a wizened old lady, very ancient, her godmother, another princess, all in black. It reminded me of a fairy story, but her godmother was a kindly old lady who had helped to raise the princess. Everyone rose and stared at her as she entered the royal box . . ."

Silva longed to ask him what a royal box was; it sounded so beautiful, like a jewel being put into a velvet setting. But she did not utter a sound as she listened raptly, longing to hear more. The deep, smooth voice went on and on, as though he talked half to himself.

"The portraits on the walls of the castle were of the family that had lived there for five hundred years," he was saying. "The men were in tartan kilts, with dirks in their belts, and their sporrans swinging. You could almost see them step out of the frames, with their dark, arrogant faces, their flashing eyes, their long legs. Theirs was a proud heritage, back in the mountains of Scotland. Oh, those mountains, covered with the purple heather, gloomy in the valleys, with dark little tarns, and ice-cold streams where we would fish for trout, and grill and eat them on a fire we started ourselves. A purple mist lies over the hills at times, and in the mist one could imagine a figure coming from one of the old battles, starting up with a cry . . ."

She remembered then that his ancestors had come from Scotland, and all she knew of it was that it was a purple patch on the map in her one geography book. Below it was an orange patch for England, such a tiny place, and her father had pointed out London, which was not far from the village where they had lived.

"The daughter of the house sang Scottish ballads for us, all dressed in a white gown to her ankles, with a scarf of plaid tossed about her shoulders, her red head high. She played the harp and sang songs, and we listened for hours and joined in when we knew the words. You would have liked that, Silva, I know."

He finally looked up, into her fascinated green eyes. The silvery hair had been tossed back over her shoulders, and she hugged her knees with her arms. She felt all shivery with emotion at what he had described, these glimpses of another life, another people, so remote from the dusky islanders she knew. He smiled, and the grave-gay smile was charming and understanding.

"You would like that, Silva," he repeated. "And the beautiful mountains there, and the cool green valleys, and the silvery-gray rivers running swiftly through them. And the people, with their quick tongues and quick tempers, and their pride and their music. Have you never thought of returning to England?"

She shook her head, still dumb, but now longing stirred in her for that cozy cottage where it had been warm and close and full of family feeling. Home. So different from the whitewashed thatched house where she lived with only Tyrone of her family. But Maria Luisa was practically her mother, and Liane her sister.

"Do you remember any songs your mother sang?"

Long lashes veiled her eyes for a moment. She sighed. "Yes, a few."

"Which ones?"

She thought. Then she sang, softly, self-consciously, a ballad her mother had sung, something about "My mother bids me mind my wheel—"

He listened, smiled, sighed, his blue eyes softer than usual. "Ah, yes, and there is the one about the last rose of summer. Do you know it?"

She had not thought of it for a long time, but she nodded, and sang some of it in her clear, pretty voice, true and soft on the tropical air.

After she had finished there was a little pause, a slight tension. Then his shoulders relaxed and he lay back on the sand easily, gazing up into the gray-blue sky. "You have a pretty voice, Silva. Thank you. I wish you could hear a good concert in Paris sometime, or Italy. Oh, Italy is the place for wonderful, theatrical opera. It thrills you to the bone. I can remember nights in Rome and in Florence when I would waken to hear men singing in the streets on their way home, rowdy songs, or romantic songs, their voices echoing through the narrow old courtyards and against the stone buildings."

He went on to describe Rome, which had buildings nearly two thousand years old in its center, and she listened eagerly, and asked him questions. He told her, without being patronizing, about the ancient Roman civilizations, and ballet he had seen, and art exhibitions, flitting from topic to topic so quickly Silva could barely keep up. She questioned him about art and he told her about an exhibition of her father's work in Miami that he had seen, and of an artist friend of his in Miami who would like to meet her because he admired her father's work.

She listened and drank it in for a time. He was so nice and pleasant, but finally her suspicions were aroused. Why was he being so nice? What did he want? Men always wanted something, she thought with distaste as she recalled Pedro's touch last night.

Did he want her? Was this his way of easing around to the subject of making her his mistress? She studied him furtively as he closed his eyes and continued talking dreamily. He was a handsome man; other women probably wanted him, the way Oona wanted handsome admirers and they wanted her.

Or was it something else he wanted from her? He talked of taking her and Tyrone away to the mainland, away from Desirée. Was it the land he wanted, the land his father had sold to Valerian Armitage? Could he be after the entire island? He admired the pretty lagoon, and seemed to look on the hills as his own. Perhaps that was it: Once they were gone from the island, he meant to take it all for himself.

"Did you know," he changed the subject abruptly, "that Rodrigues has been after me about cutting the cane?"

"Oh, has he? I knew he was worried about it," she said casually, aware that he had opened his eyes, turned his head, and now studied her face keenly.

"Did Maria Luisa get after him about it?"

She stiffened warily. "Maria Luisa does not tell Rodrigues what to do, especially about his work," she said coldly. "It is not her place."

"I told him to take a few men and go ahead and cut the best cane. But that's all."

So the cane was being cut, Silva thought as she glanced absently at the lagoon. Rodrigues would take it to the sugar mill where they would make molasses, and then distill the rum. Once again they would go out and make the rumrunning trip to the mainland. Tyrone might be involved!

Ooooh, it was that Pedro Ortega—she felt it, she knew it. He had worn red last night: the scarlet of war, of blood. He wanted trouble, he craved it. He wanted to fight them all, and make them bow down to him. He was dangerous.

"Will that please Maria Luisa?" asked Brian with irony.

She shook her head before she thought. "No—no—no," she whispered, thinking of the trouble that rum brought.

He frowned and sat up. "Why not? I thought she wanted the cane cut down, that it would please those gods of hers."

Silva shivered. It was as though some cold finger had run down her spine. She stood up. "I am cold, here in this wet dress. I must go home," she said swiftly. "I bid you good day."

"Darn it," he said, without rising. "Every time I try to ask you something, you prickle like a porcupine!"

She hesitated. He was looking so pleasant, grinning up at her like a nice boy, almost like her twin when he was feeling good. She could have stayed and let him talk about beautiful things he had seen. But it was dangerous—he wanted something from her, something she probably could not give willingly.

"I'll go home now. Maria Luisa will worry," she said primly, smoothing her drying dress.

"She doesn't worry enough about you. Does she know you bathe by yourself in the lagoon, without any clothes on?"

Swift color stained her tanned cheeks. Silva stared down at him, green eyes flashing dark and angry. Then she turned and ran into the underbrush, among the dark trees and the thick vines, where he could not follow.

Halfway up the hill she paused to peer back at him. She saw him still sitting on the beach, his arms about his knees, gazing out at the lagoon. He seemed somehow—alone. A fragile emotion touched her; she tried to brush it off like a mosquito. He was alone, but he could go back to his big, beautiful Cameron Hall, and be with that lovely lady in white lace, any time he chose.

She made her way home, troubled, involuntarily thinking of all Brian had said that day. The music of his words as he had told her of paintings, and purple hills, and opera—whatever that was—and singing in the night . . .

With all her thoughts mingled a certain knowledge. Whatever he had said that day, the casual, friendly way he had acted, Brian Cameron had meant to do this. She realized suddenly that he was a man who did nothing without meaning. He had come to her, spoken in that way, for a particular reason. He wanted something.

If he wanted her, she thought fiercely, she would resist his hard strength to the last breath of her body! She would fight and kick and scratch as she had scratched Rodrigues with her fingernails. She would never give in to those cold blue eyes. He would only bully her and force her to his will. She would not give in, not ever!

Back at the house, Liane sat idly by the hearth. Nathaniel had gone to work at Cameron Hall. She smiled as Silva approached.

"Breakfast is ready," she said, and poured coffee

for Silva. They drank in companionable silence and then set to their chores. After they had weeded the vegetable garden, they walked together in the cool of the trees, arms linked, as they often did.

Silva felt herself slowly calming. Liane was like her own sister, and would explain away her doubts. "Liane, tell me, if you will. How—how does it feel to you when Nathaniel comes, and seeks you out?" she asked shyly.

The dark girl smiled, her mouth gentle. "Oh, it is good," she breathed. "I feel soft and warm. He wants me and I want him to be close. He holds my hand, and the blood runs quickly through my body. I am alive, and joyful, like the fish that play in the lagoon, like the birds that fly in the sky, so free and beautiful." Her hand squeezed Silva's impulsively.

Silva sighed. "Shall I ever know this feeling, Liane?"

"Yes," said Liane. "You are a woman. When your man comes, you will feel like this. You will know."

They strolled arm in arm, talking or silent as the mood came, comfortable with each other. Silva thought of Brian's rugged dark face, his rich low voice as he spoke of strange and distant lands, naming sights like rare jewels. He moved her with his voice, so smooth and clever. He must know she was hungry to hear of beauty, to see loveliness.

What else did he want of her? Why did he seek her out?

She remembered again how he had pulled her to the hardness of his body. She felt her hot cheeks, where he had pressed his mouth on her. The clean masculine scent of him, his virile whip cord strength . . . and those kisses searing her flesh. His hands had stroked over her dress as though he felt her body through the cloth, as though he desired to strip the cloth from her and touch her innocent nakedness. He had spoken of her bathing naked in the lagoon. He had seen her!

Oh, he made her feel so hot, so angry, so unlike her calm, satisfied self! Would nothing ever be the same as before? The touch of his mouth had lingered, the memory of his kisses haunted her dreams.

Chapter 8

Pedro Ortega's plans were progressing well. He was satisfied with himself. He would rule all of Desirée. He would own the sugar-cane fields, the women. All would bow down to him, Pedro Ortega, who had been thrown out of Jamaica by jealous white men, and forced to leave other islands by them. They would see, those damned white men, when word drifted to them from across the ocean, that Pedro Ortega was great, was King!

He touched his scarred face and grinned to himself, his yellowed teeth bared. They believed in him now, ever since the voodoo ceremony, when his scarlet had conquered the white of Maria Luisa and she had been forced to leave.

He thought of the white girl, slim and beautiful, whirling about the sacred pole, her silver hair like a halo around her lovely face. He had had to reach out and touch her, she had seemed like an unreal thing, like a pale white ghost, so lovely and wraithlike. He had touched her waist, felt her warmth, felt for a moment her terrified breathing as he watched the slight but sensuous breasts heaving under the white dress. Oh, there was fire under that white. He would like to have possessed her that night! Through the girl he had conquered Maria Luisa, and the woman had known it, and had fled from him.

He waited in the shade of the trees for Oona to come. He saw her approach, look about coquettishly, then anxiously as she did not see him lying on the beach where they had arranged to meet. He grinned to himself and made her wait. After a few minutes he strolled out lazily and greeted her.

"Ho, there, Oona, I am over here," he called.

She pouted her luscious red mouth at him. Her eyes had narrowed to angry slits. "You make me wait. No one makes Oona wait."

She was so obvious. He looked at her with hidden contempt. Sure, there was fire in her, but it was available to any man who touched her. She was cheap. She was not a queen, like the unattainable Silva. He glanced at her rounded body, the curves emphasized by the wrap of brown and gold she had carelessly fastened about her in a style that left her brown shoulders bare. He reached out and stroked his big hand along her shoulder to her chin, then around to her back.

Oona shivered, and her eyes went soft. Pedro drew her down on the sand, and flicked open the wrap. She wore nothing under it. His hand went deliberately over the rounded breasts, and he pinched the red nipples cruelly. She cried out, slapping his hand.

He grinned down at her. "You have missed me, yes?" he murmured.

She murmured in protest, but put her arms hungrily about his neck. She hung on him, and he stroked his hand down to her bare brown thighs. He was thinking.

"Did you meet Tyrone?" he asked her abruptly.

"He would not come. He say he must fish for his family," she said absently.

He frowned, and gave her a rough spank on her buttocks. "I told you to meet him. Why don't you do what I say?"

She rubbed her buttocks and sat up, her eyes flashing. "You don't own me! Nobody owns Oona!"

"Don't I?" Anybody owned her for a moment, he thought with vast contempt. He had met her sort in the ports of Havana, in Kingston, in any port city of the Caribbean, along the wharves, where the boats came in and the women strolled along, giving the eager sailors their flirtatious looks, their hands out for money. One day she would go there, and sell what was left of her body, and be old before her time. She was not the kind to marry, for no man could be sure whether the child was his.

"I want you to meet Tyrone," he repeated with controlled patience. "Make the fuss over him. You know how. I wish him to think you love him. Make him feel peaceful, and secure with you. I will need the boy one day. I want him to do what you will with him. You understand?"

She didn't, so he repeated his words, emphasizing the importance of Tyrone's trusting her. Finally she nodded; yes, she would do what he asked.

"One day," he continued, "I shall be king of this island. Everybody will obey me. I shall be the *houngan* also. You will be *mambo* with me. The gods will listen to us, and we shall have much gold and jewels. All the sugar cane will be at our command. We drink, laugh, make love all the day and night. That will be good, yes?"

Her black eyes glistened. She nodded emphatically. "You will be king, I will be queen," she chanted.

He did not mean that, but he was not so foolish as to tell her. Let her wait and see. He drew her roughly to him, and flipping back the cotton ties of his belt, opened his trousers. He took her ferociously, making her cry out and writhe under him. He enjoyed making his woman scream out, and beat at him, before she melted into moaning ecstasy. It made him feel like a powerful king already.

One day soon he would take that Liane also, that cool girl with the slim brown body and long black hair. He would wind that hair in his hands and jerk her face to him, and make her kiss him as he wished. It would be good, the first time in that slim body. He buried his face against the golden flesh of

Oona, and lay there thinking of Liane, and how she flicked her gaze contemptuously away from him. She would pay for that look, and pay well.

He thought also of the silvery girl. He had not planned on leaving any white alive on this island. They must all go. But he could use Tyrone, providing he could whip the boy into obedience. With Oona's help, he was sure he could.

And Silva, she knew the island ways. She entered into the dances, she felt the *loa* on her. She might be spared—if she became his woman.

He pictured the slim white girl, her soft flesh against him, her white dress ripped open to admit his bold hands, his dark legs. He leered down at Oona, then crushed her full mouth under his and dreamed of the soft pink mouth of the white girl, opening to his reluctantly, crying out when he forced her to accept him, as Oona was doing now.

Women liked Pedro Ortega when he had once taken them. They begged him for gifts, as Oona did. He would have Oona, then Liane, as his queen, and he would have the white girl also, a slave to him as his ancestors had been slaves to hers! That thought pleased him, a white girl his slave, coming humbly to do his wish. He would have a harem of beautiful women, all of them as willing as Oona as he thrust deeper into her, wild moans of pleasure escaping from her lips.

On the beach, two miles from where Pedro lay with Oona, Liane lay in the shadows with Nathaniel. She had not been with him for five days, and she was hungry for his reassuring touch, and anxious to know why he had not come to her.

"Why do I not come?" Nathaniel repeated, lying on his back and enjoying the feel of Liane's soft hands on his broad chest. "I am very busy! I am important in the household of Brian Cameron. Mr.

Cameron, he say I serve good. He say I learn fast. He needs me every meal."

She sighed with longing. Tyrone had been doing all the fishing for them lately—Nathaniel had no time for it. She yearned for the old days. She hoped Mr. Cameron would tire of the island, and leave it soon, and Nathaniel would return to her arms.

"You make much money?" she asked hopefully. "Then Maria Luisa will let us marry soon."

He grinned broadly. "I make much," he said, with satisfaction. "Mr. Cameron, he pay well for good work, he say. Maria Luisa will give her approval, sure."

She stroked her hand over his chest. He stirred and sat up. "The water is good now, hot later. Let us swim."

He caught her slim hand, drew her up and held her close for a moment. Then they ran down to the water and into it, up to his waist and her breasts. Naked, they swam, then dived and came up again laughing, her black hair streaming to her waist. Liane shook it back as Nathaniel kissed her wet face, holding her close in the water. To tease him, she pushed away and dived under a wave. He came after her, breathing hard. When he caught her, he pulled her to him more roughly.

Presently, to touch and kiss playfully was not enough. They went up on the beach and lay down in the sunshine. As the sun beat hot on Nathaniel's back, he took Liane gently, moving slowly and surely in his love. Her arms clasped about his back, she breathed more and more quickly, happy in his embrace. She caught her breath, then cried out. He moved with her, and they were as one, the way she loved to feel, the way only Nathaniel had ever made her feel.

Yet a part of her mind felt troubled. There was something of Maria Luisa in her, more and more as she grew older, she thought as she curled up beside

Nathaniel while she watched him sleep. Her hand lay on his thigh, caressing slowly as he slept. Part of him was away from her. He did not tell her all, as he used to. His eyes would sparkle, and he would dream, and sit and look over the lagoon, then remember that she was there.

He did not speak now of the golden-haired woman of the household of Mr. Cameron. He talked of the food and how he served it, and complained once that the food Maria Luisa cooked was becoming all of one kind. Then, shocked at himself, he begged her pardon, but all was not well.

Was he becoming spoiled in the household of the rich man? Did he wish for more than what he had known? Or was there more to this than she knew? Darkness hung over her at night when he did not come to her and she slept poorly.

Sometimes when she slept she had terrible dreams, of Nathaniel drifting away from her in a boat with a golden sail. She knew what it meant, but she pushed the knowledge from her, proudly, desperately. Nathaniel was handsome, kind, good; it was no wonder other women would want him. But he had been drawn to Liane, and they had been close friends and lovers for some time now. How could anyone come between them?

Liane closed her dark eyes. Although it looked as if she slept, a tear trickled from under her long, dark lashes. It dried on her cheek, mingling with the salt waters of the lagoon.

Brian rode out to the end of the rail lines that afternoon, conscious of the darkness of the sky, the whirling winds. Would a storm come up? Smoke rose from the volcano, the Mountain of the Cat. It would play the devil with their plans, should that mountain erupt. It had not erupted for years, but the volcanoes of the Caribbean were uncertain, prey to the earthquakes of the area and to the tidal waves that often followed, bringing devastating destruction.

The smelter was built. It was causing much curiosity among the islanders, and Brian smiled grimly as if at a bad joke. They would soon learn. It would mean jobs for them, but jobs they were not accustomed to. Digging in the earth for the copper, piling the ore into the little rail cars, drawing it down to the smelter. Someone would have to learn to run the small engine. He considered his new houseboy, Nathaniel. The boy learned quickly, was taller and more sturdy than the usual native.

Rodrigues was upset about the cane fields. Brian had not given the overseer many hands to cut the cane, and the man was grumbling. Brian was curious about that also. Rodrigues said the cane was being cut and taken to the sugar mills, but he had not asked for freighter transportation to take the molasses and crushed sugar to the mainland. So what was he doing with it?

Was it true, what he suspected? Was Rodrigues making it all into rum? That was the devil to pay, if true. That meant he was involved in rumrunning. Not surprising. There were few enough ways to make money on the island. And the island was not far from Miami; with a swift launch it was only five hours. Damn, it was high time Brian returned to Desirée, if that was what was going on in his absence. Perhaps that was what Maria Luisa's dark hints had meant.

If only he could get some straight answers from Silva. He had tried to soften her that morning, by talking of other matters. She had listened to him like a child to fairy tales, her green eyes wide and incredulous, her mouth so soft and pink, slightly parted as though his stories left her breathless. That damned silver hair had given her a haunting aura. Lord, she was a pretty girl, and practically unaware of her beauty.

Yet the minute he brought up the matter of the

cane, or asked questions, she was up and darting away into the brush and trees, like a silvery bird afraid of a hawk. One day he would catch her and get some answers out of her.

By the time he reached the docks and the newly built smelter, the winds were raging and the sky was growing darker. Mickey McCoy looked up at the sky and shook his head.

"Coming on to storm. How severe are the storms hereabouts? I'd best cover up the engine and the cars."

"I don't know what good it would do if a hurricane strikes," said Brian dryly. "It would pick up everything—covering, engine, and all."

Mickey sighed. "Might have known the weather was too good to last. Say, does that mountain ever erupt?"

One of the men working on the smelter caught the words. He whispered to his mate, and the two of them stared at Mickey. They were frowning and shaking their heads worriedly.

Brian beckoned Mickey away with him, and they talked quietly, heads together. "That mountain is sacred to them," Brian told him. "I'll get around that superstition, but it will take time. Meanwhile, mate, soothe them with talk about the money they will make when the jobs increase. Until everything is ready, don't say anything about copper. Time enough when we get the smelter in operation."

"You know what you're doing, boss." Mickey shrugged, his hands spread. "I'll just take the orders. But I'll keep my revolver loaded, if you don't mind!"

"Good idea. I do always," said Brian quietly. The men exchanged the understanding looks of friends who had been through more than one adventure together. Brian stayed around for the rest of the afternoon, making sure everything was as tied down as possible in readiness for the storm.

By the time the men rode home on their weary

horses, the winds were swirling the dark clouds and foretelling ominous possibilities. Brian kept looking at the sky, but could not tell if it meant hurricane weather or not.

In the evening, Brian showered, changed from his khaki work clothes into a pale blue linen suit and a white shirt, and sauntered out to the patio, where a canopy had been raised. It was starting to rain.

"I thought it never rained in the tropics, darling," Astrid complained as soon as she saw Brian. Arms swathed in blue lace, her body encased in a blue silk Empire gown showing all her delectable curves, she took his arm possessively. A sapphire set in a silver heart swung as a pendant at her creamy throat.

"I didn't promise no rain, did I, Astrid?" He smiled as he detached her clinging hands from his arm and walked over to greet the Leonis as they came out to the patio. "Dinner inside tonight, I think. It will probably storm. I hope you don't mind thunder and lightning."

Mickey, looking unfamiliar and out of character in a striped blue and white suit, joined them and cracked, "Mind a storm? It's normal procedure around Brian. If the weather don't provide one, he does."

Brian laughed easily with the others, and poured Scotch for Mickey, a lime and soda for himself. "What about Irishmen? I thought you liked a good, rousing fight."

"I do, me lad! The thunder 'minds me of the time in Argentina when a storm came up right out of nowhere and scattered cattle from hell to breakfast, right over the land we were surveying, and me trying to take a measurement with a giant bull big as the Minotaur breathing fire down me neck."

Mickey rattled on with his stories, and had them laughing for a time. Brian encouraged them all to talk, and Giovanni contributed a tale of his youth in

Rome. Keller, who had slipped in quietly, listened with a smile, but said little.

A dark horse, that one. Recently, Brian noticed, he went out on his own a lot. Brian wondered where he went. He had seen Keller slipping in at dawn one morning. Had he taken a fancy to one of the native girls? The next time Brian wrote to Miami, he would order a couple of his men to check on Keller. He realized it had been stupid not to have done so earlier, but the trip to Desirée had been so casually planned. It was a pity there was no telephone or cable on Desirée.

There were too many mining tycoons about. Any of them would be eager to learn of Brian's copper mine, and find some way to take it from him, or cause him trouble over it. But Desirée was his! He would be merciless with anyone who tried to take it from him! It should not be difficult to find out if Keller was really a stockbroker on Wall Street.

As they were dining in the formal dining room, a great puff of wind blew out half the lamps and candles. Astrid shrieked and jumped up from her chair.

"What is it? What is it?" she cried, pallid with fear.

Mrs. Leoni seemed as frightened. Brian soothed them. "The storm is coming," he said calmly. "But don't worry. These walls are thick, and have stood for two hundred years. Nathaniel, draw the drapes."

The dark native went on silent bare feet to the windows, drew the silk draperies slowly, easily on the rungs. As Astrid's gaze went to him, the wide, frightened blue eyes became speculative. Brian noted how Astrid's gaze went up and down the man, and her fear was quickly forgotten. She couldn't resist looking at a man—doing more than looking, he thought—and Nathaniel was a splendid figure of a man though he was young.

By nine o'clock the winds were howling about the huge old Spanish-style mansion. Brian ordered the windows closed and locked, all the draperies drawn. The group played cards in the long, low living room, where precious Persian carpets lay on the blue-green tiles and wide silk couches of green and gold and silver were scattered about the room in comfortable, intimate arrangements. Astrid started and complained at every bolt of lightning, every growl of the thunder. But Brian was listening keenly to the wind.

It grew louder and closer. Nathaniel came into the room, carrying a tray of lime drinks, ice clinking in the glasses, sprigs of mint a gay decoration on the top. Brian stared at him.

"Nathaniel, why didn't you go home?" he asked sharply. "What about Maria Luisa and the others?"

The handsome face of the native went defensively blank. "It storm, sir," he said plaintively. "I no go in storm. Nobody mind. They not worry about me."

Brian bit his tongue to keep back lashing words. That was not the point. Maria Luisa, Liane, and Silva were alone with only Tyrone to aid them.

"I'll just go see to the horses," Brian said curtly. "If I don't come back, don't worry. They get restless in a storm."

"Darling, I get more than restless in a storm!" wailed Astrid, but he left, and he was raging.

Damn the boy, why couldn't he have left early and gone home? When Brian thought of Silva alone in that stupid thatch-roofed hut of hers, with only women and a boy to help her if anything happened, he wanted to swear. He went to his room, found his revolver and belt, clapped them on, slapped a sombrero on his head, and went out to the stables.

The horses were tramping restlessly. His black stallion was quiet, head alert, lifted. The brown eyes gleamed as Brian came to him.

"Whoa, boy, good boy," Brian murmured, stroking the long silky nose, giving a pat to the tossing mane as he got out the bridle. "You won't mind a ride in this, will you?"

A stable boy came from the darkness of the straw mats to help him. "You no go out, Mr. Cameron? There be bad winds tonight. The gods be angry," he murmured anxiously.

"Don't worry about it," Brian reassured him. "Go back to bed. I'll take care of myself."

"Yessuh." The boy watched him leave, shaking his head dubiously.

Brian went out into the black night, with the rain lashing at once on him and the stallion. He headed west, beyond the sugar-cane fields, toward the hills. On the other side of the hills lay the house where Silva lived. Damn it, he should have insisted at once on Silva and Tyrone moving in with him. It was ridiculous. He had dozens of empty rooms. There was no reason why they should not move in. Besides, it would give him pleasure to see Silva moving about his home. She loved pretty things—she would enjoy the silky sofas, the faded Persian carpets, the ivory, jade, and ornamental glass he had collected.

He smiled involuntarily, his head bent against the wind, the sombrero fastened under his chin, the brim lifted again and again by the swift gusts. He could see her wide, wondering green gaze as she looked at the beautiful objects. He could hear her singing softly in the living room in the evenings, maybe playing her lute. He had never heard her play, only the guitar when she was a child. She would lend grace to his home, a silvery wisp of a girl who moved like a tree bending or a flower swaying.

He had reached the low hills that lay between his house and Silva's. He put his stallion to the rise, and it responded nervously, rearing as a wind-whipped tree lashed at them both. "Easy, boy, easy," Brian soothed, his hand stroking the wet silky neck. The rain was coming down steadily, but still the winds increased. He cast a look at the sky, noting uneasily the wide black whirling clouds.

They took the rise, found the paths that lay faintly

marked among the trees, and finally reached the top of the hill. Brian paused to breathe the stallion and make sure of his way. This cursed darkness! Not a star, not a sliver of moon, just the white sheets of ocean whipped into caps far below, the black lines of trees before him.

The stallion reared unexpectedly, and Brian was almost thrown. He gripped with his knees, steadied the horse, and looked about. There above him in the great oak tree, lying on the limb, was a huge yellow cat with flaming green eyes! The jaguar was bigger than he had ever seen, its tail lashing furiously—

He heard the *ugh, ugh, ugh* of a strange coughing sound. He remembered what his father had said: "If you're ever close enough to hear that cough, my boy, you're too damn close! Get moving!"

He dug his heels into the sides of the nervous, trembling stallion and swung away from the tree limb. Behind him he heard the snarl. He crashed away into the trees, recklessly, the stallion's fright giving him fresh speed. God, that had been close!

Tree limbs, wet and whirling, lashed Brian's face and the head of the stallion. They went down the hill as though pursued by the devil, he thought afterward. Finally he pulled up the stallion and glanced back. They were both breathing heavily. There was no sign of a racing yellow body behind them. Maybe they had merely disturbed the big cat's sleep and it had returned to its slumbers. But Brian was stunned by its closeness. Why had the animal been there, in the hills?

Brian knew the cats always lingered close to the sacred mountain, rarely coming out into the plain or farther north and west into the hills. So the jaguar was away from its territory. Why?

He pushed back his sombrero and wiped his wet face with his scarf. When he and the animal were breathing more normally, he urged the stallion on.

The horse knew the way now, down the hill partway and into a shelter in a fold of hills.

There were no lights in the thatch-covered house as Brian rode into the yard. All was quiet. He swung down and called softly, "Anybody home? Silva? Maria Luisa?"

He heard a grunt. Maria Luisa padded out of the house, stared up at him and stared at the horse. "You crazy, Mr. Cameron? It storming, big storm. Why you come?"

It seemed a little silly now. They were safe and he had come through more danger than he cared to think about. A jaguar was a man-eater of a beast. He grinned weakly. "I thought you might like a man about the house for the storm, Maria Luisa. Or maybe I just need a place to lay my head."

"Huh. Mighty crazy," she grunted frankly. "I get cloth for horse. He wet, huh?"

"Both of us," Brian assured her gravely.

"No corral for him. I get long rope. He stay." She went inside and came back with a rope, which she fastened to the neck of the beast as Brian unsaddled it. Brian accepted the cloth, and wiped the horse down thoroughly. The stallion was trembling and cool, sweat standing on him. They tied the end of the rope to a tall pole standing in the middle of the yard. The horse seemed to settle down, with chickens cackling about its feet, as unsettled by the late arrival as they were by the storm.

"I find room for you. You come," said Maria Luisa. They turned to the house. At the doorway a silvery-haired girl raised a lamp above her head to light their way, and Brian gazed at her. A faded cotton nightdress just covered her knees, her feet were bare, her hair streamed about her shoulders. The coal-oil lamp shone over her, making a halo of her hair.

He caught his breath. He had seen beauty, but not like this: the grave, curious face, the shadowed eyes, the pale bright hair, the slim figure of the girl outlined by the radiance. He halted so abruptly that Maria Luisa was five steps ahead of him before she realized he was not with her.

"Silva, Mr. Cameron needs a room. You get sheets, darling. We make up your papa's room for him. Go, girl."

"Sí, Mamacita," murmured Silva, and turned away. She padded lightly on bare feet to another room, then returned with two sheets and a blanket on her arm. She gave Brian a shy, curious look as she went past him. "You're wet, Mr. Cameron. Why did you ride out on a night like this?"

"You'll think this funny," he said ruefully, "but I thought you might be in danger. Nathaniel is staying overnight at the hall. I think it might be a very big storm tonight."

"It storm," said Maria Luisa. "We live through it," she added placidly. "Bathroom here. You take towels, get dry. You want coffee?"

He was shivering from the cool rain and the wetness in the tropical night and wind. "Unless you have something stronger," he said.

"Not in this house," said Maria Luisa definitely. "I get you coffee."

Silva murmured to her, and Maria Luisa finally nodded, frowning. Brian went to the bathroom, carrying the lamp with him. He noted the primitive system of pipes, the mat for washing, the bowls, the whitewashed walls, the clean austerity of the room. So this was how the girl lived! It was all she had known in her growing-up years.

When he came out, Maria Luisa beckoned him to the bedroom she had prepared. "Silva, she find a bottle for you," she said. A jug of rum was set on a tilted table in the sparsely furnished bedroom. Beside it, Maria Luisa had set a battered tray with a cup and saucer and pot of coffee.

Brian grinned. "That should do me fine," he said

wryly. "I'll drink that and not even hear the storm!"

As he said this, Silva came in, moving through the darkness to the lamplit bedroom with sure feet. "I brought you bread and cheese. Would you like something else?" she added anxiously. "You are hungry?"

"Yes, I think I can eat this. Thank you, nothing more. Won't you have coffee with me?" he added gravely. Maria Luisa was blinking with sleep and Silva was yawning, but they sat down politely on the side of the bed they had just made and drank coffee with him.

He thought, What an odd night! He had come to protect them, but they were here, comfortable and sleepy, and he was the guest, being helped to warmth and food and drink.

When they had finished, he bade them good night, and they departed to their own rooms. He lay down, and with his arms under his head, he mused sleepily on the house, the odd family under its thatch roof, and himself. Curious. And that big jaguar, ready to pounce, its green eyes enraged at being disturbed.

Brian slept. Then he was awakened by a high, howling wind. He got up and looked out the small window. It was set deep into thick walls of wood and stucco. Outside, the winds were blowing the trees double and lashing the swaying palms. But here against the side of the hill, tucked into the leeward side of the island, the wind seemed to pass right over their heads and down to the sea, where it whipped up the waves wildly, but leaving them untouched.

Squawking and indignant cackling roused Brian from his fascinated attention to the storm. He went out in his pants, bare-chested, into the hallway. The sounds seemed to come from a room in the back. He went back there, to find Tyrone shooing the hens into the room.

The boy looked up in the semidarkness. A lamp shone fitfully on the table. "Oh—hi, Mr. Cameron," he said, with some surprise.

"What are you doing?"

"Brought in the chickens," he explained gravely. "They got a bit fussy with the storm. Sometimes the wind picks them up and shoots them down the hill and they get all upset."

"I don't wonder." Brian went outside in his bare feet and helped the boy bring in the last of the hens. His stallion was moving restlessly, and he paused to stroke its neck soothingly. "It's all right, boy, easy now. It's protected here," he murmured.

He looked up at the sky, and was stunned. The lightning was cracking in wide white streaks, showing breaks in the dark clouds. And the winds were whirling in that ominously familiar pattern—a hurricane!

He watched, the wind whipping his black hair, holding the neck of the stallion, stroking its nose. The wind struck a giant palm, lifted it out by the roots, and flung it like Jove's thunderbolt right at the beach. It struck hard and went deeply into the sand. Tyrone was beside him, watching.

"Isn't it glorious?" cried Tyrone, his face alight. "I love to watch storms! It isn't so much fun when you're out at sea, though," he added. "I like being here. We get some protection from having the hill at our backs."

Silva and Liane came out, barefoot, rubbing their eyes, looking about. Brian grinned at them. "Come to watch the excitement, girls?" he teased them gently. They looked like two young children, holding hands, the one so dark, the other so fair, both so touchingly young and trusting.

Silva gave him a guarded, enigmatic look. Liane blinked at him, then gazed up at the sky. "The gods are very angry," she breathed. "They know something is wrong. Look how they hurl the lightning at the island! We must make sacrifices tomorrow."

Her voice was grave and serious. Brian could not make mock of her, but he shook his head impatiently. They took this voodoo too seriously. He hated for Silva to hear her, and believe her. He saw the look she gave him, as though she dared him to say anything to Liane.

"I saw a jaguar tonight, on the way here," he said between the crashes of lightning, the rumblings of the thunder. He had to shout to make himself heard. "I didn't know they came up here."

"A jaguar!" Liane put her hand to her breast. "Where? Near here?"

"Up on the hill," said Brian, wishing he had said nothing.

The rain began to splatter down again after a brief pause as the lightning flashed brighter and closer. Then it began to rain wildly, the wind lashing the rain in their faces. Maria Luisa called from the doorway.

"You all crazy, you children? Come in, come in, don't get wet and silly! Come in and get some sleep."

Liane called to her as she came. "Mr. Cameron, he sees a sacred jaguar up in the hills, Mamacita!"

"Huhhhh," Maria Luisa took a long, grunting breath. "So the signs get bad, do they? We make offering tomorrow. Tonight we hide from the wickedness outside. Come in, Mr. Cameron! Your horse be all right."

Brian was meekly following Maria Luisa when he suddenly realized she was treating him like one of her children! He grinned down at her as they got back inside, and she reached up and patted his cheek, gently, like a nurse or a mother. "You go to sleep," she repeated. "All be okay, till tomorrow."

Chapter 9

Brian slept long and hard then, on the narrow iron bed, with its hard mattress. It was late morning when he awakened.

Moving his head sleepily, he opened his eyes and blinked, remembering all of a sudden where he was and why. Sunshine flooded in through the narrow windows, onto the whitewashed walls. Painted on them were huge flowers, giant palms, gay yellow golden-shower trees, strips of golden sand, blue sky.

Valerian Armitage must have painted these walls, Brian thought. If only he had painted them on canvas, he could have sold them for a good price. The flowers were excellent, so detailed, yet fantastic, larger than life, flaming with energy and beauty. He lay awake, studying them, then finally moved his long legs, and swung himself erect.

His arms felt stiff and sore, his back and hips tired from the strain of riding after the long day of work. But he felt relaxed and easy, somehow, as though his heart was lighter than usual. From somewhere came the sound of soft whistling. A horse nickered. Someone called, in a girlish voice, then he heard giggles.

He grinned, remembering the girls last night, so enchanting and innocent of knowledge of their beauty, so young and gentle. Like two fillies, just growing up, free and wild in their pasture. A shame to let them change, to grow up, he thought with a moment of regret.

He went to the door and peered out. All was quiet, but he could smell the fresh, sharp, hunger-making fragrance of perking coffee, and frying pork; someone was cooking over the wood fire.

He went to the bathroom and washed briskly, using the towel that hung there and the liquid soap. He washed his hair, dried himself, and got into the clothes he had worn last night. They had dried over-night.

Ravenously hungry, he walked out the back into the sunlight and stood, hand to his forehead to shield his eyes against the brightness. Silva was bending over the cooking pot. Liane was squatting on a mat, neatly shelling peas and dropping them into a smaller pot. Maria Luisa was feeding the chickens, tossing them grain. Silva turned, straightened on seeing him, and gave him a grave, questioning smile.

"You slept well?" she asked with a shade of doubt.

"Very well, thank you." He came forward. "Am I too late for breakfast?" As he watched her, he suddenly remembered the dream he had had last night.

He had dreamed of the great yellow jaguar, glaring down at him with brilliant, angry green eyes. As he had started to run from it, the animal had changed slowly to the form of Silva in a green dress, her emerald eyes shining and frightened. He had held out his hand to her, but she had drifted away from him, into the trees. He had tried to follow, but vines held his feet in place, and he had to stand and watch helplessly as she drifted away into the darkness.

He was aware that he was staring at her. She was flushed—from the fire or embarrassment? She turned back to the pot.

"There is plenty," she said. "Tyrone is taking care of your horse. You do not mind?"

There was a quaint, grave formality to her speech. She was not at all like the pert, fresh girls he knew on the mainland, with implications in their speech, words that could have double meaning. He looked toward his black stallion. It was contentedly munching a pile of hay, and its black coat gleamed like silk. Tyrone must have brushed the horse all over, lovingly, from its silky flying mane to its long tail, down over its slim black thoroughbred legs to its white socks.

"I'm grateful. I'm fond of that horse," he said. He walked over to the animal, stroked its neck slowly, and murmured to it. "You got good care here, hm? You are happy, yes? Good boy, you rode hard last night, all through that storm."

The stallion nuzzled its master's shoulder affectionately, the long nose bumping against him. Brian gave the beast a final pat, and turned back to them. Liane had stood, and brought him a cup of coffee on a saucer.

"You wish milk and sugar?" she asked. "Please be seated."

Brian sat down on a mat, his legs crossed. "Thank you." He took the cup from her and watched Silva gravely dishing up some pork and beans from the smoking pot suspended over the fire on a crane. Was this how they lived, so simply, such a quiet outdoor life? He felt sorry for her, briefly, then wondered at himself. Was it so bad? Or could it be a good life? With sunlight in their faces, the wind in their hair, talking and laughing after a good night of sleep, thankful that the storm had passed over them and not harmed them.

He noted the chickens cackling in the crude wire run. "They were not hurt last night?" he asked.

Silva shook her head. "They are all right. Tyrone got up."

Brian did not mention he had risen also. He drank the coffee, fragrant and hot, with milk and sugar in it. It tasted better than his own drunk in fragile Limoges cups, with lace on the table. He set it down and started on the pork and beans.

Tyrone came from feeding the pigs and gave Brian

a grin. In the morning light he looked older, though still young as Silva. The twins were much alike, he thought, with the same sensitive faces. He wondered what the boy found to do on the island. A paradise island for the young, yet a restless prison for someone who might long for more.

Maria Luisa came. She appraised Brian with some satisfaction and a hidden speculation. What was the woman thinking now? Brian wondered what went on in that graying head. She was a good woman, but too much given to the voodoo. How much had she filled Silva's head with it? Too much for redeeming the child? Valerian must have been mad to allow a native to bring up his children.

They all sat down on mats about the fire and had coffee with him. As they did not eat, he figured it was for politeness, that they must have had their breakfast earlier.

He addressed Maria Luisa after he had set down his empty plate. "I thank you for your hospitality last night and today," he began.

She inclined her graying dark head. "You are most welcome here, Mr. Cameron."

"I wish also to speak to you about the children."

Her expression did not change. Her wrinkled face showed more lines today around her eyes, but that was all. She looked as she had looked for years. Silva lifted her head to stare at Brian. Tyrone looked puzzled.

"Yes, Mr. Cameron? What do you wish to say?"

"I wish Silva and Tyrone to come to stay at Cameron Hall—for a time," he said deliberately, gazing straight at Maria Luisa. "I have guests there I wish them to meet. And they should learn the ways of their kind. Later, I would like to take them to the mainland. Perhaps they should go to school. At least, they may have a tutor."

Tyrone broke the sudden quiet with a laugh. "Go to school? I'm eighteen, Mr. Cameron! Father taught us all we need to know about books and arithmetic and all that. And Maria Luisa taught us, and Nathaniel, and Rodrigues—"

Brian shook his head. "That's not what I'm talking about. I mean schooling, to learn about life in the United States, how to make a living, get a job . . ."

"On Desirée?" snapped Tyrone, with a wry grin. "All you need to know is how to fish and take care of chickens."

"You won't always live on the island."

Silva started to speak, but Maria Luisa waved her to silence. The girl subsided on the mat, but her green eyes were sparking fire.

"No, they not always live here, Mr. Cameron. But change come slow. No need to hurry," she said deliberately.

"There's no time like the present," he said easily, sipping his coffee. Liane was intensely quiet, her black head bent. "I'd like the girls to come over, Silva and Liane, and Tyrone with them," he added on impulse. "I'd like to take them all to Miami for a couple of weeks, get them some clothes, show them around. Maybe they'll change their minds."

"Liane not go," the dark girl said so softly that he was not sure she had spoken.

Maria's sad dark eyes held some humor. "My children not always do what they told," she said easily. "Mr. Cameron, you wait. Maybe later the children come. You wait."

He decided to be satisfied with that. Evidently they could not be pushed. They would have to talk it over among themselves. Meantime, he would talk to Silva on the beach whenever he met her, get her over to his side, speak to her of music and art and traveling, intrigue her. Then she would come, and he had a hunch her twin would come also. If Liane came, so much the better.

"We'll wait," he said, with a smile. "Well, I must get back home. Thank you again for your hospitality."

He got to his feet. They rose also. Silva went to stir the pot, Liane went back to shelling her peas, and Tyrone, with a wistful look, patted the neck of the great stallion before unfastening the rope that bound the horse.

Brian saddled up, then said casually to Tyrone, "Thanks a lot for taking care of this brute. He seems to have taken a shine to you. You must come over and try riding him soon."

The boy's gray-green eyes lit up. "Really? You mean it? I never rode with a saddle before, but I could learn!" He stroked the soft nose as Brian mounted. Maybe he would be more easily won over than his stubborn sister, thought Brian. She had not said a word for a time. He looked toward her—the bent silvery head, the slim body in the worn cotton dress, the long brown legs, the native sandals.

He pictured her in a slim long dress of green lace, her hair bound in coils about her small head, the graceful hands holding a fan, high silver heels—

"Silva," he said commandingly.

She turned about and looked at him. There was something strange in her eyes.

"Silva, good-bye. Perhaps I'll see you soon."

The wide eyes did not seem to blink. They gazed at him, in fascination, in wonder, with something else in those depths . . .

She raised her hand slowly in farewell as he waved to her. Then he put the horse at the hill, and was bounding up it and into the thick brush and trees.

He was at the top of the hill before the thought struck him: The look in her eyes had been fear.

Fear! Why did she fear him? The thought of those clear green eyes with fear in them did something strange to him. He felt a little sick to think that she feared him. Or did she fear what he offered? He thought of her hot anger, her words flung at him. Did she think he wanted to seduce her, make her his mistress, that child?

Little fool! He scowled across his lands, his eyes lingering on the ripe sugar cane. Thin spirals of smoke came from them where the men were burning the dampness from the cane before going into the fields and cutting the ripe stalks. He rode easily as the horse plunged down the slope, then into the open flatlands. He galloped across the plain to the slight rise, then the hill where stood the proud white and red Spanish villa that was Cameron Hall.

At the stables he dismounted. The stable boy greeted him with a wide grin. "I think you get wet last night, boss," he said with a curious look.

"Very wet," said Brian. He patted the horse, then turned away. He went by a side door to the wing where he had his rooms. He was glad of a shower, thinking as he used it of the primitive bathing facilities in the house where Silva lived. Not even a tub. Her tub was the lagoon.

He changed to a brown silk suit and broad brown tie with a streak of gold in it. Then, impatient, not wanting to answer questions from his guests, he went out to the lab. He unlocked it and went in, leaving the door open. It was hot, and he soon shed his jacket, bending over the ore samples he and Mickey had gathered the day before.

He worked for several hours over the test tubes and burners before he was satisfied. Yes, it was high-grade, all right. It was running more than six percent, the best he had seen in his days of mining. He was studying the figures when he became sharply aware of someone behind him. The smell of a man, of sweat—

He turned. Rodrigues stood there, a cup and saucer in one hand, a small pot in the other.

"I bring you coffee, boss," beamed the overseer. He gave a curious look at the equipment as he stepped to the table to set down the cup and pot. He sniffed sharply. "What is that, boss?"

"Just some experiments," Brian said. Drat the man.

Curious as a cat, his ears and eyes as big as an elephant's.

"What you do with it? Something on the island?"

He moved to pick up a piece of the ore. Brian, hand upheld, stopped him. "Don't touch anything," he said mildly, holding his temper with an effort. "Might be burning hot."

"Why, boss? Why you burn the dust?"

"Just experiments," he said again. "Listen, Rodrigues. How is the cane coming? You get it all cut?"

The man gave him a grieved look. He was an artist at looking hurt, Brian decided. "I work hard, boss. All the day and half the night," he said dramatically. "We work hard. We burn the cane yesterday, today. Then the rains come, make it all wet."

"Better go out and see what the damage is," said Brian curtly. "I want to have a better yield than last year, or I'll plow it all under."

"You not plow under the cane!"

"If it doesn't produce better. You go out and look at the fields, make me a report tomorrow. Tell me if it's worth harvesting."

It gave him a feeling of cold amusement to see the forlorn look on Rodrigues's face. If the man was turning the cane into rum and selling it on the mainland, then he was truly caught between two grindstones. If he did not have a good harvest—for Brian Cameron!—then the boss would plow under the cane; no cane, no rum for Rodrigues to run to the mainland!

"Go on out, and I'll expect that report tomorrow. Tell me how many fields are worth harvesting. Get some more of it burned off, and see how much can be taken to the sugar mills. Oh—and how soon will you need the freighter to haul the sugar to the port in Florida?"

The man's face was a study in conflicting emotions. He twisted his sombrero round and round in his brown hands, faltering. He looked everywhere but at his master. Brian waited, with cold patience. Would the man admit what he was doing, or wouldn't he? He should dismiss him at once. But he could deal with a man like Rodrigues; he had met his kind often before.

"I—I—work it out, boss," the man stammered at once. "I tell you—maybe tomorrow, maybe next week," he added hopefully.

"Tomorrow I will ask you for a full report. Go on now, and let me know in the morning." With that, Brian turned back to his table of experiments.

Brian ignored the coffee as Rodrigues slunk away. He went on figuring rapidly, thinking about the mountain full of copper. The world needed copper, for cables, electrical wires, parts of machinery, many vital items in the global economy. And he would make a fortune from the Mountain of the Cat.

A momentary picture of the snarling jaguar came into his mind. He dismissed it with a shrug. Just because he was on a small, superstition-filled island was no reason to get jittery. He would be more careful where he rode in the future. And if any more jaguars came near Silva's house, he would go out with a rifle and kill them. He wasn't having Silva in danger from one of those beasts just because the natives thought they were powerful gods.

Again he was aware of someone entering the small lab. This time shoes rang on the cement. He turned around casually, to find Donald Keller coming in, looking about with interest.

"So this is where you hide yourself night and day while beautiful blondes languish around the pool and weep," said Donald with a grin.

"Can't you console her?" Brian asked, watching the man come forward and sniff at the mixture in one of the tubes. He made a face and stepped back.

"Me? No, she wants you—'only you, only you,'" Keller crooned in a reasonable mimicry of a popular singer. He seemed disappointed as he sniffed another tube, and another. "What the devil are you doing, anyway? You can't tell me a smelly lab is more interesting than blondes and flowers and swimming pools—can you?"

"That would depend on the man's hobbies, wouldn't it?" Brian turned off the last of the burners, checked the others, then picked up his papers and stuffed them into his briefcase. "Come on. I'm done here for a time. I'll see if I can console Astrid. Or I'll give you lessons on how to do it in my absence."

Keller responded with another light quip as he preceded his host out of the lab. Again he sounded disappointed, thought Brian sharply. He didn't act much like a stockbroker. Why hadn't he checked up on the man before he left Miami? His story had seemed plausible; Brian had met him at many of the parties his friends gave. Astrid seemed to find him amusing at times.

Brian found he felt distinctly curious about Donald Keller, who offered no hot tips to his friends and was not winding himself about a gorgeous lonesome blonde. If he wasn't a stockbroker, what was he? And why had he come to Desirée?

Brian considered this dispassionately as they walked to the house through the shaded gardens of golden allamanda, red poinsettias, bleeding heart, lantana, coral vine. Purple bougainvillea splashed against the white walls of the house, contrasting sharply with the red tile roofs. Once they stepped onto the veranda, into the shade, he was aware of the coolness of the tropical trade winds.

If Keller was in cahoots with one of his rivals, they couldn't get Desirée. At least the title to the land was secure; Brian had made sure of that. Valerian Armitage had bought the right to use a portion during his lifetime, but he did not, never had, owned a piece of Desirée. The children did not know that, and Brian did not mean to tell them just now. Desirée was big enough for them all.

They entered the cool lounge. Astrid uncoiled herself from a silk sofa and launched herself at Brian. Brian held her by the arms, not letting her luscious body touch his, and gazed down at her with cool amusement.

"Where have you been? You were gone all night! I was worried sick! Where did you go, Brian?" She was half furious, half relieved.

He gazed into the blue eyes, and wondered if she really loved him or if the money from her previous husband was running low. The latter, he thought. "Why did you come, my sweet? I warned you I was coming here to work," he said calmly. He nodded at Nathaniel, who had come in. "A rum and lime," he said.

Nathaniel prepared the drink carefully, adding just the right amount of lime to rum, swirling the ice cubes professionally. He had fit in well, thought Brian. Only he didn't like it that the lad had shown no anxiety over his fiancée, if Liane was that.

Astrid sat down, her mouth sulky and full and red. "You are ignoring me on purpose," she said into his ear as he sat down near her. "Do you think I'm going to just sit back and wait until you come around and pay me a little attention, like a patient puppy?"

He grinned at her. "No man would call you that, Astrid." He let his gaze travel meaningfully down over her full form, clad in a striking blue-green silk print dress with full sleeves and low-cut bodice.

She pouted, but seemed appeased, and consented to banter with Donald Keller while Brian leaned back and enjoyed his drink. The Leonis came in. Flora was looking more rested and relaxed, Brian thought. The red on Giovanni's face had faded somewhat. Perhaps he was not drinking so much here in the tropics.

Mickey McCoy did not come to lunch. Brian changed afterward to a riding outfit and rode out to the end of the line to join Mickey. They worked all the afternoon and into the evening on planning the line up the mountain and deciding how to recruit workers for the mine. It could open as soon as next week, they decided. The line would be ready, and the smelter was ready. It remained only to start digging out the precious ore. When Brian told him of the quality, Mickey jumped in the air and clicked his heels before coming down, to the delighted surprise of the natives watching him.

After dinner Astrid begged Brian to walk with her in the gardens. To humor her, he went. He lit a cigar, and as they strolled she put her arm into his and hugged it to her. She was warm and soft, and the air was sweetly scented by flowers and her perfume. What was wrong with him, he wondered, that he felt utterly cold toward her?

She was a desirable woman. He had enjoyed showing her off to friends and enemies, sitting with her at the opera, sharing late-night suppers. But bed with her—he had not wanted her since he had come to Desirée.

"Darling," she began, gently serious, "I don't want to interfere with your work."

He could have told her there was no danger. He never let a woman interfere with his work. He smiled around the cigar.

"But, darling, I do hate it that I see you so little," she continued, softly plaintive. "I came to be with you, and this island has so little to offer! When are you leaving?"

"Not until the work I am doing is completed," he said mildly.

"What work?"

He wondered if Donald Keller was working with her, and both of them with one of his mining rivals. "A secret, sweet. And you wouldn't understand it anyway. All will be revealed in due time," he said lightly.

"Oh, don't be like that! I don't really care about your beastly business secrets. But when you go off—and you're gone all night—" She paused suggestively.

She thought he had a native woman! The realization amused him. He had never been interested in that sort of dallying. He dallied only with women who knew exactly what he was about, and would accept recompense in cash or jewels.

He said nothing. They strolled on. Abruptly, at a jog in the path, she turned and pressed her voluptuous form against him. "Darling—Brian—I have been thinking about you all day—"

I'll bet you have, darling, he thought silently. Firmly he detached the smooth arms that tried to latch about his neck.

"I'm tired, Astrid. Not interested tonight, I'm afraid."

"Just kiss me," she breathed.

He hesitated. He had enjoyed kissing her in the past; she was very kissable. But today and this evening he had been thinking of Silva, how she would have enjoyed the startling crimson and pink sunset, what she would have said to the exquisite dinner of braised chicken on a bed of asparagus and cream, crowned with mushrooms, to the ice cream pertly shaped into pink roses and green leaves at each place, the French pastries turned out so deftly in their delicate crisp shells and the lightly fluffed filling. No, Silva was probably eating more pork and beans, maybe some greens. And going to bed early, as soon as it was dark, so money would not be spent on oil and candles. To bed on a hard iron stead, with a thin mattress . . .

Brian brushed his lips briefly against Astrid's cheek, and turned her firmly back toward the veranda. He was aware of her anger and frustration, held in check only because she wanted to stay in his good graces. He wondered dispassionately what about her had ever attracted him.

In the living room Donald looked up knowingly as they entered. "The Leonis retired early, tired out. They didn't sleep well last night."

"Neither did I, with that storm," said Brian. "You'll excuse me? Don't turn in on my account." He smiled, and left them.

Astrid did not remain to meet Keller's grin. She left the room and stalked angrily on her high heels to her bedroom, slamming the door so the vibrations rang along the hallway. In the lovely room of cream silk and gold, shadowed with blue draperies, she flung herself across the bed, heedless of her fragile dress.

Damn him, damn him, damn him! There was no getting close to him when he was in one of his cold moods. And she had been so sure that coming to the island was the right move. She would have him alone, aware of her, on a seductive tropical island, with a big moon and exotic flowers—

Brian Cameron, wealthy and able to give her everything she wanted, within arm's reach, and she couldn't grab him! Damn him! She lay kicking at the precious coverlet, until she finally kicked off her shoes and flung her arms above her head. She would have to plan how to bring him to heel! Her blue eyes snapped fire.

She thought and thought, but her restless body would not permit cool planning. She finally showered and put on a filmy blue gown of silk and lace, and went to bed. For long hours she lay awake, making up one plan, discarding it, making another. It did not help that her body was intensely sensual, wanting what she had denied it for too long.

She had chased Brian Cameron from New York to Miami to Desirée, and she had ignored and rejected other men to do it. Damn him! No sex, all this time on Desirée. And she just wasn't built like this, to do without sensual delights. That was how her first husband had caught her: She had thought he was safely away on a business trip, but he had returned early, on purpose. At least he had had to pay high for the divorce, she thought angrily.

She would capture Brian Cameron, and keep him

also, whether he blew hot or cold. She had a feeling that under that cool exterior he kept a furnace banked. One day she would burst through his reserve, and really let the volcano roar! A small pleased smile parted her full mouth as she recalled his fiery caresses, and she finally slept on that thought.

She wakened late in the morning, blinking sleepily at the sunlight that crept through her opened draperies. She had forgotten to close them last night. She stretched, kicking back the light sheet that covered her. Damn, it was going to be another hot, stinking day!

A tap at the door. She called, "Come in," without interest.

She turned her head as the boy came in. He started at seeing her and began to back out with the tray.

"Oh, come in, come in," she said impatiently, sitting up. "Shut the door, Nathaniel."

She gave him a long calculating look from under her lashes. He was handsome, a young native, unspoiled and blushing, she did believe. Surely he had had native girls. God, he was handsome, long and lithe.

"I b-bring your coffee, madame," he stammered.

"Set the tray down. Am I last again this morning, Nathaniel?" She smiled sweetly. She leaned over, giving him a look at her voluptuous body in the thin silk as she bent to the coffeepot. He was looking everywhere in the room except at her.

"Y-yes, ma-madame."

"Is it late? Do you go home now?"

"Yes, madame."

"Then you can stay and talk with me," she said softly. "I enjoy talking with you, Nathaniel. Do you know you are a very intelligent man? I couldn't believe it when you said you had never gone to school."

His chest swelled under the thin cotton shirt. He finally looked at her, his gaze lingering on the large, full breasts under the blue lace. He was staring at the way her breasts showed in the hollow where the lace parted and at the faint outline of hard, ripe nipples straining through the silk. She smiled into her cup.

Astrid leaned sensuously back against the lace-trimmed pillows. She drank a sip of hot coffee. Her gaze roamed frankly over him, from the strong head, the long throat, down over his broad shoulders to his brown hands, to the lithe waist and long, lean hips and thighs, down the long legs to the bare feet. She shivered with delicious pleasure at the forbidden thoughts rioting in her brain.

No one would know. No one. This boy wouldn't talk. He would know Brian would whip him, dismiss him. But he would not resist her—she would see to that.

"Lock the door, Nathaniel," she murmured.

He started. Gracefully she slid her long limbs from the bed and went over to the door as he stood shocked and still. She flipped the latch, then turned back.

"There, no one will disturb us." She smiled up at him. "You know, I noticed you the first day. How—how intelligent you look—how smart. Not like the others. A woman always notices men like you—"

She came closer to him, touched his chest with her slim hand. He started and trembled like one of the stallions. "You—should not—do this," he began. "This—this wrong. They no like—"

"I do what I please." She shrugged, coming closer. "I bet you have plenty of girls," she whispered. "Do you?"

He shook his head. He was staring at her arms, her bare shoulders. "Touch me," she breathed and took his brown hand and put it on her neck. She bent her head so her cheek caressed his hand, and trapped it between her throat and head. His free hand went to her waist, slowly, closing around it.

She ran one hand down his chest, slowly, sensuously, to his waist. Slowly she unfastened the cord that tied his trousers. They fell to the floor, and he kicked them off.

Nathaniel's hands went to her rounded thighs, and he drew her roughly to him. Desire flared in her as he brought her close to his brown body and fondled her buttocks. She began to unfasten his thin cotton shirt. He wore nothing under it.

He gulped. "You—mean this? You—white lady—" he began.

"I am a woman, you a man," she whispered. Her blue eyes were bright with desire, her lips full and moist. She was impatient for him; she could sense he was going to be good . . . "Take me, take me," she urged. "I want it, I do want it—"

Nathaniel waited no longer. He pushed her down on the floor, pulling up the lacy blue nightdress as she lay back invitingly. Astrid saw the hard brown body lowering toward her and smiled with anticipation. The carpet and floor were hard, but no matter. Another time the bed—

The room was silent but for his gasps and her moans as his mouth roamed over her creamy neck and shoulders. She managed to push down the nightdress until her breasts were bare, and he began to go wild with pleasure.

Oh, God, she had been crazy for sex. She closed her eyes and pulled the heavy head to her full breasts. He was licking her ripe nipples with sensuous flicks of his large red tongue. She moved her soft body under his lean hardness, and wrapped her legs around his sturdy back.

His hand moved slowly, with delight, over her curves, over her waist, to the full thighs. He stroked her gently. A considerate lover! And him a brown native boy! Why hadn't she noticed him before?

Damn Brian Cameron! He had ignored her too long.

Her firm hand caught at the slim buttocks, pulling

him urgently to her. He groaned, pressed to her roughly, then drew back in alarm.

"I hurt you—too big—"

"No, no—go on—go on—" she urged.

He nuzzled his big head against her. His lean hips pressed deeply against hers, and she felt the smooth fullness as their bodies joined. Blood throbbed in her temples as he rose and fell rhythmically, faster and faster, pressing her to the floor. She cried out, muffling the sound against the brown neck. God, he was good!

Chapter 10

Brian lay awake that night also, but he was not thinking of Astrid. He had forgotten her completely.

He lay on his back against the cool sheets, gazing about his luxurious bedroom at the silken draperies pushed back to let in the cool trade winds, the heavy mahogany furniture, the paintings on one wall, the wall that was hung with green and silver tapestries.

And Silva lay in a room with whitewashed walls, on a narrow iron bed, and it was all she had known since childhood. He closed his eyes in something like pain. He felt intensely frustrated.

It was not his nature to be patient. When he wanted something, he set about achieving it as soon as possible. But for Silva he had to hold hard patience to himself, and control his wish to give her everything in the world she had ever lacked, force upon her the luxuries she had been denied. He could see her in velvet dresses, lace sleeves, and silken nightgowns—huge drooping hats of cream straw and ribbons of green satin—jewels glinting green and diamond-white on her beautiful slim fingers. She was so lovely already. Dressed properly, with her natural grace and dignity, she was going to be a stunning girl.

He sat up and reached for a long, thin Havana cigar and lit it from the candle that burned beside his bed. The bedside table was of sandalwood, the top intricately inlaid with mosaics of green, silver, gold, blue, and crimson. The antique candlestick was of hammered silver, the candle of the best wax, fragrantly scented, perfume-treated beeswax.

And she was lit to bed with a whale-oil lamp.

"Damn," he muttered, smoking the cigar fiercely. The face pressed against the white satin pillows with lace edgings was as if carved teakwood, fierce as a Maya Indian's from years in the sun and stubborn fighting for what he desired. His vivid blue eyes glimmered in the single light of the candle, and the smoke from the cigar trailed upward in a thin blue line as the wind caught it. One arm lay idly across his knees as he narrowed his eyes in intense thought.

There must be some way to bring her here to a civilized house. To give her garments more suited to her beauty, to persuade her to be educated in a gentle way. If it meant bringing Tyrone with her, well enough. If it meant Liane, or even Maria Luisa, he would bring them all. But he *must* plan her future. No one else did; they let her drift. And she was like some precious treasure that must be displayed properly on a velvet backdrop.

Brian had wondered at first, cynically, if such a beauty could be untouched by the island men. Now, thinking of her grave delicacy, the wonderment on her face, the virginal purity of her look, he thought she was still a child. Liane was not—he knew the wise look of her eyes. And Tyrone also had tasted headily of the passion of the island women.

But Silva was still the pure child she had seemed at first. If he moved quickly enough, he could get her away from the temptations of the island, this pagan island of desire, and remove her to Cameron Hall, or even to Miami or New York. A chaperon, a tutor, someone to teach her the ways of the world without spoiling that lovely virginity . . . And what a wife she would make for some man!

He smiled slightly at himself. He had never thought about any girl in this way. Before, they had all been a sort of prey for him, the only question being, Will she, or won't she, tonight? But Silva was different.

He lay back, crushed out the end of the cigar, and

blew out the candle. In the moonlit dusk of his room, he lay with his eyes shut, thinking. On the huge wide bed, much too big for one, he was wondering how it would be to have such a girl—a pure, innocent girl—and teach her gently what love was about.

Love? He had not used that word seriously for years. What was the matter with him? Why did he lie awake like a lovesick courtier, a vague, undefined yearning in him for something he had never known?

He had stopped believing in love many years ago. Cynicism had taken its place. He defined any marriage as a good one—meaning the partners fit physically—or a bad one—they did not. Women were used as they indicated they wanted to be, and forgotten as easily as a flower of yesterday with petals that drooped.

Silva. Soft and fragrant. Her mouth when he had kissed her had been cool and salt with the sea. Surprised, slightly opened. Flinching from him. A sea nymph afraid of him, and of herself. He yearned now to run his fingers through the long length of silvery silken hair, to touch the sun-kissed shoulders, run his hand over the slim softness of her thigh. What if she lay with him now?

He turned restlessly in the bed. He must be going a little tropic-crazy. He had not thought of a girl like this since—since never, he realized. He had been born with a sure knowledge of his own power, his own attractions. As he had grown more wealthy, women had been more attracted to him. Partly for his lean, hard-muscled body, partly for the gifts he would give them.

Silva had not wanted his gifts. She would fling them in his face, he thought with a small grin. She had a proud chin, a tilt to her face, a straightening of her slim shoulders when challenged. How small she was, after all. She needed protection. He longed to hold her, to reassure her that the world was not so bad a place, when a strong man held her, and protected her.

No woman had ever obsessed him so. He could not get her out of his mind. He lay awake another hour, impatient of his sleeplessness, unable to stop thinking about her, to stop planning how he would get her to come and stay at his home. He wanted to embrace her, protect her, keep her from all harm. Those damn native boys! They would treat her like their other women, to be used and discarded, or made to burden themselves with child after child. He thought of her beauty blurred, her spirit quenched, the green eyes sad. No, not that for her.

He turned and tossed again and again. He would get her to come here to Cameron Hall: step one. Next he would take her to Miami: step two. Then what? A chaperon, a tutor. He would take her to concerts, to art galleries. He might take her to Europe with him. How her eyes would glow with wonder when she heard a real concert, saw the beauty of Scotland and its purple hills. And to France, where she would be a wonder to all with her grave, slim, silvery beauty. She would be called chic, svelte. But none of that mattered. He wanted to show her the beauties of the whole world, and watch her expression as she saw them. He wanted to be with her when she saw the world beyond Desirée for the first time, and he realized that she was one person whom he could not buy.

Silva was worried. Tyrone had not come home that night. There were no boats that had gone out—she had ascertained that. And Oona belonged now to Pedro Ortega. So where had Tyrone gone?

She went out about midday, when Tyrone did not return for breakfast. After the chores she was so restless that Maria Luisa had sighed deeply and told her to go out and search.

"Go, little one. The signs are bad, have a great

care. Search for your brother, but have a care of yourself."

"Sí Mamacita," Silva had assured her as she set out. Now her feet were weary, and she had searched their usual places—the lagoon, the hills, even gazing out over Brian Cameron's land.

Not a sign of Tyrone. She was about to give up and go home for lunch when she heard voices. She was on a slight rise above the lagoon, having gone back there again. She might get in a swim before returning, she had thought.

But someone was there. Cautiously she peered down between the thick bushes, parting the clinging liana that held bushes together and swarmed up the thick trunks of oaks and mahogany, and saw them: Tyrone with his arm about the plump, round body of Oona, slowly walking along the beach with her, gazing down into her face.

They were both mussed, covered with sand, laughing a little. As Silva stared, unable to believe it, Tyrone reached out with his free hand and brushed sand from Oona's long black tresses.

She was about to creep away, troubled and embarrassed, when Tyrone's arm dropped. Around the bend in the beach at Half Moon Bay came Pedro Ortega. Silva caught her breath, her hand to her slight breasts.

He would kill Tyrone! Frantically she looked about for a weapon. She reached for a dead stick near her in the deep grass as the three figures met down on the beach. Tyrone's hands were on his hips. Pedro held up his hand in a friendly gesture, though his scarred face, which was turned toward Silva, looked sinister.

They stood together for a time, talking. Then Oona laughed, flinging back her black head, and sped away, coyly turning to wave at them both. Puzzled, Silva watched. Then, deliberately, she crept like a cat farther down toward the beach, always keeping bushes between her and the two men.

Tyrone's silver head was bright in the sun as he faced the older man, dark and worn, somehow evil, in his red shirt and black pants, the scarred face twisting his personality in her eyes. There was something about the scar on his face that drew down one eye into a menacing glare.

Tyrone was talking to him earnestly, hands waving now. Pedro nodded crisply, said something in a short, sure tone. Tyrone nodded eagerly. What the devil were they talking about?

Silva was as close as she dared to come. She could not leave the shelter of the tree-strewn hillside. She strained to hear, but could make out no words. They talked in low tones, their faces serious.

They were not angry with each other, and that puzzled her deeply. Surely Pedro Ortega would not endure another man touching the woman he had designated as his own. Oona had even worn his scarlet to the voodoo ceremony.

What did he want with Tyrone?

Silva watched and listened, straining, but made out nothing. Finally Tyrone, giving a little laugh of excitement, lifted a hand in farewell and strode up the hill toward her. He passed within five feet of her, but did not see her. He was not looking for her. His eyes blazed with excitement.

Pedro remained on the beach, standing with hands on hips, gazing out to the sea. Then he, too, turned and strode up the hill. However, his eyes and attention were more keen.

He saw the girl, veered from his path, and came straight to her. She crouched, paralyzed, in the bushes. He came right at her, grabbed her shoulders, and pulled her up.

"What the devil? How long you been there?" He shook her roughly, his fingers biting into her tender flesh.

"Long enough to see you talk to Tyrone," she said bravely. "What do you want with my brother?"

She could smell the unpleasantly strong scent of him, masculine and sweaty, and she tried to back away. He held her more tightly, his black eyes going over her boldly, from her silvery hair to her slim thighs.

Pedro shrugged, and a slight grin came to his thick lips. "Just business, between men," he said. "None of this for your little head. What are you doing, spying here?"

"I came to look for Tyrone! It is—it is late," she stammered.

She was beginning to be afraid. His eyes blazed so oddly. He kept looking at her, as he had the night of the voodoo. She remembered his hands on her waist then, and her fear.

"Let me go," she demanded, with a quaver in her tone.

"When I please," he said softly. "You give me a good kiss, huh?"

He pulled her close to his warm body. She felt the hot pulsing of his hard form, sensed the blood pounding through him. She saw the queer flare of his eyes, the redness of his scar, and she was afraid.

"Let me go!"

He pulled her to him, one hand moving to her thigh and yanking up her dress. For one horrible moment she felt his palm against her thigh. She slapped him, then clawed him. He swore, let her loose for an instant, and wildly, like a driven animal, she sped from him into the bushes.

She heard his booted feet crashing into the underbrush behind her. Fear lent wings to her slim feet. She raced up the slope, panting, her heart in her throat.

He was following her! She slipped into an especially dense patch of undergrowth and stood intensely still, like a hunted deer. He crashed past her, growling a curse. He went up to the top of the hill. Presently the silence flowed back, and birds began their singing.

A flock of tropical birds swung out and winged their way like a flash of emerald through the blue midday sky. Little animals crawled out, hunting for food. A sleepy iguana flickered past her foot.

Finally, when she thought it was safe, she crept up the hill, peered about, then dashed from bush to bush to the safety of the path above her house. Then down she ran, on frantic feet, like a small scared bird, to the safety of the house.

Maria Luisa was minding the pot over the fire. She looked up sharply when Silva ran into the open yard. Her dark eyes narrowed.

"What happen?" she asked sharply. Silva flung herself into the comfort of warm, plump arms and laid her cheek against the soft breast that had always been her refuge.

"Oh, Mamacita, oh, Mamacita" was all Silva could say for a time.

Maria Luisa stroked her hair, patted her back, and waited patiently. Finally Silva gulped out her story. Maria Luisa's face hardened in wrath and concern.

"It was like snakes about, Mamacita!" She shuddered violently. "Oh, horrible! Like snakes crawling. I hated his touch!"

"He might have taken you, there in the bushes, my Silva! You must never go near him again!"

"I know, I know. Oh, men are hateful!"

"Some men, yes—some, no," sighed Maria Luisa. "One day you will know the difference. But about your brother . . . You think he was all the night with Oona, who is now the woman of Pedro?"

Silva nodded. She drew back. "I saw them, the way they were with each other," she said drearily. "Oh, foolish Tyrone. What mischief will they take him into?"

"Much trouble," muttered Maria Luisa. "That is where they will take him. But you, Silva. You stay away from them! That Pedro Ortega is not like the natives here, always singing and laughing. That one plan grim plans, and make mischief with the devil. He will bring down evil on Desirée—I know it."

Silva sighed. She would have to stay by herself at home, or go out only with Liane or someone else to the lagoon, she thought. It was too dangerous. She must not be so careless again. Pedro might have caught her, raped her.

She was eighteen now, and full-grown. Men desired her on this primitive island, where passions could run hot under the Caribbean sun. The heat of the tropics seemed to waken harsh desires in men, and they acted like animals.

Liane came up from the hill below them, her head drooping, every line of her body sad. "Where is Nathaniel?" asked Silva, concerned. Liane always met him near the favorite fishing beach, and they laughed and talked and caught fish for luncheon or supper.

"He did not come," said Liane, tears in her soft dark eyes. "He say he come. He do not come. He forget Liane. He forget me since the new job which is so important to him." She spoke with unusual bitterness.

Silva put her arms about her friend, her own troubles forgotten. "Oh, Liane, he has not forgotten you. He is making much money, so he can marry you! He said so."

"His work was finished hours ago. He does not come." Liane would not be comforted. She sat down on a mat with her slim brown legs crossed, and tears rolled down her lovely face.

Maria Luisa groaned. "All trouble, all trouble. I see trouble when the moon hides her face last night," she muttered. "I call to the gods, they do not answer. Much trouble comes to us on Desirée."

"He has acted funny since he get that job. I hate that job," said Liane with passion. "He has changed. He think more of the women there than me. He eat on a plate, he drink from china cup. He despises our food! Oh, what will become of me? Nathaniel is under a bad spell."

"We can make sacrifices to the gods tonight," suggested Silva hopefully, her arm again about Liane. The dark head on her shoulder lay limply. Liane's arms were outstretched before her, palms up, as though pleading for help. Silva thought the youth and freshness and hope seemed dashed out of her friend.

"I did, last night," said Maria Luisa. "They not listen. They despise my sacrifices. The smoke flare up, the fire go out. All bad. Much trouble come to Desirée."

"Is it from Brian Cameron?" asked Silva fiercely. "I'll tell him to go away!"

Maria Luisa shook her graying head. "Not from him, child. Because of him, partly. But not from him. It was to happen, the gods decreed. But I not know what to do to drive away trouble." She rocked back and forth on her mat and looked forlornly at the two sad girls.

Chapter 11

The October night was cloudy. The moon was obscured, and no stars shone to light them on their way. Pedro Ortega followed the compass intently, a scowl on his scarred face.

Tyrone, behind him in the wheelhouse, felt the nervous excitement chilling him along with the trade winds of the tropical night. He wore black pants, a dark shirt, a black windbreaker, but his blond hair glistened in the dim light of the cabin.

The launch was heavily packed with all the rum that was ready. Pedro, Rodrigues, and Tyrone had loaded the casks at the dock just after dusk, then set out slowly into the sunset. Tyrone stared ahead at the fading light of the reddish sunset and felt the shivers of apprehension and turmoil that always shook him when they made a run.

It had been this way from the beginning. No matter how many rumrunning trips he made, he thought he would always feel this tremor of keen anticipation of danger, the thrill of challenging the sea and the Coast Guard and the other rumrunners, out on the open waters between Desirée and Miami. Forty miles of trouble! Sharks swam these waters, and other fish cast their phosphorescent glow as the launch skimmed over the dark waters.

Rodrigues sat on the deck, his knees cradling a machine gun. He had oiled and loaded it, with the absorbed interest of a child, fascinated by the weapon he handled so well. In his belt was a pistol and a long knife. He wore only trousers cut off at the ankles, a thick sweater, and a cap pulled over his head. His dark face gleamed when he looked toward the wheelhouse, where Pedro steered their course.

Their boat was one of the finest in the waters, a thirty-foot launch painted dull gray, with power in the engines that they had tested time and again. They could go faster than the Coast Guard, no worry about that! Their biggest worry, thought Tyrone, was the jealous men of Cuba and the Bahamas, who knew that Pedro Ortega got the best prices for his good Desirée rum.

They had tried to force him to join them, but Pedro was a loner. He turned up his nose at those cold-eyed men from the syndicates and the gay, devilish runners of the Spanish Main, those modern-day pirates who carried the liquor over to Florida for the thirsty mainlanders who hated the Prohibition laws.

Tyrone stirred, and came forward as Pedro beckoned to him.

"Hear anything?" muttered the dark native.

Tyrone shook his head, then bent it to listen better. Rodrigues crouched against the deck and listened also, his head twisted so his good ear was to the south.

Then Tyrone heard it, a slight throbbing sound in the tropical stillness, faint, faraway. His whole body thrilled to the sound. He looked questioningly at the head of Pedro Ortega, slightly bent as he held the wheel in his huge, powerful hands.

They all waited tensely as the boat skimmed lightly through the waters. Pedro had the best boats. Tyrone wondered where he had obtained them. One usually had to pay a high price for these fast-running motor cruisers, especially one as large and as fast as this one. But Pedro had appeared with it about three months ago, and never mentioned where it came from. The slower launch they had been using was now used for fishing trips.

Pedro confided in no one. He was a lone wolf, as

Rodrigues said, a lone *tigrero*—like the jaguars that stalked the Mountain of the Cat. He was tough and he was mean, but one felt safe with him, because he was clever, and protected his own.

Tyrone had been with him once in a Miami port, and when someone attacked Tyrone, holding a knife at his throat, Pedro had flung the man into the water with a flip of his strong arms, then spun Tyrone around with him, to run back to their cruiser.

He had tried to thank Pedro. Pedro had said, "You will pay me with your loyalty!" Tyrone had tried to do that.

He flinched, thinking of Oona. She had tempted him beyond endurance and he had had to have her. Oddly, when he had seen them together that morning, Pedro had not been angry. Tyrone was puzzled by that. It didn't make sense, for Pedro was a very possessive man.

The thrumming sound was closer, and brought Tyrone abruptly back to their present danger. Pedro bit out a snarling curse. He beckoned to Tyrone. "Take the wheel," he commanded.

Rodrigues looked up at them from his crouch on the deck. He lifted his hand. Pedro shook his head, and took down the other machine gun, fastened to the bulkhead behind his chair. Holding it, he caressed it mechanically, checked the load, then stalked out on deck on the other side from Rodrigues.

Tyrone was alone in the wheelhouse, only the top of his head a shining silver halo above the steel-lined little cabin. He felt the boat quivering with energy in his hands as he let out the speed gradually, increasing it as Pedro motioned him to do.

Such tremendous power in his hands! The sleek boat raced through the waters, leaping above the waves like a tiger shark! He loved the boats, the water, the smell of the sea in his nose, the feel of the wind in his hair, crisp and cold and tingling.

Abruptly a light shone across the wheelhouse like a

silver sword. A voice hailed them through a megaphone. Tyrone started and jerked the wheel.

"Ahoy, there, heave to! This is the Coast Guard!" the voice called. Tyrone let the throttle out all the way, his blood racing frantically.

As the slim boat leapt faster through the waters, a line of tracers rattled across the bow. The boat jumped in Tyrone's hands, and he faltered a moment.

"Blanks," Pedro barked at him. "Get moving! Keep it going. Turn north slightly."

Tyrone corrected their course, his ears drumming as the tracer blanks were followed by a hail of bullets from a machine gun. Rodrigues still crouched behind the protection of the rail. Pedro was intensely still, waiting.

Someone yelled through the megaphone, but the words were obscured by the increasing distance. Tyrone glanced behind them. He could see the gray cruiser dimly behind them. The clouds hid any light that might have come from the moon and the stars. Pedro Ortega knew what he was doing, making a run on a dark night like this!

They raced farther and farther away from the roar of the megaphone and the hail of bullets that lit the night briefly. A spotlight shone across the waters, tossed and angry between the ships. But they soon left even the searchlight behind them.

"Keep to the north," ordered Pedro briefly.

Tyrone steered the launch tensely, and was soon able to slow down as they left the Coast Guard behind them. They were only going about eighteen or twenty knots per hour, and this beauty could make up to thirty. Pedro was smart, all right.

Tyrone's throat was dry; he swallowed convulsively again and again. The encounter with the Coast Guard had been so close, closer than ever before. In the dim light of the wheelhouse he noticed a hole in front of him, and examined it closely. Yet, it *was* a bullet hole. The law had used real bullets the last time they had fired. Tyrone's head had been missed by inches!

He stared ahead for a long time as he directed the boat toward Miami. Pedro came into the wheelhouse, hung up the machine gun behind them, and took the wheel again. "Get some coffee," he ordered curtly.

Tyrone said, "Yes, sir," and went down to the cabin below. He lit a small lamp in the galley, and then the tiny stove. His hands were shaking. He had never been that close to death before.

Why had Pedro ordered him to take the wheel just then? Had he known that Tyrone was in danger of death? Any man who had to steer the cruiser and keep that speed would have to keep his head up above the protection of the steel. Or did Pedro feel he himself had to man his machine gun, and he trusted Tyrone at the wheel?

Tyrone prepared the coffee mechanically and brought up cups to Rodrigues and Pedro. Rodrigues looked up at him keenly, thoughtfully. "You shook, boy?" he muttered.

Tyrone took pride in the nonchalant way he shook his head and shrugged his shoulders. He went below again, to the closeness of the cabin, and drank his coffee down there, and held a blanket about himself to still the shivering.

Pedro turned south after half an hour, and the boat ran smoothly along the reefs. He knew those waters, but any man could make a mistake. He watched closely.

Tyrone was with him near the wheel when Pedro cursed. "Damn. They're waiting for us at the key."

Tyrone felt cold. This night was damned. Maria Luisa was right: There was trouble in the stars. He peered ahead and saw the tiny running lights of the Coast Guard patrol boat.

Pedro put out to sea, and the boat followed, like a gray shark, waiting for them.

They gave chase for three hours. Tyrone's blood felt cold, his hands numb from relieving Pedro at the wheel. As dawn approached, they had still not been able to land their expensive, damning cargo.

"What we going to do?" asked Rodrigues plaintively. "Soon there be light. We cannot remain. We go home?"

"Like hell," said Pedro. "I know a place—" He went silent again, glancing about the open sea. The gray dawn was creeping over the dark, still waters, turning them to steel-gray. Soon the sun would rise and dance golden and orange over those waters, and they would be seen plainly.

But Pedro had turned inland. There was no Coast Guard cutter about. He ran for a time between two small islands, in water so shallow that Tyrone hung over the side of the rail, holding his breath for fear that the boat would catch on the mangrove roots.

"Swamps," muttered Rodrigues in disgust, staring with fear at the thick mangroves, the lianas, the entwined trees, the hanging gray Spanish moss. "Bad in there, very bad."

Pedro heard him, and gave a grin that showed his yellow teeth. "But safe."

He slowed the boat and finally halted it near a series of worn wooden planks that led back into a vague darkness. It was gray-black in there, with a stink of swampy waters and fish. As they halted, mosquitoes came to swarm about them. Tyrone slapped himself again and again, but felt the sharp stings on his tender flesh. The others did not seem to mind it.

Pedro motioned to a place. "We land the stuff there. I know a cabin—it will be safe."

They began to unload, carrying the heavy cases of rum from the cruiser to the rotting landing dock, which threatened to give way under their booted feet. Tyrone carried case after case ashore to the shelter of a small wooden hut, dumped it down, stretched his aching arms, and went back for another load. Lianas flung themselves in his face and he was feeling the sting of the mosquitoes as he fought his way through the junglelike growth toward the hut and back again. He swore and jumped back as he almost stepped on a snake that seemed to be slithering toward him. Goosebumps came up on his flesh, and he shivered violently when he regained the safety of the cruiser. He had to force himself to go out again.

When he was finally done and they were aboard again, Tyrone felt exhausted. Pedro was cursing in an angry monotone.

"I got to go to Miami next, and tell my fellow where to meet me. Goddamn, that mean another trip. The Guard, they watch for me today. I come tomorrow in fishing boat," Pedro decided. He scowled and grunted as he backed the cruiser out of the narrow passageway.

"You find this again?" asked Rodrigues worriedly.

"I know my way around hell and back," snarled Pedro, and neither Rodrigues nor Tyrone spoke to him again, preferring the safety of the open deck to the confines of the wheelhouse and Pedro's nasty temper.

They were finally out on the open sea. Full dawn was spinning golden threads on the blue and silver waters. Foam dashed against the rocks, and more foam was spun in their wake as the cruiser darted through the waters, faster now because it was relieved of its heavy load.

Tyrone scratched his face and arms, and tried to make himself quit. He was feeling frantic with the sting of the mosquito bites. Rodrigues, watching him, shrugged and grinned. "Get Oona to put stuff on you," he advised with a curl of his lip.

Tyrone retreated to the cabin below and lay down. He was weary, the excitement gone. And he had much to puzzle him. Why were both these men, lovers of Oona, so willing to let Tyrone have her? Was she part of a plot, and if so, what plot?

Pedro called him when Tyrone was almost asleep.

Staggering with weariness, the boy went up the stairs.

"I get something to eat," Pedro said curtly. "You steer, and if you or Rodrigues see anything, call me at once. At once, you hear?"

He turned over the wheel to the lad and went below. Rodrigues caught Tyrone's gaze, shrugged, and sat down on the foredeck, where he could stretch out lazily in the sun and still watch all about.

No ominous Coast Guard cutters came into view. Only a few fishermen were out early, some in expensive white trawlers or yachts, with lines over the bow. Tyrone steered clear of them, wanting no curious eyes to rest too closely on the cruiser that had made the rum run into the keys.

It was early afternoon when they landed at the dock at Desirée. Tyrone had steered for most of the five-hour journey, and his arms were weary, his body exhausted. He was hungry, tired, mosquito-bitten. And his conscience plagued him.

He had the feeling that Pedro was playing him out on a line like a fish; maybe the lovely Oona was the bait. Pedro was not one to let someone have his girl, and Oona was going along with her role. If only he was not so tired, maybe he could figure it out.

Tyrone had to walk about five miles to get back home. Weary as he was, he went slowly, staggering with exhaustion by the time he stumbled into the yard. Silva was there, and she started up with a cry.

"Tyrone? Where have you been? What happened? Oh, your poor face!" She touched him with gentle fingers, but even those hurt, and he flinched.

"Leave me alone. Just got a couple of mosquito bites," he muttered.

Maria Luisa came to him as he went into the house. All he wanted was sleep, and relief from the bites.

"Got good medicine?" he asked gruffly to her reproving dark eyes, so sad and so knowing.

"I bring," she said.

He went into the small bathroom and showered, pouring cold water from the basin over his head and body by the bucketful. That was some relief. Maria Luisa came in unceremoniously as he was still pouring water over himself. She made him feel like a small boy, he thought resentfully. "I can take care of myself."

She paid no attention to his petulance. She patted his face dry, then began to apply the cool salve to the bites on his face, his arms and shoulders, his whole body. Mosquitoes must have bitten through his clothing.

She shook her head over him maternally. "You get in a swamp, huh, Tyrone?"

"Maybe," he shrugged. "Maybe so."

She gave him a sharp spank on his bare buttocks, and he glared at her over his shoulder. "Don't you talk like that no-good Rodrigues," she admonished. "What would your father say to you now?"

"He isn't here," Tyrone said flatly. A wave of desolation swept over him. He had never been able to talk to his father. Valerian had always been so absorbed in his art or his grief that his children seemed to exist only as small silver ghosts to him. There was no one for Tyrone to talk to, no one who could advise him. No one with whom he could discuss his doubts and his fears, the sharp worry that haunted him.

"You get some sleep, you get better temper come morning," said Maria Luisa. "I bring soup to you in bed."

He slid between the sheets of the bed, feeling with relief the hard mattress under him. He was almost asleep when Maria Luisa came in with the steaming bowl of soup. He sat up to drink it, then lay back down again, smiling like a child. Warm, dry, fed, comforted. "I'm sorry, Maria Luisa. I was cross with you," he said before he drifted off.

He felt her warm palm on his face. "You good boy. Go sleep now," she murmured.

She went back out to the fire. It had just gotten dark. Silva and Liane sat on mats before the fire, and looked up at her questioningly. Maria Luisa shook her head. "That Rodrigues, he take him to swamps," she said with a scowl. "All over bites. I fix him. That Rodrigues, he no good for Tyrone."

Silva did not tell them of her fear, that Pedro Ortega had taken both Tyrone and Rodrigues out in the boat, that he forced them to help with the rum-running. She knew Pedro was a cruel man, that there was no gentleness or goodness in him; but Rodrigues was different. He had been good to them at times. He was a happy, laughing man most of the time, whereas Pedro was somber, cunning, always planning mischief—or worse. The war god was his god, and he was content only when he made trouble. She gazed uneasily at the fire until she grew weary.

She thought for a long time that night, and could not sleep well, tossing on the hard mattress. The night winds cooled her body, but could not soothe her.

In the morning, Silva was up early. Tyrone still slept. She had peeked into his room, to find him in a deathlike sleep, his fine features relaxed, the silver hair tossed on the sheet. All red and swollen with bites. She bit her lips. He would get in worse trouble than mosquito stings if he kept on with Pedro.

Liane had gone off to the beach after breakfast to wait patiently for Nathaniel. Her eyes had been sad and dark this morning, as though she did not really expect him to come. Silva felt sad for her friend, and indignant with Nathaniel. He was getting grand ideas, and hurting Liane. Maybe it would be better to let them marry soon, but Maria Luisa would not be hurried.

Silva fed the chickens and the pigs, for Tyrone

still slept. Then she hoed the garden until the heat of the day drove her back into the shade. She longed for a swim in the cool lagoon but dared not go alone again.

How things were changing from her earlier carefree days. When her father was alive and she was as young and thin as a boy, dashing about in her loose cotton shifts and sandals, she had had few fears and worries.

Growing up could be dreadful. Small troubles became great ones, unsolvable ones. She brooded on her mat, watching the meat and turning it occasionally on the spit. Maria Luisa had decided on roast chicken today. A treat for her young ones, thought Silva. A special treat to chase away the gloom.

It seemed inevitable when Rodrigues came. He walked down the hill with a long swinging stride and grinned to find her alone for a change. Silva knew Maria Luisa was inside the house, taking a little nap in the coolness. Silva watched warily as Rodrigues approached, and when he came into the clearing, she stood up.

"Good day to you," she said formally, and went to pour coffee for him and for herself. She added milk and sugar and handed him the cup. He tried to take her hand along with the cup, but she was ready for the move and slipped her fingers deftly away just before they could be grabbed.

"Tyrone sleeps?" he asked, squatting on a mat.

She nodded. "He was very weary. Also he had mosquito bites all over his body. Maria Luisa was very displeased."

Rodrigues grunted and sipped the hot coffee. Silva drank a little of hers, watching him cautiously over the rim of the cup.

"Did Pedro go with you?" she asked suddenly.

"It is Pedro's boat," Rodrigues said after a pause.

Silva swallowed a sip of the hot coffee. "The three of you, it is dangerous for you," she said slowly.

He shrugged. "Men enjoy danger, and your brother has become a man. Ask Oona," he added with a grin.

Her lashes covered her eyes. When he talked like that and looked at her up and down her body, she wanted to run and hide from that knowing gaze. "He is only a boy. I wish he would not go out with you men. He enjoys danger, yes, but he does not know how to protect himself—yet."

"So—he will know one day."

"I wish he would not go," she repeated.

He opened his black eyes wide and challenged: "So? What do you ask?"

She put her hand to her throat, where the betraying pulse beat. "I want you to—to prevent him from going. Persuade Tyrone not to go out on those—those trips. They are not good. He is in danger. I would be —very sad—if anything happened to my twin."

He was silent for a little time, surprising her. She wondered what was going on under that thick thatch of coarse black hair. His black eyes had narrowed, and he stared at her over his cup.

Finally he said softly, "It could be arranged, for Tyrone to not go out again."

"How do you mean?" she asked tensely, her slim body erect. She set down her coffee cup beside her, her green eyes eager and appealing. "What—? How—?"

"I could arrange it. I could persuade Pedro to take someone else. Tyrone not like it—" He shrugged eloquently, one hand outspread, palm up. "But he must do what Pedro say. And I, Rodrigues, can talk to Pedro."

"Would you, Rodrigues?" She was passionately grateful, but still a little wary. "I would be so grateful! He does not need that money. He can get along, fishing—"

"Sure, sure, he get along. All it take is a word from you."

She took a deep breath. He followed the movement of her cotton shift as her breasts moved under the thin covering. "What—do you mean?" Her voice was stifled; she felt as though she could not breathe without pain to her lungs.

"You marry me," he said bluntly. "If you marry me right away, I get Pedro to start alone. He no take Tyrone again. Okay? I protect my family, yes? My wife, and wife's brother."

Shocked, she sprang up, lithe as a startled fawn that sees a jaguar approach, stalking it. "No, no, no! I cannot!"

He got up also, and approached her. He grasped her wrist. "You say no. You shy of Rodrigues. I teach you not to be shy."

He pulled her toward him. She hated his touch on her wrist, hated the wetness of his red lips, the way he licked them as he stared down at her. She hated the greed in his black eyes, their speculative glint, the smell of his masculine body—

She tried to pull away. "No, no, I won't marry you! Never! Never! It is impossible! Besides, you want Oona! Why don't you marry Oona?"

"Oona is the girl of Pedro now," he said, scowling, his eyes suddenly fierce.

She wanted to ask why, if that was the case, the girl made such a play for Tyrone, but her own safety was in jeopardy. She yanked at her wrist, but he pulled at her cruelly, yanking her to him. She cried out at the pain. "No! Let me go! Let me go!"

"You marry me, Tyrone be okay!" he panted, pulling her closer to him. She kicked with a sandaled foot; against his boot it made not the impact of a fly. He laughed down at her. "You want fight, eh? Okay!"

His arm slipped about her slim waist. Behind him, Maria Luisa had slipped up with a stick. She cracked him sharply on the head. He sagged, let go of Silva, and fell down. Silva stared down at him, half crying, shaking with fright.

But Rodrigues had a hard head. He sat there, rubbing it, glaring furiously at the two women. Silva backed away from him, backed farther when she saw the anger in his face.

"You'll be sorry for that!" he told Maria Luisa. "You be very sorry, old woman! I could break you in two with my hands!" And he held up his huge hands, shaking them at her.

"You let my Silva alone, or *I* break *you* with the help of the gods," said Maria Luisa. "I see shark come for you! That is in my dream. I see sharks gather about you, if you keep after my Silva! You go, and stay away!"

He got up, grumbling, furious. He picked up his shabby hat, pushed it down on his head, and started away. He turned at the edge of the clearing.

"You will be sorry, Silva," he said to the girl. "You be very sorry. Tyrone has no help now! You must hate your brother, to be so mean to him!" He grinned at her threateningly, and laughed mockingly as he left, stamping up the hill.

Maria Luisa stared at Silva. "What he talking about?" she demanded sharply.

The girl's shoulders slumped. She sat down and put her head on her knees. "Oh, Mamacita, I tried to get him to promise to leave Tyrone alone. He said he would if—if I—I marry him—" She shuddered with revulsion. "I hate his touch! I hate men—I hate them all!"

Maria Luisa sighed, picked up the cup from which Rodrigues had drunk, and began to scrub it fiercely in a pail of water. "You must let Tyrone do his own fights," she said simply after a while. "I think he wake up pretty soon. Maybe he have clear head once again. He pretty damn fool, let Pedro and Rodrigues lead him around by nose. Maybe he wake up."

Silva wrinkled her nose in perplexity. "Do you mean—" she began.

"You no worry about Tyrone. Let him be. You worry about Silva!" Maria Luisa told her sharply. "I told you about them men. You stay away from them. When a good man comes to you, you be clean and fresh and pretty for him."

"I don't want any men," muttered Silva sullenly. She rubbed her face with weary hands. "All men are bad. All men."

"Not all men," said Maria Luisa more gently. "You wait for right man, girl. You wait!"

"I'll wait, all right," muttered the girl. "All my life, and hide from them!"

Maria Luisa stroked the long silver hair with a gentle hand. "You my lovely girl," she crooned. "A man come to you one day. He love you for your good heart; you love him and make him happy. That is good. You will see."

But Silva was not so sure. She was even less certain when Liane returned at lunchtime, alone, her face sad, her eyes red and swollen from weeping.

Silva nursed her bruised red wrist and thought savagely that no men were good. They just made women cry. Better to stay away from them all!

After lunch she returned to her neglected paintings. In the living room she worked on one of the paintings she was doing, finding satisfaction in creating a beautiful flower on the fragile material. There was happiness in this. Where men were concerned, there was no joy or gladness. Only trouble, trouble, trouble.

For no reason she thought suddenly of Brian Cameron—his vivid blue eyes watching her alertly, the hated pressure of his strong mouth on her lips. Yes, he too was like all the other men, wanting to have his own way with a girl, then laughing and discarding her when he was through.

She would avoid him also. That was best!

Chapter 12

Tyrone rested for the next few days, brooding before the fire, smoothing more ointment on his bitten skin. He seemed quiet, thinking and frowning. Silva hoped that something had made him consider his actions. Maybe he would get some sense and not go out with those men again.

He did not confide in her. He had not these past several years. They had been close when they were younger, close because their father was so distant and strange and unapproachable.

Maybe one day Silva and Tyrone would be close again, she thought with a sigh. If only she could tell him her troubles. She wished there was someone besides Maria Luisa in whom she could confide. Liane was preoccupied now with her own worries and fears.

Silva was pleasantly surprised when Tyrone came back one noon in time for lunch, without fish but with a pleased grin on his face. He was dusty, his trousers dirty, but a gleam shone in his gray-green eyes.

"Where you been?" asked Maria Luisa sharply. "You get dirty like a child!"

Instead of taking offense, he laughed at her and at himself. "I've been horseback riding!" he announced. "Wait—I'll tell you about it." He disappeared into the house.

He bathed, changed, and returned in fifteen minutes. Silva had time to consider fresh worries. Horseback riding—he must have been with Brian Cameron!

Her fears were confirmed when Tyrone returned and sat down on a mat to be waited on. Silva filled his plate with pork and beans, with greens fresh-cooked in ham broth.

He ate hungrily. Between mouthfuls he said, "I went out early to go fishing. Met Brian Cameron at the lagoon, riding that big black stallion of his. A beauty!"

The lagoon. Silva's fork paused above her plate. He had gone down to the lagoon. Thinking to meet her? She was wise to stay away from that place! Resentfully she wished Brian Cameron would return to the mainland, so she could swim in peace once more.

"He let me ride the brute. God, what a marvelous animal! Then we went back to his house. He showed me around his stables. Would you believe he has ten horses there? A fine mare he said Silva could ride. She is a little brown beauty, Silva, gentle and high-strung, but you could ride her. You're lightweight."

She compressed her lips. Maria Luisa shot her a warning look. Silva took a gulp of hot coffee, almost burning her mouth. Tyrone chattered on, his cheeks flushed, his eyes blazing with pleasure.

"Brian showed me how to saddle up, and then we went out again after breakfast. We rode for miles. I fell off a couple of times, but he just waited for me and I hopped up again. He said I was a natural rider. He said I could come every day and ride. He said—"

Silva could eat no more. She was seething. Brian Cameron was taking her brother in hand, as he had threatened, and Tyrone did not even see it! For breakfast—breakfast in that big house?

Maria Luisa asked the question. "You eat in Cameron Hall?" she said mildly, squatting on a mat with a fresh cup of coffee in her brown hand.

"Yes, yes. We ate on a patio. Glass-topped table, beautiful bamboo chairs with wide fan backs. A pool like I've never seen," said Tyrone, eloquently moving his hands. "Silva, you would go mad there. You never saw such tiles and paintings in the house, and tapestries—Nathaniel showed me around. We had breakfast—hot coffee, and eggs and bacon, and fresh pineapple brought in on the freighter, and finger bananas—I ate like a pig! And the guests—"

"They nice to you?" asked Maria Luisa.

"Nice! They were like—like friends," he said, sighing. "There's a nice older couple, Mr. and Mrs. Leoni—Italian, Brian said. And Donald Keller—he's a stockbroker in New York."

"What that?" Maria Luisa demanded.

Tyrone didn't know. He had just picked up the term and waved it before them grandly. His eyes shone, and his voice rose to a high pitch, then wavered and came down again. "And when we came back from riding, this lady was there! Wow! You should have seen her in a swimsuit. All sleek in her white suit, and diving into the water. Blonder than you, Silva, yellow-blonde with big blue eyes—"

The blonde lady in the cream lace dress, thought Silva, feeling a strange choking sensation in her throat. That beautiful lady, blonder than Silva, with golden hair and blue eyes like the sky, all dressed in beautiful clothes.

"Finish your meat, Silva," ordered Maria Luisa. "What Mr. Cameron talk about, Tyrone?"

"Oh, gosh! About Miami, and New York City, and horses, and college." Tyrone gobbled the rest of his food, then set down the plate. "It's too late to go fishing. How are we for food, Maria Luisa? I promise I'll go early tomorrow. Silva and I are going out tonight."

Silva set down her plate carefully. For the first time in quite a while she said something. "Going out? Where? To New York City?"

Tyrone looked amazed at her sarcasm, the bitterness in her voice. "Gosh, no—don't be silly. We're going to Cameron Hall for dinner. I promised to bring you."

She swallowed. "I don't want— I won't go," she said flatly.

"Oh, Silva, I promised! Don't go all stiff and proud! Come on, Sis, you never go out. It'll be fun. You'll be amazed at the house. Nathaniel will show you around."

Go to Cameron Hall, where her father had never gone, where they had never been invited in the old days—and have the house servant show them around? No, thank you, she thought violently.

She was about to reject the invitation once more when she saw Maria Luisa's urgent look and gesture. Silva closed her mouth again and let Tyrone rave on. Finally he jumped up and went away to look over his clothes and figure out what to wear.

Then she said fiercely to Maria Luisa, "I will not go! He invited Tyrone, and Tyrone can go. But I will not set foot in that house! He is a bully, a devil—"

"Child, child, do you not see? How happy is Tyrone. He forgets Oona and the men for today. Do you not see?"

Silva stared at her excited face. "What do you mean?"

"Maybe Tyrone forget Oona now. He meets others. He friend of Brian Cameron. Maybe Brian take him in boat to Miami. Forget the black schemes of Pedro Ortega. He good boy. Brian clever man. Brian get him away from those no-good men."

Silva took a deep breath, her hands were shaking. "But, Mamacita, I don't have to go for that! I don't want to go. They—they will laugh at me," she added in a low tone.

"Laugh at my beautiful Silva? Why? Will she not outshine all the others? No, no, my lovely one. They not laugh at you."

Silva squeezed her eyes shut, forcing back tears. She pictured herself in a faded dress, with sandals, while the other ladies were in lace and silk, glittering with jewels.

"You wear the new blue and pink dress we made," said Maria Luisa with great satisfaction. "You wear new sandals. Your hair shine like the moon at night. You keep your head high, you proud girl. They all fall over each other, like the men here, only they good men. They white men, white like you."

Silva sighed. She had wanted somewhere to wear her new blue and pink dress with the shining lines in it. Only, to put it on, get dressed up—and walk miles over the hills and across the plains, past the burned cane, to Cameron Hall? What a joke. She would arrive as dusty and dirty as Tyrone.

"Walk there," she said drearily. "Walk and get dusty? No, no, Maria Luisa. It will not do. I would be too ashamed."

Tyrone came out. Maria Luisa challenged him with Silva's question, and he looked surprised. "Didn't I tell you? Brian is sending a carriage for us. About five o'clock. We'll have plenty of time to get there for drinks and dinner. He'll drive us home."

"Drinks and dinner," muttered Silva as Tyrone dashed away again for a swim in the lagoon. "Drinks—what does he mean? Am I to drink the fiery rum?"

Maria Luisa looked worried and advised her not to drink anything but tea or coffee. Then she went with Silva to look at her dress and sandals, and worry about whether to bind up her hair or leave it loose.

Brian Cameron himself drove his carriage for them. He arrived before five. Silva came out uncertainly when Tyrone called for her, yelling, "Hey, Silva, he's here. Come on!"

Brian was grinning when she came out. She hated the look on his face as he gazed critically up and down her. The dress was long and slim and left her shoulders bare, showing the lovely sun-gold arms, the tanned throat. She wore no jewelry; she had none but a silver chain left her by her mother, and it did not suit the gown. On her bare feet were new green sandals.

"Good," said Brian, but Silva thought defensively that he was disappointed in her. Did he think she had a lace dress? "You're bringing your guitar, aren't you?"

Silva stared at him. Brian moved a hand impatiently.

"Didn't Tyrone tell you? We want you to play and sing. Can you still play the piano?"

She shook her head. "It is too many years," she said slowly. Did they expect Silva and Tyrone to sing for their supper? In a storybook she had there was a picture of paid minstrels sitting in a gallery playing while the grand folk ate their dinner. Was that what he wanted? She could have hit him and wiped the smile from his lean, hard face.

Tyrone snapped his fingers. "Forgot," he said gaily and ran back into the house. He emerged with two guitars, a lute, and a slim reed pipe. Eagerly he put them into the carriage, then hopped in himself in the front. Brian handed up Silva into the back, as there was no more room on the front seat except for him as driver.

Silva clung to the carriage side with one hand and waved to Maria Luisa and Liane with the other. Liane's face was wistful. Why could she not go also? Did Brian not want her because she was not white? Silva felt colder and angrier as they went along, the carriage lurching up the hill, then down again into the valley on the other side. Down into the valley, where the sun shone on the wide fields of sugar cane, burned and ready for harvesting, on the wide fields, the green paddocks where the horses ranged, on to Cameron Hall.

She said nothing at all on the way. The men did not seem to notice. Brian was busy showing Tyrone how to hold the reins to keep control of the two horses that drew the carriage. Tyrone laughed and talked eagerly. For his sake Silva was glad she had agreed to come, for Tyrone alone might not have gone to an evening dinner, as Maria Luisa had said. And this might wean him from Oona.

Silva felt strange, sitting high up in the carriage, gazing out at where always before she had walked. She had never ridden in a carriage in all her years on the island. She remembered vaguely riding in a carriage in England. Mostly they had walked the cobblestone streets of their little village.

All too soon they arrived at Cameron Hall. What would have been a long, dusty walk had been a short, somewhat pleasant ride. Brian helped her down in the stableyard, as though she were a grand lady. She bristled and pulled away at once from his arm. He gave her a narrow-eyed look.

"You look beautiful, Silva," he said pleasantly.

Trying to soften me, she thought belligerently, and went ahead of him into the garden, through it, past clumps of roses, bushes of bleeding heart and golden allamanda and red poinsettias, past frangipani in white and pink. Brian reached up, broke off a pink frangipani, and thrust it into her hair. She flinched from his touch. He took her shoulder firmly in one hand and settled the flower with the other.

In her ear he whispered, "Stop it. Be a good girl, or I'll spank you. Tyrone is enjoying this. Be good!"

She gave him a glare of green eyes, and he laughed softly and gave her a gentle push in the center of her back, to urge her ahead of him. They walked to a cool patio at the side of the white walls.

The house was much larger than it had seemed from a distance. It was two-storied, with the outer walls like a fort, with barred windows. A red tiled roof covered the center and both wide wings. On the interior part of the courtyard, graceful iron balconies and stairways led to the upper floors and outlined the larger windows, which stood open to the trade winds.

Silk and satin curtains billowed from the open French windows.

When she saw the guests gathered about the table in the cool patio, Silva hesitated. Brian urged her on, a big hand around her slim arm. Tyrone was going ahead, happy and expectant, as though quite sure of himself in his gray trousers, short-sleeved shirt, bare ankles, and sandals. Can't he see the difference? thought Silva passionately, wanting to turn and run.

As though feeling the urge in her, Brian's grasp grew tighter, and he held her so hard it hurt her arm. The men stood up as they came, and the ladies looked up and smiled—like cats, thought Silva.

"Here you are, friends," said Brian easily. "The mysterious and lovely girl of the island of Desirée: Silva Armitage. This is Mrs. Flora Leoni and her husband, Giovanni, friends of many years."

The dark-haired lady gave Silva a warm smile and a cool clasp of her hand as Silva held out hers gravely. "Lovely to meet you," murmured the woman, a critical look going over Silva from silver head to bare heels. The man beamed more broadly and bent over her hand as though he would kiss it. Silva snatched her hand away.

"Mrs. Astrid Larsen," said Brian, and Silva turned to the golden-haired lady sitting at the far edge of the table. The beautiful woman was wearing a dress of silvery-blue, with glittering jewels at her ears and throat. She did not hold her hand out, and neither did Silva. There was antagonism in the blue eyes, and Silva flashed her own cold message. I don't want to be friends, not with you, thought Silva. The disdainful look was appraising and made her even more conscious of her simple dress, her bare legs.

"And Donald Keller, a stockbroker from New York City, who loves your island," murmured Brian in her ear. Silva bowed her head gravely to the young man who stood smiling pleasantly at her.

"Happy to meet you, Silva. Please call me Donald,

or I shall feel elderly. I understand you play beautifully."

"Thank you," she murmured, not knowing what to say.

He went on easily, "I play the piano. I thought we might try to find out if we can play anything together."

"I'm sure you can, Donald," said the beautiful golden woman in a sharp voice. Mrs. Leoni laughed aloud, then gulped.

Brian seated Silva. Tyrone sat down. Nathaniel came out with a tray of drinks, beaming at Silva and Tyrone. He started to set a glass of bronze-colored liquid before her, but she shook her head.

"Come on, Silva, try it. It's quite mild," Brian urged gently.

She ignored him. "A cup of tea, if you will, Nathaniel," she said. The man looked puzzled, then nodded, smiling. He padded back into the house. Silva noticed that Astrid Larsen was following him with her cool, calculating look. So this was the woman of whom Liane was afraid.

Tyrone took a glass of rum and lime. As he drank it, his face colored and his speech became more animated. Silva grew more and more quiet, her head lowered. She resented being invited here; she resented the looks of the women. She hated Brian Cameron for putting her in this position.

"What a charming—outfit," Mrs. Larsen drawled after Nathaniel had brought Silva her tea. "Did you make it yourself?"

Silva raised her head and appraised the blonde woman with a long, slow look. Deliberately, insultingly, as she was looked at. "Have you seen many dress shops on the island?" she asked cuttingly.

Brian put his hand on Silva's, which lay on the table, and gave it a warning squeeze. "She makes her own clothes," he said. "A very clever girl."

"I'm sure of that," smiled Mrs. Larsen, the glitter

of her eyes matching her jewels. She raised her glass, saw it was empty, and called sharply, "Nathaniel, fill my glass!"

Nathaniel came at once, bent over her devotedly and filled the glass from the bottle he carried. He did not bother to add the seltzer from the other bottle, or lime juice, Silva noted. She saw the woman drink easily, as though accustomed to the liquor.

Donald Keller said, in the brief silence, "I understand you came from England."

He seemed nice and easy to talk to. She turned to him gratefully. "Yes, thirteen years ago. When our mother died."

"It must have seemed very strange after the small villages and big cities of England," he said calmly, tapping a cigarette ash into a white alabaster ashtray. "Did you find the change hard to make?"

"No, not especially," she said. "Father—called it a paradise."

"Ah, but he was a painter," said Mr. Keller. "I have seen his work in New York. A friend has two of his paintings, and is very proud of them. Are there any of his paintings left now?"

"Just two," said Silva. "One of my mother, one of Tyrone and me as children. They were all he kept. The rest he sent to Miami to be sold."

Donald Keller kept the conversation flowing easily on the subjects of art and music, Miami and New York, and the stockmarket, until Nathaniel padded in quietly and announced that dinner was served.

Brian rose at once, his hand on Silva's arm. He directed her into the huge dining room just beyond the patio and seated her at his right. She had never seen such an ornate table. The room was huge, and the table filled it from one end to the other, except for mahogany cupboards displaying silver and glassware and a sideboard from which Nathaniel served the dinner.

Mrs. Leoni took the other end of the table, with

Tyrone on her right, as though they emphasized that the children were honored guests. Mrs. Larsen sat at Brian's left, and Donald Keller beside her. Silva could scarcely find a word to say, she was so busy drinking in the beauty of the room, the exquisiteness of the silver and glass, the lace tablecloth.

In the center of the long table was a low epergne of chased silver with carved figures of gods standing freely: Neptune with a trident, Diana with her hunting dogs, sea nymphs, Zeus with a thunderbolt. It was filled with white frangipani, lantana in many colors, and several enormous red poinsettias, all deftly arranged. Before her was a set of small silver salt and pepper pots with elaborate carvings on them. Her silverware was so heavy with carved handles that she almost dropped it.

A china plate was set before her, with an assortment of appetizers: chunks of pineapple lightly cooked in bacon rounds, tiny red tomatoes stuffed with mushrooms, something odd and gray that looked like eggs, a salty narrow fish. With it were various sauces that she dared not try—they all looked very spicy.

Brian was watching her carefully, and occasionally he leaned over to urge her to eat, or told her what things were. The eggs were something called caviar. A rubbery white thing was octopus. She tried everything politely, but left most of it on her plate.

The others were drinking sparkling golden wine. She shook her head, and stayed with the fresh cold water with ice chunks in it. Brian frowned and ordered a glass of wine poured for her, but she left it. She would not attempt that.

A short red-haired man joined them after they were well started. He had a pleasant though weary grin, and was introduced as Mickey McCoy.

"All unloaded?" asked Brian as the man sat down between Silva and Mr. Leoni.

"Aye, that it is, the lot of it," said Mickey. "And,

darling, if I had known you was waiting for me, I'd ha' run all the way back home." He gave a puckish grin at Silva's startled look. "There now, ye remind me of dear old Ireland, all silvery in the morning, with dew on the white roses."

"Now, Mickey, none of your blarney for the girl." Brian laughed. Astrid looked cold and contemptuous. "Mickey has been with me for many years, Silva. Believe about half of what he tells you."

"Half, is it? I've been restraining meself," Mickey protested, helping himself lavishly to the plate of appetizers. "I could write a poem to those lovely huge eyes, green as the Emerald Isle."

Even Silva had to smile as the others laughed or groaned. Yet she felt nervous and stiff under the critical enmity of Astrid Larsen's gaze.

"There now, darling, ye'll have a bit more of the food, or ye'll surely pine away, and leave me desolate," murmured Mickey, giving her a kindly wink and a keen look.

Nathaniel removed the plates and returned with clean china of creamy-white with blue and gold rims. Silva was more fascinated by the plates than with the food, crisply fried fish with candied yams. After that, he served thick chunks of roast beef, mashed potatoes, and a mixture of beans and corn. By this time she could eat little; it was too much, and too strange.

She tasted everything, then pushed the food from one side of the plate to the other. Astrid Larsen kept watching her, with an odd little smile curling her red lips. Such very red lips—they looked as if they were painted with red dye, all shiny, and they left red smudges on her white napkin and crystal glasses.

Finally dishes of finger bananas covered with a mixture of mangoes and nuts and an orange glaze were served. Silva ate some with relief—at least she knew what she was eating. Then Nathaniel brought coffee; she could drink that.

"We'll have the brandy in the drawing room," said Brian.

Silva glanced at him, then away. More to drink? When could they leave? It was dusky-purple dark out now, and she wished she were home, curling up on a mat beside the fire while Maria Luisa told her stories. How long did they have to stay?

The drawing room was even larger and more elaborate. Silva was afraid to walk on the beautiful rug with its faded blue and red and green and brown designs. Astrid walked across the rug on her high-heeled silver shoes, not caring that they dug into the fabric, and she sank into a large blue chair that set off the golden color of her hair.

Along the side away from the fireplace stood a huge grand piano of rosewood with beautiful black and white keys that were not yellow from age but magnificent and shiny. Silva dould not refrain from going over to stare down at it.

Brian was at her shoulder. "Would you like to play it? Go ahead, sit down," he urged.

She shook her head, with longing. "I have not played much for many years."

Tyrone brought over her lute, which had been placed with the guitars on a side table. He grinned at her. "Let's play, Silva. I was talking to Donald—he wants us to play with him. He's keen on the piano."

Brian broke in. "You two play first. I want them to hear how it sounds, just the two instruments."

Sing for our supper, thought Silva again, bitterly. But she said nothing, not wanting to spoil Tyrone's obvious pleasure. Masculine and boyish, he saw nothing wrong in the contrast of their clothing with that of the others, in their bare legs and suntanned faces, their native air compared with the complicated sophistication of the mainlanders.

Silva curled up instinctively on the rug near the fire. It was a cool evening. She tuned her instrument, leaning her ear close to the plaintively twanged strings as she worked, then nodded to Tyrone. He started out with a gay air of the natives, singing lustily of work in the cane fields and the joys of relaxing in the evening with a pretty girl. She played along without singing.

Tyrone beamed at the polite applause. He was happy tonight, thought Silva. She must make the best of it, encourage him to come and ride the horses and go out on Mr. Cameron's boat—leaving her out of his plans. Yes, that might work. Tyrone could be weaned away from his no-good friends, and from Oona.

"Now the ballad of the fair lady," he murmured to Silva. She was reluctant, but he started the plunging chords and she had to join in. The lute sang sadly, sweetly, and Silva began to murmur the words, singing with more confidence as she progressed. Brian led the applause, and they asked for more.

The twins sang for a time, then Donald Keller got up and went to the piano. He played a few chords, then began a song Silva did not know. Tyrone got up to watch Donald's fingers curiously, picked at the guitar, and joined in. Finally Silva caught the melody, a pretty one, and she joined in also.

When they finished, they heard Astrid's acid-sweet voice. "I never heard such an odd arrangement of that song! 'A Pretty Girl is Like a Melody'—nobody would ever recognize it!"

"You did," Mrs. Leoni pointed out. "I thought it was charming. Donald, do you know 'Avalon'? That is one of my favorites."

He gave her a charming smile and started to play again. Tyrone and Silva caught the melody, which was very lovely and sweet. Giovanni Leoni, surprisingly, came over to the piano, and in a very fair tenor began to sing. A ripple went down Silva's spine, a tremor of surprise and pleasure. The big red-faced man could sing with passion and a true voice.

Then Donald played and Giovanni sang—songs called "Japanese Sandman," "Swanee," and "Look for the Silver Lining." Silva played on, her cheeks blooming with color and excitement. Tyrone's eyes sparkled. Presently he was able to join in the singing, and he loved it.

Silva would have loved it, too, if Astrid had not leaned back, yawned, and blown cigarette smoke into the air in little rings. She was evidently bored with the whole thing. But Brian listened and watched with a grave smile. Mrs. Leoni applauded enthusiastically and looked happier than she had all evening.

"Giovanni, I didn't know you had such a voice," said Brian once. "I would have made you sing for me before!"

He gave a shrug, hands out, evidently pleased. "All Italians sing, even Momma," he said with a bow to his plump, dark-haired wife. "Only she is shy. Me, I am not shy. I get up and sing my heart out. Give us another, Donald, *prego!* This is most enjoyable!"

They all did seem to enjoy it, except Mrs. Larsen. Brian smoked a long Havana cigar and supplied drinks to the men when they proclaimed they were dry. Silva could have played and sung all the night. She was relaxed at last in the admiring company of those who loved music as she and Tyrone did.

Mickey McCoy, fortified with a tall glass of whiskey and ice called out for some Irish airs. They sang some, and he thumped his foot along with them and joined in with a growly, uncertain tenor.

Brian kidded him, "An Irishman who can't carry a tune! I've told you before, Mickey, you're a disgrace to the Emerald Isle. Maybe ye didn't come from dear old Ireland after all."

"We can't all be talented in the same way," Mickey protested, stretching out luxuriously. "I got no voice, but the girls always fall for me good looks and me charm."

Mrs. Leoni leaned over to pat his hand. "If I was

ten years younger, I'd be falling for ye meself," she said, a twinkle in her black eyes.

Giovanni frowned at her and came back from the piano to sit down possessively beside her. Brian gave Silva a broad wink. Mickey looked smug.

Why, they could be fun, she thought in surprise as they laughed and teased each other in a good-humored way.

Mickey leaned confidingly close to Silva. "Did I ever tell ye about the time, Brian," he said across her, but obviously directed to the girl, "that this dear little girl in Brazil run away from her cruel father, and come to me for protection? Such a sweet, pretty girl she was, and trusted me on sight, she did. She took one look at me handsome face, and—"

But Brian laughed and so did Silva, rather shyly.

Then they wanted to hear Silva play the slim pipe. She took it out, blew a few tentative notes, then began to play for them. She wove a melody of some of the songs they had sung, and the room was silent but for the delicate, plaintive notes of the single instrument, like a cry of the lost and forgotten, a memory of melody, a wisp of music. All were silent; even Astrid forgot her cigarette, and it burned down to her fingers before she stubbed it out in the ashtray beside her.

"Lovely. Anything else would be anticlimax," said Brian when she set down the pipe and pushed her fair hair back. He stood up. "Come, I want to show you some of the house, Silva. You must be weary, and I'll take you home soon." He held out his hand, and forgetting her dislike of him, she placed her hand in his and let him pull her up. He was smiling, his most charming grave smile, with the odd light in his vivid blue eyes.

"You come too, Tyrone," she urged then, turning to her brother.

"I want to try the piano," he said absently, sitting down as Donald Keller got up. He tried a tentative chord. "Wonder how much I have forgotten . . ." He struck a wrong note and winced.

Silva looked about desperately. Brian was drawing her toward the door. Astrid looked daggers. "Mrs. Larsen, do come also," Silva said, knowing the woman did not want her to be alone with Brian.

The blonde smiled lazily. "But, darling, I have seen all the house already—many times," she drawled.

Mrs. Leoni stood up. "So have I, but I adore looking about." She smiled and came with them. Silva could have hugged the motherly woman.

"Fine," said Brian, and took the two of them on a short tour. He opened doors, showed them a suite on the first floor, a glimpse into a darkened bedroom with cream draperies and a massive mahogany four-poster. "My parents slept here," he said. "They had the sitting room next door, and Mother used to do the accounts there."

He opened other doors, showed them briefly a study and a huge library with more books than Silva had seen in her life. There were curio cases filled with silver objects, a cupboard with glass doors and behind the doors precious objects of gold and amethyst and coral and jade. She saw statuettes of ivory, little temples of fragile olivewood, some strange clay people with odd faces which Brian said he had found in Central America.

"Well, that is roughly one-fifth of the house, Silva," he said, leading the way back to the drawing room. "You can see it is a huge place, and I rattle around in it like a lost soul. No wonder I feel I have to fill it with guests, eh? You and Tyrone must come over and stay for a while," he added casually as he led them into the room.

"It is a beautiful place," said Mrs. Leoni enthusiastically. "Our bedroom and sitting room are so charming, Silva, with cream walls and roses everywhere. I shall hate to leave when we return to New York. It is so peaceful here."

"Thank you for showing me around," said Silva politely to her host. She did not know why he had that odd gleam in his eyes and a hint of a smile about his lips. "We must go now. It is late. Tyrone?"

He finally got up reluctantly from the piano and gathered up the instruments. Mrs. Leoni insisted that Silva take her shawl with her, as the evening would be cool. The men said the twins must really come back soon and they would have more music. Mrs. Larsen blew more smoke rings.

In the carriage Brian said, "Did you enjoy yourself, Silva?"

"Yes, thank you," she replied in a muted tone. She had not at first, but later with the music she had forgotten her antagonism.

"Good. I want you and Tyrone to come often. Tyrone, how about coming over tomorrow and trying the horses again? Silva, there is a little mare just right for you."

"I shall be busy tomorrow, thank you," she said, her tone even.

"Come the next day, then," he said easily. "Come any time. I want you to feel free to drop in."

Tyrone was yawning behind his hand. Brian drove the horses warily through the night, up the hill through the bushes. He kept glancing up into the trees sharply, Silva noted from the back seat. She wondered if he had seen another jaguar.

At the house, Tyrone slipped down. "Thanks a lot for the dinner and all," he said. "Gosh, I'm tired. Coming, Silva?"

"She'll come in a minute," said Brian, getting down. He lifted up his arms, and before Silva knew what he was about, he was picking her easily from the seat and lifting her down to the ground.

Tyrone carried the musical instruments into the house, calling "Good night." There was no sign of Maria Luisa or Liane. They had probably gone to sleep in the house, as the night was cold.

Silva shivered, then took off the shawl. "Please thank Mrs. Leoni for me," she said. Brian tossed the shawl into the carriage, blocking her way past him.

"Just a minute." His voice was soft, with a ring of steel behind it. "You did enjoy tonight, didn't you? No smart cracks, now, Silva."

"Thank you, yes." She stood tensely, warily.

"I want you to come again soon. It's time you and Tyrone were more with your own kind. Eventually you will move in with us. I want to take you to the mainland, you and Tyrone, change your lives. This is no life for a girl like you."

She stared up at him. Her hands were at her shoulders, hugging herself against the chill in the air. Goosebumps prickled her skin. "What—do you mean?" she whispered. "I belong here—I live here."

"You live here, don't belong here," he corrected sharply. "We'll talk again tomorrow or soon. You're tired tonight."

"We don't have to talk again," she said firmly. "If I had thought you were going to talk like this, I would not have come, even for Tyrone!"

"Tonight I thought you looked like a rose, just budding. Now you're all thorns," he said, a cold, exasperated amusement in his voice. "Grow up, Silva! You can't go on like this."

"I can! I shall!"

He stared down at her. She tried to move past him, but he caught at her arms. Suddenly she was swept to him, held against his warm body. She felt the hard beating of his heart, the frantic drumming of her own. Then his head ducked, blotting out the moonlit sky.

His lips found her neck, brushed it with fire, then moved up to her chin, to her ear. She struggled frantically against him, kicking. He did not even feel her kicks, she realized, her soft sandals against his boots. It was a nightmare repeating itself. Then his mouth found hers.

It was a hard, angry mouth, warm and fiery, pressing urgently on her lips. He forced her lips apart and her head back on his iron-hard arm. She struggled weakly, felt his hand on her back, moving down to her hips, slim and silky in the new dress. She felt dizzy, odd, with the touch of his mouth, the hard pressure of his demanding lips against hers.

He raised his head, said thickly, "God, you are sweet—" His head bent again, and his mouth burned on hers. She tried to turn her head, frightened of his strong arms, the passions he had unleashed. It was as though a jaguar had sprung suddenly, and she was helpless.

His mouth slid down to her throat, drank the frightened pulsing of the heart that beat there. She cried out, "No, no, no," and tried to claw at him with her fingers. He caught at her hands, but it took all his strength to hold her now. She fought and kicked and clawed at him.

"Stop it, stop it," he raged. "You little mule! Stop it. I'm just kissing you—"

"I hate it!" she cried. "You are a beast! You are alike, all you men! I will not be your mistress! Go back to that Mrs. Larsen. She wants you—I do not!"

"Little devil!" he muttered as she kicked and tried to scratch him. He folded her arms behind her deliberately and held them with one hand as he pulled her closer to him. Furiously his mouth held hers, his hand on the back of her neck held her head so she could not turn it. She was compelled to endure his kisses as he took a leisurely toll of her mouth, her cheeks, her throat, up to her silvery hair.

Then suddenly he let her go, and stood back. "Go inside," he said curtly, breathing hard, glaring at her as though she infuriated him. "You are an unreasonable, childish girl! Grow up! We'll talk another time. But you can see why it is dangerous for you to stay on this island."

"Only because of men like you!" she whispered,

her hand against her bruised mouth. "Because of men like you! All was well—until you came!"

He stared down at her upturned face, clearly visible in the moonlight. He reached out one hand, then dropped his arm to his side. "Go inside, or I won't be accountable!" he said thickly.

She turned and ran. From the safety of the hallway, she heard the carriage as the horses turned it and he left. She was weeping silently, tears streaming down her cheeks.

She rubbed at them angrily. That he should make her cry! She hated him, and his hateful touch. He was just like the other men, like Pedro Ortega and Rodrigues.

She went to bed but could not sleep, terribly stirred up by the scene, by the evening, and Brian's kisses. Something boiled and erupted in her, like a volcano that wanted to spill out terror and destruction on the man who had insulted her.

She lay awake until dawn, tossing and turning on the bed, her face streaked with tears, her body aching from his rough embrace. He had wrenched her arms —bully, beast! He had bruised her mouth, scratched her chin and throat with his rough face. Beast! All men were beasts! She would never go near him again, never!

Chapter 13

Brian was working hard these days, getting the smelter ready for when the first loads of ore came down from the mountain. Tyrone came over early each morning to ride, and Brian enjoyed his company. He was an eager lad, bright and companionable, no little prickly thorns about him.

Silva was a different matter. She did not come, and he did not see her at the lagoon or in the hills. Little entrancing devil! He had enjoyed those kisses, angry though he had been. She was smooth and soft and fragrant, so young and fresh and unspoiled! Still, he supposed he should not have kissed her.

She had been so angry. And he thought she had been frightened also. Her heart had been beating wildly under his hand, and the pulse in her throat had raced beneath his lips. But he wasn't really sorry, though he cautioned himself to show more control around her. She was as easily frightened as a wild doe, a little nymph of the woods who would turn into a slim tree rather than endure the caresses of a man.

How lovely she had looked that night, slim and rounded in the close-fitting dress, her ankles bare, her silver head bent over her lute as she curled up on the rug before the fire. How pretty, how entrancing—

She could be lovelier yet, dressed right. He pictured her in a gown of sea-green chiffon, foaming about her ankles, silver slippers on the slim narrow feet. Or in a dress of frothy white lace, like the foam that had curled about her in the lagoon, curling about her breasts and waist and arms. Or in a negligee of palest green and cream, showing the slim form beneath, while he kissed her breathless. He pictured her, the eyes half shut, glinting green with passion, in his arms, held close so he could feel every quickened breath.

He laughed at himself, shook his head, and plunged into work again. He was mooning over a girl, like a young lad, like Tyrone. He should know better. She was probably cold and selfish like all the others. Yet —yet she had felt warm and shy and soft, and she had been concerned about Tyrone.

He went to the lab, unlocked the door, and entered. He had lit two lamps before he realized there was something wrong. He stared about grimly.

All the ore specimens were gone! He knew he had left them neatly arranged on the tables, graded, with the papers that showed the ore content. "Damn," he said aloud. "What the hell would anybody want with those?"

He felt furious and frustrated, and a little worried. Who would walk off with those? Who could get into the lab? Not his guests, probably; they were not interested. But perhaps Rodrigues . . .

He locked up again, got a horse from the stables, and rode down to discuss it with Mickey McCoy at the smelter. The red-haired Irishman listened, hands on his hips, eyes thoughtful.

"Well, the boys will know soon enough what you're doing," he said practically. "If the natives are a-wondering, they'll know. In fact, we might as well recruit the boys for the mines. Tell them what to do and how much money they'll get."

"Is the smelter far enough along?"

"It'll be done in two more days," Mickey assured him. "We might as well get the men up to the mine and start them digging. It'll take them a bit to catch on to what we want and learn how to load the cars. I've got a fine boy learning how to run the engine.

We'll have it all going smoothly. Had another idea."

"What's that?" Mickey had worked with Brian for years, and his ideas were usually practical and good.

"Have a company store. Bring in goods from Miami for the ladies—dress lengths, thread, foods, stuff they like. Not rum, though. That makes trouble."

"And they make it right on Desirée," said Brian dryly. "Right out of my good cane! So no need to bring in drink."

"Thought so," said Mickey, with no surprise. "I'll be sending the word to Miami. Want the freighter to bring back some goods for a store? We could build a shack in a day or two."

They discussed the idea, made out a list of goods, and took it down to the freighter captain. He set off that afternoon for Miami, and would return again in a few days, as soon as he could get all the goods together. Brian gave him some letters for his Miami office staff, to take care of other business in New York, London, and Caracas, and then returned with Mickey to the smelter.

By the next day they had workers employed to work the mines. The men were curious but willing, though apprehensive, it seemed, about working on the Mountain of the Cat. Brian arranged for them all to ride up in the open little coal cars that would later be loaded with copper ore, and they were pleased to be riding in that.

Mickey showed them how to work the picks, how to choose the ore veins to follow, and spent the time giving them directions for the next week. Brian wore his oldest clothes and worked the smelter, directing the operations, firing the furnace, taking care of the slag, showing the natives how to cast copper into ingots.

By the time the freighter returned, they had the first small load ready, ingots of ninety-five percent copper to go back to Miami for shipment to a refinery for further purification. The slag cast aside was making a small hillock beside the smelter. Brian thought he might use it to fill in a portion of the bay, to make larger docks for ships.

Smoke trails showed the location of the smelter already. Dense black smoke rose daily from the furnaces, and Brian worked at it early and late, returning home only to wash, change, and have dinner with his guests. He noted that the grass near the smelter was dying. Too bad. But that was the penalty of progress, he knew. One had to have the copper; it was necessary for industry. And there was enough copper in the mountain to make him a millionaire several times over, if he had not been one already.

The natives were well paid, but Mickey said they were grumbling and whispering among themselves. They were not used to that kind of work. But Brian would be generous with them. Already several of the women had come to the makeshift hut that would be the temporary store and had purchased goods for dresses, using their husband's wages for credit.

It would work out well. When it was well started, he would take a vacation, he thought. His guests would be ready to return to the mainland. He would collect Tyrone and the sulky Silva and take them along, too, he decided. It was time the girl got civilized! He hadn't seen anything of her for more than two weeks. When he asked Tyrone about it, the boy turned red and stammered that Silva was shy.

Shy! The girl was a mule!

At dinner Astrid pouted and complained of his neglect. Donald had been curious about the smelter and had come to visit it several times, sniffing and turning up his nose.

"So this is why you came back to the island!" the stockbroker kidded him. "Smelly stuff!"

"It was one of the reasons, yes," said Brian, drawing luxuriously on his long Havana cigar, thinking of Silva as he gazed out at the sunset over the bushes of flaming hibiscus and golden allamanda.

"I suppose you will make another fortune," murmured Astrid. He could read her transparent mind, and bit back a grin. She would forgive him all his neglect, if he solaced her with more diamonds and her favorite sapphires! She had a surprise coming, he thought lazily. He had become weary of her presence. On an island, she palled.

He would drop her after they returned to the mainland. Silva would occupy his mind for a time. He would dress up Silva and her twin, show them about. They might even go back to England with him, he thought, tapping the ash into a brass ashtray. He would enjoy watching their faces when they saw their old village, and London, and some plays and concerts. Silva and music—and stunning in some evening gown he had chosen, with emeralds in her little white ears . . .

Pedro called some of his trusted friends together for a meeting that same night, off in the hills above the village, near the new railroad tracks. They could smell the smoke in the air, and they had seen the damage to the grass and flowers.

Rodrigues had brought to Pedro the little samples of ore and the small pieces of paper. Pedro had poured over them helplessly, not showing his frenzy of apprehension. Something was going on, and he did not understand it. How could he control these men, when Brian Cameron gave them fat sums of money, and clothing and food at the company store! He had thought Brian Cameron would want only the sugar cane, maybe a share in the rum.

However, something bigger was going on. Until the men were finally employed and Pedro knew what was going on, he was helpless. Now he could act.

He called them together and looked them over, his sharp black eyes comprehending their puzzlement. He had not been hired. That red-haired man had studied him and shaken his head. "Not today," Mickey Mc-

Coy had said, and dismissed him. Pedro's mind burned with fury at the dismissal.

He had some jugs of rum there, and they all drank and talked easily for a time. Rodrigues was important, passing out the rum, kidding the men, asking about their families. But when Pedro was ready to talk, he slashed his hand through the air at Rodrigues, commanding him, letting the natives see that he, Pedro Ortega, was the one who had called the meeting, the one who would make the big talk.

"You have lived on Desirée all your lives," he began slowly, taking a position before them, legs apart, head up, commanding. He had watched some politicians talk on Haiti, moving their hands, flashing their eyes, making soft talk, then louder, and bolder, and moving the crowds. The thought intoxicated him more than the rum he had drunk, making fire in his head the way the rum made fire in his stomach.

"Yes, yes, the island we love," they murmured, drinking more.

"Listen to me! This white man, this Brian Cameron, he will ruin everything here! I know. I who have lived on other islands, and came here for the peace I wanted but could not find elsewhere! Where else is it so peaceful? Where else so beautiful? No, only on Desirée do all live in peace with much to eat and drink—fish from the sea, much fruit from the trees. You can laugh and drink and make love from night to morning to night again, all you wish! It was good here!"

He paused, looking about. Rodrigues was staring at him with admiration at the big words that rolled from Pedro Ortega. Pedro's chest swelled. All the bitterness he had felt at being driven from other places was gathering into one volcano of action. It was the whites who ruined everything. Natives could live together quietly. It was the whites: the grinning businessmen who cheated them, the pallid missionaries who scolded them for voodoo, the white women who drew aside their skirts when the natives passed! Those ruined a place like Desirée.

He said all this, and they nodded and nodded, though many of them knew no other whites than those who had come to Desirée: the pale artist who had come with his silvery-haired twins; Brian Cameron, who had lived there with his parents; and Mickey McCoy, who worked beside them and paid them money. But they nodded and nodded. "Yes, the white man ruins all," they chorused agreeably, and drank more rum from the huge jugs.

"They will tear down the sacred Mountain of the Cat," said Pedro solemnly. "Already he tears at the heart of the mountain with the sharp picks, and teaches you to do so! What will happen? All the mountain will be gone soon!"

They frowned and looked at each other. Papa Henri had said much the same thing, urging them not to work at the mines. But Maria Luisa had said, "Wait and see what happens."

"How can this be?" asked Auguste, who worked with Papa Henri and was considered wise himself. "How can one man tear down a mountain!"

Pedro held up his hands. "You yourselves have loaded the mountain onto little cars and seen it go down the mountain to the sea. There it is burned up! How long will it last? How much have you torn from the sacred mountain already?"

"It is a huge mountain. It will last forever—our ancestors have promised this," said another man, nodding solemnly.

"It will last," Pedro said, his voice ringing out in the quiet night, "if you all will protect it. How long can this be, if you meekly submit yourselves to the dictation of the white man? He tells you where to work, and you toil all the day even in the heat of the day! Your back runs with sweat! All because he promises you money!"

"He give us the money, and we buy at the store.

My woman is happy, and she give me much love," laughed one man. Someone beside him kicked him into silence.

"I hear the jaguars scream at night," Pedro said solemnly. "Have you not heard the big cats cry out? It is the spirits of the big cats which are protesting at the removal of their sacred resting places! I have seen the yellow cats roaming in the hills far from their sacred mountain. They are restless. They mourn, and they cry out for peace!"

There was silence. Others had also heard the great cats crying out, snarling in the night. Only in the daytime did they dare to climb the mountain and hack at its sides with their shiny picks, then load the ore by the light of the setting sun into the funny little cars that whined down the mountainside to the sea. At night the workers would lie awake, uneasily aware that the cats were coughing their displeasure. The gods were awake! They heard! They knew!

When Pedro spoke again it was in a voice so low that the men had to lean forward and strain to hear him. It was deadly quiet in the little clearing, and they stopped drinking to listen.

"The other night I was walking on the sacred mountain," he began, pausing dramatically so they would take in his words. "I walked along, and then I heard the *cough, cough* behind me of one of the jaguars. One of the sacred cats was following me! Of course, being a man and a human being, I was frightened."

He paused and looked around slowly. They were gaping at him.

"So I wanted to run, but fear locked my legs. I did the only possible thing. I turned and faced the great animal. I stared into his green eyes." He crouched down, imitating how he had stared into the eyes of an animal.

"I said to him, 'I am Pedro Ortega. What do you want with me? Do you eat me?' I said this to him, and he understood me, as the animals will who are the gods."

There was a whisper among the men, a slight restless movement, as though a chill wind of fear swept through them. They listened intently.

"He said to me, this sacred cat, 'Pedro Ortega, I am displeased with my people.' "

The men began to chant fearfully, rocking back and forth, praying to the gods to forgive them.

"But what could I do—I, one humble man? I asked this animal, so fierce before me, his great body stretched, his yellow coat shining in the light of our mother, the moon. His eyes flashed at me, and he said, 'It is the white man who offends me, and you permit it! You will dig in the belly of my mountain! You disturb my rest. You frighten away the prey on which I live!' And I knew it was so."

Pedro paused for effect. Rodrigues had his head back, his mouth open, drinking in the words. Pedro felt the tingling sensation of an orator who knows he has his audience in the palm of his hand.

"What can I do? I say this to him. I knew it was so. He spoke the truth. And he said to me—he said—" Pedro hesitated, then hissed the words: " 'Drive the white men away!' "

They started, jerked.

"I say to him," Pedro went on rapidly, his voice rising, "I say to him, 'How can this be? What can one man do?' " Pedro reached out his hands to the men. " 'I will ask my friends!' " he cried out. " 'I will do whatever you say, oh, jaguar, the god of the sacred mountain!' And he say to me, 'Drive out the white man! Kill him, kill him—kill them all!' "

They moaned, staring wide-eyed at him.

"You mean, the white man, the Mr. Cameron?" one of the bolder men asked.

"All the white men," said Pedro hoarsely. "All the whites must go!"

"Yes, the white man and the man with red hair.

But what about—Tyrone? What about his twin, the girl with the silver hair? They are one with us—they know the voodoo; they are under the protection of Maria Luisa!" Auguste said gravely, a troubled look on his face.

There was a silence as men looked at each other, nodding and muttering. Yes, yes, the silver-haired twins, they were like their own. They were good and kind. They made music. They danced at the voodoo. They were magic.

"But of course the twins should not be driven away," said Pedro finally, looking about. "Are they not one of us? Have they not lived here many years?"

Inwardly he cursed. He wanted to be rid of Tyrone. He would make Silva his own woman, and use her. But Tyrone would be a nuisance. He had not been blind to the early-morning rides, the sight of Brian Cameron riding beside Tyrone. With Tyrone out of the way, he could control Silva. Well, that would not be difficult.

Tyrone could be taken on another rumrunning trip. He needed one more trip anyway, to buy guns and ammunition for his plans. On that trip, he would dispose of Tyrone.

When he had worked up the men, whipped up their fury on behalf of the sacred mountain, Pedro would drive them to riot and destruction. No white man would be left alive to report to the mainland about the deaths.

"When must we do this?" asked Auguste.

Rodrigues had been silent. He had been listening, watching, his soul troubled, struggling against his impulse to follow where Ortega led, and his own reluctance to create violence. He wanted no one killed, no one driven from the island. The island had been peaceful. Now Brian Cameron promised money to them. It could be a good life, but for the digging out of ore from the mountain.

Perhaps the gods could be appeased by offerings.

Would that not do instead? But Ortega was not one of them; he had lived here only a short time. Why did he suggest that the whites be driven away? And why did he say that the twins would be saved?

Rodrigues watched Pedro narrowly.

"I will go to the mainland. I will buy guns and weapons," said Pedro. "After I return, then we will rise up and drive out the whites. If they resist, they will be killed! Only the silver-haired twins will remain, for they are one with us. They will live with us, and the woman will be part of us." His eyes gleamed in the firelight. "She may claim one of us as her mate. That would be natural and good. She will bear our children. Eh?"

Rodrigues caught his breath. So he had been right in his fears. Pedro Ortega also craved the lovely Silva! He had looked with eyes of lust on the beautiful girl, and he also wanted her. His ambitions were high. Not only would Pedro, an outsider here, drive out the owner of Desirée, he would be the ruler of those left.

"Why do we need guns? Will not our knives be enough?" asked one man, touching the curved machete at his belt. "One blow, and the head is gone!"

There were some murmurs against the idea, but others cried out and drank and their eyes sparkled. It sounded like a grand plan.

Rodrigues was silent, listening as Pedro told how the white house on the hill was a fortress. He had looked at it, and if the whites retreated into the house, they would need guns to shoot them out. They planned the attack, some of the men so sodden with drink they did not know what they said. But Rodrigues remained quiet, listening, outwardly respectful to Pedro but troubled in his soul.

"The island must be kept for us, those who love Desirée," said Pedro solemnly, his head uplifted, his eyes flashing at them. "It is our own sacred trust, to preserve this beautiful island. Only we can do this!

We must be strong and brave, and do what the gods command! Or we do not deserve to live here on this sacred place, where the jaguars command."

"Oh, *sí, sí!* How you are right!" they chorused eagerly, chests swelling. Even Auguste was nodding earnestly, swayed by the oration.

"Are you with me, then?" Pedro cried. "Will you help me keep the sacred island clean and beautiful for our children and our children's children? Forever?" He roared at them, his chest out. "Shall we keep Desirée sacred to the gods? Shall the jaguars be content with us? Answer me!"

"Aye! *Sí, sí!* Aye, aye, we will do it!" They chorused eagerly back to him, drunken, swayed by his words. They enjoyed listening to the echo of their words roaring through the trees.

"So. It will be done!" cried Pedro Ortega, satisfied.

Chapter 14

Silva had been watching the lagoon in the early morning for several days. Brian Cameron had not come. Some mornings he rode very early with Tyrone, she knew that. But he did not come to the lagoon.

Finally she judged it safe again and resumed her swims. Perhaps life would return to normal. Surely Brian Cameron would weary of life on an island and return to his many interests about the world. Silva felt sure of it.

On a mid-October morning she lay on the beach in her wet cotton shift after her swim, sunning herself lazily. Her silver hair was spread out around her on a thin towel. She closed her eyes against the brightness of the sky, then opened them again happily to see the little white clouds scudding across the blue, the waving of the green palms, the flash of a scarlet parrot, the white foam of the blue-green waters as it dashed against the white beach. Life was good these days. Tyrone was happy, and he did not seek out Oona. Rodrigues was busy working, so he did not come to disrupt her peace. Only the smoke from the smelter disturbed their days, drifting over the island in blackness more dense than the burning sugar cane.

Her thoughts turned reluctantly to the night of the dinner at Cameron Hall. How beautiful the rooms had been! The huge mahogany furniture, the precious rugs, the magnificent piano, the gowns of the ladies, the silver and crystal and glass. She had never dreamed that in this world there was such loveliness. And Brian Cameron treated it so casually! He was accustomed to it!

The crash of the horse through the undergrowth startled her. She jumped to her feet and turned apprehensively toward the trees behind her. Too late to run. Brian Cameron on his black stallion came out of the trees and reined up, staring gravely down at her.

She picked up her towel, her gaze searching for her sandals.

"Don't run away, Silva," he commanded. "I want to talk to you—about Tyrone."

That halted her. She watched him with wide, round eyes as he dismounted, tossed the reins over the head of the black horse, and came to her.

"Sit down again," he said. He sat down himself on the sandy beach, careless of his faultlessly tailored riding suit of cream, only a shade darker than the sand. He pushed back the sun helmet he wore and stared at Silva again.

She sat down, curling her legs beneath her. "What is it?" she asked shortly.

"About Tyrone," he insisted quietly.

"What about him?"

"You know he is very restless. Unhappy."

She gazed at him with distress in her green eyes. "But I thought he was happier. He rides your horses—"

"Yes, and fishes and swims. But what kind of life is that for a boy shortly to become a man? He is thinking of the future, and does not know what to do. He needs more education, Silva, and training to learn a profession. I want to take him to Miami."

She was silent, her lashes long over her eyes, one slim hand picking up sand and pouring it out slowly. He watched the move as intently as she did.

"Could—would you—take him there?" she asked finally. She did not want to ask him for any favors. But for Tyrone . . .

"He would not go without you," Brian said gently.

She jerked back. Perhaps she longed to see Miami, her father's paintings, the streets of a city, the life and action . . . but not as a favor to her!

She bit her lips. Brian finally went on. "I think you must face this eventually, Silva. You two cannot remain on Desirée indefinitely. It is a beautiful paradise, but not for young eager ones such as you and your twin, when you have your lives to live, the world to see. I have talked to Tyrone. He might like to finish high school, then go to college and train for something. Would you go with him, at least to high school?"

Her bright head drooped. "I—don't—know—" she muttered. What conditions would he make for his aid? It would be expensive. Life on the mainland was very expensive, her father had complained when he returned from taking his paintings over to be sold. He had been glad to return.

Brian waited a little, then went on. "And you, Silva, you are lovely, and one day you will marry." His tone sounded calm and dispassionate. "You will want to learn the ways of civilization—how to dress right, how to go out, and give parties yourself. You might want to attend high school, and fill in the gaps in your knowledge. You could take tests, find out what you lack, and just take those courses. It might take a year or two."

She bit back angry questions: Where would they live? On what money? She hugged her knees. It was all impossible—unless Brian Cameron was offering charity to them—charity she could not accept!

"Tyrone is interested in engineering. He has asked me about my work as a mining engineer," Brian continued casually, as though he conversed about the weather. "I think he is a bright lad, and I should like to sponsor his education. I have a friend who teaches in a university. Tyrone could live with that family, be guided by my friend in his high-school and college work. Would you like that?"

Silva hugged her knees tighter. Her head was bowed almost to her knees. She could not answer, and tears stung her eyes. Was he tempting her? Did he want her as a mistress for a short time, as payment for favors to Tyrone? She wished she knew more about men, was as clever as—as Mrs. Larsen!

"Tyrone is very restless," said Brian again. "I want you to think about this, Silva. He will not leave the island unless you come also; he has said so. He is your protector, he says."

She stiffened. "Yes, he is! He and I belong together," she said sharply.

"Of course," he agreed smoothly. "I realize that. And you have always been together. But if he remains much longer, the chance will be gone. He will fall more and more into the ways of the natives. He won't want to make the effort to go to high school and college. Don't you see? He should go soon."

She swallowed, then raised her head. Tears blurred her vision. Leave the island? Leave Desirée? Leave Maria Luisa and Liane? Desolation swept through her.

He said, more gently, looking at her, "Don't look so sad, little one. There is a beautiful world out there, and you can always come back and visit Desirée. You know that. Think about it, and we will talk again. I know you would enjoy seeing Miami, and the paintings your father did. You know, I bought several of his paintings recently."

She started. "You—did?"

"Yes. They were in a gallery in Miami. I ordered my agent to purchase them. And now they hang in my apartment in Miami. You shall see them when you come with me to Miami." Before she could object violently that she was not going, he said easily, "And I'll show you about the city. You shall meet some friends of mine. I think you would like to meet a man who was an associate and friend of your father, Julius Payne. He is an artist also. I have several of his paintings in Miami and New York City. He paints differently from your father, in a style that is called abstract. But his use of color is marvelous."

Brian talked to her about art, in a way that she had hungered to hear. Her eyes were wide and wondering, her gaze intent on his face as she strained to hear every word of the wonderful talk. She had missed this so much since her father had died.

"I wish you could visit Venice, little one," he said. "You would enjoy the colors there. It is a city built on water, with canals between the little islands. Small boats weave in and out of the canals, and one can ride in a boat from the dock out to an island called the Lido, where there is a beach like this one, and one can swim all day. When one is hot and weary, there are little stands that sell ice cream."

"What is that?" Silva asked eagerly.

"Ice cream? Well, it is a cold custard, with many flavors, sometimes with chopped fruit in it. Very refreshing on a hot day. There is another island, Murano, where skillful glassblowers work with the most beautiful glass in the world, making drinking glasses and statuettes and small figures of glorious colors. I have watched them by the hour, and never tire of it."

Silva knew he was tempting her to leave the island with all this talk of the world. Nonetheless, she could not resist listening and asking eager questions.

He spoke of England, of London, and asked again of the village where the Armitage family had lived. "I know of it—I was nearby at Bath once. You shall visit it, you and Tyrone, if you wish. I plan a trip to England next May. I wish you both would come with me. We shall see concerts in London, in the grand concert halls. They are magnificent, with many seats, and crimson velvet boxes where the lords sit. Sometimes the king and queen come, with their children, and listen also. One hall is where your mother once played, when she graduated from music school."

"Oh, I wish I could see it," Silva whispered, her eyes shining, little golden flecks in the green. He studied her eyes, then turned away again to gaze out at the sea.

"There is so much beauty in the world, Silva," he said, almost dreamily for so tough and masculine a man. His tanned hand scooped up the sand and let it sift through his fingers as he spoke, as she had done. "I have traveled in the Orient also. You know where that is?"

"It is the purple and yellow spot on my atlas," she told him eagerly.

"Ah—yes. Well, the lands there are different. The people are small and have slanting eyes. The babies are the cutest you have ever seen. They look like little golden dolls with black hair in a fringe, and big dark eyes. They have artists who love their art as your father did. Their art is that of massive mountains and small people drifting about on the little lakes in boats. They attempt to show how great is the universe, and how small are the people in it. They picture the great swans, which are lovely graceful birds with white wings. The hawks and the herons are in their pictures. They can take a piece of ivory like a small ball, and carve it around and around until every speck of it is a graceful carving of a tree, a flower, a bird, a tiny house."

She listened and listened, drinking it in hungrily. She held her breath to hear all the words. How wealthy he was, to have seen all this! What a store was in his mind! Her father had taught them that true wealth was not in money or gold. True wealth was what was in the mind and heart, the memories stored, the beauties seen and appreciated, the friends one had, the goodness of life.

Did he appreciate all this? Did Brian Cameron understand how rich he was in memories and friends?

Silva wondered. Sometimes he seemed cross and angry and unhappy. Perhaps making much money had blurred the memories of the goodness he had seen, the loveliness of the earth he had been privileged to witness.

Yet now he seemed to be happy as he lay on his elbow and talked of riding on a boat down the Yellow River in China and seeing tall cliffs rising about him, feeling like one of the small people in a Chinese landscape on a silken scroll. Or riding on a camel in Egypt, staring up at amazing pyramids that had been piled up stone by stone thousands of years before. Or floating in a huge boat across the sea, into the blue Mediterranean, seeing on one side the bleak sands of Africa, and on the other the huge carved profile of Gibraltar. Stopping in a bazaar in Tangier, seeing dark men in white turbans making a snake rise out of a basket, or a wood carver making delicate marks in olivewood, or a woman veiled in gray from head to foot, only her eyes showing.

He talked of working in the wilds of Central America, digging ore out of the ground, pestered by mosquitoes and insects that stung like crazy, seeing crocodiles moving their prehistoric shapes up onto a sandbar, then slithering down into the waters again. He told her of hacking his way through jungles where no white man had ever gone, coming out through the lush growth into a silent city built a thousand years ago, huge pyramids of the New World, with bloodstained altars and massive grotesque figures of the gods of war and of rain and of the sun. Shivers went up and down her spine as he talked, describing all he had seen, the dangers he had faced, of jaguars and snakes, and of pumas and piranhas, of plants that would suck the arm from a man should he venture too close, of delicate orchids blooming in the darkest jungles.

"A whole world, Silva," he said. "I would like to show it to you—and Tyrone, of course. How your green eyes would shine." He smiled up at her teasingly. "Just as they are shining now, only more brightly, because you would see these places yourself."

She took a deep breath. She felt as though she had been wandering in an enchanted forest, seeing beautiful objects on every side—here a delicate green orchid, there a sandalwood tree, over here a boat sliding through silent waters. Now she must come down to reality.

"I do—worry about Tyrone," she admitted in a low tone, looking away from him down the beach. "He is restless, I know it. Couldn't you—would you take him away? By himself, I mean? I must stay here with Maria Luisa, with Liane—"

She could not read his expression; his face seemed to have become a teakwood mask. Only his blue eyes glittered, narrowed against the bright sun of midday.

"Why must you?" he asked.

"I—I belong to them. Maria Luisa—she is getting older. Her hair turns gray, and she talks much to herself," she confided simply. "And Liane—is worried." She paused, did not say why. Liane's love affair with Nathaniel was her own concern.

"Perhaps they can be persuaded to come with us," he suggested.

"Liane, perhaps. But she would never—*we* would never leave Mamacita."

"Yet you worry about Tyrone," he murmured after a brief pause. "Don't you think he should go away with me?"

"If you would trouble yourself with him," she told him simply. "He needs to go, I believe. But where will he go? Perhaps the world outside would—would amaze him—frighten him—I don't know."

"I wish to take Tyrone with me the next time I leave," said Brian thoughtfully. He studied her with narrowed eyes. She seemed so simple and forthright, but was this all a ploy to make him beg her to go with him? "However, he will not leave without you. You must plan to come also."

She worried her lower lip with her teeth. He watched the changing expressions on her creamy golden face, the way she tossed back the drying silver hair with a movement of her small head. Was she really so unconscious of her beauty and grace?

"Are you frightened of going?" Brian said finally.

She nodded, her head down. "The world outside—can be cruel, Father said," she admitted.

"Yes, I know that. But I will be nearby, as long as you like," he told her gently, amazing himself. He had promised this to no woman in the world! "Will you trust me?"

She hesitated, finally whispered, "I don't know."

He felt impatient, cross with her. But he crushed down his feelings. He was intent on persuading her. "Think about it. We should go soon, before Tyrone becomes too involved with—other people. Talk to Maria Luisa. Tell her I will take care of you both. I will come and see her soon—tell her that."

He stood up decisively. She stood also, and balanced herself on one foot to adjust a sandal. She had the easy grace of any wild thing, her arm upheld to maintain balance, her wrist and hand as beautiful as the studied gesture of a ballerina.

He looked at the pink mouth, remembering its cool sweetness, like the first taste of a passionfruit. He stepped closer and put his hand to her head. She jerked back, her eyes wide, wary as a bird about to take flight.

"Silva, I will be good to you, I promise," he murmured. He embraced her easily, his arms steel hard. One hand at her head, one on her waist, he held her before him, then bent his head to take her mouth. She tried to pull herself away, but he took his kiss and found it as sweet as before, salty from the sea, cool as the trade winds. No passion there—she was like a child.

He stepped back, smiling. "Think about it, Silva," he said casually. He kept his hand at her waist, looking down at her, and she caught him off guard, pushing at him fiercely with both strong little hands. She knocked him down to the sand, and fled into the bush.

"Drat the girl!" he said aloud, sprawling on the sand. She was gone in an instant, lost in the underbrush, the faded cotton of her dress merging with the undergrowth, her hair mingling with the silvery leaves. But he had had his kiss, and he had put words into her ear. He got up, brushed himself off, and went over to the black stallion, still waiting rather impatiently for its master. "If you had tried that, I'd work it out of you, old boy," Brian growled at his horse, and stroked the nose. "But she's wilder than you are—she'll take more taming. But I'll do it if it takes a year!"

He swung up and turned the horse to the hill. As he rode up he kept glancing about for Silva, but he knew from previous experience that she could merge with the brush and be invisible to him. He was frowning as he reached the top of the hill and started down again.

He must meet her again soon, talk to her persuasively about music, art, the beautiful cities of the world. He had watched her shrewdly as he talked. Like Tyrone, she had no interest in money or gold or jewelry. They meant nothing to these wild children. But beauty, music, art, adventures—they both craved them. Tyrone seemed more interested in music, Silva in art and the cities. He would persuade them soon! For their own good, he thought savagely. Armitage must have been out of his mind to think he could leave them here forever.

He was making plans as he rode along. The mine and smelter were well started now. He would leave

Mickey McCoy in charge, and he could trust the freighter captain to bring him any message of trouble. He would pack up the two silver-haired savages and carry them off to see the world. It might be fun—a vacation for himself, a big adventure for them. First New York City, then over to London, and to their old village. Then to Paris, and Silva to be taught dancing and how to walk in high heels, and taken to fashion shows, dressed in the latest garments from the best houses. He could picture her in a beaded silver dress, spangled, dancing in some shaded nightclub with him, slim and lithe in his arms, perhaps welcoming his kisses on the moonlit ride home. The picture was very pleasant.

Halfway back to Cameron Hall, on the wide plains where the sugar cane lay in its burned field, he met the carriage. A groom drove it, and in the back seat sat Astrid, radiant in a silvery-blue gown, with a parasol shading her golden head. Her sapphires glittered at her wrists and throat. Only a scowl marred the beautiful face, as she lay back in a languid pose.

He stopped his horse and dismounted. He motioned for the groom to change places with him. The groom took his stallion and went on. Brian helped Astrid to the front seat with him, then took the reins.

"Impatient?" he murmured in her beautiful ear.

"Darling, you know you promised to spend the morning with me! I was going wild! Where have you been?"

He smiled ahead of him, at the sleek grays in the harness. "Surveying my property," he said, thinking of Silva curled before him on the beach.

"Over there?" She pointed skeptically. "There's nothing over those hills but more beaches! Have you been seeing that white native girl?"

There was venom in her tone. He thought dispassionately that it was time to send her home to New York. "What concern is it of yours whom I see, Astrid?" he asked curtly. "I have much work to do, and the whole island is my concern. I warned you that you would be bored here with nothing to do!"

She bit her lips. "I do believe that girl has charmed you," she said petulantly. "They tell me she goes in for voodoo. Has she been practicing her charms on you?"

"No," he said curtly, thinking of how Silva ran from him, evaded him, how her green eyes shone with fear of him when he came too close. "Who said anything about her involvement with voodoo? Where do you hear such talk?"

She hunched her beautiful shoulder. "Oh, I hear things," she said vaguely.

Yes, I'll bet you do, he said to himself. He had noticed that Nathaniel fell all over himself waiting on her, how his eyes dwelt longingly on her, how her bedroom door remained closed until noon with Nathaniel missing. The little bitch, he thought. She was having an affair with the boy, and encouraging him to talk to her. Brian felt a strong distaste for her. He could do something about her, by sending her away. Until she was gone, there was something he could do about Nathaniel.

Back at the house, Brian sent for the boy, who was preparing to serve luncheon. Nathaniel arrived in the master's study eagerly, as Brian was studying a packet of papers.

"Yes, sir, Mr. Cameron?"

Brian looked at him. He was a handsome lad, and not stupid. He wasn't the first man who had fallen into the wily trap of a seductive older woman. Brian realized only too well how easily he himself had been taken in by Astrid's abundant boudoir charms. "Nathaniel, you have done well here. You learn quickly," he said levelly. "How would you like to earn even more money?"

Nathaniel looked at him warily. His bare feet shuffled on the thick carpet. "Yes, I think so, boss," he said finally.

"Good," said Brian heartily. "I want you to report to Mickey McCoy this afternoon. Tell him I sent you. He wants to train someone to be his assistant. I think you'll do just fine."

"Me? Work in the mine?" Nathaniel asked, his doe-brown eyes intently staring at the floor.

"Would you rather be just a houseboy?" asked Brian, as though disappointed in him. "I thought you would want to work your way up."

Nathaniel hesitated, wondering when he could see his blonde-haired mistress if he didn't work in the house. "Yes, boss, I want to work up, like you say," he said finally, realizing he had no choice.

"Fine. Serve the dinner here this noon. Then afterward, go to Mickey McCoy. That is all." Brian turned back to the papers on his desk.

The boy left the room slowly. Brian grimaced at the pages—more problems. He must get Astrid and the others away from the island, quickly. He himself would go with the twins as soon as he could persuade them. McCoy would take the copper out of the mountain; he should be able to keep things going smoothly here. And Brian felt like a vacation—a holiday with eager green-eyed Silva.

Chapter 15

A red-gold line of tracer bullets shot across the stern of the cruiser. They had been trying to shake off the two Coast Guard cruisers for over an hour. Tyrone shook his head, dazed.

One had been waiting in the secret darkness of the Florida keys, dashing out of a cove when they came near, the other cruiser trying to herd them in from the open sea.

Pedro was crouched at the port side of the boat, his machine gun ready, a scowl on his dark face. On the starboard side Rodrigues and Auguste were hunched down with their guns. Auguste looked nervous and apprehensive; it was his first trip. But the money lured him, as it did all of them. Papa Henri would be furious.

A bad omen: the clouds had slid apart and a sliver of moon shone through, lighting up the waters. Tyrone chewed nervously on his lips as he eased the wheel slowly toward the open sea. He knew their boat could outrun the cruiser in the open waters.

"Turn down the coast. I'll watch and tell you when to turn in," Pedro ordered tensely.

They were followed on both sides. How would they escape? Tyrone wondered, but knew better than to protest. He kept the cruiser sliding along the keys, watching as carefully as he could at the speed they were going for the treacherous mangrove roots that stretched far out, and for the shelves of razor-sharp coral that could rip the bottom right out of the cruiser.

A voice called angrily through a megaphone: "Come about, come about! You won't get away! This is the United States Coast Guard! I order you to come about!"

The voice grew fainter as they sped away from the gray cruiser. A final tracer of red bullets hit the stern, some striking the back of the wheelhouse. Tyrone felt his flesh shuddering as though it had been hit. A quiver went through him, cold excitement chilling his very bones.

Then they were away. Pedro indicated where he should turn toward shore. Tyrone obeyed, watching intently to make sure they did not founder on the coral.

"Shut off the motor," Pedro ordered, and stood up. He was alert, listening. Then they all heard the faint hum of a boat, then silence as it passed them by. He finally nodded.

Oh, thank God they went by, Tyrone thought. His wet hands slipped on the wheel, and he wiped them on his pants. He had not wanted to come on this trip, but Pedro had glared at him with his cold black eyes and threatened him.

"You want me to tell Brian Cameron what you been doing?" he had demanded. "He stop being friends with you and with Silva!"

Tyrone had said, "This is the last trip, then. I give you warning, I am not going out again." He had been rash, he realized now, to get involved in the rumrunning, but at the time Rodrigues had first suggested it, he had felt wild and reckless.

"This is my last trip also," Pedro had said easily, dropping a hard hand on Tyrone's shoulder. "There is no more rum on the island. We move on somewhere else, make more rum. No, Brian Cameron grows no more sugar cane. But I promised this rum to Miami. We go."

And so they had gone that night, with a heavy load of rum. Jugs and jugs had filled the hold and had held down their speed. He had been able to get only twenty-five knots from her tonight, Tyrone realized. But so long as this was the last trip, and they had made it, it was all right.

They waited in the darkness, all lights off. Then Pedro said, "Rodrigues, lower the motorboat."

Rodrigues started, then went over to the motorboat and began lowering it over the side. They never questioned Pedro's orders on ship—he was the captain. Auguste went to help. The boat dropped into the water with a faint splash.

"We put ten jugs of rum on it," Pedro said, and took Tyrone below to hand up the jugs. The jugs were put into the boat, but there were still about fifty jugs of rum left. Tyrone wondered what Pedro was about.

On deck then, Pedro turned and faced a puzzled Tyrone. "You know the waters; you can run the motorboat," he said quietly. "I trust you."

Tyrone felt an apprehensive shiver tingle through him. He hoped it went unnoticed in the darkness. Tyrone moistened his lips and said, "Yes, Pedro? What do you want?"

"I want you to take the motorboat with the rum to Miami. Take it to the dock where my friends wait. This will satisfy them for tonight. I promise it. You will keep the promise of Pedro Ortega to his friends?"

How could he refuse? Pedro trusted him. Rodrigues moved slightly, then stilled. Auguste said, "But I go with him! He should not be alone in the open waters."

Pedro shook his head. "Better he go alone. Nobody notice a young man alone. You take fishing rod. If you stopped, you are fishing, a young white man out from Miami. They not hold you."

So it was settled. Tyrone put on his heavy jacket, took the fishing rods, and started the motor. He was comfortable and familiar with the boat—he had worked over the engine, run it into the harbor at Desirée, and raced it about when he pleased. Pedro had been generous.

He waved his hand in silent farewell. Pedro peered down from the deck of the cruiser, watching him as he slid out from the canal between the little keys. Then he was alone, out on the open sea, fleetingly wondering whether anyone would believe he was out fishing several hours after the sun had set.

Tyrone kept to the keys, moving in and out, avoiding the coral reefs, whose presence was signaled by the darkness of the waters below the surface. The moon was out again. Odd. Pedro usually avoided the moonlit nights.

He grew more confident as he moved slowly up toward Miami. At his speed he figured he would reach the port several hours before dawn, and then be able to get away.

He was stunned when the cruiser ran him down. All of a sudden a gray shape was sliding up beside the motorboat, and a megaphone-muffled voice commanded him:

"Stop! Pull over to us or we'll run you down! This is the Coast Guard!"

Tyrone could not hope to outrun them and cursed his own carelessness. He silenced the motor and held up his hands in the white glare of the searchlight shining accusingly at him.

He was drifting alongside. One man jumped down into the motorboat, making it rock dangerously. From the cruiser, two sailors held rifles on him.

The portly sailor in the motorboat pushed aside the sacks, lifted a jug, opened it, smelled, tasted. "It's rum, all right!" he yelled back.

"How much?"

The sailor counted. "Ten jugs!"

"Okay. Take him in tow! Bring the lad up here!"

Tyrone went resignedly up the rope ladder they had

lowered and faced the hard-eyed captain of the patrol boat.

Auguste took word to Silva in the morning. He was red-eyed, shocked, stumbling with weariness as he told her.

"Your brother, they took him. We hear when we get to Miami early, at dawn, Miss Silva!"

She felt as though the blood drained from her head. Silva put her hand to her breast to still her pounding heart. "No, no, not Tyrone! What will they do with him?"

"He is in the jail," Auguste said simply. "He should have stayed with us. Pedro, he hid for a long time. We go to Miami, no trouble. We heard about Tyrone then." His troubled gaze studied her, then he dropped his eyes. Maria Luisa stood there, hands on hips, her contempt visible.

"You do not try to get him out?" she queried, too gently.

Auguste shook his head. "Too dangerous, Pedro say."

"Pah!" She spit on the ground, said something vile in the native tongue, and Auguste flushed with shame.

Silva stood frozen. She could not imagine Tyrone in jail in far-off Miami! He would rot there! She knew that rumrunners were often sent to prison for many years—Liane had whispered of it. Auguste made his apologies again and left. Only Liane had the kind words to thank him for coming to tell them. Rodrigues had not come, nor Pedro.

And Silva knew she could not go to Rodrigues or to Pedro for help. They would demand a very high price for any help. And if they had not helped Tyrone at dawn, they would not help him now. Had they deliberately let him be trapped?

Liane put her arm about her, but Silva could not weep. She was thinking, thinking desperately.

Only one man could help her, but his price also

might be high. He might demand that she become his mistress. Better Brian Cameron than Pedro Ortega! She had no choice. Silva shuddered at the thought of the scarred man and his greedy looks at her.

So she went to Brian Cameron. Tired and dusty, she arrived shortly before noon. He was there, the new houseboy said, and took her to Brian's study.

He rose quickly as she came in. "Silva? What is it?" He took one look at her face and immediately ordered the boy to bring her some coffee.

He set a chair for her, which she sank into gratefully. Then she told him the story. As Brian listened, his face turned hard. "Miami? And he is in jail!"

The houseboy entered quietly with coffee, but Silva could not touch the steamy brew. Brian told her curtly, "You will drink. Bring sandwiches, pack up a lunch for us," he told the boy, who nodded and left.

"You will—do something?" Silva asked faintly. She clasped her cold hands together. Then Brian did something strange for him: He lifted her hands and put them gently to his lips.

"Don't worry, child, of course I will. We'll set off for Miami at once." He smiled faintly at her expression. "You want to help with your brother, don't you? We may have to pull some strings to get him out of jail. Rumrunning is a serious charge. It is a federal offense, you know."

Silva did not know what a federal offense was, but it sounded dreadful. In her sleeveless cotton dress she sat and shivered. Her green eyes were huge and she looked somehow lost. He patted her arm briefly.

"I'll get a sweater and coat for you, and a hat and scarf. It may be colder on the water. In Miami we'll get whatever else you need. Wait here, and drink that coffee!"

He was gone for about an hour. Silva wondered anxiously if he had changed his mind. The kindly houseboy urged her to eat some sandwiches and drink the coffee. She nibbled enough to satisfy him and huddled fearfully in the big armchair, waiting.

Finally Brian returned. He carried a basket of food and some heavy clothing for her. He was wearing a dark suit and boots and carried a sailor's cap.

"The carriage is ready," he said briskly, giving her a keen look.

"But Maria Luisa—" she faltered.

"I'll send word to her. Come along."

She did not see his other guests as they set out. He took her out a side door, to the stables, where a carriage was waiting. A sleek dark suitcase was set in back. He installed her beside it, with a sweater about her, a coat on her lap. "All set?" he asked, and she nodded numbly.

Brian took the reins from the coachman, and they traveled at a smart pace, along the cane fields, along the dried ruts of the roads that led from field to field, turning then toward the docks at the southwest side of the island, near the native village.

The smoke from the smelter rose dark against the sky, and the smell was stronger as they neared the docks. Silva's nose wrinkled. So this was what the natives now did, working in the copper mines and the smelter of Brian Cameron. How—how ugly it was! How different from the tender green of the cane, the brightness of the blue sky. How many changes he had made in the short time he had been here!

Brian helped her onto the white cabin cruiser, settled her in a comfortable cabin, then left her. Silva peered from the odd round window, a breathless feeling running through her. Was this a wild dream? Was she really going to Miami, when she had resisted the idea for so long?

Miami! And the world beyond! She had seen nothing but the island for thirteen years. She was to see the odd buildings Tyrone had described, all the brightness and beauty Brian had told her about. But Tyrone was in jail, on that peculiar thing, a federal offense.

All that mattered was to get him out again, to rescue him.

Again Brian was gone for almost an hour. She grew restless. He finally came aboard, and Mickey McCoy waved at him from the dock as Brian came up the rope ladder.

"All set," said Brian cheerfully, seeing her silver head poking up from the cabin below. "Want to come up while we cast off? If it gets too cold, you can go below again."

She put on the sweater and the hat, and came up shyly to cling to the white railing as he set the cruiser in motion. Two native boys had come along to help him, and they gave her white-toothed grins, recognizing her. The word must have gone out. "Tyrone be okay now, Silva," one said to her.

She nodded, and managed to smile. She watched Brian's brown hands on the wheel, so sure and confident as he was. They swung away from the dock and out into the open blue sea. The cruiser cut through the blue waters, making white foam rise behind them. Then they were out in the blazing sun of the afternoon.

"Silva!" Brian called and motioned to her. She managed to come forward, her sandals slipping on the wet deck. "Get me a sandwich and cup of coffee, will you, like a good girl? Bring them up—I'll be at the wheel till we get to Miami."

She nodded, glad to have something normal to do. She went below, fighting to keep her footing on the narrow steps, then, quite pleased with herself, managed to get back up again with sandwiches in wax paper in one hand and a cup of coffee in the other. She brought them to Brian, and held the coffee while he ate, his eyes intent on the blue sea before him.

He spoke little, evidently thinking of plans ahead. She did not trouble him with her own doubts. Time enough when they got to Miami, and found out what condition Tyrone was in.

In about five hours, the cruiser slowed and began to maneuver into a landing dock. Men caught the ropes flung by the island boys, and a tall, well-dressed man waited for Brian. Silva put her sweater about her again. It was very big—probably one of Brian's, she thought—and the warmth comforted her in the cool of late afternoon as the breezes grew stronger.

Brian helped her ashore, spoke briefly to the man, and then they went out onto a busy street. Silva's eyes grew wider and she wanted to look everywhere at once. There were so many buildings! Some were so tall—she could count three rows of windows on some, and farther on there was a building with eight rows! It was huge.

At the road were some odd-looking carriages. Years ago she had seen a few automobiles in England. But these were different, sleek and long and powerful looking. Brian opened the door of a shining dark car. "A Pierce-Arrow," he said to her questioning look.

She kept silent rather than admit she did not know what he was talking about. He got behind the wheel, and they slid away from the curb after the boys had set the baskets and suitcase in the back. She bit her lip to keep from crying out at the noise—automobiles honking, people shouting, the whine of machinery as they passed a group of men repairing the road.

The roads were muddy from recent rains, but Silva scarcely noticed the lurching of the car or the low suppressed curses of Brian. There were so many people! More people than she had seen in her life. As they swept down a main street, lined with palm trees and shops and blazing bright signs, people were walking along the road on shiny white walks, and they halted at the street corners. Lights winked in the middle of the street. Bright lights, not candles.

She looked everywhere at once, turning and twisting in her seat. Brian glanced at her as they paused at a red light, and he finally grinned.

"Young one, you will break your pretty neck if you keep twisting it around like that! Calm down!"

"Oh, everything is—so strange," she whispered. "All the noise, the people— Where did they come from?"

"They live here, and work here," he replied. Finally he drew up in front of a very tall building. She peered from the automobile window to see it had eight rows of windows. "I live at the top of this building. We'll go on up," he said casually.

"But where is Tyrone?"

"I'm going to leave you here in the care of my housekeeper while I run around and check on matters," said Brian absently. They got out of the car. A man dressed in a dark blue uniform with golden buttons came hastily, to take their luggage, and he bowed to Mr. Cameron as though he were a great man.

"But do they know you are coming? Will the house be dusted and food brought in?" asked Silva. She could not imagine dashing into such a huge place without word. When one gave a dinner, one notified people.

"What? Oh, they are always ready. They never know when I'm coming," said Brian impatiently. "Come on—here's the elevator."

She was walking across the thick red plush carpet and wanted to pause and see how her feet sank in. He was waiting at the door of what looked like a small room. Innocently she entered it with him, then gave a gasp as the door closed, the smartly dressed man in blue pressed a button, and they moved upward! She pressed her stomach. It felt very odd. Brian noted her dazed look, the wild amazement, and took her hand gently.

"Poor Silva, everything is new," he said quietly. "Calm down, honey. This is an elevator, and we're going up to the eighth floor. Okay, here we are. Step out."

She was glad to get out of the strange beast. She never wanted to get in one again. Surely there were steps somewhere. He opened a gilded white door, and behind it a man came forward and bowed. "Mr. Cameron, sir, welcome."

"Ah, Bowles. This is Miss Silva Armitage. Silva, this is Bowles, who takes care of me in grand style."

Silva held out her hand gravely. The man swallowed, looked very embarrassed, and finally touched her fingertips.

"Fred phoned you from the dock? Good. Is Mrs. Bowles about?" asked Brian briskly. "Show Miss Silva to the gold room. She will have that. I have to go out again. Have Mrs. Bowles fix— Ah, there you are, Mrs. Bowles. This is Miss Silva Armitage."

Silva did not offer her hand again, as the woman bowed and smiled. Both of them were tall, rather plump, graying, and dressed in gray. And shaking their hands seemed the wrong thing to do, judging from Mr. Bowles's reaction.

"Pleased to meet you, Miss Armitage," murmured Mrs. Bowles, looking her over without seeming to. "The gold room is ready. And you'll have tea or coffee?"

"Fix her some coffee and something good to eat. I'll be back in a couple of hours if all goes well. Bowles, get one of my robes from my room—bundle up Miss Armitage. She is cold and a bit damp from the sea. Silva, take it easy—I'll be back presently."

And then he was gone, leaving her to the two strangers. Mrs. Bowles showed her to the gold room. Silva stood in the middle of the large bedroom, staring at the gold and white painted bed, the pretty mirrored dresser in matching gold and white, the billowing white silk draperies at the large windows, the glimpse of the sea and the city of Miami from the windows. She was afraid to go near the windows. She had never been so high up before, and she thought she might fall.

"Shall I unpack for you, Miss Armitage?" murmured Mrs. Bowles.

"Unpack? Oh—no. You see—there wasn't time to pack. I just came along to help Tyrone," explained Silva.

The woman looked blank. Silva sighed. She wanted nothing so much as to lie down. Evidently her weariness made a silent appeal to the woman, for she forgot her surprise and said comfortingly, "I expect you'll want food and then rest, Miss Armitage. You just make yourself at ease. Here is your bathroom—" And she pushed open a mirrored door to reveal an immense claw-footed tub, a toilet of white, and a matching cosmetic stand with colorful little glass jars on it. "You'll want to wash up. There are brushes and cloths— I'll come right back with your coffee!"

She departed. Silva explored the wonders of the bathroom, sniffing at the contents of the jars, fingering the sand in them wonderingly. Perfumed sand! Whatever could anyone want with that? She used the pink scented soap, washed and dried her face and hands, brushed back her silvery hair, and came out.

Mrs. Bowles knocked and entered with a tray. Mr. Bowles followed with a huge green and gold robe, miles too big for her, and the word that Mr. Cameron had telephoned and would not be back for about five hours.

"You might as well sleep, then, miss," said Mrs. Bowles, and helped Silva change to the robe from her wrinkled cotton dress. She carried the dress away with her, perhaps to wash it. Silva ate and drank a little. Then, wrapped in the warm robe, she lay down to sleep.

But even this high up she could hear the shrill honking of the automobiles, the cries of the street vendors, the whine and noise of the huge city, so unlike the musical whispering of the sea. She tossed restlessly, thinking of Tyrone in a jail cell. What were jail cells like? Was he comfortable? Was he in chains, like the men in her picture books?

She slept lightly, uneasily, and finally awakened, to night and the strange room. She sat up abruptly, with a quick intake of breath, until she remembered where she was.

The sound of masculine voices came to her. "Tyrone," she said aloud. Forgetting her large robe and her bare feet, she dashed out into the hallway and to the huge living room. "Tyrone!" she cried, to pause abashed in the doorway.

Brian Cameron turned to her, drink in hand. Behind him was not the familiar thin form of her brother, but a tall older man, maybe in his midforties, with graying hair, keen dark brown eyes, in a beautiful suit. It could only be described as beautiful, of brown velvet, with a pale pink silk shirt and a flowing mocha-brown tie!

"Where is Tyrone?" she whispered blankly.

Brian set down his glass and came over to her. He drew her into the room. "Things did not work out so quickly, my dear. This is Julius Payne, an artist, who knew your father well. He is going to help us."

Julius Payne held out his hand and smiled at her like a kindly father. Silva felt safe putting her slim hand into his.

"We must get some new clothes for you, Silva. You are charming in that robe, but it is trailing the ground," drawled Brian with amusement. Her cheeks flushed hotly and she retreated, but he caught her hand again and drew her to a creamy armchair of thick, soft silk and velvet, and set her down. "I'll get you a drink."

"No—no drinks!" she said hastily.

He frowned down at her. Bowles came in, discreetly. "Some tea, then, or a fruit drink, Silva?" asked Brian.

"Fruit drink, please. Oh, tell me about Tyrone," she begged, her hands clasping each other nervously.

She curled up in the chair, her legs under her, under the wide skirts of the green and gold robe.

Julius Payne seemed unable to keep from staring at her. "I should paint you like that, Silva," he murmured.

She gazed at him. Brian shook his head. "She would come out all curves and angles on your canvas, Julius," he said. "No, I'll get a portrait painter for her."

"But I am one, my dear Brian!" laughed Julius. "I can do both. And Silva cries out for a painting. I can see her, a little woods nymph, gowned in silver-green, stepping from out the woods, lianas clinging to her feet, violets in her hands."

"Um. Maybe. We'll see," said Brian, finishing his drink. Bowles brought a tall cool glass to Silva. She tasted it, decided she liked the mixture of fruit with a slice of lime on the top.

When they were all settled with their drinks, Brian said, "Now, Julius, you might explain the situation to Silva. She is very anxious about her twin."

Julius set down his glass and got out a silver case. As Silva watched, he opened it, took out a white cigarette, and lit it from a strange little matching silver case. He blew smoke in the air. He hadn't even used a match, she thought, with astonishment.

And now that she thought of it, the dusky room was not lit with candles or oil lamps. Light bloomed from the mantel, from beautiful crystal chandeliers in small round bulbs of a strange frosty look. And no one had lit them with a match! How very odd.

Her fingers clenched on the silk of the armchair. She took in the luxury of the large apartment room—the thick red carpets, the creamy armchairs, the draperies blowing at the windows, a closed glass case of precious ivory and porcelain vases and strange figurines in clay. The little table beside her was inlaid with tiny colored fragments, cunningly fit together into patterns of flowers and leaves.

"Tyrone," said Julius deliberately, and her attention jerked back to him. "Tyrone is in jail, and likely to remain there. Evidently this was not his first rum-running trip. The Coast Guard fellows recognized his silvery hair from other trips, when he steered a very fast dark gray cruiser away from them, even though they fired upon it."

Silva's little fist clenched against her heart. She could feel it beating like a panicky wild thing, yearning to be free.

"Tyrone? Fired upon?" she whispered.

Brian scowled at Julius.

"Ah—yes. Once," said Julius. "And it seems that the charge is serious. However, he is very young. If someone like a relative—an older man—would guarantee his behavior, would take charge of him, be responsible for him, they might release him into the custody of such a person."

Silva kept on staring at him. An older person, a man. Who? Would Rodrigues? No, she would not ask him. Maria Luisa? No, they had said a man. Papa Henri?

Brian said, "Julius Payne knew your father well. He has offered to take charge of Tyrone and straighten him out. The boy has promise, I assured him of that. Tyrone could go on to school, then to college, as I want for him. I think the boy has learned his lesson. He assured me he had meant to make this his last trip."

"Oh—would you—do that?" whispered Silva with a great effort, passionate gratitude in her eyes as she gazed toward Julius. "I am sure Tyrone will be no trouble. He is a good boy—"

"I'm not so sure," said Brian dryly. "He can get into a lot of trouble very quickly. He was just telling me a few days ago that he wanted to go to college and become an engineer. Now here he is in jail."

"We'll discuss it comfortably," said Julius when Mrs. Bowles called them to dinner, just as Silva wanted to plead again for Tyrone. She sat silent, scarcely able to force down the delicious fried chicken, the mashed potatoes, the green salad, the chilled fruit bowl. Brian wanted her to try the white wine, but she shook her head.

He frowned at her, but she was obstinate. Wine made the heads of people go queer, and they did strange things. She wanted none of that, nor of the forsaken rum either.

After dinner Julius remained for about half an hour, and they finally did discuss Tyrone and what might be done. Then he left, assuring them he would come again tomorrow, and also talk to Tyrone.

Silva curled up in the chair, feeling desolate and frightened. She had thought it would be so simple. She and Brian would come to Miami, he would talk to certain men, and Tyrone would be released. But it had not happened like that at all.

When she looked up, Brian's gaze was on her thoughtfully.

"We'll go shopping tomorrow," he said. "You need some clothes. We may be here quite a while."

"You mean—you might not be able to get Tyrone —out of jail—soon?"

"Silva," he said patiently, rising to pour another glass of glowing topaz brandy for himself. "It could take a week or two, and be grateful it isn't longer! In the meantime, you can't live in one dress and pair of sandals. We'll go out tomorrow."

Deliberately he drew up a chair near to her and sat down, gazing frankly at her. She flinched from the keen look of his vivid blue eyes, so startling in the deeply tanned face. His curly dark hair was brushed smoothly, yet a small lock of curl hung over one eyebrow, giving him the rakish look of a pirate.

"Silva, we must talk frankly," he said. "This has brought on something I have wished to discuss with you soon anyway. You recall what I said about leaving the island, seeing the world. You need to get away from Desirée as much as Tyrone does."

Her voice seemed choked in her throat. She half closed her eyes, but she could still see the imprint of his forceful dark face, the obstinate thrust of his chin. He drank a little of the brandy, then set down the bulbous glass beside him on the inlaid table.

"I have been thinking for a long time. You need someone to take care of you. Tyrone is too young, too reckless—he needs looking after himself. Maria Luisa—well, she won't leave the island; it is her life. That leaves—me."

She could not speak. She felt paralyzed as he leaned forward and took her small hand in both of his. What did he mean? Would he make a mistress of her? Oh, the shame of it, and the horror! She wanted to be free, to roam the woods, to swim in her blue lagoon, to be lighthearted and happy again, the way she was before Brian Cameron returned.

"Silva, I want you to marry me," he said firmly. "I have decided that is the only solution. You are a lovely girl. You are bright and quick. You will learn quickly what is required of you as a wife, the mistress of my home. We will travel—I'll show you the beauties of the world." He began to speak more rapidly, holding her hand cruelly tight. "I want to show you the loveliness I told you about. England in the spring, Paris and the clothes in which you will shine. Italy: Venice with its boats, Florence and its art, Rome and its grandeur and history. Then on around the world, going where we please. What do you say?"

She could say nothing, struck dumb, confused, frightened. She wanted to marry no one. Yet something strange was stirring in her heart. She had thought he would claim her as a mistress, use her, discard her, forget her. This was—was different! Marriage! To belong to this great forceful man, who waved his hand and made things happen. He would take charge of her, and change her life so drastically she would never find herself again!

"Silva, you will enjoy it." His voice sank to a wooing, charming note. "You should wear beautiful clothes, look the way you were meant to look—a fey sweet girl in the right dresses, the prettiest shoes and coats and little hats. You should learn to dance, to play the piano—" He waved his hand to a beautiful rosewood piano in the corner of the huge drawing room, sitting in the shadows. "I will always take care of you. I'll take custody of Tyrone, and straighten him out, see him into the care of my professor friend. He'll want for nothing, I assure you."

As she sat numbly, his grip loosened, became coaxing. His thumbs stroked over her soft flesh. He was gazing keenly at her—at her face, her throat, her slim form lost in his great robe. He wanted her, she realized. Just as Pedro Ortega and Rodrigues Estavez had wanted her. He was a man. A brute, a beast! He already had Astrid Larsen, maybe dozens of other women! Why did he want her?

"Silva, say something," he urged.

She gave a long, shuddering sigh. It was a nightmare, the way her bones seemed to be turning to water as he gripped her hand. She felt feverish, light, strange. "No, no, no," she whispered.

He scowled. "What do you mean?" he asked harshly.

"No—I cannot—marry. I don't want to marry—" She stumbled over the earnest words. "I don't want to—oh, Brian, I don't want to. I want to be free!"

He got up, and pulled her easily with him. Surprised, her body fell against his, and he gripped her roughly. His arm about her, his hand behind her head, he kissed her lips deliberately. The sensuous warmth of his mouth startled her from the nightmare, into another fright. She fought to turn her head, but he gripped her more tightly, hurting her.

She kicked out at him, kicked his shins, and hurt him. He swore, almost dropped her, but grabbed her again, kissed the white ears, the suntanned throat, opened her robe to kiss the tops of her soft breasts. She fought him in earnest then, afraid he would take her right there in his elegant living room!

When he would not let her go, she made claws of her little fingers and scratched at him. He ducked just in time, and swore. "You little hellcat! Stop that! I'll spank you if you don't stop!"

"Let me go! Don't touch me! I hate your kisses—I hate you!" she cried. "You're just using me. You use Tyrone—you use people. You want my body—you can't have it! I'll run away, I'll run away! I swear I'll run—"

"Oh, you will?"

For a moment she thought he would carry out his threat and spank her. He looked grim and terrible. He picked her up as she kicked and scratched at him, and carried her into the hallway, back to her bedroom. He dumped her on the bed, and she bounced and glared up at him.

He was breathing heavily. "You be quiet and think, Silva!" he said ominously. "Get some sleep. I'll talk to you in the morning!"

"I won't be here! I'm going home!" she cried hysterically, and burst into tears.

"In that case, I'll lock you in. You get some sleep. Stop crying, for the love of God!" He stormed out, and she heard the irrevocable grinding of the key in the lock and his muttering as he stalked off down the hall.

She cried, curled up in the bed, lost and frightened, until sheer weariness sent her off to sleep. In all her nightmares of that night, she was helpless.

Chapter 16

Liane roamed slowly along the beach, her heart heavy, her head aching. Again Nathaniel had not come. The lagoon shone blue and green in the shallows, and foamy white waves crept up over the creamy-colored sand. She leaned down, examined a shell, tossed it again from her.

Nothing mattered very much. She had lost Nathaniel. She had not seen him for three days now, and then he had come only to say he could not come the next day, looking red-faced and embarrassed.

He was working now for the red-haired man, Mickey McCoy, he had told her proudly, and he would make much money. But he had not added the words she longed to hear: "Then we can marry, Liane!"

Auguste said he had seen Nathaniel in the company store, looking at silver bracelets, and buying one. Auguste had looked at Liane's wrist significantly, seeing it bare. No, Nathaniel had not given her the bracelet he had bought. Someone else had claimed that bracelet—as she claimed his heart, his arms, his hard body that could make her so happy.

Her dearest friend Silva had left the island in the company of Brian Cameron. He had sent word to Maria Luisa that they were going to Miami to find Tyrone, but they had not returned. They had been gone for four days now and she had not heard from them. Only silence.

Liane paused and gazed out to sea, toward the far land that was Miami. She had never been there. Somehow in her bones she felt chilled and apprehensive. Something was very wrong. Her mother muttered over the fire morning and night now, rocking herself back and forth. Liane had suggested they go to consult the gods, but her mother had not even seemed to hear her words.

Ah, things were very bad, very bad. The gods must be very angry with them all. Perhaps it was the doing of Brian Cameron, that he had ordered the belly ripped from the sacred Mountain of the Cat, and ore taken from it to the evil-smelling building near the docks. More than two dozen men worked for him now, deserting their own patches of vegetables and fruit trees, working hard, making much money, talking of buying, buying. It had not been like that in the old days. Even Nathaniel worked with the ore, digging and directing others, as an assistant to Mr. McCoy. Liane shook her head sadly. She did not understand anything any more.

All the old peace was gone. She and Nathaniel had lain under the shelter of palm trees and made lazy love, laughing and giggling, then being serious and happy together. No more. Now as she walked alone, she felt coldness in her heart, and a terrible fear that nothing would ever be the same again.

Brian Cameron had brought the golden-haired woman to Desirée, and she had woven a spell over Nathaniel, Liane knew it. She had seen them in her dreams, with Nathaniel's strong hard arms about the foreign woman, her red mouth laughing up at his ardent face.

Liane shuddered, clasped her arms about her, and walked on, in a daze of unhappiness. At first she did not hear the man who called her name.

"Liane! Liane!"

She flung about swiftly. "Nathaniel?" But hope died

as swiftly. It was not Nathaniel who loped along the beach, scarred face flushed and excited.

Pedro Ortega came eagerly to her side. He gazed down at her. Her eyes were half shut against the morning sun. Dully she waited for him to speak, uninterested.

"Where have you been? I have searched for you yesterday and today," he demanded.

She shrugged. "About," she said coldly. "You have heard something of Tyrone?"

His face closed up, looked hard and impassive. "Tyrone? Why should I hear about Tyrone? Is he not in jail in Miami?"

Pedro Ortega cared nothing about Tyrone, Liane thought. It confirmed her suspicions. She had wondered if Pedro had deliberately betrayed Tyrone to the Coast Guard. If Pedro had led Tyrone into a trap, it was because the boy was reluctant to go on anymore rumrunning trips. Maria Luisa had said he did not want to go out this time, yet he had gone, and been captured.

She waited.

Pedro stared down at her hungrily, then reached out and ran a caressing hand down her slim brown arm. She jerked away.

"What you want?" she asked sharply.

"Talk with you. Serious talk."

"What about?"

"Sit down with me here," he urged, trying to draw her into the shade of some palms. She had often lain there with Nathaniel, beside the sparkling waters of the blue lagoon.

"No." She shook her head. "It is nice here in the sun. What do you want?"

"To talk. And talk long." Deliberately he pushed her ahead of him, one hand on her arm, another on her waist, to the shade of the palms, and forced her to sit down on the sand. She was too indifferent to him, too intent on her own pain, to care what he did just now. "There, that is better. We have much to say."

She waited.

"I plan to rule this island," he began expansively. "I am Pedro Ortega, and I have much rule over the men here. They respect me, they follow me. Rodrigues follow me, and Auguste. Many others listen to my words."

She gazed out to sea.

"You hear me, woman? I will rule here," he said rapidly. His black eyes burned with fanatical intensity. "Already the men listen to me. Brian Cameron will not return. The work on the sacred mountain will halt! The whites will be driven away. I say it—Pedro Ortega."

She began to wake from her sad dreaming. She felt a chill trembling through her. What did he say? What did he mean? She turned to stare up at his dark scarred face, scrutinizing the ugly jaw and mean black eyes.

"Yes, you are surprised! You do not know Pedro Ortega! I shall drive the whites from this island, and rule it as my own. You shall see this in a short time!"

"I shall see it never!" she scoffed. "You talk foolish! Brian Cameron, he rule this island—he own this island. All work for him. He is good man."

"He is white man! He is bad! All whites want to rule blacks! It is bad! You do not know what I have seen on other islands! We are the ones who are beaten; we receive the scars!" He pointed to his face with his big brown hand. "You will see! The whites must be driven out, so we can be free!"

"This is scare wild talk. You foolish man! The whites never go! They rule everywhere," she said positively.

"You are a stupid girl! But you will see. Pedro Ortega will conquer this island! And rule it. And you shall be my queen! You, Liane, I shall take for my queen."

He paused, breathless. He stared at her, waiting for her to be impressed. She flung back her smooth brown throat and laughed harshly. Strangely, she sounded like her mother, husky and deliberately toned.

"Never in the world! You know nothing! The gods will not permit this! You are a stranger here, and you do not listen to the gods! If you try this, they will destroy you!" she told him slowly, as though speaking to an idiot, her eyes flashing.

He made a harsh inarticulate sound, enraged, like a beast. "You—you—mock me," he whispered when he could speak clearly. "I show you—you do not mock Pedro Ortega!"

His big hands grabbed her, and he pushed her down into the sand. Too late she realized that her apathy had led her into a dangerous situation. She had never before remained alone with Pedro Ortega—she had wisely feared him. But now they were alone at the lagoon, with only the birds to hear her cries, only the fish to listen.

He held her arms tightly with one hand as he straddled her with his heavy body. He yanked her dress up to her thighs. Liane gasped for breath, tried to roll away. He held her there, greedily looking down at her under him. His big hand held her thigh, squeezing the flesh tightly.

"I show you— You are—my woman!" he said thickly, undoing his trousers.

"No—no—never—" She cried out, screamed, as he thrust himself upon her.

She writhed and yelled, but he bent and pressed his thick red lips to her mouth, stifling the cries in her throat. He lay on her, crushing her under his hard hot body, running his hardness up and down her thighs, enjoying the struggle as she twisted and tried to throw him off. She was a strong girl, lithe, muscular, but he was a man, and much tougher. And he was not afraid to hurt her—he seemed to enjoy causing her pain. He twisted one of her brown arms behind her, yanking it upward until she cried with the exquisite pain of it.

Tears rolled down her cheeks, into her open mouth. He licked her lips greedily, pressed his mouth again to hers, and thrust his big tongue into her mouth. When Nathaniel had done this, it had been sweet. With Pedro, it was bitter, bitter.

Then he ripped her dress up from her thighs, tearing the cloth in his lust to get at her. She tried to keep her legs together, but one of his knees came between her legs and pressed cruelly, until she had to give in, and part her legs.

She did not want him. Her body was not ready and softened for love, the way it always was by gentle Nathaniel. He forced his way in, and tore her tender flesh. She moaned, and he laughed against her mouth.

"Good, huh?" he mocked as he began to move inside her. "Good, huh? Yes, again—fight with me—I enjoy this—" He ripped the top of her cotton shift and began licking and biting her breasts as he jerked his body to hers—again, again, again—until she was dizzy with the pain. He grabbed her buttocks tightly and rode her higher and higher . . . Then his body lurched forward, he moaned with great pleasure, and fell limply on her.

Finally he rolled off, and gasped for breath. Liane was too hurt and stunned to move. He sat up, grinned down at her, and passed a possessive hand over her naked body, over her soft taut breasts. He pinched the red nipples cruelly, and laughed softly when she flinched from his fingers.

"You my woman now," he said roughly. "Remember that, Liane! You my woman!"

She was fearful he would remain. But he got up, pulled on his dirty white trousers, and fastened the rope belt, all the time gazing boldly down at her. He had what he wanted; he had proved himself a man with her. He was pleased with himself.

"I come again," he said. "You my woman now, Liane!" He finally strode away, cocky, his head up.

Liane felt torn in soul as well as body. He had violated her. Only Nathaniel had had her before, and he was a good gentle man. She finally staggered to her feet, tried to fasten her dress together to hold until she got home.

She was weeping, her eyes blurred with tears as she stumbled over the hills. It seemed endless, that trip. Blood dripped down her legs to her sandals.

Maria Luisa was at the cooking fire when Liane stumbled into the clearing. The older woman dropped her wooden spoon and sprang at her daughter fiercely.

"Who did this? Who dare touch my Liane? Tell me his name, I kill him! Not Nathaniel—no, not him. Who did this?"

"Pedro Ortega," muttered Liane. "Oh, Mamacita, I hurt so much!" She collapsed onto a mat, shuddering with sobs. She had never been treated so cruelly in all her days. Her mind revolted from the memory of what he had done to her.

Maria Luisa brought cool water and cloths. Her mouth tightly pressed against her fury, she bathed her daughter and smoothed cool ointment on the wrenched, stained thighs. Then she drew Liane to her and soothed her like a baby, rocking her back and forth, crooning to her.

The two women slept little that night. They had talked for a time, then been silent for long hours, thinking, worrying about what to do. Maria Luisa had asked Liane if she would tell Nathaniel of this, if he would avenge her.

Liane had replied, "I don't know, Mamacita. I don't know." Shame and dread held her back. She wanted to crawl into a black hole and hide from the world. Would Nathaniel even want her again knowing how a cruel man had held her, forced himself on her?

And if she did tell him, what could he do? He was a gentle man; he knew little of knife fights and revenge. Perhaps Pedro Ortega would attack and kill him! She shuddered heavily.

They sat before the fire in the evening and held to each other in wordless comfort. Liane lay with her head on her mother's breast, and felt the warmth and gentleness of her mother's arms, thought of the years her mother had been her fierce defender, her thoughtful and wise mentor. Always there had been Maria Luisa, standing between her and the world. Maria Luisa would aid her.

If only Nathaniel had not failed her . . .

Morning came. They rose, washed, and began to prepare the breakfast. Maria Luisa spoke of Tyrone and of Silva, worrying about them. "Way off over the water in Miami. What can be happening to them? Will Brian Cameron protect my silver baby? Oh, he must have a care of her!"

"He is a strong man. Maybe he will protect her," said Liane listlessly. Some strong men protected, some defiled. She shivered.

They drank hot coffee, ate hot corn bread and pork. Liane was hoeing in the garden when Pedro Ortega came jauntily into the clearing.

She dropped the hoe and ran back to her mother. "He comes again—oh, Mamacita," she panted, terrified as never in her life.

Maria Luisa took hold of her big knife with which she chopped meat. "He not touch you again, not in my life," she said fiercely, her dark eyes flashing. "He pay for this."

Pedro walked up to them, grinning, his scar shining red in the sunlight. He looked at Liane with longing. She had been good for him yesterday. He had enjoyed the way she struggled, the softness of her flesh, the tears in his mouth, the sweet perfume of her body.

"Hallo, there, halloooo," he said, mocking the white men, cockily. "You got coffee for me today, eh? You tell your mama you are now my woman?"

Maria Luisa thrust Liane behind her. She held the knife firmly in her hand. "You go away. You have done wrong to my child," she said. "The gods will answer you! The shark god will attack and kill you, if you touch her again! You go away!"

Pedro laughed at her, without mirth. His eyes flashed. "Get away from me, woman," he said, and tried to thrust her from his path. "You come, Liane. We go swim together, eh?"

"She goes nowhere with you!" Maria Luisa was inflamed with anger. She stuck out her lip at him. "Go, evil one! You brought nothing but trouble to the island with you! No wonder they throw you off other places! You evil. You must go!"

He lost his smile. He thrust her aside ungently and reached for Liane. "She come with me—now!"

Maria Luisa lunged at him with her big knife. Pedro took it from her easily and thrust at her. She jumped back. Snarling with rage, he followed her, took her by the shoulder, and plunged the knife into her heart. Maria Luisa coughed, gave a guttural cry, and swayed in his grasp.

Liane screamed, reaching for her mother. Pedro pulled out the knife from her chest. A great gush of blood came from the woman, and slowly she crumpled to the ground.

Liane crouched over her, trying frantically to stem the blood. "Mamacita! Mama—Mama—" She used a cloth to press against the horrible big wound. Maria Luisa's eyes were staring up at her, large and dark. If only she would speak—

Pedro reached down, felt her arm. "She dead. You come away," he said, a rough angry note in his voice. "Come!"

Liane did not move. "Dead? No, no, no, no—"

She pressed back her mother's graying dark hair.

She bent and pressed her cheek to the warm cheek. She was not dead—she was not—she only had fainted with her eyes open. The blood spurted, then finally slowed to a trickle.

"Get Papa Henri," Liane urged. "She must live! She will live! Get Papa Henri to help me."

Pedro snarled, "She is dead, I tell you! Listen, Liane, you tell Nathaniel about this, I kill him too! You understand?"

He yanked her back toward him by grabbing her long hair, so she half fell before him. Liane stared up at his scarred cruel face, hearing the savage words but scarcely comprehending them.

"You tell—nobody! Understand? The woman die by accident! I not here! I go now! If anyone hears of this, I come back and kill you too!"

He let go of her long hair, tried to force her to her feet, but she could not stand. With a curse, he let her sink again to the ground, beside the body of her mother. She bent over Maria Luisa, pressed her cheek to the cooling cheek. Frantically she felt for a heartbeat. There was none.

"You come with me, that is better," urged Pedro. "Come—you be my woman. I take care of you!"

Liane scarcely heard him. She was in shock. She could not believe it. She began to moan and rock beside her mother, holding the lifeless body to her breast. "She was alive but a moment ago. Oh, gods of my mother, aid me! Aid me!"

Pedro shook her by the shoulder, but she did not hear or understand him. "I go now. I come back later. You be my woman, and you come with me then!" he said emphatically, and finally strode away.

Liane held her mother close, crooning to her, begging her to listen. "Mamacita, you will be better soon! Come now—breathe, smile, tell me you hear! Mama! Breathe, Mama!"

But the woman lay limp in her arms, blood staining her dress, her flesh. Liane bathed her tenderly with cool water. No more blood spurted. Surely she would recover if the blood had stopped.

But no breath stirred her chest. No sound came from her lips. Liane knelt beside her, washing her face and her arms with cool water, calling to her.

"Mama, you cannot leave me! What shall I do? How can I live without you to help me, to advise me, to protect me, to comfort me? Oh, Mama, wake and tell me that you live!"

She called to her in English, then in her anguish in the island patois. She called on the gods, on Erzulie, the *loa* of her mother. "Make her wake again! Oh, Erzulie, bring her back to us, the living. She cannot die now! Surely it is too early to call her to yourself! She is needed yet on this earth! Bring her back to me, oh, Erzulie, I beg of you! I will bring you whatever you desire—the sweetness of honey, the best of rum, the white chickens you like. Oh, ask what you will—" Liane cried, but the body in her arms did not stir. Its coolness struck cold fear into her. Finally she laid down her mother and flung herself to the earth to weep, to mourn, to beg the gods for aid that did not come.

Pedro looked back twice before he disappeared into the trees. He was furious at the flaw in his plan. He had not meant to kill the old woman; he had just wanted Liane again. He had thought of her most of the night—the silkiness of her flesh, the perfume like flowers of her body. Urgency had driven him to her. Only this had gone wrong!

Well, he reasoned, Liane must become accustomed to the idea of being his woman. He would have her, and no one on the island was strong enough to prevent him. His chest swelled. It was not a bad morning's work. The old woman had never liked him. He was rid of her now.

She would get used to being his woman, this Liane with the petal-soft skin and silken hair. He would use her hard, and she would bear his children, and he and his sons would rule this island!

Late in the afternoon there was a massive explosion at the copper smelter. The natives had gone home for the day, and only Mickey McCoy was there, tending the fires, examining the day's work.

McCoy was blown from the building by the force of the explosion. Men came running, and took him, unconscious, from the rubble. They brought him back to Cameron Hall in the carriage. Mrs. Leoni and her husband took care of him, cleaning him up. When Mickey regained consciousness they asked him what had happened.

"Damned if I know!" he said, and cursed some more before he could calm himself. He lay helpless with his one leg broken, cuts on his face and body, blood all over him. "Damn—the whole thing blew up! No reason—"

Astrid refused to come near him; she shuddered and said it was all too dreadful. McCoy just grinned up at Mrs. Leoni and said he was fine. But she conferred with Donald Keller, who was of the opinion that they should send Mickey McCoy to Miami on the freighter at once.

He refused to go. "No, I got to stay here and get them boys back on the job. How bad is the building damaged?"

They could not tell him that night, but the next day Donald Keller and Giovanni Leoni went down in the carriage and saw that the smelter was almost a complete wreck. They conferred gravely.

"We must send word to Brian Cameron at least," said Keller seriously. "The captain is ready to sail today, at any time, isn't he?"

"I wish we could get McCoy to go also. What if he gets worse? What if his wounds are infected? And I'm worried about his leg," growled Leoni, scratching his head. He wanted a drink badly.

McCoy would not leave. They sent word by the freighter captain and asked Brian to send a doctor over to the island if he could find one to make the trip. In the meantime Keller tried to get the natives together to start repairing the smelter. But they had disappeared.

He reported to Mickey that the men had gone and the little coal-car train had not made its regular trip up to the ore mine for the day. Mickey let out a lurid stream of colorful words.

"Damn them all!" he cursed, in spite of Mrs. Leoni's presence. "I'll show them the fine edge of my tongue when I get on my feet again!"

But that would be some time. Meanwhile the men had not turned up for work. Keller told McCoy he thought it was unwise to follow them to the village and try to force them to return to the mine.

"Something is going on here we don't understand," Keller said slowly. "If there was nothing to cause an explosion in the copper smelter, then someone must have set an explosion—right?"

McCoy stared at him. "You're a wise boy," he said dryly. "You'd think you had been in the mining business all your days! Yes, there must have been someone a-setting the explosion, and not wishing me any good! We'll have to wait for Brian to get back to get to the root of it."

He had noted that the houseboys were strange and quiet, whispering among themselves. He had thought they were worried about the mine, but he did catch that they were talking about Maria Luisa. Had that old woman urged them to set the explosion? Maybe Brian should know about that also. It was a puzzle for sure. Brian paid them well; why should they get upset?

Chapter 17

Silva had slept little in the night. She had wakened again and again to the sounds of automobile horns honking, shouts, laughter, screaming in the streets. What a wild place it is, this civilization, she thought.

Civilization. She had thought of it eagerly, especially after Brian Cameron had told her of the beauties of London and Paris, the marvelous music of the concerts, the lakes and rivers in blue beauty, the imposing pyramids against the sand of Egypt. But this was not what he had said. It was terrifying, loud—ugly sounds and people who stared at her, making her cringe.

In the morning, at dawn, it turned cooler, and she finally slept, only to have nightmares where jaguars were prowling about, green eyes flashing in the night, ready to pounce on her from sinister dark trees. The sacred mountain erupted with smoke and fire, and everyone was screaming. Maria Luisa was screaming soundlessly, her mouth open, blood streaming from her—

Silva wakened, covered with sweat, and jerked upright in the bed, staring about her in a daze. She could scarcely remember where she was. Then she saw the huge white bed, the white sheets, the billowing curtains at the windows—and remembered.

Tyrone was in jail. Brian Cameron had demanded that she marry him. He had kissed her hatefully, making her feel hot and uncomfortable and terrified, and then he had locked her in her room. She shuddered, and got up. She went to the bathroom unsteadily, and felt like vomiting. But the moment passed, and she felt more comfortable after she had splashed cold water on her face.

She had nothing to wear but the green and gold robe. She wandered back to her room, took a sheet off the bed, wrapped it around herself, and sat in a chair far from the window. She stared out gloomily, amazed by the bright ugliness of the city of Miami. Was this the paradise beyond Desirée?

Someone unlocked the door, rattled the handle, then came in. Silva stiffened, turning a frightened face to the door. Mrs. Bowles came in timidly, her anxious face lightening when she saw Silva.

"There you are, dear, wide awake at last. I wondered how you slept," she said comfortably. She smiled at the girl, but Silva stared back at her sullenly. This woman was in the pay of Brian Cameron.

"I'll bring you a tray of breakfast. It is almost noon, but I expect you'd rather have bacon and eggs and coffee, wouldn't you?"

Silva nodded. "Yes—thank you." Coffee did sound good. The woman left, to return in a few minutes with a silver tray, which she set down on a table near the window. Silva was afraid to go near the window, but she was hungry. She finally got up, trailing the bed sheet.

The woman disappeared again, to return with boxes and dresses over her arm. "Mr. Cameron sent out for some clothes for you," said Mrs. Bowles, as though she had not noticed the girl's silence. Silva sipped her coffee, watching the woman from the corners of her eyes. "There—isn't that pretty?" She held up a green cotton shift, much like those Silva wore on the island, only it had bands of darker green stripes around the hem.

The woman took out sandals from the box, and other things Silva had not seen before. She explained that they were slips—whatever those were—for under her dresses, and stockings, and several thin girdles for her hips. Silva fingered them curiously, not at all sure how to put them on. She went on with her breakfast. She was not hungry—she felt sick—but she must have energy if she was to run away from Brian Cameron. And somehow she felt that sooner or later she must do that.

He was like Pedro Ortega and like Rodrigues—he wanted her body. Only he paid in different coin. Like them, he would force her to his will if he could. She resolved to fight him with all her strength. If only she had not left the island! Maria Luisa would have helped her hide from him.

When Silva had finished her coffee, Mrs. Bowles said encouragingly, "You can have a nice wash, and then I'll help you dress. Mr. Cameron wasn't sure you would know about all these clothes."

"I just want my own dress and sandals, please."

Mrs. Bowles looked uncomfortable and flushed. "Well, Miss Armitage, I'm— Well—you see—I can't get them. Mr. Cameron took them to a dressmaker, and the people at the shop are using them to figure out your size. Do try on these clothes, and if they are right, they will go ahead and find some other dresses and pretty things for you."

Silva wanted to flare out angrily, but the woman looked so unhappy, and she could not go about in a bed sheet all day. Her mouth compressed, she washed herself, glaring at her angry face in the mirror, her green eyes flashing with rage. She came back naked from the pretty bathroom, and stood silent as Mrs. Bowles explained how the garments were worn.

The girdle was hot in the warm day. The stockings were impossible—they were filmy and sticky, and Silva ripped one as she tried to put it on. She flung it across the room, and it lay like a silvery snake on the pale carpet.

"I won't wear it—I won't!" she cried out in despair. "Give me just a dress to wear."

"Oh, dear, oh, dear," mourned Mrs. Bowles. "Well, it is hot today. Just put on these dear little panties," and she indicated some filmy bits of pink and green and white. Silva reluctantly donned one pair, then a pink slip, and over that she put on a pink and white striped cotton dress, with a square neck and no sleeves. She felt naked on top and too dressed below. She sighed.

"There now, you look sweet," said Mrs. Bowles in relief as Silva finished dressing. "Now, here is the brush and comb Mr. Cameron bought for you."

Silva wanted to fling them across the room also. Mrs. Bowles looked apprehensive as the girl picked up the silver brush and surveyed it with angry eyes. He was buying the presents as though she were his woman, like Rodrigues would have done. There was a beautiful silver hand mirror to match. Silva finally sat down on the padded dressing-table bench and brushed her hair vigorously before the long mirror. A golden girl faced her, with vivid green eyes and silvery hair spinning about her head like fine gossamer webs.

She had never seen such a beautiful big mirror before. She admired the shiny dark red dressing table, and matching bench, and a huge cupboard in which Mrs. Bowles began to hang the dresses. Silva watched warily as one dress followed another: a silvery dress with sparkles on it, a white cotton dress with round neck and little red berries embroidered on the skirt and sleeves, a long filmy green dress that floated like a cloud.

There were half a dozen pairs of sandals and slippers, some like her own, but others strange, like those Mrs. Larsen and Mrs. Leoni had worn, with silver buckles and satin sides and toes that were pointed. Could she wear those without falling down?

The silver hair hung about her shoulders to her waist. Mrs. Bowles looked at her, then finally stepped up to her. "Now, dear, Mr. Cameron said I should show you how the ladies wear their hair. I could braid it and fasten it up, or you could wear a chignon at your neck."

Silva stared at her. "Why? I'm going back to the island soon," she said simply.

"Well, I think he means to take you about," said Mrs. Bowles. Her quick fingers worked at the hair. Silva was too numb to fight. She stared at herself as the woman bound and fastened the silvery hair back into a neat chignon at her neck. The hair was parted in the center and drawn back tight, and it felt hot and uncomfortable. Civilization was tight and hot and binding, Silva thought.

Someone called, a deep booming voice. "Oh, there's Mr. Cameron. He's home for lunch as he said," cried Mrs. Bowles, giving Silva a quick but thorough look from head to heels. "It's too bad you couldn't wear the stockings yet, dear, but I'll explain."

She urged Silva to the door. Silva wanted to hang back. She was afraid of this new Silva, this tightly bound Silva. Her shoes were not her own, her clothes clung tightly and were uncomfortable. But most of all she feared Brian Cameron, who picked her up and threw her about as he pleased, and locked her into rooms.

She followed Mrs. Bowles slowly to the living room. Brian Cameron turned from scanning the piles of envelopes before him, to look at her critically from head to foot. Then he smiled and nodded, as though pleased with the goods, she thought sullenly.

"Have you seen Tyrone?" she asked bluntly, without greeting him. She was here for one purpose, and he must be reminded of it.

"Not this morning. Julius is going over to see him this afternoon with a lawyer," said Brian. "Yes, you look very nice, Silva."

"She couldn't wear the stockings yet, Mr. Cameron. She will learn in time," said Mrs. Bowles, with satisfaction in her voice. "Do you like her hair this way?"

"Yes, very nice and neat. We're going shopping

this afternoon, Silva," he said with a smile, as though he did not notice her scowl. "You will need lots of clothes for Miami. It is a smart town. How do the dresses fit, Mrs. Bowles?" he asked as though Silva did not matter.

"We just put on the one, sir. We'll try the others later."

"No matter. I'll take her to the shop with me, and we can fit her out. Ready for lunch, Silva?"

"I just ate breakfast," she said sullenly, jerking back when he touched her arm lightly to guide her to the dining room.

"You can have something with me," he said firmly, and pushed her ahead of him to the dining room. The room was large and brightly lighted, with a white cloth on the table and silver settings. The china plates were of cream and gold, and the glasses shone bright and sparkling. She sat down reluctantly, her head bowed.

Mrs. Bowles brought a cold clear soup for Brian and a cup of fresh fruit for Silva. "She did just eat breakfast about an hour ago, Mr. Cameron," she said cheerfully. "So she won't be very hungry yet. Good to have her get some sleep, wasn't it?"

"Yes, I'm glad you slept well, Silva."

She opened her mouth to say she had slept badly, then shut it before the cold, mocking gleam of his eyes. He only wanted his own way, and he was stronger than she, knowing smart words and twisting her meaning. Her heart felt heavy in her breast.

Mrs. Bowles brought some meat and vegetables for Brian, offered some to Silva. The girl shook her head in silence.

Finally the woman left her alone with a cup of coffee, and disappeared in the kitchen, closing the door behind her. Brian stirred sugar and cream into his coffee. "Well, Silva, have you thought over what I said last night?" he asked quietly.

"I won't marry you," she said baldly. "And I won't be your mistress, either."

"And Tyrone can rot in prison for twenty years," he said, sipping his coffee.

She started, and put her slim hands to her face. Oh, he was as bad as Rodrigues or Pedro any day! She hated him! All had been well before he had returned to the island.

"Come, Silva, be sensible," he said impatiently. "This isn't such a bad lot! You couldn't stay on the island forever. I told you I wanted you and Tyrone to leave, and come to the mainland."

"Why? So we could be made deaf by the sounds of those horns?" she cried out and flung her hand to the window. "Or be run over by those horrible automobiles? Or be put into jail by bullies? Is this the civilization you wish us to know? Is it? I prefer my island!"

He bit his lips and seemed to fight back angry words. He drank his coffee slowly, then stood up. "Come to the other room. We can talk before we start out," he said evenly.

She went before him, her head back, the unfamiliar weight of the heavy chignon on her slim neck like some shackle from iron chains, like her picture books of the pirates and their prisoners. He went to the window in the drawing room and beckoned her to look out. She shook her head and backed away, her eyes frightened.

"What's the matter?"

"It's too far— It—it makes me afraid," she whispered.

"Oh—I see." He left the window and indicated that she was to sit down on one of the silken sofas. She perched uneasily on the edge. He lit a long Havana cigar, regarded her keenly through the smoke. "Well, Silva, there is sure to be much to make you afraid here, but I will always be around. You won't need to worry. We're going shopping. I'll show you the shops of clothing, jewelry, hats, shoes. I am a wealthy man—you can buy whatever you choose. Presents for Liane and Maria Luisa, too—whatever you want."

He thought to buy her, just as some native men tried to buy the favors of Oona, and succeeded. She thought of the bracelets and earrings of Oona, and felt sick with nausea.

"I want only to be free," she whispered desolately. She wanted to be free to sing on the beach, to swim in the cool waters of her lagoon, to listen to the songs of the birds, to pick the flowers, to dance lightly when she was alone. Her world seemed immensely far from her.

He moved impatiently, and the smoke wafted toward her. "You are grown up, Silva, or will be soon," he said, his voice taut. "I want to marry you, to protect you."

As Nathaniel had wanted to protect Liane—until he became entranced by the golden-haired woman at Brian's house! Now in the arms of another woman, he forgot Liane, and she wandered alone.

Perhaps that was Silva's answer. Perhaps Brian Cameron would soon weary of her. He went on talking, soothingly, about taking her to concerts and plays, of traveling with her to New York City, of showing her beautiful things—

"I will make a bargain with you," she said suddenly, interrupting him rudely. He blinked, laid aside his cigar.

"A bargain? What bargain?"

His tone was sharp. She bit her lips and forced herself to say it.

"I will not marry you. But I will—live with you, a short time—be your mistress—if only you set Tyrone free." She held her breath, watching his face.

"You don't know what you are saying!" His face had turned dark and angry red under his tan.

"Yes, I do," she retorted stubbornly, feeling the blood draining from her head. She felt light and dizzy, but she went on. "I will be your mistress for a time, so long as you like. Then when you tire of me, you take another mistress, and I return to Desirée."

There was a long silence. He stared at her, at her lowered lashes, her flushed face, her tense body. Then he got up and paced back and forth over the thick carpet with its patterns of strange curlicues and red flowers, and golden borders and blue leaves.

Maybe he would agree. He just wanted her body, she knew. She held her breath, waiting, her hands clenched together. Oh, it would be bitter and terrible for a time, but then she would be free again, and so would Tyrone. That was all that mattered, to be free and alone, to be able to walk the island lightly and at peace.

"I cannot do that," said Brian. He had finally stopped and picked up his cigar again. He drew on it savagely, making smoke whirl about his head so she could hardly see his face. "No, we will be married. That is final. Do you accept or not?"

"I do not want to marry you!" she whispered. "Oh, please, do not make me do this!"

"It is your freedom or Tyrone's," he said arrogantly, his eyes flashing. "What do you choose? He is in a small cell with another man who is a thief and a robber, an older man, who is mean. Do you wish to leave him there?"

She cried out, pressing her hands to her heart. She bent her head, and tears ran down her cheeks. He showed no mercy, watching her closely, his lean hard body tense.

"Well, Silva?" He was merciless, pressing her.

She finally nodded her head.

"You will marry me? Say it!"

"I will—marry you," she whispered desolately. "You will get Tyrone from that—jail?"

"Yes, as soon as possible," he said briskly. He crushed out the cigar. "Come now, wash your face and get your hat. We're going out."

"Where? To Tyrone?"

"No, shopping for pretty dresses, so I can see you looking lovely," he said with cold cruelty.

She left the room without a word. She had only his promise, and she did not know if she could trust him. She washed her face in cold water, drew deep breaths to calm herself, and found the pink hat that matched her dress. It was wide of brim, like those the men wore, but softer, with a pink ribbon about it. She crushed it down on her head, and came out of the room.

Mrs. Bowles met her in the hallway and readjusted the hat. "Dear, we forgot a pretty pocketbook for you. Be sure to get one."

"What is that?" Silva asked blankly.

"We'll get some pocketbooks," said Brian with irony. "Don't worry about it. Come along." He took Silva's arm possessively, with iron-hard fingers that pressed into her flesh.

They went down in the frightening box called an elevator, and her stomach seemed to have left her. Silva pressed her hand to her waist, in agony until they had arrived and the doors slid open to allow her to leave. She sensed that Brian was watching her with amusement. She wanted to cry. He was so cruel, so—so terrible!

He took her arm again, and led her out into the bright sunlight. A man drove up in an automobile, a silver-colored one, long and sleek and powerful looking. Brian gave him some coins, and the man beamed at him, looking curiously at Silva. Brian helped Silva into the front seat, where she sat tensely on the edge of the seat. He got in and started the engine, which whined and roared. She quivered.

"Sit back," he ordered, without looking at her. She tried to lean back, but every time the car stopped, she jerked forward. Finally she gripped the edge of the seat with both hands, holding on.

"You'll get used to it," said Brian, and brought the

car to a halt right in the street. He got out, strolled around, and helped her out. He was looking different, in a sleek suit of cream silk with a soft golden-brown tie, a wide-brimmed straw hat that looked new and fresh, quite different from those the natives wore, of straw that was green and raw.

He helped her out, gripping her elbow with hard fingers, as though he feared she would run away from him. But where could she run? People walked past them on the sidewalks, staring at her, and at him. She dared to glance up at him to see if he noticed. He stared straight ahead, his blue eyes vivid and flashing, his curly dark hair just visible below the rim of the cream hat.

They entered a large store, bigger than the house where she had lived. It had soft gray carpets, and rows of clothes, on funny wire racks. A smartly dressed thin woman came toward them, moving on black shoes with pointed thin heels. Silva wondered how she could walk on them.

"Ah, Mr. Cameron, how delightful to see you again." The woman smiled with a stretching of her thin red lips. She glanced at Silva, then looked her over, seeming to take her to pieces with her gray eyes. "And this is the little fiancée. How sweet!"

Silva wondered how the woman could know so soon that she was a fiancée. She had just promised to marry Brian Cameron! Did it show in her sad face?

Brian moved Silva smoothly over the carpet to where two dove-gray chairs were set. He motioned her to sit down in one, and he sat in the other.

"You have the dresses ready?" he inquired.

"Yes, sir. At once!" She clapped her hands, and Silva jerked in alarm. The sound was sharp and startling in the quiet room. Two girls came out, so tall and thin they looked as though they were hungry. They carried dresses over their arms, reverently, like babies.

Brian looked them over critically, then motioned to

two of them. "Silva, try them on. Go with the girls—they will help you change," he explained as she gave him a blank look.

"Change my dress here?" she whispered. He nodded.

She swallowed. The ways of the civilization he liked so much were odd indeed. She followed the girls to a smaller room, where they stripped her, marveled at what they called her "tan," and put on her a dress of silver-gray gauze. Then one girl led her back to Brian, who nodded his head.

The thin woman poked at the dress, pulled at it critically, her head on one side like a crane. Silva wanted to laugh, but no one else seemed amused. They all took it very seriously.

"Yes," said Brian. "That one. Now the other. And have you found a white wedding dress yet? One with layers of white lace?"

The woman beamed and nodded. Silva tried on a rose-colored lace dress, and Brian approved of that. Then they put on her a huge white lace dress, with layers and layers of fabric that weighed her down. It was made with filmy long sleeves that fastened at her wrists, and the thin woman threw over her head a white lace veil that covered her completely. Silva struggled to push it away, but the woman held her hand firmly. "No, don't disturb it. Perfect, perfect! Mr. Cameron will be pleased."

Silva started out to show it to him, but they held her back. "No, no, it is bad luck!" they cried.

Would it displease the gods they worshiped? Silva longed to ask which gods they followed. Instead she stood and turned, and put on one dress after another, showed them to Brian obediently, walking on high-heeled shoes that made her feet ache. They put on her one of those warm detested girdles, and fastened stockings on her legs, and made her walk in high silvery sandals made only of straps. Brian nodded and his eyes gleamed with approval.

Silva became very tired. She seemed to have done nothing all the day but put on one dress, take it off, put on another. And her legs hurt with the walking after her simple sandals.

She finally sat down in the dove-gray chair. "No more," she said wearily. "Oh, please, no more!"

Brian frowned, took a look at her face, then said, "All right, my dear," in a surprisingly gentle voice. "Madame, add pocketbooks in the matching colors, be sure they all have shoes that match, and add the lingerie and nightwear I ordered. You'll have it all delivered?"

"Oh, yes, Mr. Cameron, I'll take care of it all. Don't worry about a thing!" The woman seemed radiantly happy. "Some of it will go out this very afternoon. The rest in a couple of days. How soon do you wish the—ah—wedding garments?"

"Send it in a couple days," said Brian, and took Silva's arm again. He squeezed it as they walked to the door. She was wearing a pale green linen frock, as one of the girls had called it, with flat green sandals and those horrible green stockings and hot girdle. But she didn't want to bother to change again.

"You look lovely, darling," he said gently as they went outdoors. The green hat hid her expression; it flopped nicely over her face, she thought.

She sighed deeply. "Can I—see Tyrone soon?"

He frowned again. "One more errand," he said. They walked down the wide street past the car. More people than ever were on the street. She started to step down off the curb, but Brian grabbed her arm. "Wait for the light," he said.

"What light?" she asked blankly.

He showed her patiently a red and green light in the middle of the street and explained that she must not go when it was red, only when it was green. Cars swished by again and again, honking in her ears. It was deafening. She clung to his arm involuntarily as one car came very close to turn the corner. He patted her hand reassuringly.

They crossed the street and then another, and walked on. He seemed to know just where they were going. Every store looked alike to her, full of strange objects, more dresses, hats, white stiff figures wearing clothes, tools in one window, cans of groceries in another, piles of fruit in another. Didn't everyone have good fruit on their trees? she wondered, seeing people go in and choose fruit from shelves where it must have lain for a time.

Then she saw another shop window, and every other thought flew out of her head. She stopped, clutching Brian's arm in her excitement. A window full of canvases, palettes, paints, a rainbow of delicious colors, and in the background a painting.

"Oh, look—look—paints! I need paints! Oh, may I have a blue color, please?"

Brian seemed startled. He pushed back his hat and looked down at her in a puzzled fashion. "You want some paints, Silva?"

Wild frenzy possessed her. Inside the open door she could see more canvases, more beautiful frames for stretching the canvas, and her own was in pieces! She practically dragged him to the store.

He followed, amused and puzzled. She darted down one aisle and then another. Her hands fluttered over paint tubes, and greedily she picked up one and then another. A beautiful blue, a carmine, a golden-yellow—

"Oh, Brian, may I have them? May I have them? I am clear out of blue! I made some, but it isn't good. Oh, please—"

"Darling, you may have whatever you like," he said indulgently. "But I didn't know you painted. I thought your father—"

A tall man in a gray suit came toward them. "Yes, sir? You wish some paints?"

"The lady wishes some," said Brian. "And while

you're at it, some canvases, drawing pads, whatever the lady wants." Seeming highly amused, he followed Silva about as she and the clerk gathered up rolls of canvas, pads of drawing paper, a box full of beautiful paints, drawing pencils, pastels, and sticks of charcoal. Silva felt as though she were going mad! All these gorgeous materials, and she had been starved for them.

Whenever she looked at Brian to see if she could buy something else, he just nodded to the clerk, his blue eyes shining, and said, "Go ahead, put it on the bill."

He patiently waited while she chose the colors carefully. When she puzzled over which green to take, Brian said, "Take them both. Oh, put in an assortment, to let her play with them," he added to the clerk.

When she had finally calmed down, a huge pile of material was waiting. Brian gave the clerk a little piece of paper which he wrote on, and said, "My car is two blocks back, the silver Rolls-Royce. Put them all in the back, will you? We won't be long."

"Oh, yes—yes, sir," and the clerk bowed them out of the store.

"Oh, thank you—thank you so very much," said Silva finally, happily, as Brian took her hand to lead her away. She squeezed his hand, radiant. "Now I can paint again! I had only tree bark which Tyrone found for me."

"I had no idea **you** painted," said Brian slowly, still holding her hand closely.

"Oh, yes, Papa taught me, and then I went on with his canvases after he—he died. But I don't have any more canvases, and the paints were all gone. I tried to make my own, with berries and from squeezing flower petals," she explained, her glowing face upraised to his, "but you have to work fast, because they dry out so."

"I see. I—see."

He turned her into another store, but she did not mind now, her thoughts full of the marvelous possibilities of the canvases. She could paint again!

The store was quiet, whispery quiet, with glass cases about the room. A man came forward, and seated them in beautiful golden chairs. He set a black velvet cloth before them on a table, and brought out some cases. Brian opened them with a flick of his fingers and examined the contents.

There were stones inside, beautiful bracelets and necklaces, rings and earrings. Oona would go wild with delight, thought Silva, a little excited herself at the beautiful objects. She noticed a silver butterfly with blue enameled wings that sparkled. She touched it with her finger, and the clerk smiled.

"Does it please Mademoiselle?" he asked.

"It is pretty," she said shyly. "But not so beautiful as a real butterfly."

The men exchanged amused looks. Silva drew back, her sensitive spirit flinching from their humor. Brian was picking up bright shining rings. He took her left hand, and tried one and another on her finger, looking at them critically. Some had bright stones in them, some were plain gold bands.

One of the thin gold bands fit her slim finger perfectly. Brian nodded at the clerk, and the gold band disappeared into a dark blue box with a white velvet lining. Then they studied various other rings—a green one, a blue one, a sparkling white one.

"Which do you like, Silva?"

"I don't want any, thank you," she said politely. She was thinking of Oona again, and the earrings which Tyrone had bought for her.

Brian frowned. The clerk hid his mouth and coughed gravely. Brian jammed another ring on her finger, a little roughly, and looked at it. It was a huge green stone, with sparkling white ones on either side.

"We'll take this one," he said shortly. The clerk nodded. Silva started to take it off. "Leave it on,

Silva. It is your engagement ring," he explained as the clerk went away to bring over another tray.

"Oh." She wondered what that meant. There seemed so much she did not understand, and she thought Brian got tired of explaining. Perhaps she could ask Mrs. Bowles; the woman seemed nice and understanding.

Brian bought for her a set of green shining stones on a necklace that felt heavy on her slender neck, and some bright green earrings to match. Then the clerk found a bracelet of gold with more green stones to set on her wrist. Brian finally nodded, and had the clerk wrap it all up for them.

"Mademoiselle might like this also," said the clerk, almost shyly, as the procedure was concluded. He opened a box, and showed them. Inside was a jeweled butterfly, something like the first one. Only this was of gold, with the little wings quivering as though alive, and shining with some of the green stones for eyes, and golden feelers, and a green enamel body. "This looks more—alive—for Mademoiselle," he said gently.

"So you like it, Silva?" Brian took it out and put it in her hand. Her sensitive fingers stroked it gently.

"Oh, yes, yes, better than all the others," she whispered, and Brian smiled down at her. He fastened the pretty butterfly on her dress, where it quivered and shone like a live thing, ready to fly away—like her freedom, thought Silva.

"There you are, my dear. I am glad something pleases you," he said dryly as the clerk left them again.

"Oh, I am happy with the paints," she said innocently. Brian stared at her, then flung back his head and laughed. She had a feeling he was laughing at her, and she shrank back once more.

If only she might soon talk to Liane and Maria Luisa. Surely they would advise her what to do. She felt so lost and strange.

She would talk and consult with them, and then everything would be better. Maria Luisa might even talk to Brian—she was not afraid of him—and explain that Silva was too young to marry now. Maybe Silva would not be compelled to marry him after all.

Chapter 18

It took three of the smartly uniformed bellboys at the hotel-apartment to carry up the boxes from the silver Rolls-Royce. Silva was weary, and her feet hurt. She clung to the railing of the elevator as they zoomed upward again. She longed to lie down—on a beach somewhere, preferably on her beautiful island—go to sleep, and not wake up until she was in her own home once more.

But it could not be. Brian Cameron kept watching her sharply, holding her arm or her hand, and she could not even run from him.

They went into the beautiful apartment hallway, and Mrs. Bowles came out beaming at them. "More dresses have arrived, sir, and some pretty accessories. I put them in Miss Silva's room."

"Fine. And take these supplies and put them somewhere. Oh, do you have some room where she can paint? What about the storage room behind the kitchen? That has some good light, I think."

Mrs. Bowles looked blank, as did the butler, then they both nodded. "Oh, yes, sir," Bowles said gravely. "We'll put the ah—supplies—there. So Miss Silva paints?" He looked down at her in a kindly fashion before resuming his polite mask. "Mr. Payne has arrived, sir, and is waiting for you."

"Then we'll go right in. Come, Silva." Brian took her by the arm again, urging her toward the drawing room. She was reluctant, watching her precious canvases being carried away.

Silva was still thinking about painting as they walked into the drawing room. If she could paint, away from Brian Cameron, she might be able to feel calm and almost contented once more. Two men stood in the drawing room. The older man came forward with a smile. The younger silver-haired man hung back shyly. The lights dazzled Silva, she could not see, then—

"Oh, Tyrone!" She flung herself into his arms. He stared down at her, then his comforting long thin arms closed about her. "I didn't know you. Oh, Tyrone, you are out of that horrible jail!"

It was worth all the fear and worry and weariness to have him out of jail, to be holding him close to her. He nuzzled his face against her mussed hair.

"I didn't know *you,"* he said, in an odd way, strange and mature. She drew back and gazed up into his face. "You are dressed so—"

He broke off, glanced at the other two men, then said rapidly in the native patois, "What happened to you? Why are you here? Why are you clothed like this?"

She answered swiftly, "He brought me here. We have a barter—"

"What barter? Is it to be his woman?" asked Tyrone bitterly, still in a native tongue.

She hesitated. There was no word for marriage in that tongue. "I have agreed to marry Mr. Cameron," she said bluntly, in English.

Tyrone started, his face white under his tan, the lines of his mouth carved deep. He seemed older, worn, thinner. She put her hand anxiously to his cheek, to the scratchy feel of it, the deep lines beside his nose and mouth. "Why have you done this?" he whispered, speaking in the native tongue again.

Brian interrupted. "Speak English," he barked furiously.

Tyrone turned to him, his arm protectively about

Silva. "What have you done to her?" he asked. "She is my sister. You must not harm her!"

Brian's face softened. "I shall not harm her," he said, more gently. "I want her to learn civilized ways. Look at her—isn't she beautiful?" He waved his lean hand at Silva.

Tyrone gazed down again at his sister, at the smart green dress, the new hairdo, the hat which had tipped back from her face. "She was always beautiful," he said slowly.

Now Silva realized that he too looked different. He wore a tropical white suit like Mr. Payne's, and a silken shirt of green which made his eyes look more green than gray today. He wore a darker green necktie that flowed broadly over his chest. He looked—strange, different, smarter, older.

"Come, sit down. Silva is weary from shopping," said Brian, crisply taking charge. "Come, Julius. Tell me how you did it. I wasn't sure you could get Tyrone out of jail today."

"I signed my life away," said Julius Payne with a grim smile. Silva thought that she had, too. "Promised to look after the young man with my life. Ah, well, a good cause. Silva, I want your promise to let me paint you."

Silva and Tyrone sat down stiffly on the edge of a silken sofa. Their hands were still clasped tightly, like two children afraid in the woods. Tyrone fingered her left hand, and felt the huge ring. "What is this?" he asked. He lifted her hand, staring at the ring.

She could not remember the word, so she looked at Brian for assistance.

"Her engagement ring," said Brian. "Emerald, like her eyes."

"Very nice," said Julius, gazing across at the two of them. He turned to Brian. "I'd like to return to Desirée with you. I could paint Silva's portrait, and still keep an eye on Tyrone, as I promised in about a dozen documents today. What about it?"

Brian leaned back, and accepted a drink from the tray Bowles was handing about. "I'm not sure of our plans yet," he said. "We are going to be married in a few days. I want to take Silva to New York, then to Europe. Why don't you and Tyrone stay in Miami for a time. Then he can have a tutor to prepare him for college."

Silva clenched Tyrone's hand tightly. They were going to be separated! A wave of panic swept through her. Tyrone also listened in silence as the two men—practically strangers—casually discussed the twins' future as though they had no say in the matter.

"By the way, Silva paints," said Brian, turning to her with a smile. She was shaking her head at the tall cold drinks Bowles was offering. "Come on, Silva, try a mild one. You'll like it."

"No—please," she whispered to Bowles.

"I'll bring you a cup of tea, miss," he murmured to her, comfortingly. "What about your brother?"

"Yes, please, tea," said Tyrone, in spite of Brian's frown. "Of course Silva paints. I think she is better than Father ever was."

"That is an amazing statement," said Julius Payne thoughtfully. "I should like to see your work, Silva."

Both of them looked at her as though they examined her under a bright light. She flushed, and drew back against Tyrone.

"No, I am not better than Father. My—painting—is different," she said quietly.

Tyrone said to Brian, "When you stayed with us, in Father's bedroom, you must have seen the walls. Silva painted those. Father did more conventional things, you see," he explained eagerly. "Mr. Payne and I looked in some windows at the art. I saw some that looked like Father's. But none of them looked like Silva's. They make you think of cool forests, and brilliant flowers like you see in a dream. And birds that never were."

The men stared harder, from Tyrone to Silva. She

bit her lips and squeezed Tyrone's hand to keep him still.

"Well—I am interested," drawled Julius Payne. "Silva, what about it? If you let me do your portrait, I'll see if I can instruct you in any fine points of painting and mixing paints, and all that. What about it?"

"Oh—I would like that," breathed Silva. If he came with them, surely she would not be left so alone with Brian, who frightened her, the way he looked at her. It was as though he possessed her with his eyes.

"We'll see," said Brian, and got up abruptly. "If all you want is tea, we'll have dinner soon. Silva, change to that silver dress with the beaded top, and the silver shoes. Tyrone, you talk to Julius. I'll see about dinner." And he went out.

Silva swallowed angry words. She did not want to change to the silver frock. But she must keep Brian pleased with her, not angry. And she had a feeling he was angry now.

She went to her room. Mrs. Bowles soon came in, and got out the silver dress, cut in a square neck, with no sleeves, just straps over her shoulders. The top was covered with shining beads and sparkly stuff that scratched her arms. But Mrs. Bowles cooed over it, and said she looked like an angel. The high heels were higher than before. Silva felt sure she would fall over and hurt her ankles in them. Mrs. Bowles opened a box and took out a small beaded object.

"This is your pocketbook for this dress," she explained gently. She put inside a little white handkerchief and a small round thing she called a powder compact, and showed Silva how to use the tiny puff to brush across her nose if it got shiny. Silva refused to put red stuff on her mouth—it tasted funny—and Mrs. Bowles finally sighed and let her alone.

Brian met her in the hallway as she came out. He put his hands on her slim waist, where the loose shift dress emphasized the soft lines and curves of her figure. He gazed down at her, then deliberately bent and brushed his mouth over her cheek, moving slowly to her lips. She tried to turn her head away, but he forced her to accept the kiss.

His eyes blazed bright blue as he drew back. Before she could say anything, he told her, "I'll show you where your painting equipment is. You can paint tomorrow for a while in the morning. I have to go back to the office until lunch."

She willingly went with him, though his hand clasped hers cruelly tight and the high heels made her wobble on the soft carpets. They went past the kitchen door back to another white-painted door. Brian opened it, and they walked inside.

It was not a large room, but it contained only some packing cases, shoved to one side. Two large windows let in some good north light. Someone had set up a frame, and the canvases were in rolls there, alongside her cartons of paints, pads of drawing paper, and all the rest.

Brian looked about critically. "I'll have a table and chair put in here. What else will you need, Silva? A lamp, yes," he added himself.

"Oh, it is lovely, just right," she said eagerly, her hand squeezing his spasmodically, as she might have Tyrone's. "Oh, thank you very much! I have so longed to paint."

"I'll be curious to see what you do. You will let me see your paintings, won't you?"

"Oh, yes—if you really want to."

"Tyrone thinks you are very good."

"He loves me," she said simply.

Brian smiled, slowly, and turned her to him. She stiffened. He took her in his arms, and she felt crushed against his starched white suit and white shirt, with the small black tie in a bow at his tanned throat. He kissed her deliberately, his hand on her back pressing her to him. He pressed his lips to her throat, up to her ear, over her cheek to her mouth again. She trembled, wanting to fight him, afraid of the heat in herself, the passion in him. She did not know what a man did with a woman.

Maria Luisa had warned her. "When you marry," Maria Luisa had said, "I must be there. I will tell you what to do with a man, and what he does with you, and there will be no fear."

But Maria Luisa was not there, and Silva felt terrible fear of this unknown thing. She felt very panicky. She put one slim hand on his chest and pushed. He drew back a little, his vivid blue eyes darker than usual, almost as dark as the night.

"You must get used to me, Silva," he said, his lips thin and hard.

"How can I? You are a stranger to me," she said, meaning she was not accustomed to white men and their ways, only to the natives.

"Not for long," he said curtly. "Come in to dinner. It is ready."

At dinner she felt better. She was hungry, and the churning in her stomach had almost stopped. Tyrone sat next to her. When the other two men talked of business, she and Tyrone could speak softly in the native patois, and she learned of what had happened to him.

"Why did Pedro leave you at the dock?" she whispered.

"It was not that way," said Tyrone. Rapidly he explained how they had been chased by the Coast Guard, and how Pedro had persuaded—or rather, ordered—him to take ten jugs to Miami.

"Did he know you would be taken by them?" she murmured, forgetting to eat in her distress.

Her little hands clasped each other. He put one hand on hers. "I think so, Silva. I think it was a trap. I think he hates us whites on the island. Auguste warned me that Pedro is talking of throwing all whites off the island. I think it is foolish talk. The men do not like him. They know he makes trouble on other islands, and gets thrown off. But still I am worried. He tricked me, and I ended in the jail."

"Eat your dinner, Silva," said Brian sharply. She started, and turned her distressed face to him. His blue eyes seemed to see right through her.

Tyrone changed the subject. He had seen a gallery, he said, where their father's pictures were hung. Her small face lit up at once.

"Oh, where was it, Tyrone?" she asked. "I long to see them."

"Not far from here. Mr. Payne got me from the jail, took me to his apartment, sent for clothes, then we went out after I had had a bath and changed. We came to the apartment here, only we stopped about —about four blocks from here. I think they call them blocks."

She absorbed all this. "And you saw Father's paintings?" she whispered reverently.

"Yes, the gallery, named the Gallery of the Brothers, had about a dozen of Father's. Some were marked 'Sold,' but he—the man in charge—said they would be held for another week, so people could see them."

She memorized what he said. She longed to see them before they went away. Julius Payne turned to them, and began speaking of art, of Miami, of music.

Bowles brought more food. They had a hot soup called chowder, made of shrimp and potatoes. Then he brought slices of roast beef, a fresh green salad with a strange dressing that shone red but tasted delicious. For dessert there was the thing called ice cream, which Brian had once described to her. It was very sweet and delicious, and she ate all of hers. Brian watched her with satisfaction as she ate, and seemed more mellow as they rose from the table.

In the drawing room, Bowles brought coffee and poured it for them. Brian came over to her. "Watch how he pours, Silva. Later on you will learn to do this for our guests," he said casually, and sat down beside her instead of Tyrone. He put his hand casually on hers at times. Sometimes he put his hand to her waist, and touched her with the warm possessiveness that made her uneasy again.

He kept looking down at her, in the slim silver dress, as though he enjoyed looking at her. Tyrone got up to study the pretty things in the glass-covered cabinets. "Look at any of them, Tyrone," said Brian. "The cupboards are open. You'll enjoy the ivory. Show him, Julius."

And so Julius and Tyrone looked at the objects, and talked about them. Tyrone brought over a small round ball of ivory, and Brian showed it to Silva, explaining how it was made of hard material which was carved by Chinese people, round and round, with small figures in it. She touched it delicately with her fingers afraid, she would hurt it.

All too soon, Tyrone and Julius left. At Silva's expression, Brian said, "You'll see plenty of Tyrone, don't worry. He'll come over tomorrow evening."

Tyrone kissed her good-bye and whispered, "Don't worry, I'll see if I can get you out of this," and with that she had to be comforted.

When they were alone, Silva said uneasily, "I think I shall go to bed. It is late."

"Not yet," said Brian calmly, and drew out his cigar case. "We haven't had a chance to talk yet. I am planning the wedding for next week."

She gasped, staring up at him. He frowned, and put away his case.

"You might as well get used to this," he said, and drew her into his arms, kissing her neck and throat, and her face, until she was breathless and frightened.

It reminded her of Rodrigues and Pedro, how rough and greedy they were, how their eyes shone with dark hungers. But Brian would get furious all over again if she pulled away. She stayed in his arms, passive, only her fingers clenching on his sleeve to show her unease. He grew more gentle, and his lips caressed her forehead, where the hair was drawn back smoothly.

"There, that isn't so bad, is it, darling?" he whispered. His hands lingered on her back, smoothed over her waist and rounded hips. She swallowed a protest. He had a right to touch her; she would be his woman —she had agreed.

Tyrone was out of jail. Brian had kept his promise, and now she must pay for it. Oh, if only Tyrone could think of some way to rescue her! But how could he, when she had promised to give herself in exchange for the freedom of Tyrone?

"I wish," she began hesitantly, "that we can soon return to Desirée. I wish to talk to Maria Luisa before I marry. I promised her—"

"No. We will be married here."

She gazed at him anxiously, her fingers twisting together. "Then Liane and Maria Luisa could come here? To Miami, on the boat?"

He frowned. She wished she knew what he was thinking, to make him look so cold. "They would not feel right here, Silva, among my guests," he said at last, curtly. "These people are very—well—social-minded—"

"Maria Luisa will not mind! And Liane— Oh, but they must come to my wedding! I cannot imagine— to be married without them. Maria Luisa raised me. Liane is like my sister." She licked her dry lips. She felt in a nightmare, caught in a web of hot passions and strange emotions. She longed to fight free and run back to the island, to the safety of Maria Luisa's arms.

"It is impossible, Silva," he said flatly. Then he added harshly, "If you think they will get you out of the wedding, forget it! You have promised. We made a bargain. Now Tyrone is free, you must keep your word."

Then he pulled her close and kissed her again, till

she felt weak and limp. He seemed more furious than loving. Maybe that was how men were.

They finally sat down on the sofa, and he talked of the wedding. It would be held in a church. Her thoughts wandered away. It had been thirteen years since she had been in a little country church in England. It had been of gray stone, she remembered, and her mother was buried in the churchyard under a slab of white marble with her name carved on it. Green leaves grew over the gray stone of the church, and the churchyard was dark and it had rained the day her mother was buried.

She realized Brian was still talking. "There will be a reception afterward at a hotel. Some of my business friends are coming, and some others I want you to meet. Presents will start coming in. You may have fun unwrapping them. I'll have Bowles bring another table in here to set them on."

What are presents? she wondered, but dared not ask. Another question to save for Mrs. Bowles.

"I was hoping to get away on a honeymoon with you soon," Brian went on, smoking his fragrant Havana cigar and drinking from the glass of golden-brown liquid beside him. He leaned back, surveying Silva's still form. "What are you thinking about?" he asked sharply.

"I—I was wondering—about things," she finally sighed. "Sometimes you use words I do not know."

"What words?" he asked.

She flushed, and bent her head. It shone silver in the lamplight, and Brian's gaze lingered hungrily on her. "Oh—like 'reception,' and 'presents,' and that other—'honeymoon.' "

He gave a short laugh. "I think you will learn all that in time. Anyway, it meant that I had hoped to go away with just us together. But I have to wait until I hear from the island, how things are going there. If Mickey McCoy has business well in hand, we can get away."

"Where?" she asked.

"I haven't decided yet. I still want to take you to Europe. You would like Venice, darling," he said, and put his free hand on hers. Presently he set aside his cigar, and it burned in the white ashtray while he pressed his mouth to hers, and she tasted the smoky passion of his kiss.

Finally he let her go to bed, and she sighed with relief at being alone. He had not locked her in tonight. She slipped into the silky nightdress she found laid out on her bed, of white silk with ribbons at the throat. She washed and brushed her teeth with the strange stuff in the tube that Mrs. Bowles had shown her. It did not taste nice, like the twigs she used on the island. It had a strong flavor, and she tasted it for a long time as she tried to get to sleep.

In the morning she wakened, thinking about her father, and his grave smile, and the paintings he had done. She wished she could see his paintings. Surely she could find the way herself! Brian had said he would go to the office today.

She waited until she heard his voice in the hallway, curt and businesslike, speaking to Bowles. Then the closing of the door, the murmur of Bowles and Mrs. Bowles. He had left.

Silva got up, took a bath in the strange big tub which still frightened her. She dried herself with the huge fluffy green towel, and put on a fresh set of the underclothes. She must look smart, she thought, or they might not allow her to see her father's paintings.

She put on a tight white girdle, and silver stockings, tearing the first one but managing finally to put on two stockings alike. Then she put on a green slip, and a green silk dress with a round neck and cap sleeves. She found green shoes that did not have too high heels, and a green hat to match.

She listened carefully at the door. No sounds. She

stole out softly, and escaped from the front door, which was not locked. She dared not use the strange elevator that went up and down so fast. She had located a sign marked "Stairs," and those she went down. They seemed very long, going round and round, down and down, but finally she emerged into sunlight, blinking, at the back of the hotel-apartment complex.

She walked briskly, past the curious stares of bellboys and men in dirty white aprons over their trousers. She emerged from a dirty street into a wider one, and with relief recognized the front of the building. Now to the left, and four blocks—

She walked along briskly, watching eargerly for the gallery Tyrone had told her about. She walked —and walked—and walked.

She remembered to stop for the red lights at the street corners. It helped to go with the crowd—they surged forward in a frightening reckless manner when the light changed, and she let herself go with them. She crossed streets, and streets—and finally she realized she had gone much more than four blocks, and she had not found the gallery.

She hesitated, frightened, and looked about. There was a dress store, and she gazed into the window to see if she could see the thin red-lipped woman, but it was a different woman there, and a different arrangement, and the carpets were green. So it must be a different store. She was deafened by the noise of the traffic as it speeded up. Someone honked impatiently at her as she hesitated at a crossing, and she put her hands to her ears. Oh, they hurt! And her feet hurt—the heels were too high. Oh, where was she?

She could not stop; she must go on. She finally turned and started back, but something was wrong. She could not find even the dress store with the green carpets. Instead, she came to some stores with much fruit in the windows, and one with a great fish staring blindly at her from glassy eyes.

It repelled her. She had just begun to feel very hungry, but the sight of that dead fish staring at her made her feel sick. She began to run, panic-striken. She must get back to the apartment—she did not know anywhere else to go.

She ran and ran, dashing out recklessly into streets, causing automobiles to honk blaringly at her. A policeman stopped her. She halted before him, gazing up at the stern face, hearing nothing but the blare of horns and the yells of people. "I'm all right," she gasped. "I must go! I must—go—"

She darted past him. He looked irritated, then returned to his traffic corner, waving his white-gloved hands imperiously. She trudged on and on, getting more weary and feeling rather faint and scared now.

She was in some strange part of town. The streets were more narrow, and the alleys were littered with garbage. Why didn't they clean it up? she wondered. The smell of it, turning her more sick, made her turn and run in the other direction. Small boys played in the streets here, and someone yelled something obscene at her, a small boy, yelling something terrible.

She clapped her hands over her ears, and tears began to spill down her cheeks. She was so totally lost. If only she were on Desirée! She would know exactly where she was! She never got lost on Desirée.

She longed to sink down and rest, but there were only hot sidewalks glaring in her eyes, and the noise-filled streets where automobiles honked at her and men glared and cursed her for being in their way. Tears were rolling freely down her cheeks now. She longed to scream and run and run, but her feet hurt so. . .

A car slid up behind her. Someone grabbed her arm. She turned, protesting, and saw Brian Cameron, his blue eyes blazing with fury.

"Ohhhhh," she cried, and collapsed into his arms.

She clutched at him and sobbed, "I'm lost, I'm lost!"

He opened his mouth, then closed it grimly. He picked her up and put her into the car seat. She cried quietly, and he put a white handkerchief in her lap. She wiped her eyes, but still the tears came down.

At the apartment, he drove into the back, then turned to face her. "Why did you run away, Silva?" he asked grimly. "Don't you keep a bargain?"

She stared at him over the edge of the damp handkerchief. "I wanted to see Father's paintings," she said simply. "I went out to see them. Oh, my feet hurt," she sighed.

"God, you crazy little girl," he said. He leaned over, took the handkerchief, and gently wiped her face dry. "Come on, I'll take you upstairs. I've been hunting for you for three hours, ever since Bowles said you had disappeared."

"How did you know I was lost?" she asked.

Brian groaned, but said nothing. He helped her out of the car, then picked her up and carried her inside. He put her into another elevator, one that was not so fancy and brightly shining, and pressed a button. She leaned against him, and for the first time was glad he was strong and lean and hard.

"How did you know where to find me?" she asked again.

"I don't know, Silva. I just drove and drove like a maniac," he said. She noticed he seemed rather pale and shaken. Maybe he had gotten hot and cursed at also on those terrible streets.

In the apartment he delivered her to Mrs. Bowles. Bowles came also, looking concerned and pale. "She got lost on the streets," Brian said tersely. "For God's sake Silva, you don't know your way around! Don't go out alone again. Promise?"

She nodded. "No, I won't go again," she said desolately. "I was very frightened. Thank—thank you for finding me."

He bent over, brushed her mouth with his lips.

"You're welcome, darling. Don't scare me to death again, okay? Now I'm going back to the office, to try to get some work done. You feed her, Mrs. Bowles, and tuck her into bed."

He departed abruptly, slamming the door. Mrs. Bowles sighed and shook her head, and helped Silva to take off the tormenting shoes and tight clothes. She tucked her into bed, and Bowles brought a tray of tempting cool dishes and a hot cup of coffee. It was such a relief, after the horrible feeling of being lost, that she cried again, and they almost cried with her.

After that she dared not go out alone. She stayed in the apartment. When Tyrone came, they talked eagerly, quickly, like children frightened in the woods, holding hands tightly. Tyrone could not think of anything to say to comfort her.

During the days, when she was alone, she went to the white room in the back and painted. She painted a woods scene, with huge dream flowers of soft cream and gold and purple, with a mournful child wandering about, her hand on a tree, lianas catching at her feet.

Brian was more gentle with her. But whenever he came to find her, he put his arms about her and pressed kisses on her neck and throat, or made her kiss him back, and she was frightened of that wedding day soon to come. He could not seem to keep his hands from her, could not resist touching her with his lips.

Only in painting did she find refuge and forgetfulness of the ordeal that was yet to come. She thought of Brian's kisses and shivered.

Chapter 19

Brian was tired and impatient. He was working hard to get everything cleared up before the wedding. If all went well, he could be off on a long trip with Silva immediately after their marriage.

He paused in his work, picked up a cigar, and lit it. Eyes narrowed, he thought of Silva. She was very quiet and pale these days, and he felt vaguely troubled about the changes in her. She wasn't used to being cooped up in an apartment all day. He must get her out more often.

Still, the wedding was in four more days. They would both last, he thought, though sometimes the urge to make love to her was violent in him. She was so sweet, so gentle, and sometimes when he kissed her, the soft mouth moved and she pressed her lips to his in hesitant response. But she still trembled when he touched her. God, she had such soft skin, like a baby's, and he loved to run his fingers through the loose silky silvery hair and study her beautiful oval face and the large green eyes.

How pretty she had looked last night, curled up in a corner of the sofa, wearing the loose green shift that she seemed to like. In sandals, her hair loose, she had seemed more like she had on the island. Tyrone could always bring a sparkle to her eyes and a pink bloom to her cheeks. She was upset at being separated from her twin, but Brian was determined to break that bond. She was going to be his *wife,* and he must come first with her.

John, his assistant, came into his office. "Pete Johnson just arrived," he said significantly, and Pete followed him, his young tanned face filled with suppressed excitement.

Brian nodded curtly at him. "You're late."

"Yes, I'm sorry, But as I was starting out I saw Flavio. Couldn't believe it—I'd heard he was in Peru." Johnson was out of breath, bubbling with excitement.

"Flavio!" Brian repeated sharply. "Okay. Where was he?" He swung around in the swivel chair, eyeing Pete keenly.

"In the same neighborhood where he always hung out. Bragging as usual. Said he had a gold mine in Peru, and was tossing gold nuggets around."

Brian's eyes narrowed. He had thrown out Flavio and his gang from his own mining area in Peru two years ago, and had continued to mine emeralds. Was Flavio on to that operation again? He had told him never to return to Miami. Was Flavio so stupid, or overconfident, as to return? Or did he have someone over him? Brian wondered briefly.

"Let me follow him," Johnson urged eagerly. "I found out plenty." He told Brian with whom Flavio was living, the girl friend he had with him, the men he had met in midmorning.

Brian mused, smoking his long cigar in short puffs. Flavio was stupid. So he had found himself a "protector," probably in exchange for some of his precious gold.

The price of success! All the sharks came after one. They wanted to bring down the whale. Briefly his mouth curved at thought of himself as a whale. "A big tycoon," some journalist had written of him in a newspaper in New York City after Brian had successfully beaten off attempts to take a jewelry business from him. He had copper mines, gold mines, emerald mines in Latin America, contacts abroad, part interest in three jewel firms, a cautious interest in a diamond mine in South Africa.

As a mining engineer, he had started out fast. He had a keen eye for the opportunities in mining, the opportunities for wealth in putting together the right operations. No middlemen for him. He organized the mining, formed companies to sell the products, oversaw the industries that handled the copper and gold, encouraged jewelry designers to work for him, and gave them a free hand in designing unusual gem settings. His diversified interests had made him a millionaire at twenty-five, and now he no longer knew how much he was worth.

Of course, other men were jealous. There were some Latin American and European businessmen jealous enough to try to bring him down.

He listened to the report, thinking at the same time of the various possibilities for disaster. He would cope with them, as he had coped before.

"No," he said as Pete suggested again that he would follow Flavio. "You know too much; you have been seen near him. I think I'll put Marco on the job. He has been wanting to prove himself. Pete, you'll be his contact. John, you have the concert tickets for tonight? You'll come with Antonio—he likes music."

Marco was called in and briefed by Brian and Pete. It took more than an hour. Then Brian called the dress designer.

"You have something my fiancée can wear tonight?" he asked. "We are attending the symphony tonight, Madame."

"But of course! The silver gauze will be ready, the one of green and silver like the sea foam, which you so admired, Mr. Cameron," she caroled over the telephone. "And the little silvery-green slippers, and an adorable jacket of white ermine that I have just gotten in from Paris."

"Good, good. Get it over to the apartment, will you?"

"Oh, yes, Mr. Cameron. And—if you will permit—" She sounded as excited as Pete had.

"Yes, what is it?"

"The most charming dress has just arrived from the Middle East. A soft sheath of peach color, with darker bands of Oriental design—a long robe for at home, Mr. Cameron. I can just see it on your most beautiful fiancée. Shall I send it with the gown and jacket?"

"Absolutely, Madame. I trust your judgment completely. And you have finished the wedding dress, and the trousseau?"

"They are almost complete. I have seamstresses working day and night. Oh, the lace on the edgings, the soft tissue silk—oh, Mr. Cameron, they are a dream!"

"Yes, yes, thank you! I count on you, Madame," and he hung up impatiently. But he was smiling a little, thinking of Silva in white tissue silk.

He rang Mrs. Bowles, told her of the dress and jacket, and asked her to have Silva ready for dinner. They would go to the concert immediately following dinner. The housekeeper promised to have the girl ready.

"What is she doing now?" he asked involuntarily. He wanted to picture for himself what she did, how she looked.

"Oh, sir, painting, as she always does," sighed Mrs. Bowles.

"I see. Well, get her to stop in time to dress!"

He hung up, thinking of the painting he had seen, her first one. It was gorgeous, spectacular. She did have a tremendous and unusual talent. He had not told Julius Payne, for it had somehow disturbed him that Silva had such a talent. Would she be satisfied to be a wife, and later a mother, with a talent like that? Still, she could keep on painting.

But he did not want her in the public eye. He was jealous of her, possessive about her. She was his find, his pearl, his special girl. He thought of a popular song, shook his head in despair at himself. He was going soft as a crooner. He wanted to keep Silva to himself, watch her face as she discovered the beauty of Venice, of Paris, of Persia. He wanted that white bud opened up slowly for his own delight as she came to know the world, to experience love and desire and passion and beauty. He did not want to share her with anyone, certainly not a public avid for the newest artist.

He was late arriving home. He came wearily into the drawing room, to find Silva sitting at the piano, her head bent over the keys. He paused, startled once again by her beauty. She wore the silvery mist-green dress, which floated about her like sea foam, as Madame had promised. Her hair had been drawn back into soft curls, with golden clips fastening the wings from her delicate face. She glanced up as he came in, the green eyes timid and unsure.

"Silva, my dear, you look lovely." He forced himself to speak briskly. He wanted to gather her up and carry her away where they could be alone. He satisfied himself by coming over to her, taking her little chin in his big hand, and tipping up her face to kiss the pink mouth. She hated lipstick and would not wear it. He did not mind; it was all the easier to kiss her.

The soft mouth quivered, responded slightly. Then she drew back. He let her go. She would learn one day what he wanted from her. There was all the time in the world to teach her.

"Sorry to be late," he said. "I'll go and change. Are you looking forward to the concert?"

Her eyes lit up and her face bloomed in soft pink color. "Oh, yes, Brian," she breathed. "I want so much to hear the music."

"Good." He smiled at her, went off to his bedroom to change, and whistled in the shower. In half an hour he had returned, feeling more fresh in a cream jacket and dark trousers, a black tie at his throat. Bowles had the dinner ready to serve at once, and they went in. Brian had Silva sit on his right, as she did when they dined alone.

"What did you do with yourself all day?" He frowned slightly when she shook her head at the wine. He wanted her to learn to drink a little, to enjoy the good things of life, of food and liquor, of wines and exotic appetizers. She still nibbled cautiously at caviar, made a face over borscht, and refused rum cakes.

"Oh—I painted. And I played the lute for a while. Thank you very much for the lute." She always thanked him conscientiously for his gifts, but she displayed much more enthusiasm over the lute, the pipe, and the paints than over her dresses and shoes, and the jewelry that cost one hundred times what the lute had. He smiled a little at his own thoughts. Silva would always be a little innocent about some objects in her new environment, he hoped. He had no wish to destroy her naiveté.

"I should like to hear you some evening. Tyrone now has a guitar. Perhaps he will bring it when he comes tomorrow night."

"Shall we see him tonight?"

"No, Julius is taking him out somewhere." It was to a nightclub, and Brian fingered his wineglass thoughtfully. It was part of his campaign to separate the twins. He hoped it would not backfire.

They ate, then departed for the concert. Brian drove himself, watching automatically ahead and beside and behind him for any car which stuck too close to him. He noted that John and Antonio were following him carefully, and they parted nearby in the lot. He wouldn't take any chances.

Silva looked adorable in the little white ermine jacket over her gauzy green skirts. His emerald shone on her hand, and she wore little emerald earrings in her delicate shells of ears. How beautiful she was, and no wonder everyone stared as he walked in with her on his arm. He was proud of her. No one would think that until a week ago she had never worn high heels, never worn a gauzy gown or a fur jacket, never gone to a concert, never set foot in such a marble hall.

He led her to their box, glancing about casually to make sure John and Antonio were in good seats just below and behind them, where they could keep watch. The news about Flavio had worried him somewhat. The man was either too foolish or too confident. He wondered who was behind the man this time. Then he dismissed the thought as he helped Silva remove her ermine jacket and set it on the chair behind her.

Her cheeks were flushed pink under her golden tan. She looked more alert and happy than she had for the past several days. He had been tender and understanding with her, leaving her alone to paint, not being too passionate with his kisses, though he had longed to crush her in his arms at times. She was so adorable, so little and sweet.

He showed her the program and explained it quickly before the hall darkened and they settled back in their seats. The conductor came out. Silva caught her breath. Brian put his hand gently over hers, clenched in her lap. She felt almost too much—he could feel the vibrations of her emotions.

There was a brief overture. He enjoyed it, but more he enjoyed the wide, wondering look of Silva as she listened to the first concert she had ever heard. The music seemed to be rippling about her. He must teach her to dance, he thought. She would be like a wind child, moving with the music.

She started when the applause came, shrinking in her chair. He leaned to whisper, "They clap their hands like that when they like it. It doesn't last long."

"It is so loud," she murmured in his ear, and inadvertently touched his ear with her lips. He felt himself shaking inside. God, he thought, he had better pull himself together, or he would scare her! He scared himself with the force of his feeling for her.

The applause died. Then a young violinist came out

and bowed. The applause came up again. Brian pressed her hand reassuringly, and kept his hand on hers as the music began once more. It was a beautiful Mendelssohn violin concerto, and he could feel her thrilling to the music, growing more and more excited, so that she trembled.

He delighted in her delight, watching her face unobserved, pretending to keep his attention on the stage, feeling the music vibrate through them both. He kept her hand in his, and sometimes she squeezed his fingers, unconscious that she did so, in intense pleasure at the music.

When the intermission came, she clapped with the rest, earnestly, her whole face smiling and flushed. She turned her pretty eyes to his when the hall was finally noisy with the pleased babbling of the audience. The conductor and soloist had left the stage, and the other musicians got up and moved about.

"Oh, is it over?" Silva whispered, in regret.

He shook his head, smiling. "No, there is more to come. After the intermission they will play again, some music of Tchaikovsky I think you will enjoy."

"How wonderful, how beautiful." Her eyes were shining.

He touched her flushed cheek gently. "Would you like something cool to drink? I could get something—"

She shook her head, but got up and strolled the hallway with him, earning them curiously envious looks. He was proud to have her on his arm. Some friends paused, and he introduced her.

"My fiancée, Miss Armitage!" She had little to say as they laughed and exclaimed and wondered.

"I thought you were never going to marry, Brian! But I can see why you changed your mind!" one man teased, eyeing her boldly.

Brian covered Silva's silence, answering his acquaintances pleasantly. He drew her closer to him when he felt her tremble. She was not used to crowds like this. He made sure John and Antonio were leaning near the box before he himself relaxed.

They ran into an old business acquaintance of Brian's.

Bill Hartman and his wife begged to be introduced to Silva. Brian had always liked Bill—he was a decent sort—and his wife was the kind of nice older woman Brian wanted Silva to meet.

He watched Silva respond to the kind cordiality of Mrs. Hartman. She smiled faintly at the praise of the woman for her gown.

"But getting married in a few days!" the gray-haired Mrs. Hartman exclaimed. "Brian, you have to let us have a dinner for you. You haven't even come to see us for months, and then you spring this on us! I don't blame you a minute, but do let us entertain!"

He hesitated, thought of his engagements, then agreed. It would be good for Silva to be in a crowd different from those she knew. She would begin to blossom in their admiration, become more confident of herself.

They returned to their box after saying good-bye as the house lights darkened. "What did she mean?" whispered Silva shyly.

"What? Oh, I'll explain later," Brian said. He had to remind himself continually that all their talk was as though in a foreign language. She simply didn't know what they meant by entertaining, by giving a dinner for them, by engagements and honeymoons. It would be sweet to teach her what getting married meant!

On the way home, after enjoying a symphony by Tchaikovsky, he told her briskly about Bill Hartman and his wife. "I used to work with Bill—he taught me a lot. His wife is very pleasant. Her own children are grown up. She gives a lot of time to charity organizations and all that. I think you will like her."

"And she wants to—to give us a dinner party—because you are friends," said Silva, with a little satisfaction in her voice. "I think I understand. It is like on the Island, when someone marries—" She faltered.

He continued swiftly. "Exactly right. When someone marries, it is an important occasion, and all your friends wish to celebrate with you and be happy. So, it is not so different, is it?"

"Yes, I understand."

"I have been thinking about tomorrow, Silva. I am free in the morning. You want to see your father's paintings, don't you?"

"Oh—yes. Would Mr. Payne—would he take me over—?" She was frightened of the city streets, and just as well, now that Flavio was back in Miami, he thought grimly.

"I'll take you myself, Silva. I want to see his paintings again," said Brian. "My own purchases should be framed before long. Which reminds me, we must see about buying a house somewhere. Perhaps Bill Hartman will have some suggestions. You see," he said as she turned her head toward him, "when we are married, we will wish to have a house of our own. I have an apartment in New York City, one in London, and so on, but we want a house."

"But—there is Cameron Hall—" she whispered.

He ignored firmly the wistful note in her voice. "That is a house, to be sure. But we will often be in Miami. You be thinking about what kind of house you would like to have."

He drove up before the hotel-apartment entrance. A bellboy came to take the car. Brian helped Silva out, took a quick keen look about, his free hand casually on his jacket pocket, which bulged with the small revolver. All clear. Perhaps Flavio did not have his plans made; he was slow. But he would make an attempt one day. Brian resolved to make sure Silva never went out alone.

The next morning she was ready early, eager, wearing a smart new dress of pink and mauve, with a matching pink hat. It made her look all the younger. She wore cream silk stockings and pink slippers with pointed toes.

Brian smiled his approval. "Very smart, Silva," he said. He talked casually at breakfast about her father's collection. She hung on every word, and absently ate everything on her plate and drank all her juice. He was pleased, for this week she had eaten little, and there had been shadows under her great green eyes, as though she did not sleep well.

They went out to the collection, walking slowly. As they went he pointed out things for her to remember. He reminded her again of streetlights, told her about grocery stores, how people shopped, how they went to work in big office buildings. She listened intently, as to a fairy tale.

But once inside the Gallery of the Brothers she was suddenly animated and excited. She went from one of her father's paintings to another. Brian followed her, watching to see which ones held her attention longest.

When she hesitated for a long time, he raised his finger to the gallery manager, who beamed and nodded. Brian had warned him ahead of time that he meant to purchase more of the paintings of Valerian Armitage.

"Oh," said Silva wistfully, coming to a halt. "This is Mama, in our cottage in England." She studied it with caught breath. There was a scene of a simple room, of chintz and oak, and a woman at a piano, her silver head bent to the keys. There was a loving intensity to the painting—it vibrated with charm and silvery-rose colors, one of Armitage's best works. Fortunately, it was not sold yet. The gallery manager had put a high price on it, and rightly so. Brian raised his finger, and nodded. The manager nodded.

"Do you remember her very well?" asked Brian, when that was done. The woman in the picture looked like Silva, though older.

Silva nodded, then shook her head. "Sometimes—like it was a dream," she murmured. Tears shone in her eyes as she finally reluctantly turned away.

He took her arm and drew her to him. "Silva, when we have our house here in Miami," he said deliberately, "I shall have these pictures I have just bought put on the walls, so you will enjoy them all our life together. Shall you like that?" He had meant to keep it for a surprise, but he could not bear the lost look of her small face.

She turned in his grasp and gazed up at him unbelievingly. "Oh—did you—have you—oh, did you buy—?"

He nodded smilingly. "The four paintings I think you like best. The one of your mother, the church at home in England, the one of you and Tyrone as children, and the one of the village street."

"Oh—Brian—" She still stared at him, not quite believing, her face lightening into radiance. The manager turned away discreetly. Impulsively she reached up. He leaned down. She kissed his cheek, very shyly, her lips lingering on his face for just a moment. It was like being touched by the wing of a butterfly. "Thank you, Brian. Oh, thank you." She glowed.

They went around and looked at them all again. Brian would have bought the entire gallery if it would have brought that same reaction. He watched her flushed face, the sparkle of her eyes, the easier way she spoke to the gallery manager about her father and his work. Yes, she was gaining confidence, and she was not so afraid of him.

Afraid of him. Yes, she had been afraid of him, still was. It sent a chill down his spine, but he resolved to ignore the feeling. She would learn to love him, he swore it.

Chapter 20

The next day, Brian received an urgent call from the freighter captain, who had just docked. Brian told him to come right to his office. The captain reported in detail. Brian listened gravely, upset and furious, and concerned about Mickey McCoy.

"How badly is he injured? Why didn't the fool come with you?" he interrupted once.

The captain shook his head. "Wouldn't leave the works," he said. "We all begged him. But he was obstinate. The men disappeared; they went back to their huts and refuse to work. Probably some superstitious nonsense about the Mountain of the Cat—El Gato, as they call it. McCoy has a broken leg, but it seems to be a simple fracture. Still, he must be in pain. And I don't know about their antiseptic for his open wounds."

Brian reached for the telephone. He rang several doctors before finding one who would go to the island for a few days. He made arrangements with him, then turned back to the captain and asked more questions. As Brian noted down the damage, Antonio listened, leaning against the door frame. Pete came in, bursting with his own news. Brian finally let the captain go back to his own work.

"All right, Pete, you're bursting—go on," said Brian, still scribbling on the note pad. He dared not think yet what this meant to his own plans to get away.

"About Flavio, Mr. Cameron. I found out what he

is up to, or Marco did. He just reported in, and it confirmed what I guessed last night."

Brian stopped writing, and looked carefully at the young man. "Go on."

"He's joined with some outfit from up New York City way, for some rumrunning. It's getting to be big business. He is advertising for young men who will take chances, know how to run motor launches and cruisers, know how to fish, can swim underwater. Today Marco found out he is hiring Cubans, Haitians, any number of islanders, for a big operation. Promising them two hundred dollars per month and bonuses."

"Oh, God," Brian said. He rubbed his forehead thinking about Tyrone's involvement in rumrunning. Was there a connection?

When Pete finished his report, Brian told him to relieve Marco with another young man, Paul, who wanted more dangerous work and higher pay. Antonio still leaned on the doorframe as Pete left with his instructions.

"Well, Antonio?"

Antonio shut the door gently, came to the desk, leaned over, and spoke in his usual soft manner. "Some men have been asking about you, Mr. Cameron. Some New York types. I think they be the same men who hire Flavio."

"They think I'm in the rumrunning business?"

"Maybe. It is big business now. It makes much money. They want to know if you interested too. I let word go back to them. Big boss not interested. He straight."

"Were they Coast Guard?"

Antonio shook his head. "No, not that type."

Brian rubbed his nose. "Well, keep on letting the word go back, and make it convincing. I'm strictly legitimate. And I stay that way. Tell them I don't need the money from rumrunning. And warn them to stay away from me—and mine."

"I tell them strong, boss," murmured Antonio, and slipped away by the back door.

Brian laid down the pads after he had studied them. His mouth was set grimly. Trouble all around. He could handle Flavio. Maybe the man would not bother him if he became convinced that Brian Cameron didn't want a cut of the rumrunning business. But about the island . . .

"Damn," he said aloud. "That blows my plans for the honeymoon."

He could not go off with Silva, leaving Mickey McCoy with a broken leg and other injuries, to cope with the island. And the smelter would have to be rebuilt. Damn it all. Were they crazy on that island? The men had seemed to enjoy the work, after their first superstitious mutterings about the mountain. Maybe someone was stirring them up.

He thought of the scarred man, who had stirred his own suspicions. He had seen the type before, the would-be dominant personalities, the ones who drifted from place to place, stirring up trouble, trying to be big shots. He would have to check up on him—What was his name? Pedro something? Yes, he would have to look it over. Antonio was good at ferreting out information on the islanders.

Damn. He thought of the longed-for peaceful honeymoon with Silva, the wedding just two days from now, then off to New York and Europe. He couldn't take her away now; it would have to wait.

They would have to go back to Desirée at once. In fact, he would have left that day if it were not for his wedding.

He phoned some more instructions to the dock, wrote out a message for Mickey McCoy, sent it along, stayed until seven o'clock clearing his desk, then went back home.

Silva was sitting in the front drawing room, curled up in a corner of the huge sofa near the piano, strumming her lute. Her green eyes looked up gravely as he came in. The soft plunk of the lute was stilled.

Well, she was one who would be glad to return to Desirée. He would tell her after the dinner tonight. He bent over her, brushing his lips over her soft childish forehead, where the blonde hair was drawn back into waves.

"How are you, honey? Sorry to be late."

"It's all right. You—look tired," she said slowly.

It was the first time she had expressed any concern over him. His heart leaped up a bit—foolishly, he thought. But he was glad. "I'm a bit tired. Tell you about it later. I like that dress," he called back as he went to shower and change.

He studied her as they started out for the Hartmans' party. She was like a rose tonight, in a deep rose-colored gauze gown with a full skirt, the bodice of dark rose spattered with pearls. She wore pearls with it, small ones in her little ears, a double-strand choker about her slim throat, a large pearl ring on her right hand. Rose slippers to match, pink stockings. Yes, Madame knew her business.

At the Hartmans' he watched her proudly as she stood with a tall cool glass in her hand, smiled faintly, and answered politely the sometimes rude questions of the social crowd. Amy Hartman hovered around her protectively, as though understanding she was new to this, and a sweet person. He noticed Crystal Woodruff, sleek in a slithery gown of green scales all the way down to her feet, with a cigarette holder of green jade tilted in her scarlet mouth. Hadn't she left her husband already? He thought he had heard the rumor, but hadn't paid much attention to it.

Crystal came up to him, seeming to glide like a cat. "But, darling Brian, you must be out of your mind," she murmured to him, right in front of Bill Hartman and another man.

"Just don't let the rumor get around in the business world," he hedged, and Bill chuckled.

"Darling, I mean the girl! She's a baby, an infant!"

Her sharp green eyes were keen for his reaction. He smiled faintly. Her bobbed auburn hair swung in spit curls on her cheeks.

"Eighteen, as you could see by the license published in the paper, Crystal," he said. "Sweet as can be, a real honey. Don't find them like that much any more —that's why I'm marrying her fast, in two days time."

Bill slapped him on the shoulder. "Right you are. Reminds me of Amy at her age."

From Bill there was no higher compliment. The Hartmans were, some said, ridiculously fond of each other for having been married almost twenty-five years.

"A beauty," murmured the other man, studying Silva appreciatively.

Amy was receiving more presents at the door, and she came to pile them on an overloaded table. "Brian, darling, you really must help Silva open them all. She'll be all evening!"

Brian went over to her at once. Silva was looking rather overwhelmed. The dinner had been splendid, but she wasn't accustomed to the smart chatter of twenty people in her ears.

Silva was opening a large box, a solemn expression on her face. She slid off the lid to reveal an enormous silver teapot and tray, with matching creamer and sugar bowl. She stared down at it.

Brian helped her lift out the creamer. "Beautiful silver, darling. We'll use it often in our new house."

"Oh—yes, beautiful," she murmured, and caressed the silver creamer with her slim fingers. She studied the design closely. Then her face lit up. "Oh— it's a mermaid and dolphin. How lovely!" she said spontaneously.

Amy and Bill Hartman beamed. The gift was from them. "I thought you looked like it, honey," said Amy fondly. "Just like a nymph from the sea."

"Thank you so very much. You must come over and I will serve you some tea soon," said Silva.

Amy hugged her. "After your honeymoon, of course," she reminded. She seemed very pleased.

Brian opened up a long box, found a set of cocktail forks, and thanked the donor. Silva opened another box and exclaimed politely—she seemed to be catching on to how to act—over a set of crystal wine glasses.

Then she opened another large box and lifted out a ceramic bowl done in vivid blue and green. She puzzled over the design. Then she dropped it abruptly. "Oh, it's a snake!" she exclaimed in horror. "Oh—a snake!"

A green snake writhed in a lifelike manner through the blue flowers of the gaudy bowl, up over the handle, so the head reared in realistic imitation. Silva backed away from it, as though it were real.

Brian found the card in the bowl and read the name. "Mrs. Crystal Woodruff," he read, iron in his tone. "Well, Crystal—"

Silva turned on the red-headed woman smoking her cigarette right into Silva's face. "A snake. I was bitten by a snake once—I almost died," she said fiercely. "How could you give a snake to anyone?"

Conversation and laughter died abruptly as everyone in the room caught the clear accusing voice. Crystal flushed an ugly orange under her thick make-up.

"Really, dear, it is a very smart bowl. Everyone has them these days," she said. "How unfortunate that you were bitten!"

"You mean, you're sorry that I didn't die!" accused Silva fiercely. Brian caught her arm, and was surprised to find her trembling.

He set the bowl back in its tissue lining in the box and put on the lid. "How about this box, Silva," he directed her quietly. She was shaking so much he had to open it for her. He quipped lightly over the set of toasting forks. When the conversation had started up again and people had stopped staring at Silva, he motioned to Amy. "Take that one away—give it away," he muttered, handing her the box that contained the large ceramic bowl of the snake design.

Crystal put her hand on his arm as he returned to Silva. "Darling, you're not furious with me, are you? I thought surely you would marry someone as—sophisticated as yourself! How could I imagine you would tie yourself down to a child!"

He looked down at her, wondering at himself that he had ever found her attractive. She was a bitch, and that was that.

"My good fortune," he said, removed her hand, and turned back to Silva. He pointedly ignored Crystal the rest of the evening. He felt as angry and upset as Silva was. He wondered at himself. He was as protective toward Silva as someone to a child, but not because he thought her a child. He knew she was capable of deep emotion, of adult feeling—somehow he knew that. And he would waken her to love, if it took a long time, a lifetime.

He was not sorry when Crystal left early with a man about ten years her junior. Amy Hartman caught Brian's look, raised her eyebrows, and shrugged.

"She's off my list for good. Sorry about that, Brian," she murmured.

"Not at all. You've been good to Silva—I can tell she likes you. I hope you'll be about when we return to Miami," he said.

Her face lit up, her honest lined face. "I'd adore to be. I'd love to show her about. When do you plan to return, Brian?"

"Our plans are indefinite now. I've asked Bill to look for a house for us, though. You might listen for us," he told her with a smile. "Something big, well designed, with plenty of garden space, and a pool."

"Sounds marvelous. I'll be on the lookout for you. Do let us know where to write. Silva, you look so beautiful tonight. I adore your gown. That deep rose makes you look like a rose yourself," smiled Amy as Silva came up to them.

"My sentiments exactly." Brian put his arm about Silva's waist. It encouraged him that she no longer flinched so much from him, just a quick stiffening of her body, then she would force herself to relax as he held her.

They left before midnight. At the apartment, Brian paced from one end of the drawing room to the other. Silva was watching him with grave puzzlement.

"Darling, go change into something comfortable and come back," he said finally. "I have something important to tell you."

"All right." She went away quietly, returned in ten minutes wearing the new peach Oriental-flared outfit with full skirt, tiny mandarin collar, and bands of exotic design at the hem and full sleeves. She curled up in a corner of the sofa, pushing cushions behind her. He paced back and forth, then came to a halt before her. He had a drink in his hand. He felt he needed it.

"Do you want one?" He indicated his drink. She shook her head in silence. He wondered if she knew how restful she was, how peaceful, with her quiet, her understanding.

He sat down opposite her. "I had disturbing news from the island today, Silva. The smelter was blown up. Mickey McCoy was injured!"

Her hand went to her breast, pressed there, her slim fingers spread wide against the peach fabric. "Oh—no, Brian. How—badly—was he hurt?"

"Broken leg, cuts and bruises. I have sent a doctor to him. The freighter went back tonight." He swallowed another gulp of the liquor, then leaned back with a sigh. "Mickey is a good friend of mine, and a smart man. I can't understand what happened."

She studied him with her wide, clear green eyes. "Did—anyone else—get hurt?" she asked anxiously.

"No. No one else. The men had gone home for the day. Now they won't come back. We have to rebuild the smelter."

She was silent. She bent her head and began to fiddle with the wide sash of the gown. Her face had paled.

"I just don't understand it," he said, half to himself. "We paid them good wages. They seemed to like the work. It isn't as though there are any other jobs on the island."

"It is—the Mountain of El Gato," said Silva unexpectedly, raising her head. "The jaguar will not permit the mountain to be devoured. It belongs to the jaguar."

Brian stared at her. Just when he thought she was getting civilized, she would come up with that! He bit back a harsh reply. The silence flowed between them.

Then she said, "Do you know the girl Oona?"

He frowned. Her mind seemed to flit from one thing to another. Then, alerted by something in her face, he replied mildly, "No, I believe not. Who is she?"

"She was the woman of Rodrigues. Now she is the woman of Pedro Ortega. She—she reminds me of the woman tonight, the woman who gave me the snake on the bowl."

He was silent. He had a feeling she was conveying a subtle warning to him, but he didn't get it. Pedro Ortega. That was the name of the scarred man they had not hired.

He groped to find her meaning. She was as complicated as Maria Luisa at times! "Did Rodrigues object when Oona became the woman of Pedro Ortega?" he asked.

Silva gazed at him with her wide green eyes, the

lashes fluttering. "No. That is why I wonder," she said. "He did not make a fight."

He rubbed his face. He must be tired. He couldn't get it all. "What does that have to do with Mrs. Crystal Woodruff?" he asked.

The clear green shuttered. "She reminds me of Oona, that is all," said Silva. "Was she—was she your woman?"

God, could she be jealous? He stared at her, but could not figure it out from her expression. "Never in the world," he said, with emphasis. "She repels me. I gave away her bowl, by the way. We don't want it."

He leaned back and finished his drink. "You wish more?" Silva asked, stirring as though to rise and fetch it for him.

"No—no, thank you. Silva, this means we will not be able to go away to New York and to Europe for our honeymoon, as I had planned," he said slowly. "We must return to Desirée after our wedding."

She put both hands on her breasts, and her face lit up eagerly. "We—return—to Desirée?" she whispered in rapture.

"Yes, for now. I must find out about Mickey McCoy, how badly hurt he is. Then the smelter must be rebuilt, the men persuaded to work again. It will be some time. I'm sorry. I want to show you the beauties of the world, Silva, but it seems that work comes in again."

Her eyes were sparkling and happy. "But I wish to return to Desirée," she said simply. "I wish to see Liane and Maria Luisa and my friends once more. When can we go, Brian?"

"After the wedding, a few days later," he said brusquely, intensely disappointed. He had been talking about Paris and London, Venice and Florence, and the Orient, to her for hours. Had it all meant nothing to her?

"Then—then much later, we shall go to Europe,

maybe?" she asked. "Maybe Tyrone can come with us!"

He was tempted to exasperation, then realized she still did not understand what a honeymoon was. "Yes, perhaps later, Silva."

"I am sorry—about your friend, Mr. McCoy," she murmured. "I hope he is much better when we arrive."

He rubbed his hand over his forehead. Mickey, his right-hand man. Maybe he would recover soon.

"Your head aches?" whispered Silva.

He nodded without opening his eyes. Everything seemed to be going wrong. He felt immensely depressed. The smelter blown up. McCoy injured, he didn't know how badly. And no honeymoon, where he could be alone with Silva and teach her to open up to him, and love him.

She reached for the lute and began stroking the strings very gently. "Will this help, a little music? Sometimes it helps Maria Luisa when she is weary and sad," said Silva, and played the lute for him.

He leaned back again, eyes half shut, watching her face as she bent lovingly over the shining instrument, her slim hands making the music of a pretty old English tune. And it felt better, it really did, to have her sympathy and gentleness, to hear the music soothing him.

Silva felt some strange emotions in her as she played. She longed to help him, comfort him, as she would have Maria Luisa or Tyrone or Liane. He did not seem his brisk, confident self tonight. No, he was weary, his face drawn and tired, his hand going again and again over his head as though to stroke away pain.

It was late, past midnight, but she played on and on. She saw him begin to relax, put his head back against the chair, close his eyes. The lines of his face smoothed out. He had a large, generous mouth, she thought.

She had liked some of his friends tonight. Mrs. Amy Hartman had been kind, something like Maria Luisa, though slim and in a smart blue gown. Perhaps it would work out after all, to live sometimes in Miami.

She had sensed Brian's great disappointment that he must return to the island and straighten out more work. He had been working very hard. She wondered what work he did, all the day, skipping luncheon, coming home too late to relax before dinner. Was this also civilization, to work very hard from early morning to late at night? The natives on Desirée did not work so. They got up early only to fish, they slept in the heat of the afternoon, they had the feasts at night and laughed and danced often. Brian talked on the telephone for an hour at a time, saying crisp things about selling stock or buying gems or putting someone on the payroll. She herself was afraid of the black talking box they called a telephone, and would not speak into it. It might be enchanted, or haunted, that voices could come out of it.

A clock softly chimed one o'clock in the morning. She paused, listening to the pretty sound. Brian opened his eyes and smiled over at her.

"Very lovely, Silva, thank you. I think we had better go to bed. I'll be off to work early. Don't bother to get up for me. What shall you do tomorrow?"

"Oh—paint and play music," she said. "I feel very foolish. On the island, I would cook your meals and have coffee ready for you when you came home. I do no work here."

"Time enough for that when we marry," he said, and stiffened as he saw her flinch, the little gesture of her hand to her heart. But he stood up firmly.

"Off to bed, Silva," he said. "You did well tonight. Everyone was charmed with you."

"Everyone except that Oona-woman," said Silva unexpectedly, and gave a charming little chuckle that he had not heard before. Her green eyes shone with mischief. "I think she wants you for her man, Brian. That is why she hates me!"

He tapped her cheek with his finger, then stroked it gently down over the peach of her skin. He bent and kissed her lips lightly. "Good night, little doll. Dream of me, and no one else, hear me?"

She gave him another enchanting smile. "I cannot order my dreams, Brian," she said, in a sort of rebuke.

He gave her a mock scowl, took the lute from her, and drew her up from the couch. He wanted to snatch her into his arms and crush kisses on her pink mouth. Instead he led her to the hallway and gave her a gentle push in the direction of her bedroom.

"Good night, darling," he said, watching her go.

She glanced back over her shoulder at him, her chin upturned in the dusk of the hallway, her silver hair gleaming softly about her lovely face. She gave him a half-smile, dreamy, sleepy.

"Good night, Brian," she whispered.

He went to bed with her face haunting his memory, making him smile, letting him forget the problems for a while. He lay back in bed, his hands under his head, thinking of her. In just a few more days, a few more days, they would not sleep apart.

Chapter 21

The white lace and satin wedding dress fit tightly at the slim waist. More lace covered Silva's arms, with a lace bodice about her young bosom. Then the satin flowed to the floor, and lace panels swept about the satin. It was a charming, beautiful dream of a dress.

Mrs. Bowles smiled at her in the mirror, at the grave-eyed girl she was dressing. "There, now, you look like a dream," she murmured. She handed Silva the pearl earrings for her small ears, set the single strand of creamy pearls about her throat. The silver hair was set in a coronet about her head, the wedding veil fastened to it, flung back just now. The fragile lace of the veil made the silver hair shimmer.

There was no color to the girl except her pink mouth, yet she refused to wear any rouge. Mrs. Bowles dabbed a little powder on the short nose, then stood back to look critically, anxiously at Silva. She had come to be very fond of the girl in the brief time she had been staying there. Quiet, young, but a lady. You could always tell a lady, Mrs. Bowles had said to Mr. Bowles.

Mr. Cameron had left early for the church. Impatient, he was, thought Mrs. Bowles with a wise silent chuckle. No wonder. He wasn't used to waiting for what he wanted. Quick enough, the wedding was, and all his friends calling and asking why the hurry.

He didn't want this little girl to slip through his fingers, that was it, said Bowles to his good wife, nodding sagely. Pretty and smart and gentle. Just the kind of wife to quiet him down a bit, get him to settle down. She's the kind who will want babies, he predicted, and soon, and be a fine mother at that.

Julius Payne arrived. Silva could hear his voice, and the murmur of the other man, Tyrone. "There they are, dear. All ready now?" asked Mrs. Bowles.

Silva stood up, reached for the edge of the dressing table, and gripped it for a minute, her eyes shut. Was the girl going to faint? Mrs. Bowles stood watchfully, ready to catch her. She was a bundle of nerves, that was sure. Better when the wedding was over. She knew plenty of girls who got thin and nervy over their weddings. And this was going to be a big one, in a huge formal church, with the reception at the biggest new hotel in Miami. The Biscayne Peabody Hotel was a real sight, and Mrs. Bowles was eager to see inside it.

Silva finally opened her eyes and smiled faintly at the housekeeper. "Thank you for all your help, Mrs. Bowles."

If Maria Luisa had been there, Silva could have hugged her, and found comfort in her arms. And Maria Luisa would have said something with wisdom and gentleness in it, and comforted her and given her something to hold to. Now she must straighten her spine, and go through by herself.

"There now, dear, you're welcome." Mrs. Bowles stood back, then scurried to open the bedroom door for her. Silva swept out, careful of her wide wedding dress. Mrs. Bowles followed her with the white prayer book and the white orchid with the green heart to carry on the book.

Julius Payne and Tyrone were in the drawing room, looking unfamiliar in white tropical suits and white shirts. Tyrone kept shrugging his shoulders. The suit itched, and his shoes hurt from walking the concrete. Brian had said they were going back to Desirée in about a week. It couldn't be too soon to suit him. He had had enough of Miami.

He turned and gazed at his sister as she entered. She was so different, he could not believe it was Silva. The pearly-white face, when she had been a golden tan, the sweeping white lace and satin gown, the large sad eyes.

He started toward her, then stopped. "Silva," he said, his voice choked. Would she ever believe he had tried to stop the wedding? He had talked persistently to Brian Cameron, but the man would not listen, except to set his hard mouth.

Silva gave her brother a sad smile, like a wisp of sunshine flitting through a cloud. "Tyrone, you look wonderful," she murmured.

He gulped and ran his finger around his tight collar. "I tried, Silva," he said, in the native patois. "He would not listen to me. He wants to marry you."

Julius caught the English word *marry* in the speech and frowned. If anything went wrong now, Brian would kill him! "Here we are, then, off to the wedding," he said, very heartily, stepping forward. "The car is ready. Let's go." He hurried them out, his hand under Silva's arm.

It was not far to the church. Silva caught the curious staring at her as she sat in the back seat of the silver Rolls-Royce, Tyrone beside her. Julius sat with the chauffeur, the man Antonio, whom she had seen leaning against the wall at the concert hall. Why had Brian not looked at him or spoken to him? It was a puzzle. But all life was a puzzle now—she could not understand any of it. She just groped along, trying by instinct to do what was right, with Brian, with his social friends, even with Tyrone. Tyrone was unhappy and anxious for her. She took his hand in hers, and he warmed it swiftly for her, clutching at her as he had when they were children.

The church was huge, a great gray Gothic edifice of which Miami was immensely proud. Silva shrank back as she saw the immense crowd of people waiting outside. She didn't know she was a "society" bride. There were smartly dressed women in their little cloche hats and sleek suits, and men in formal garb with flowers in their buttonholes. There were others on the outskirts, peering at her, commenting. There was a man with a flash camera setting it off in her face and making her wince from it.

Julius rushed them into the church narthex, and paused for breath. Silva felt the great pulsing of an organ under her feet before she even heard the music of it, coming from inside the church nave. She began to tremble. It was here, the fatal day, and she was afraid.

Tyrone kissed her cheek and left her. He was to be best man. He strode up a side aisle and disappeared into a little door.

"A few minutes, Silva," said Julius gently, his cynical face overlain with anxiety. "Brian and Tyrone will come out with the pastor and stand up at the altar, then the processional music will start. You remember?"

She nodded. They had rehearsed briefly yesterday, in street clothes. Her hands had been cold when she had met Brian at the altar and the pastor had told them about the ceremony.

Behind them, Antonio and two other men leaned at the church door, glancing about uneasily. She wondered why they did not go inside and sit down.

Then the music started again, and she gave a tremor, for it was the wedding music. Julius took her hand and placed it on his arm. She drew down the veil over her face, and wished she could hide forever in its shadow.

She had thought before about her wedding, on the island. She would have a gown of new cotton, and Liane would make a flower crown for her head. She would be hugged by Maria Luisa, and together they would go to Papa Henri. A vague stranger—only he would be close and dear to her by then—would stand waiting for her, smiling as he waited. And her heart would be joyous as Liane's had been when she went off with Nathaniel.

How different this was! As they moved slowly up the aisle, her high-heeled white satin shoes making her walk unsteady, she noticed the craning heads, saw the sharp face of the bobbed redhead Crystal, who had given her the snake bowl. She shuddered. She saw Amy Hartman then, up closer to the altar, and wished she could hold to the woman. She felt Amy Hartman would understand.

Ahead of them, Brian, pale and stern, was waiting at the altar, with Tyrone beside him, unnaturally stiff and haunted-looking. And the pastor in his white robe, his gray hair, gazing thoughtfully at her. She came to a halt beside Brian, the prayer book and orchid trembling in her hands.

The ceremony began. It was really very few words, but it seemed endless. Then Brian was placing a gold ring on her left hand, and replacing the engagement ring on it. Her hand felt very heavy now. He squeezed her hand encouragingly.

She said a few words, in a choked voice, and placed herself in Brian's care and control forever. It was done. His responses had been clear and firm, and so strange: "With my body I thee worship—"

They turned to each other, and she threw her head back as he touched the veil. He took her in his arms and kissed her lips with that hard, controlled touch she knew so well. His eyes glittered as he drew back.

Julius came forward and kissed her cheek gently. Tyrone bent to his sister, kissing her other cheek. Then they turned and faced all the strangers, all the curious eyes, the grins, the smirks, the smiles, the excited chatter as they walked down the aisle again. The organ music throbbed about them. It was done.

"We'll go to the hotel for breakfast, Silva," Brian was saying in a natural tone as they stepped outside the church. "We form a reception line—"

Crack—a sharp sound. Then another *crack*—

Brian swept her hastily back inside the church. "God damn it," he said harshly. The young men fled from him, Antonio and the other two, sweeping down through the crowd, pushing people away, running to the other side of the street.

Silva gasped. "What—what—?"

"Shots!" yelled someone. "Someone shot! Who was it?"

Silva clutched at Brian's arm. It felt as though all blood had drained from her body. Gunshots. Who would shoot at them, and why?

She thought of the way Antonio and the other men were always near them, their eyes cold, empty, waiting, alert. Always searching, looking—for what?

"Brian," she managed in a whisper. "What—what is it? Shots! Why?"

He patted her shoulder automatically. His eyes were steel-hard, not looking at her, staring across the street. Then he glanced about just inside the church, calculatingly studying those wedding guests closest to them.

"It's all right, honey," he said, his voice like the harsh crack of a whip.

It was not all right. Across the street, she could see the crowd scattering, as though blown by an explosive wind. Then Brian's broad shoulders moved, to shut her off from the sight. She clung to his arm, shaking. The shots seemed to have shattered what little composure she had.

Why would anyone shoot at her, at Brian? It was a nightmare from which she could not waken. She heard sharp whispers from near them in the church.

"Shots! I know it was shots! Shots! Enemies . . . dangerous . . . these wealthy men always have enemies . . . business rivals . . ."

Tyrone came up behind them. "What is it?" he cried.

Brian thrust Silva into his arms. "Keep her inside!" he ordered, and dashed out into the crowd himself. Silva was shaking now, so hard that Tyrone could scarcely hold her. The crowd coming out was halted by the little party at the door, barring the doorway. The ushers in their smart white coats peered with curiosity out the doors as they kept people back importantly.

"What happened?" whispered Silva to Tyrone.

"Gunshots, honey," he said. "I don't know why."

She bent her head. It was all part of the terrible mystery. The smelter blown up, Mickey McCoy injured. Lost on the city streets, her mind blurring with fright. Terror and violence on the streets of Miami. Horror. If only she had never left Desirée!

Brian returned. "All clear," he said shortly. His face was a mask. "We'll go out the side door," he added in a low tone.

Silva was turned and whisked down an aisle to a side door, out the narrow passageway, and into a car waiting there, a dark car with shades on it. Tyrone followed them. Brian put Silva inside and got in after her. Tyrone sat on the other side of Brian.

"What was it?" asked Tyrone quietly.

Brian gave him a frown. "Just some nut shooting in the street," he said roughly. Somehow Silva knew it was not the truth. Someone had been shooting at Brian, or at her. The shots had come as soon as they appeared.

Tyrone said unexpectedly, bitterly, "I thought you promised to keep Silva safe! I won't have her involved in your rough plays!"

"By God, she won't be," Brian told him violently. He brushed his hand over his eyes.

The chauffeur was Antonio. He drove the car deftly through alleys, whizzing past garbage cans and dirty white walls, braking when someone paused in front of him to stare, then going on again. They finally pulled out into a wide street, and in front of the elaborate arched entrance of the hotel Biscayne Peabody.

A beaming uniformed man held the door open.

Silva was helped out, feeling trammeled by her full gown and high-heeled satin shoes. Brian took a long look about, then grasped her arm and drew her inside. His generous mouth was hard and tight. Tyrone followed them, looking about worriedly. Antonio stood at the car door, watching, his hand to his jacket pocket.

Silva was escorted into a huge hall. There were long tables at the side, decorated with white orchids and white satin ribbons and filled with huge dishes of exotic foods. They stood in line—for hours, it seemed—and smiled and greeted people, and said nothings in polite voices. She felt the curiosity in their faces like a blow, and she dared not look in their eyes. The society wedding of the season, and bullets also! What a sensation! News photographers came, and their pictures were taken, and Silva had to smile and smile.

She met businessmen who knew Brian, and their eyes were cold blue, or cold gray, or cold black—always cold and curious and wary. She met their wives, smart bobbed women in brilliant colors, or suave and sophisticated in silvery or gray tones. Amy Hartman in a gay blue dress was a brief relief, her warm hands clasping Silva's cold ones. Crystal came, with one of her boy friends, smoking into Silva's face, eyeing her coolly, enviously.

"We'll sit down now." Silva moved like a numb being to Brian's touch and direction. He directed her like a puppet to the end of the long table. He filled a plate for her with all kinds of exotic things she could not eat: the caviar she detested, the little vinegared fish, a piece of rich spice cake.

She drank a little of the bubbling champagne, smiled when she was instructed, poked vaguely with her fork at her plate. She saw Mrs. Bowles, grandly upholstered in a violently purple gown but with a genuinely delighted smile on her face, and managed a real smile to her. Speeches were made, Julius's polite and effusive and elegant, then some others with shades of meaning that made her wonder. Brian would frown a little but force himself to laugh, glancing quickly at her. She kept her face as serene as possible, pretending she was not there.

She wished she were swimming in the blue lagoon, lying back lazily in the early-morning sunlight, drinking in the dawn wind and the fragrance of frangipani . . .

She saw Brian look at her plate, and made a gallant effort to eat. But she could not. He leaned over and whispered, "Poor child, wait till you get home. Mrs. Bowles shall fix you some bacon and egg and hot tea. All right?"

She nodded gratefully and gave up all attempts to eat. She drank a little more of the champagne, got up with Brian to cut the first piece of an immense gaudy white cake half as high as herself, with a small image of a bride and groom on the top. She felt his hand over hers as she cut with the huge long knife, and he guided her deftly. Then she could sit down again. She was so tired, and her feet hurt. Oh, for her sandals!

The party went on and on. Brian took another look at her face and murmured something to Julius. Then Brian said quietly to Silva, "Julius will take you out to the car. I'll make a dash for it when you're safe. All right?"

She didn't understand, but nodded. She wanted above everything to get out into the fresh air. Julius took her arm, smiled at someone, took her over to introduce her to a fellow painter, and they withdrew to the side of the room, talking. She scarcely knew what they said. Then Julius managed to get her out of the room, and behind her she heard a great outcry. Tyrone and several other men at the door, holding back the crowd, gave her a grin as Brian escaped by another door. Julius was holding her, half carrying her through the red-carpeted hallway, out the door to the car, where Antonio waited.

Julius put her into the car. Antonio did not smile; he was looking about sharply, his black eyes alert, everywhere but at her. Brian ran down the steps. Antonio slid behind the wheel, and as soon as Brian got into the car, panting, beside her, Antonio had the car moving. A hail of rice and confetti struck them from the few people who had managed to get to the steps.

Silva looked in amazement at the rice and white stuff on Brian. "Whatever in the world—?"

"Native customs, darling," he said wryly. "More to explain later."

"On the island we throw flowers," she said gravely.

"Something like that." He was leaning back, recovering his breath. "Antonio, any sign?"

"Marco is following."

"Good. Let me know."

"Yes, sir."

At the apartment Antonio drove into the back, and they got out and went inside by the back way, up the service elevator to the top floor.

Inside the apartment it was intensely peaceful. Brian shrugged out of his coat. "God, I need a drink," he said simply. "Darling, I'll never marry again! This one has to last me a lifetime. Okay with you?"

He was teasing and normal and human. Silva finally managed to smile and nod. "Me also. Never again," she said. "Does it always hurt one's feet so much?" she added plaintively.

"Poor love! Go and change to something comfortable. As soon as Mrs. Bowles comes, you shall have your decent breakfast—and wear sandals, darling, anything you choose!"

She retreated to her bedroom, gave a sigh of relief to take off the fragile white veil, the pearls, the white gown. She struggled out of it, anxious not to damage it, and with relief hung it over a chair. She ripped off the white stockings, yanked off the horrible hot girdle, and breathed freely for the first time in hours. She stood naked, breathing in and out for a few minutes. Oh, what a relief!

He had said to wear something comfortable. She knew he liked the peach outfit, and that was comfortable. She put on a slip, then the shift with the wide sleeves, and the deliciously light fabric rippled down her tired body. She slid her weary feet into sandals and fastened them. Then she brushed out her hair into the loose waves that hung down her back.

Shyly she went back to the drawing room, hungry now and more relaxed. Brian smiled at her from the bar. He was pouring out another drink for himself with ice. "Bowles is back, and the missus. You shall have your tea pronto," he said.

She curled up comfortably in a corner of the couch and laid her head back on the cushions. Presently Mrs. Bowles brought in a tray of steaming-hot food, good ordinary food, and Silva sat up to pour the tea. Brian sat down opposite her, stretching out his legs, and sighed.

"Glad to get that over. I wonder why civilized people put themselves through these ceremonies. Do you know, Mrs. Bowles?"

"Laws, sir. It's the custom." She beamed down at him.

Silva thought again about civilization and how uncomfortable it could be. She drank her tea, nibbled at hot fresh toast, and ate hungrily of the bacon and eggs. Brian seemed as hungry as she was. They had scarcely finished when Bowles came in.

"Telephone, sir. I'm sorry, he said it was urgent."

Brian groaned and got up. "Too good to last." He paused at Silva's side, ruffled her hair with his hand. "Go get some sleep, darling—sleep away the afternoon if you like. I'll probably be tied up in calls."

He went away. She finished her tea and then took his advice gratefully, lying down on her wide bed and going straight off to sleep. The ordeal was over.

She wakened at dusk and lay watching the crimson sunset outside her window. The orange beams glinted off the deepening blue of the sea, the deep rose a reflection in the east of the scarlet of the west. Finally she got up, stretched lazily, and went to wash and put on the Oriental shift again. It was very comfortable.

Brian was in his study. She could hear his deep voice rumbling, giving an exclamation, an order, then pausing to listen to the black box. She went into the drawing room, to sit at the piano and play softly for a time.

Brian came in presently. He had changed to a pair of dark slacks and matching silk shirt, without tie. He looked informal, comfortable, the way he had sometimes on the island.

"Pink cheeks," he said approvingly. "You slept hard, darling. I looked in once, and you were dreaming, I think, and smiling."

She flushed at his possessive tone. She reminded herself that he had the right to look at her while she was sleeping, but it made her feel self-conscious.

They had a lazy dinner of white wine and chicken breasts, some green thing called asparagus with white sauce, chilled green salad, fruit custard, and coffee.

Brian seemed rather thoughtful and quiet. She roused herself to ask shyly, "Did you get your work finished, Brian?"

"Oh, what needed to be done, darling. Most of it."

She longed to ask him about the shooting that day, if they had caught the man who had shot, who he was, why he had shot. Somehow she knew Brian would evade the questions and his mouth would go tight. He told her only what he wanted her to know.

She played the piano for a time in the evening. Tonight she felt uneasy again. Brian was leaning back, drinking more champagne, watching her at the piano. And the look in his eyes disturbed her. Finally she stopped.

"I am rather tired. May I go to bed again, Brian?"

"Of course. Run ahead." He stood up, dropped a kiss on her head, and let her go. She felt relieved.

Mrs. Bowles had laid out a new nightdress on the bed, of white silky material with lace at the brief sleeves and the low neck. Silva washed and put it on, brushed her hair briskly, and went to bed. She felt relaxed, relieved that the day was over, wishing they would go back very soon to the island.

She turned over in the wide bed, punched the pillow under her head, and was just drifting off to sleep when the door opened, the door that was between her bedroom and Brian's. She sat up, startled, her eyes wide in the dusky dimness of the bedroom.

He was wearing a robe of ruby material. He came in, in a matter-of-fact manner, and over to the bed.

"Is—is something—wrong?" she gulped. Maybe he had news of Tyrone.

"No, of course not, love. It's just time to go to bed, that's all." His voice was husky, a little amused. "We're married, remember?"

She gulped, all her fears rushing back. Did he mean to sleep in her bed? Would he bother her tonight? What would he do with her? Oh, if only Maria Luisa were here, and could tell her what was going to happen!

She watched, shrinking back as he swung out of the robe, and she saw he was naked. He seemed so big, so masculine, standing before her in the dimness. A slight wind blew in, ruffling the curtains, chilling her body. He slid into the bed beside her, and reached for her.

She stiffened, but Brian soothed her with his hands and his voice. "Take it easy, honey. It'll be all right. I'm just going to kiss you. I wish you would kiss me with your mouth, hold me with your little hands." He coaxed her, murmuring with his velvety voice, charming when he wanted to be, she thought.

Silva lay rigid in his arms. His hands went over and over her, stroking over the silken nightdress, fondling her neck where the lace was shoved back. He bent over her and pressed his mouth to her throat, into the soft shallow hollow of her shoulder, brushing his mouth over and over her until she shivered with tension and something else.

His fingers stroked through her long hair. He turned her head and their lips met, as though lazily. But she felt the hardness of his, the pressure, the urgency. Oh, what was he going to do to her?

One of his big hands went to her thigh, down to her knees. He drew up the edge of the nightdress, and his hand moved deliberately over the silkiness of her leg. She tried to draw away. He would not let her go, moving her closer to him, so she felt the heat and strength of his lean long body.

She remembered the time on the beach when he had held her tightly to him, as though imprinting himself on her. It was like that—only worse. There was no running away.

He removed the nightdress, up and over her head, flinging it to the end of the bed. Then he turned to her more urgently, and his lips followed the curves of her body, from the roundness of her shoulder, over the soft mounds of her breasts, down to the neat trimness of her waist, and below. She caught her breath again and again, unable to believe what was happening to her.

A soft fire was beginning in her, amost overwhelming the fear. But still she was afraid. His caresses were so deliberate, so very thorough.

His big hand went to her thighs, parted them. Then he moved over her. She gasped in shock, to have him over her. When he began bringing their bodies together, she cried out in pain and surprise. He hurt her badly, and she began to cry, writhing and twisting to get out of his arms. He would not let her go, some fierce passion driving him to continue, even though she wept and her salty tears were in his mouth.

Finally the agony was over. He drew back, breathing heavily. He pulled her into his arms and held her against him, murmuring soothingly into her ears. But she felt hurt, physically and mentally, at his brutality.

"Darling, didn't you know what to expect?" he asked half angrily. "Didn't that woman, Maria Luisa, tell you anything?"

"No, no," she sobbed against his bare chest. She wanted to yank herself from him and run, run, run away. "She said—she would tell me—when I marry —not till then—"

"God," he muttered, and his fingers tightened on her shoulders. She felt the fury in him. Then he relaxed and pressed his hand down her back gently, over and over. "Okay, honey, take it easy. The worst is over now. It's done; you are my wife. Do you realize that?"

Oh, yes, she realized she was his woman. He had hurt her and taken her cruelly, the way he wanted. She lay passively on his body while he stroked his hands over her, and his breathing quickened. Still the tears fell sadly down her soft cheeks, and he stroked his fingers over her face and felt them.

"All right, love," he said finally. "Lie back and sleep."

She did not trust him. She lay back rigidly, her fists clenched on the edge of the sheet he had drawn up over them. Her eyes stared into the night. He lay on his side, his arm over her, as though to show his possession even in his sleep.

When she was sure, by his quiet breathing, that he slept, she got out of bed quietly and slipped to the bathroom. She was stunned to find the blood on her, and washed it off with a damp cloth, tears sliding down her face. She hurt, she felt wrenched. Could a man do this to a woman, when he was tender at other times? How could he be so cruel?

"Silva?" He stood at the bathroom door, gazing at her. She cringed, knowing the look in his eyes as he gazed down her naked body. She should have stopped to put on her nightdress and robe. "What is it, darling?" He came in, saw the blood on the cloth. His jaw clenched as he frowned. "Are you much hurt, love?" he asked more gently.

She turned her head away. He examined her, frowning, then said, "You'll be all right. Come back to bed. You need some sleep."

He drew her back with him, tucked her into bed beside him, and drew up the sheet and then a thin blanket, as the night had turned colder. He put his arms about her and felt her tension.

He sighed. "You'll be all right, sweet. Believe me, you'll be all right. I should have explained—but how the hell could I? Damn all women," he muttered. "You should have been told. I'm sorry it was such a shock, darling."

She knew he was sort of sorry, but he would have done it again, she knew that. There was tension in his body, a sort of hard control in his arms. She wished he would go away to his own bed! But if she suggested that, he would rage, she knew.

He drew her head to his shoulder, soothingly stroking her silky hair again and again. "God, you're so lovely," he murmured.

Loveliness. That brought on all the trouble. She thought of Oona and her sensuous appeal to men. She thought of Liane, walking the beach alone while Nathaniel was drawn to the more lovely blonde woman.

Brian was gentle and kind. He stroked her and soothed her, explained to her about what happened between men and women. Finally he told her to go to sleep, that nothing else would happen that night. She wasn't sure whether to believe him, but she was so tired—so very tired—

Her eyes dropped shut, and she slept. It was odd to sleep in a man's arms, to feel the hardness of them about her, the warmth of another body, lean and different, against her own. She kept waking uneasily in the night, shifting her position, and in sleep he would follow her, and draw her back to him again, possessive even in sleep.

She dreamed, wild dreams, of a jaguar pouncing on her, of a volcano erupting and burying her in its hot ash. And she was on a motor launch, going out to sea, on and on, into a brilliant sun that burned her and hurt, going to some strange place where she did not know herself and knew no one else.

She fell into a deep sleep toward dawn and was sleeping heavily, like a child, on her back, her arms upflung, her creamy face closed in sleep like a magnolia in bud, thought Brian as he bent over her tenderly. How small she was, how sweet and gentle, and easily hurt.

Maria Luisa! Damn, he thought, she should have told the child something! It had been a great shock to the girl. If he had had any idea, he might have been able to begin to prepare her. Perhaps not. She might have backed out of the wedding, run away recklessly, hurt herself, got herself lost as she had that awful day.

How lovely she was, with the dark brows so definite and winglike above the closed eyes. The creamy skin, with a lingering of its golden tan. She needed to get into the sun again, the sun of her favorite lagoon. He softly traced with one finger the line from her smooth shoulder to her pink-nippled rounded breasts, childlike, yet with a budding woman's maturity. Like a peach, just ripe, blooming—all his.

She stirred and moaned a little in her sleep. He stilled his finger, watched her face for a little while as she dreamed, then rose softly. He had a lot of work to get done before they could return to the island of desire. This time he would bring his bride back with him!

He shrugged into his robe, still gazing down at her—the relaxed body, the bent knee, the childlike curve of her arms above her head, the pink mouth relaxed in sleep. So beautiful, so innocent until last night. He had not been wrong—she had not had a man before. She was fresh, inexperienced, his to teach and to adore.

He drew up the sheet and blanket to her chin, and left her softly.

Chapter 22

Liane felt as though she moved and spoke in a nightmare. Mamacita was dead, her eyes blank until Liane had swept her hand over the eyelids and closed them forever. Her plump laughing mother, her wise mother, Maria Luisa, honored and respected and loved.

Auguste had come with other village men and carried her away to a place of honor, at the *hounfor* of Papa Henri. There she lay in a wooden box, with the lid not yet nailed on. They had dressed her in a white dress, and Maria Luisa looked peaceful.

But Liane was not peaceful. Inside her a rage swept. For the first time in her life, she hated.

She had known gentleness and happiness as a child. In the arms of her lover, Nathaniel, she had become a woman, knowing joy and the possession of a strong man, the desire of a girl for her mate. But then he had left her, and she had come to know a bewildered frenzy, a great loneliness that could not be assuaged.

Now she knew hate. Pedro Ortega had raped her and would do it again, Liane knew. She did not know how to protect herself from him. Maria Luisa had tried to protect her, and he had killed her with the knife.

Two older women had come to stay at the house with her. Liane sat on a mat, her legs crossed, her head bent, unbrushed hair sweeping over her shoulders as she mourned. They did the cooking, the sweeping, the taking care of the pigs and chickens. They spoke when she spoke; the rest of the time they were silent, respecting her grief.

She had told no one what had happened. Auguste had asked, and Papa Henri had come and sat silently waiting for her to tell him. She had kept her mouth locked tightly against the bitter gall of the telling. No, Pedro Ortega would kill no one else. But she would have her revenge. Somehow she would avenge Maria Luisa.

She had heard the talk. Pedro Ortega was stirring up the men. He had jugs of rum at a hut, and they came and talked, and swore they hated all whites. Then the smelter had exploded, injuring the red-haired Mickey McCoy. Somehow Liane knew Pedro had done this also. He was cunning, that scarred man, that devil of the Caribbean islands. No wonder he had been forced to leave other places. He was evil. Silva had gone to the mainland with Brian Cameron, and Tyrone was gone. She must face this alone.

Rodrigues had come and tried to talk to her. He was uneasy, upset. He squatted beside her at the fire and said tentatively, "You will tell us who has done this evil thing, Liane." The two women, frankly listening, pouring coffee for Rodrigues, exchanged glances with each other.

Liane stared into the heart of the fire. It had not gone out since her mother had lit it two mornings ago. It would blaze and remain alight until she was avenged, Liane vowed.

"You will tell me, Liane," coaxed Rodrigues, his eyes shifting over her. "You know I am friend to you. All the people, they love Maria Luisa. Who did this thing? Her knife slip?"

He knew no knife had slipped. It had been driven right into the great heart of the woman, taking the warm blood and breath from her, leaving her a limp thing that was nothing. Never again would she talk with her daughter, never again would she sing in the morning and evening, never again would her deep husky voice speak wisdom and courage.

From somewhere must come an answer. Liane thought intently, her blazing dark eyes focused only on the fire. The words of Rodrigues were like beads slipping away from a dark palm, meaning nothing. He finally got up, bowed, and left.

Auguste came for her and the women that night. Together they walked to the *hounfor* of Papa Henri. The wizened old *houngan* was drooping, his sad head bent, his face more wrinkled than a nut that has lain for too long. He sat in his chair, his brown fragile hands on the arms of it, and directed the ceremony for Maria Luisa.

Liane was the honored guest. So was Maria Luisa, lying in her white dress in the mahogany box, lying so still, her face upturned as though she would rise again and speak wisdom to her children. All of them were her children; to all of them had she given of herself, generously, for many years.

Thérèse had the big pot of beef cooking. Others had brought chickens, white for Erzulie, the powerful *loa* of Maria Luisa. One was killed before Liane. She dipped her fingers in the blood and made a sign on her forehead.

Legba was invoked. He was the spirit who guarded the gateway and the crossroads, and he would open the doors and make free the way for the powerful *loa* to come to the ceremony for Maria Luisa.

Lines were drawn on the floor of the *hounfor*. It was a small one, open to the winds. The people came, dressed in white for Maria Luisa, silent, respectful, tears on the faces of the women.

The drummers came, the three of them. They began to beat the drums, the big one booming, the middle one rapidly taking up the tempo, whipping the sounds into the night. The deeply purple night had come, not yet the black night. The fires sprang up against the darkness. The little drum came in with a fiery tattoo, urging the gods to come.

The candles on the altar had been lit. Liane stood up and took over to the altar a large jar of clay fired with blue and white lines that her mother had made. She bowed to the altar, bowed to her mother, then set the jar of sweet honey on the altar and backed from it to her seat again. A soft moaning arose from the women, chilling the blood, quickening the spirit.

The drums quickened, urgent. Come, come, come. A woman sprang into the lines drawn about the center pole, flung back her head, and danced about the pole. Papa Henri gestured and the woman bowed and backed away again. Still Liane gazed raptly at the altar, until the flickering of the candles seemed burned into her brain.

There must be a way, an answer. Come to me, come to me, she was saying silently to the *loa*. Come and answer, oh, I beg you. Come, spirit that my mother adored. Come and help me to avenge her. She adored you—oh, help me now to avenge her!

The boula drum was plaintive, rapidly beating. The man who beat the drum was old, but his hands flashed as rapidly as those of a young man as the spirits moved him. The drums boomed heavily, moaned, beckoned, piercing the wild sweet air of the island of desire.

At Cameron Hall, Donald Keller rose uneasily again from his chair in the comfortable drawing room. He had ordered the doors and gates of the great hall locked three days ago, and only he could allow them reopened. Giovanni Leoni had agreed with him nervously. Now the huge man got up from his armchair and moved to the window with Keller.

"What is it? Do you know?" he asked, the drink shaking in his huge fist as he thought that this vacation had turned into a nightmare.

Donald shook his head. "I don't know the drums.

The natives have all left us; only the chef is here. Might be a signal for attack. The guns are ready in Brian's study," he added in a lower tone.

"Mickey McCoy says that one of the women died. Maybe it's something for her," said Mrs. Leoni, brushing her hand over her eyes. None of them had slept much lately.

Astrid was drinking more heavily than Giovanni. "Damn him," she said thickly. "Going off to Miami without me, leaving me with those damn natives! I could kill him!"

Donald looked at her wordlessly. She was not very attractive tonight. Her dress open to her waist, she looked blowsy, red-faced as she gripped the thick glass of whiskey. Her hair hung down over her forehead, over her shoulder, and her lace sleeve was torn from her haste in dressing. He wondered when Brian would return.

The drums increased in tempo, subtly but definitely. Then there was a heart-stopping pause, and suddenly the drums were beating a rapid, heart-bursting tempo.

Liane was shaken. She jumped from her chair and leaped into the circle. She began to dance, beating her bare feet against the hard earth. She danced around and around the pole. Everything seemed blurred and shaking to her. The drums seemed to have picked her up and hurled her into the center of the *hounfor*. Someone else jumped up and followed her, an older woman, her screech echoing as she cried out.

Another followed, and another. Soon a dozen people were whirling and dancing in the center of the sacred place, dancing and waving their arms and screaming as the *loa* possessed them.

Pedro Ortega came in and leaned at the side of the room against an outside pole. He wore his red shirt, brilliant and brazen against their white. And with him came his evil god of war.

Liane felt it, she felt the shock of his impudence. He was evil, evil, and he brought the devil with him! She flung back her head, impotent, troubled, frantic. In her whirling she fell against the box that held Maria Luisa. Someone moaned aloud.

Liane turned, gripping the box, her hair falling over her face. Blindly she reached out, groped, and felt the chill flesh of her mother. Her fingers went lovingly over the still body, up to the face. The drums, pausing, sent the dancers spinning uncertainly to the ground. All waited, watching, mouths open.

Liane felt the face of her mother, the beloved features, frozen and locked in death. And as she felt, the spirit possessed her. She flung back her head. Face upraised, her black hair streaming down her back, she held one hand on her mother's face as the other arm stretched up high, higher, fingers reaching for the sky, for the god who might pity her.

She cried out, and her voice was the deep husky voice of Maria Luisa! Her companions trembled, and fell, and crawled away, yet remained close enough to hear. Papa Henri was shaking in his chair, his old eyes tragic. Auguste knelt near the altar, trembling, for this was beyond his experience.

She cried out, in the husky voice, "Oh, hear me, Erzulie, hear and avenge me! For evil was done to me, and I have been cut off from my dear ones! What have I done? Ay, ay, ay, what have I done, to be cut off too soon! Ah, too soon! Ay, ay, ay, it was an evil thing to do to me!"

"What was done? What was done?" came the mutters behind and about her. Liane did not hear, wrapped in her trance. She knew only that her beloved mother spoke through her; she felt her presence within her. She flung back her head and listened raptly for the voice to tell her what to do.

"Erzulie! Erzulie! I have served you as well as I could! Drink of the honey, taste of the white fowl!

I have invoked you all my life! Desert me not! Why was this evil done to me?"

At the doorpost, Pedro Ortega clutched at the wood, his fingers closed fiercely over the post. He longed to leap at Liane and silence her. He could catch her slim throat in his fingers and silence her forever. But he dared not go near her. They would tear him to pieces with no time lost. He could outrage them in many ways, but not like this, not here.

Still tenderly touching the cold face of her mother, still with her other hand upraised in the air, stretched, taut, supplicating, Liane cried out, "Erzulie! Maria Luisa is here! She begs for you to come—"

Another woman leaped into the center and cried out, and began speaking in the familiar way of Erzulie. Still another came, and danced. Many were possessed that night, and drank of the honey and ate of the chicken flesh, as Erzulie would have done.

Liane was content. She had made contact with her mother. The answer would come. She would know. She felt fierce inside—a fierce kind of waiting possessed her. The voodoo gods would tell her what to do. They had come tonight. They would comfort her, help her, inform her. She had reached them, as her mother had often done. They were beside her, within her, around her. They would help her. They too had loved Maria Luisa. Erzulie came, and Damballa, the snake god. A small snake crawled in on the floor and wound itself around the pole.

Papa Henri saw him first, and whispered in a hiss, "Damballa!" And all turned and were quiet, watching as the small snake wound itself around the pole, held up its head, and hissed. It was a sign, and they went into a frenzy.

There was much dancing, until some fell down exhausted. Papa Henri danced, possessed himself, crying out in the name of Damballa. Baron Samedi came also, with black death, singing his songs that made the women blush, as Auguste cried out and writhed with the *loa* that rode him around and around the pole.

It was dawn finally. Lightning cracked in the sky, and the dawn was a dark one. Thunder rumbled, echoing the drums as the exhausted drummers fell over on their instruments. It had been a meeting none of them would ever forget.

They carried the box to the small cemetery. Men fought for the privilege of carrying it, until Papa Henri told them which ones would carry, which would go ahead, and which behind. The women followed, mourning, carrying flowers. Two of the women supported the fainting Liane, who had eaten nothing for two days.

Torches lit their way through the dark brush. The dawn was not sunlit, it was gray, and the skies wept then, with the women who wept. Rain fell into the hole in the ground which had been dug the day before.

Oona had come, dressed in white, her merry face serious, her head bent. She had much sin on her, she thought, and her mind was whirling with it all.

Pedro Ortega came, but held back, his bright red shirt a mockery and a sign. He watched, but he flung no dirt to the grave. It was marked by many that he did not, and later there would be whispers.

Men set the lid on the coffin, and the tap-tap-tapping pounded on the brain of Liane. She flung herself at the box, and for the last time she embraced her mother, her Mamacita, and cried out her name. Then they held her back, with pity and compassion, and closed the lid over the serene cold face of Maria Luisa.

The box was slid into the grave. Papa Henri mumbled the words over the coffin and threw into the grave the first handful of dirt. Others came up, throwing the dirt, throwing the flowers, weeping into the grave as the rain ran down their cheeks. Rain soaked Liane, but she did not feel the chill. She sagged in the arms of a woman, half fainting now from the strain.

Auguste found a snake, cut it in half, and flung it into the grave. Then with a cry he jumped down and danced on the coffin, his long lean arms upflung. They stood respectfully, watching, waiting for him to be finished. He came up, his head hanging with exhaustion, and they filled the grave. It was done; she had been honored. Maria Luisa would not be forgotten.

Papa Henri stumbled to Liane. He passed his hand over her forehead tenderly and blessed her, his weary face crumpled and expressionless with fatigue.

"You will come and see me soon, Liane," he said.

She did not know his words. Nothing made any sense to her. The two women took her away and led her to the house, where she fell on a mat and lay there as though dead.

Yet she felt triumphant. The *loa* had come; all knew it. The *loa* would tell her what she wished to know. The gods would guide her. She had but to watch and wait and listen for the voices.

Pedro Ortega invited the tired men to his hut and gave them more drink. They talked of nothing but the ceremony, how *loa* had come, what they felt. They talked of who had done this to Maria Luisa, such a good one, such a wise one, how she had healed with herbs and her hands passing over one.

Pedro grew impatient with them as they fell down in a stupor of drink and exhaustion. He closed up the jugs of rum and carried the remainder away. They did not note his leaving. They slept heavily.

But he had plans to make. He had succeeded in blowing up the smelter. Next he would rip out the railroad tracks up the Mountain of the Cat to the mine. They were long and heavy; he would need help in this. He *must* make them follow him and obey him. He could not do it alone. He would blow up the entrance to the mine, close it off forever. They would approve of this, and they would follow him from then on.

His god was powerful, the god of war. Let them have white Erzulie, frail Erzulie, the eternal female. For Pedro Ortega, he would have power.

Nathaniel did not come to the ceremonies. He had meant to come, but he had met Astrid down by the beach in the afternoon, and she had let him swim with her. They had splashed in the water, and afterward on the beach, under the shade of the palms, he had taken her gently, reverently, smoothing her golden flesh with his hands. So white, so round, so different from himself, how beautiful she was!

Her fingernails scratched his back, and she cried out like a cat. Like a fierce jaguar did she make love with him. Ay, ay, it was good, better than Liane, though he did not want to think about her. That thought made him feel guilty and he wanted to feel good. He took the white woman again, and again she devoured him with her greedy red mouth, her long white arms. She left him weary.

At night he went to his hut and slept, waking only a little when the drums sounded again. He covered his head with a blanket, for he did not want to hear the drums. The drums tonight were not for him. He craved the white woman. She was a fire in his blood, in his loins. When he rested his brown body on hers, she would laugh up at him and encourage him to do things he had done with no woman in his life. It made him burn to think of the things he had done to her body, his mouth all over her, and her mouth on him.

He was on fire for her. Tomorrow he would see her again, and take her again. She loved him, he was sure of it. No woman would permit him to press his mouth where he had if she did not love. Even Liane had protected herself with her hand, and chided him. This woman stopped at nothing. He must have her again, and again.

Liane lay half sleeping on her mat, her thoughts concentrated on the ceremony. She had felt the *loa* riding her, her own precious *loa,* the *loa* of Maria Luisa. It must be good, for it had worked.

Briefly she thought of Nathaniel. He had not come. She felt sadness, loss. But it was burned out of her with the fire in her, the fire for revenge, for hate. Hate had burned out love. She must fulfill this hate before it also could be burned out.

Her fingers stretched out before her eyes could still feel the cold hardness of her mother's face. Death had come so swiftly. Death had come creeping in treacherously and snatched her mother away. A good woman, a wisewoman, all said so. Liane's long fingers closed slowly before her eyes. She would have the soul of Pedro Ortega between those fingers, and crush it—so!—before the hate could be burned out of her own soul. It must be done, and done soon. She would not rest in comfort and peace until that time.

The *loa* would help. They had promised. They had come to her.

Chapter 23

Brian had been at work all day. Silva had risen late, feeling weary, exhausted, troubled. Her body hurt. She bathed long in the tub, filling it a second time with hot water, and scrubbing tenderly where it hurt. How could he have done this to her? Was it what all men did?

Mrs. Bowles waited on her quietly, as though sensing her depression. She suggested that Silva put on the new green silk dress made in the Chinese fashion with loose waist, rounded high collar about her slim throat, and full sleeves. It felt comfortable. With it she wore only the green sandals, no hateful hot stockings.

When the time neared that Brian would come home, she grew trembling and afraid. She could not play the piano. She plucked at the lute, but the sounds meant nothing.

When her nerves were stretched to the breaking point, he came. The door slammed, and he spoke to Bowles in his usual growl and laughed. He came into the drawing room and bent over her at the couch. "Hello, honey, how are you?"

All as though nothing had changed between them!

He brushed a kiss on her forehead. She mumbled, "I'm all right."

"I'll change and come back. It was a busy day. I'll be glad to relax."

He went away and returned presently wearing a casual gray shirt with gray trousers, his dark hair still damp from the shower. He casually poured himself a drink from the whiskey bottle and added ice.

"Want something, darling?" He lifted his glass to her. She shook her head, meeting his eyes. They seemed darker, more intense, the blue rather indigo tonight.

He sat down in the big chair near the piano. "Come over here, Silva." It was quiet, but an order. She started.

Hesitantly she slid to her feet, padded over to him, and stood beside his chair. He put his fingers on her wrist gently, then drew her down to sit on his lap. She was stiff, apprehensive. He pulled her back so her head was on his shoulder. One hand gently smoothed back her loose hair.

"I've been thinking about the next few days, honey," he said presently. "We'll be going back to Desirée in about a week."

She felt a leap of pleasure and relief. She could talk to Maria Luisa, to Liane, take up some threads of her old life again.

"We'll have some more shopping to do. I'll take you out tomorrow morning to Madame's. I've told her what I want. Some warmer clothes for winter—some velvets—"

"For Desirée?" She sat up straight, alarmed.

"No, darling. We won't be long on Desirée, I've made up my mind. I'll get things going again, then we'll start off for New York and Europe. I mean to spend the winter abroad with you."

She gazed into his face with shock and fear. Alone—with him? No Maria Luisa, no Liane, no Tyrone—

"Tyrone is going to study hard," he said, as though reading her thoughts. "Julius will direct him. He'll catch up on his high-school studies, choose a college. We're going to roam Europe, end up in Italy by spring. And there Julius and Tyrone will come and join us. Will you like that?"

"By spring—" she whispered, her face paling. So

much could happen by spring. He was watching her keenly, the drink ignored on the table beside him.

"Yes, that will give us some time alone. Then we can show Tyrone around. Does he paint?"

She shook her head. "He—he likes music," she faltered.

"Good," said Brian briskly. "Plenty of music in Italy. We'll take in concerts and opera. You'll be able to tell him about opera by that time."

He kept on talking like that, so quickly she was bewildered. She was going to be separated from all those she loved. She was going to be alone with him —with this man who had hurt her so. How could she endure it?

He watched the changing expressions on her face. He seemed disappointed, but went on speaking until Bowles came to announce that dinner was ready. Silva picked at her dinner, mechanically. She dreaded going to bed tonight. All her innocence was gone, and she feared him now. He would not let her alone, she knew it. She dreaded the touch of his hands on her, the possessive grip of his hands, the fierceness of his eyes.

After dinner she played the piano for a long time. Brian was sitting at a desk, going over some papers. Presently he went to his study to talk into the black box, issuing crisp orders. She went on and on, not wanting to stop though her fingers were tired. When she went to bed, she could not rest, she thought. She would be hurt again.

But she could not remain up forever. Brian came back, yawning. "Time to turn in, honey. We'll have a full day tomorrow. I'm leaving you with Madame to be fitted for some winter clothes. I've made a list—"

She had to go to bed, pulling the white lace nightdress over her head with numb cold fingers. She slid into the big bed, pulled the sheet up, and lay like a figure on a tomb, motionless, until he came in. Her green eyes surveyed him over the edge of the white sheet.

He took off the dark red robe, revealing white pajamas underneath. He slid into bed and turned to her. She was stiff and cold, shaking with fright. He held her close to him, patting her back. "I'm sleepy, honey. How about you? Close your eyes, and get some sleep."

She closed her eyes, but could not sleep. She was waiting for him to attack her again. He brushed his lips against her cheek and murmured sleepily to her, "Kiss me, honey." His mouth pressed against hers, held there until her lips moved slowly in response.

Then he lay back, and seemed to go right to sleep. She could not believe it at first. She lay stiffly under his arm, hearing his even breathing beside her. His face seemed boyish now in the dim light. She studied it cautiously. Was he truly asleep?

His mouth was relaxed, its hard lines softened. A lock of black curls hung over his forehead. Gently she pressed it back. He stirred. She stopped her hand hastily. Whatever had she done that for? His flesh was warm, his cheeks rather scratchy until he shaved in the morning. How different men were from women! Sometimes she had slept in the night with Liane, curling up like two kittens together, for comfort on a cold night. Liane's flesh had been warm and soft. Brian's was hard and scratchy, and his body was lean and hard and long.

She closed her eyes, sighed in relaxation, and finally drifted off to sleep. She woke once in the night when he turned over and slung his arm across her. But he did not waken then.

She wakened to the sound of a husky masculine voice singing in the bathroom. She stirred, blinked, opened her eyes wide to the sunlight. She sat up. He had left her. It was daylight. She felt so relieved that when he came in, in his robe, she was able to smile at him shyly in response to his grin.

"Come on, kitten, get up. Rise and shine. We have much to do today. Wear that smart cream outfit, will you?" And he went away whistling to his own bedroom.

She hopped up gladly. The night was finished. Maybe the others would not be so bad. She bathed and dressed quickly, and came out for breakfast soon after Brian. He was reading the morning paper, and grunted when she said, "Good morning." Mrs. Bowles gave her a wink, and a shake of her head, as though to say men were like that.

When Brian finally tossed away the paper, there was a frown on his face.

"Is anything—wrong?" Silva asked timidly.

"Oh, some damn mining engineers got Bolivia all screwed up," he said, and she did not understand. "They have to improve their agriculture first," he began. She listened carefully to his explanation, resolving to read the paper more often. Evidently it told him things. Previously she had found little of interest in it.

Brian grew more cheerful as he ate. He was evidently thinking over plans for the day. She ventured to ask him, "Must I stay at the dress shop all day, Brian? Could I not go to an art gallery? Perhaps Mr. Payne would come, and Tyrone."

He gave her a quick thoughtful look. "Hm. I'll think about it. Tell you what—I'll leave you at Madame's this morning, pick you up for lunch, and this afternoon we'll have fun. Okay?"

"Okay," she agreed soberly, not knowing what he meant by fun.

"There now, you ought to take the girl out more," dared Mrs. Bowles. "A pretty girl like that, she ought to go dancing."

"Dancing? What is that?" murmured Silva, thinking of the voodoo ceremonies. She recalled a book she had read once where the main character had been given a ball on her eighteenth birthday, and had danced with the prince charming.

"Mrs. Bowles, you are a genius," said Brian solemnly, a twinkle in his blue eyes. "Silva, we'll go dancing tonight."

"Oh, but I don't know how!" she cried, in a panic.

"I'll teach you," he said.

Mrs. Bowles laughed, and patted Silva's fair head reassuringly. "There now, dear, you'll enjoy that. You have such music in you." She brought them more coffee and a pot of marmalade.

They arrived at Madame's shop as the blinds were drawn back, and Madame herself was just arriving in a sleek red automobile. She exclaimed on seeing them. "*Alors,* you are so early! Never were the society so early!"

"We are not society," Brian assured her. "We are business people. I am a tycoon, as you said behind my back, Madame!" He laughed at her vivid blush.

"There, you are a naughty boy," Madame said, surprised at herself. "Come, Mrs. Cameron, we look at the new gowns ready for you."

Silva did not recognize herself as Mrs. Cameron until Brian gave her a gentle nudge forward. The gowns were beautiful—of deep green velvet edged with flowered embroidery, a white satin with spangles on it, a low-necked loose gown of gray crepe de Chine trimmed with a narrow band of gray fur. There was a pretty tailored suit of golden-brown velvet, with the long tunic embroidered in gold, and a matching close-fitting cloche.

"Very good," said Brian with satisfaction. He went flipping through the dresses on the racks nearby, looking for more.

Silva wanted to say, "This is enough, this is enough!" But he would not listen to her.

She put on dresses and smart long-toed shoes that hurt her feet a little. And she put on hats and scarves, and was draped in an evening gown of black patterned lace over black satin which made her look older and more serious. Brian had lingered, seeming to enjoy the show. He sent to the jewelry shop next door, and delighted in hanging about her some of the pretty baubles from the trays the men in gray suits brought over. Long strands of pearls, earrings of jet, bracelets of gold that jangled on her wrists, then a dazzling set of diamonds that made Madame gasp.

The more excited Madame became, the more French she spoke, and the more wary the girls were of her. They scampered to bring her scarves, hats, shoes, stockings. Brian watched all with enjoyment.

A girl whispered in Madame's ear. "You have ze telephone call, *monsieur,*" announced Madame tragically.

"God," Brian groaned, and got up to go to her office. "Continue, please, Madame. Look around, Silva. Get whatever you want."

She was wearing a long gown of silver tulle, which floated about her. When he said this, she went to the rack where she had spied something. Wistfully she fingered the vivid blue dress she could picture so well on Liane. It would bring out the blue in her glossy dark hair, and she adored that color.

"That color—she is not for you, Madame Cameron," said Madame gently.

"No, I—I wanted it for a friend," murmured Silva wistfully. She touched another dress, of bright gold, simply made in the full feminine style Madame liked. "This also— Oh, if I could—"

"We will ask Monsieur Cameron," said Madame.

Brian returned, frowning. "I'll have to get to the office. You go on, Silva. Madame, you will take care of her. My man will wait outside. Silva, you are not to go outdoors at all! Understand? Not at all. Wait here until I come back."

"She wishes the dresses for a friend," announced Madame hastily. "If you approve, *monsieur*—?"

"What—what is it, Silva?" He looked at the bright blue dress, guessed instantly. "For Liane? Of course—get several things. Get some dresses for Maria Luisa also. And some beads—whatever you want. You know her size?"

Liane would be so happy! Silva smiled and nodded. Brian touched her forehead with his lips, and was gone. Madame sighed with satisfaction and turned back to Silva.

"Now, your friend, she is about your size, perhaps?"

"Yes, my height, only she is more full—here—" Silva indicated her bust earnestly. "I can wear her dresses, but she cannot wear mine."

"Um, slim of waist? Yes, bring the twelve in this," Madame ordered one of the girls. They went dashing about, and brought the brilliant blue crepe dress, and the gold one, and another beauty in a flowered pattern that Liane would adore.

It was more difficult finding something for Maria Luisa. Madame finally suggested choosing some lengths of fabric and letting her make them up. Silva fingered a number of them, finally settling on three, then with a feeling of satisfaction turned to choosing gold bracelets for Liane, and a strand of pretty blue beads, and some dangling earrings that would make Oona rage with jealousy.

When Brian had not returned by one o'clock, Madame had lunch brought on a tray for Silva, and they went on fitting and choosing, with suggestions by Madame. It seemed that Brian had left a long list of garments.

There was a fur coat of a soft silky material the woman called mink and lifted reverently to put on Silva. With it was a little mink hat fitting closely on her head. And there was a long black velvet opera cloak with a lining of white silk and a hood to fit over her hair. Madame explained about opera and how the ladies dressed up for it. When Silva asked her about the music, Madame expounded happily on the joys of the music of opera, until Silva's head was filled with gold lamé, and tragedies of women stabbing themselves on stage, and songs that went on for fifteen minutes, and a full orchestra, and how the ladies stared at each other through their opera glasses. Madame added a pretty pair of golden opera glasses from the jeweler's for Silva, and a black velvet opera purse to carry them in.

Brian finally returned at about three o'clock, looking tired and grim. Madame promised to send all to him at the apartment, most quickly, and to finish making up the other clothes he had requested. Brian glanced over Silva critically, as though she were a model he would approve or disapprove. She had the feeling she was a toy or a pet, on whom he would hang dresses and jewels, would display on certain occasions, would pick up—or set down and forget—as the mood took him. He was silent, driving, with Antonio in the back seat of the car for a change.

They slid to a stop about two miles away. Brian halted the car, and Antonio jumped out to open the door for Silva, looking about, his hand on his cream-colored pocket. He never said much; he looked about with his intelligent black eyes and seemed to see everything on the street. Brian looked past him, and Silva did also, to see two others of Brian's men sliding to a stop in their car. Antonio followed them into the great pillared building.

Then, to Silva's delight, she saw it must be a museum. She had heard about them, but had not thought to see one. She went, enchanted, from one painting to another, to gaze wide-eyed at works of Renoir, Bellini, Rubens, Van Gogh, and others she had seen only in books. She clasped her hands in their little gloves tightly together in delight, gasping at the marvelous colors. Brian solemnly followed her, not speaking unless she asked a question. His eyes were as keen as hers on the paintings, and he seemed to know quite a bit about them.

They walked and walked, until they came to an inner patio, where a fountain rippled quietly over a dolphin and a boy, and flowers of crimson and gold were set about, and some white-painted metal chairs. They sat down, in silence, gazing with relief at the beauty of nature after the beauties of the paintings.

Brian seemed to understand her mood. She was thinking how little she knew, how much more she could do. Seeing the marvelous paintings, the gloss of the colors, the contrast of vivid blue and flaming scarlet next to each other, the softness of the effect of light in Renoir and Manet—her mind was in a whirl.

Finally Brian spoke, in the peace of the mellow afternoon. "There is much more to see, Silva, but I think we'll save some for another day. There are galleries of Greek and Roman figures, masterpieces from the Middle Ages, stained-glass windows, but it would only bewilder you more. Let's go home, you get some rest, and tonight we'll go dancing. Okay?"

His smile was boyish and direct, his vivid blue eyes glinting in the sunlight. She smiled shyly back at him, and slipped her fingers into his hand and squeezed it impulsively. "Thank you, Brian. Thank you so very much."

He gave her hand a squeeze in return. "Glad you liked it. There'll be more this winter. You will love London, Paris, and Italy even more. But this is a taste of what we will see together."

She had that to think about as she lay down in her bedroom that late afternoon. She could not sleep. The colors and shapes of the figures in the paintings were swimming around in her mind. So much beauty. How had she ever dared to paint? How could she have the confidence to ever paint again, after seeing the works of the masters? She felt humbled and excited, all at once.

And Brian had said they would see much more this winter. Could so much beauty exist in the world?

It must, for he had seen it, and he would show it to her. Finally she began to look forward to going off with him alone. He was so understanding when he wanted to be.

She must have fallen into a light sleep, for she wakened to find Brian in the bedroom. He was sitting on the edge of the bed, watching her. She had the impression of warmth on her face, of lips that had touched hers. He smiled down at her.

"Sleeping Beauty," he teased. "Aren't you ever going to wake up? I came home early to take you dining and dancing!"

"Oh," she sat up with a start, clutching her robe about her. She blinked at him, and he ran a finger down her warm cheek. "Did you—did you get your work done?"

He grimaced. "It is never done. But I have stopped for today. I told Mrs. Bowles to lay out the short silver dress with the beaded top. That is correct for dancing. And the silver slippers. And wear the little white fur jacket—it is getting cooler."

He lifted her hand and pressed his lips lightly against the pulse in her wrist. She watched him gravely. "I wish to—to thank you, Brian, for the dresses for Liane, and for the—the time to go to the art museum today. I know you are very busy."

"Never too busy for you, honey," he said lightly, and smiled more gently down at her. "Mrs. Bowles will pack for you when we get ready to leave. Be sure to tell her to include the dresses for Liane. We'll be leaving the fur coats and all that here in Miami, to pick up on our way out."

"And shall we—see many more beautiful paintings in Europe?" she queried, her eyes glowing. "I have so many ideas, Brian. I want to change my paintings—to make more use of color and light, if I can."

"We'll see thousands of paintings," he told her calmly. "Julius will talk to you about techniques of painting. He is anxious to come with us, by the way. He wants to paint you before long."

"On Desirée," she said, with a little sigh of hope. Things were going better than she had feared they would.

"Right, on Desirée." He got up and left her to dress. Mrs. Bowles came in and helped her get into the wisps of underclothing, the slim sliver of shining dress that came only just below her knees. Mrs. Bowles fastened her hair in braids, then bound them around her small head—to keep them out of her way while dancing, she said.

Brian was dressed up also, she found when she came out. He had put on a suit of cocoa-brown and a cream silk shirt with a golden-brown bow tie. He seemed to approve of her. They set out gaily. Antonio drove them, though, and Silva, aware of his presence, was a little worried. Would Brian be shot at again?

They drew up in front of a smart restaurant with red and gold awnings. Inside, the head waiter showed them to a small table in a private corner, and three waiters lingered around them. One brought chilled white wine that sparkled—champagne, said Brian. Another brought a tray of appetizers. Silva bravely tackled the detested caviar and found it almost pleasant this time. Brian gave her a nod of approval. The little pastries filled with meat and rice were delicious and spicy.

By the time she had eaten half of her breast of chicken, creamed on a bed of asparagus, and a crisp green salad with hot Italian bread, she was feeling relaxed and happy. Perhaps it was the wine, zinging pleasantly in her head, making her just a little dizzy. Perhaps it was the approval in Brian's blue eyes, the smile of his mouth, the way his hand held hers between courses, his thumb caressing the back of her hand.

The music was playing softly in the background.

More couples came in, and Silva's eyes widened at the dresses of the ladies. Some were very short, with hems that looked like points and zigzags. And their hair was short, bobbed in brisk little curls, and their eyes sparkled, and their fingers snapped in time to the music. She watched them dancing, and thought she never in the world could do that bouncing about.

Then Brian was standing, drawing back her chair. "Time for a lesson, darling," he said in her ear as she stood up. "First thing is to relax in my arms and let me guide you around the floor. Let your feet move as you wish—I'll direct you."

He made it sound so easy, but it was not. She was stiff, afraid of stepping on his feet. He coaxed her, bullied her, encouraged her, and finally she closed her eyes in desperation and let him guide her around, her feet following automatically. And suddenly she felt the music whirling her around, as the drums did in the voodoo ceremonies, and it became easier. "Good girl," said Brian, and kissed her ear.

The music throbbed in her, it seemed a part of her. Brian said, "This is the waltz. You just go one, *two,* three, one, *two,* three, and sway with me." Away they went! Silva felt a delicious thrill at the movement and she gazed up at him with shining eyes. He grinned down at her, and drew her closer to him.

When she had learned the waltz, he motioned to the orchestra, and evidently they listened to what he wanted. "We're going to try a tango now," said Brian.

"What is a tango?"

"You'll see right now." He drew her into another position, so she was stiffly against him, his arm circling her closely. It was another series of movements, and she felt very awkward, especially when he held her so tightly that she could not breathe! He turned her in quick little movements, and sometimes she stumbled, but he kept encouraging her.

They finally returned to their seats. She was breathless, laughing aloud at her excitement, her cheeks rosy with the effort. "Oh, did I do so badly, Brian?" she pleaded, eyes shining.

"You did beautifully, honey. You're a born dancer. A few more lessons and we'll show them how it's done." He poured more champagne into her glass. She drank it thirstily, and her head swam all the more.

It was a lovely, strange evening. They finally went home at two in the morning, creeping in, Silva's shoes in her hand because her feet hurt her. They giggled in the hallway as Brian teased her about not waking up Bowles. She managed to get to her bedroom, take off her clothes, put on her nightdress, and wash off the light makeup around her eyes which Mrs. Bowles had showed her how to apply. Then she fell into bed.

Brian came to her room when she was settled. He did not turn on the light, just took off his robe and slid into bed with her. He drew her to him, and she found he was naked.

Her head was dizzy with the wine and the dancing. She could not think, and she did not want to fight. Emotions boiled through her, and she felt soft and weak. When he pulled her close and stroked one hand gently over her shoulder and arm, she put her hands on his lean shoulders.

"Ah, darling," he whispered, and kissed her ear and her neck, nuzzling against her soft skin. "You please me so much."

She felt strangely lighthearted and happy at his praise. Her fingers stroked slowly, timidly, over his hard shoulders. He felt so tough, so masculine. His skin was not like hers, not soft and silky, but rough and hard-muscled. She pressed her palm against his chest, her fingers tangled in the thick mat of hair as he bent over her.

He made an inarticulate sound in his throat. Silva sighed and closed her eyes as he kissed her breasts, the taut nipples, the soft flesh of her waist. She felt—oh, odd—dizzy, light as air, like a bubble blown by the wind, with colors sparkling in the sunlight. She had some power over him, she was beginning to realize. When she yielded to him, and touched his shoulders, and did not fight, he seemed to become very emotional and excited, breathing hard. He was that way now.

Made bolder by the wine, which seemed to make her feel melted and floating, she put her arms about him as her belly seemed heated and her thighs soft. He came over her, bending as he had that first night. She felt a vague sense of fear, but was too dazed to resist.

Silva's palms stroked over his back. He was pressing hard, sweet kisses on her breasts, and they felt swollen in his lips. He nibbled and pulled at her breasts. All the time she felt more hot, and the blood seemed to race through her.

She kissed the shoulder near her lips, and that seemed to set him off. He pressed hard on her, and again that hardness hurt her—but only for a few moments. She felt soft for him, and her limbs moved as he wished. He held one thigh in his hand and stroked her, and murmured to her.

"That's it—oh, my love—let me again—darling—lift up. Oh, sweet—lift up and let me—there—there—"

He gasped, and she felt him rubbing against her. Little sparks seemed to be let off in her, like the phosphorescent fish at night, sparkling in the ocean. She gripped his back, clasping him close in her arms. She was slipping away, somewhere, to a place of strange enchantment, bound up in his arms.

She felt faint at the wild whirling of her mind, the racing blood of her body. Was it the wine? Or was it Brian, so big and solid and firm?

He drew off, and pulled up the sheet over them both. He was shaking, trembling as he relaxed. She fell asleep on his firm shoulder, feeling his fingers stroking through her silvery hair.

She slept hard, dreamlessly, for a long time. When she wakened, the sunlight streamed across the bed from a high angle. She felt her head—it ached. Oh, dear, she had had too much of that delicious champagne. But she had been with Brian, and he had not hurt her. She felt quite contented when she went to take her bath, smiling a little.

Mrs. Bowles came in with a hot cup of coffee while she dressed. "Mr. Cameron will be coming to take you for a drive later this afternoon," she said comfortably. "And how did you like dancing?"

Silva whirled about the room in her bare feet, showing how she had waltzed. "One, *two,* three, and one, *two,* three—oh how I waltzed!" she laughed, her cheeks dimpling. "Oh, it was such fun!"

"There now, I knew you would like it," said Mrs. Bowles, smiling at her affectionately. "I think the silver suit today with the black trim—that is smart." And she laid it out with the silver slippers.

Silva waited happily for Brian. When he came, he looked tired, and her heart lurched. She looked anxiously at him. "You are—very tired," she said slowly. "Would you rather not go out?"

"No, I must get out, get some air," he growled wearily, and rubbed his hand hard on the back of his neck as he sat in his favorite large chair. Impulsively she got up and came around behind him.

"Let me rub your head. I think I can help," she said shyly, and timidly put her hands on his forehead. She swept deftly down over the forehead, over the temples, massaging with a hard, sure touch, down to the back of his neck—then back up again, in a slow sweeping motion, rubbing soothingly. She felt him relax in surprise at her touch. He bent his head forward, and she rubbed his neck with her small strong fingers, then pressed her thumbs over and over on the top of his spine.

"Ah, that's great, honey. Go on for a minute."

She went on, smiling at Bowles as he looked at her

in surprise. He had brought in some black coffee, which he set down beside Brian. Brian drank some, then begged for more. Silva, happy to be of some use once more after days of being nothing but a pet, rubbed his forehead, his temples, down to his neck and up again.

"You're a doll," said Brian. "Oh, you're a very doll. That feels marvelous." He shook himself like a great dog and reached out a lean arm to bring her around to sit on his knees while he finished his coffee. "And what did you do today?"

"I slept," she said ruefully. "What was the name of that thing I drank?"

"Champagne," he grinned. He drew her head down to his shoulder, gave her a hug and kiss, then stood her up again. "Okay, we're off."

He was never idle for long. They went for a long drive, which ended up at the house of some friends of his. They had dinner with them, as the hostess begged them to do. Brian and the other man discussed business over drinks in the corner, while the hostess politely quizzed Silva on who she was and where she had come from. She was nice, but Silva felt odd.

They went for another drive the next day, ending up at a sunswept beach. Madame had furnished Silva with several bathing suits, which felt odd on her after bathing naked in her lagoon. Brian came out in a pair of vivid blue trunks that left his long, bronzed legs bare. They were covered with black hairs, like his bronzed chest. She was embarrassed to look at him.

He took her into the water, slowly at first, for this was ocean water, with tides and unexpected waves foaming in white crests to topple her over. No sheltered lagoon this, but the Atlantic Ocean. She gasped again and again as a wave toppled her, but she came up again and wiped her face. She wore a funny little flowered cap on her head. Madame had said it was the thing to wear, and it matched her flowered green suit. She flinched sometimes at the way Brian gazed down at her, making her shy.

But he was kind. He took her to beaches, to more art galleries. There were more intimate evenings in nightclubs, with elaborate dinners, champagne or sparkling white wines for her and red for Brian, and then dancing. He taught her all the fashionable dances and was satisfied with her; he said she learned rapidly.

He even took her to his office one day. They had come back early from a ride out to see houses, though he only slowed, gazed critically, shook his head, and drove on. As they parked at his huge white office building in downtown Miami, Antonio came at once to the door of the car.

There were the usual men at the doors of the buildings, the usual quick, alert looks about. Silva was almost accustomed to this, but not quite. It made her skin prickle to see how they watched and looked about.

They rode up in an elevator, and Brian held her hand when she gasped at the speed of it. He gave her a wink, but he was not laughing at her, this time, she was relieved to see. She hated it when he laughed at her—it made her feel like a pet dog.

She was wearing a sleek white suit today, with a blouse of shell pink and a scarf of deeper pink tying back her hair. Her shoes were deep pink, and so was her handbag. She felt people staring at her as they went into the huge suite of his offices on the top floor of the building.

Brian released her hand casually. "Honey, sit down, read a magazine. I'll try not to be long." He went over to a desk and spoke briskly to a girl with scarlet lips, black hair, and languishing eyes with dark makeup around them. She got up quickly, went to a cabinet, and took out a file. He nodded, then went into his office and shut the door.

Silva looked at the magazines on the glass-topped

table near where she sat on a gray sofa. They all seemed to be about oil, gas, minerals, mining, and business. The red-lipped girl came over to her, smiling in a friendly fashion.

"Mrs. Cameron? Would you rather look at these?" She handed Silva several fashion magazines.

"Oh—thank you very much." Her voice seemed swallowed up in the plush velvety office. She bent her head over the magazines, turning the pages slowly. She recognized one dress that Madame had chosen for her, and studied it intently. It looked odd to see it on a slim tall model with a disdainful expression on her tilted head.

Men came in and spoke to the red-lipped secretary. She let one man into the office, and the others waited. Antonio lounged near her desk, his eyes everywhere and nowhere. The men shuffled their feet, pretended to look into briefcases, picked up mineral magazines, and made some show of reading them.

Brian came out and spoke to his secretary. "Yes, sir, at once," she said, and picked up the telephone on her desk and spoke into it. Brian left the door open. "New York on the line, sir!" she called to him, and inside his office Silva could see him picking up the telephone there.

The men got even more restless, but said nothing. Brian spoke for fifteen minutes on the telephone, Silva knew by the little gold watch Brian had clasped on her wrist yesterday. She had learned how to wind it, and he set it for her. It told time, he said. She thought of the island, where these times did not matter and no one had watches or clocks.

Brian came out of his office and studied the men. They all stood up alertly, eagerly. He nodded to one curtly, then turned back into his office. The man almost ran in, scurrying in the way people followed Brian's orders, with respect and almost—fear.

Silva turned the magazine page unseeingly. It was strange how they treated him. Everyone ran to do his orders. Antonio still leaned against the wall, not smoking, not moving, watching.

The secretary tapped on the door again. Brian called to her to come in. "New York again, sir," she said softly.

"Right. Put them on."

The door closed. Silva waited, fascinated now by the little drama of all those men straining to know what was going on, by Antonio who watched without seeming to watch, by the secretary who tap-tapped at a typewriter and made black reading marks on a page, and answered the telephone quickly, and put people on the line or told them Mr. Cameron could not be disturbed today.

Brian came out again, and the man with him left, looking a little shaky, a little furtive, creeping out. Antonio did look at him then, sharply. Brian came over to the other men.

"I'm sorry, gentlemen, no more time today. Let my secretary have copies of your proposals, and I'll try to get them read in another two days. That's all."

He came to Silva, took her arm, and left with her. They went down to the street with Antonio in the elevator with them. Silva wondered why he had sent the one man away, why he would not talk to the others. It was all beyond her. When people called on Maria Luisa, she served them coffee and listened to them.

Life in Miami was so much different from life on Desirée, she thought. Would she ever become accustomed to it? And Brian Cameron was an important man. That worried her.

Why had he married her? She was young and stupid; she knew nothing of his business, could not help him as his efficient secretary did. She was not smartly dressed with bobbed hair, like that Crystal, though somehow she did not like to think of Brian married to one like Crystal, who was as hard as her name.

"What are you thinking, darling?" In the back seat Brian put his arm casually about her waist.

"About those men, waiting all day to see you," she said slowly.

He gave a quick look down at her hair. "Oh, they want me to spend money on their projects. Most aren't worth working on," he said lightly. He ruffled her hair under the pink scarf. "You look about fifteen today. Are you sure you are eighteen?"

"I wondered also," she said deliberately, "why you married me and not one of those—those ladies who are smart, and know how to dance already. One of those—" She nodded to the smart women clustered on the street corner waiting for the light to change.

"Because I wanted to marry you, that's why," he said. "And I'm not going to discuss it in the car with Antonio listening!"

Antonio moved his shoulders, and a little red came into his neck. Silva was embarrassed also, as Brian was laughing at her.

She felt like a stranger in a strange land. Brian answered only those questions he chose to answer, and he explained only what he wished. She felt so bewildered, so confused. Would she ever learn?

And would Brian wish to continue to be married to her? Or would he discard her when he wearied of her? Then what would she do? She depended on him here. Back on Desirée, she knew her way about. Perhaps he would one day let her return to Desirée alone, and to the life she wanted.

Stranger yet, that the thought brought her no pleasure. She had tasted strange fruits, and longed for more. There was some odd security in the firmness of his arm about her waist. She had become accustomed to his touching her, holding her hand. What would she do when there was no Brian to touch her, to laugh into her eyes, to tease her?

She thought of their embrace the first night she had gone dancing. Her mind had been blurred by the champagne, but she still blushed to think how she had responded to him. She remembered his lips on her body, his mouth pressed urgently to hers, his hands possessively learning every bit of her.

Sometimes she daydreamed, idly plucking her lute, remembering the hardness of his shoulders under her fingers, the strange excitement in her body as he held her. It was more difficult to paint now. She would find herself staring blankly at a canvas, paintbrush in hand, thinking of Brian, the way he had kissed her, touched her, wanted her.

Was this what it was to be married? The mind and will gradually absorbed into that of another? Nothing clear but the touch of a lean dark hand, the memory of a night, the recalled pressure of a hard body on her softness?

She felt as though she were in a net, struggling like a fish, her golden body straining against the silken cords that closed more tightly about her each day and night. She was not Silva anymore, not just Silva, the girl. She was a woman, afraid, full of new desires that yet frightened her.

Chapter 24

For once, they stayed home that evening. Silva was quite content to do that. She changed to the peach Oriental outfit and her soft green sandals, and came to the living room before Brian. She curled into her favorite corner of the sofa and gazed out the immense windows to the scenes which never failed to fascinate her: great white Miami and the blue seas beyond. Bowles had not yet drawn the draperies.

Brian came in, ruffled her hair lightly, and got himself a drink. "How about a small one for you? With lime juice?" he asked.

She surprised herself. "Yes, please, just a small one." She accepted the glass and tasted it. She was becoming accustomed to the strange taste of rum in fruit juice.

He sat down in his big chair, stretched out, and began talking. It seemed that he was divesting himself of a mine in Peru, and selling out there. She listened intently, trying to understand everything intelligently.

"I want to get some things cleared up," he was saying. "I've worked hard for years. Now I want some fun. The business can run itself for a time, and with the telephone I can keep in contact with my various managers."

She wondered if that meant he would stop mining the sacred mountain on her island, but dared not ask. She was afraid of his scowl and his temper, though he had shown her little of that side of him lately.

But she had heard him roar at people, and she did not want him to roar at her again.

They went in to dinner, and she managed to eat well of Mrs. Bowles's delicious cooking, tonight some cream soup, then tender slices of veal laid on white rice with mushrooms and raisins mixed in. For dessert there was fruit in a compote and a crisp thick almond cookie. They took their coffee to the living room, and Brian continued to talk, almost absently, as though explaining things to himself.

He talked about weeks and years he had spent in the mountains in South and Central America, following his mining interests. He talked about living in the Far West, in Texas and New Mexico, of a winter spent in the mountains above the snow line, of trapping and fishing and hunting. It had been strange to return to college after that, he said, but he felt as though he knew then what he wanted to do. He had helped his father in business until the death of his father. He told her about that, curtly, as though the memory still hurt, of how his father has died of cancer.

His mother had died many years before. He scarcely remembered her, just dimly as a dark-haired feminine presence with a gentle voice and a hand on his head in the darkness.

"Father worshiped her. He never looked at another woman, though there were plenty to throw themselves at him as he got more wealthy," said Brian with a laugh that vaguely hurt her. She looked down into her empty coffee cup, set it aside carefully. She knew there were women like that. Oona was like that, going from man to man, depending on who offered her a silver bracelet. Did Brian think of Silva like that?

Was this why he bought her presents all the time, tossing jewels at her, dressing her like a doll? Did he think that was what she wanted? She could have told him otherwise; she had tried to tell him that all she wanted was to be on her island, free and unhampered by anyone. She had begged for her own dresses, her own sandals.

"Play to me," said Brian, with a sigh, and she picked up the lute and plucked at it vaguely, until a melody came to her. She bent her silvery head over it, and played and sang softly, the songs of the island, songs her mother had taught her in England, mixing, weaving them, as her fancy directed. He lay back in his chair, his eyes half closed, though she was conscious that he watched her.

Presently they retired for the night, and she stood at the window in her white nightdress, the lights out, gazing at the lights of the city glittering below her. They were up so high! White lights blossomed all over the city in patterns like stars, one building wearing a coronet about its head. Out on the water, ships were outlined in lights, some red and green, some white. At night she could almost love the city, with its ugliness and dirt hidden, only lights outlining it and making it beautiful. Stars twinkled less brightly than over her island. Against the black velvet of the sky there on Desirée, the darkness made them prickle like the brilliant diamonds in her new bracelet. Here they were blurred a little by the lights of the city.

Brian came up behind her, slipped his arms about her, and drew her back against his hard body. "What are you thinking?" he asked softly, against her ear.

"About the stars and the lights," she said.

"We'll soon be going on one of those ships, back to Desirée. Then another much larger ship to Europe," he murmured. "I think you will love it, all the new and fascinating things to see. You'll bring your sketch pad with you, and pencils. We can buy canvases and paints for you as we go, and leave the paintings with friends. Shall you like that?" He kept urging her to express what she felt, but she still felt reserved and uncertain with him.

"I—I expect it will be—very strange," she finally

said. He gave an impatient sigh and drew her over to the bed. She slid between the sheets and lay back. He took off his robe and lay down with her, reaching for her, and suddenly, warily, she felt an urgency about him that had been absent for a time.

He put his arms about her and drew her to him in the bed. He was not wearing the pajamas tonight. She felt his naked body next to her silken-clad one. He stroked his big hands over her shoulders and arms, clasped his hand about her neck, and drew her close, pressing a kiss on her mouth.

His lips pressed hard, urgently. She kept her lips shut tightly, a little frightened. She wished he would not do this! Yet he had been kind this week, and thoughtful, taking her about on drives, telling her things, showing her the art galleries, teaching her patiently to swim in the ocean and to dance. Perhaps if she had had champagne tonight, she would feel more relaxed.

She sighed a little as his lips left hers to seek the warm hollows of her throat and neck. He brushed his lips over and over the velvety skin. She reached out shyly, curiously, and felt the thick dark curls of his head under her fingers as he bent over her. She had been looking at his hair this week, ever since she had rubbed his forehead for him. His hair was thick and springy, not like hers, which was light and inclined to be fluffy and fine spun. She felt his curls, then pressed her hand to the back of his neck.

He muffled an endearment into her throat. "Oh, pretty, sweet darling," he whispered. "Oh, honey—love—"

Gently he drew back the strap of her nightdress, pressed his lips to the slight rounded breast. She felt warm finally, not tense, and somehow not so frightened. He kept on kissing her, down over her breasts. He took a taut pink nipple between his lips and pulled carefully on it. She felt a warmth stealing through her body, a little fire starting somewhere.

When he drew off the nightdress, she knew what he meant to do. She was a little scared yet, still remembering that he had hurt her the first night. But surely it could never be so bad again? Mrs. Bowles had talked to her one day, and Silva had managed to ask her a few questions, flushing hotly. Mrs. Bowles had been so nice, just like a mother.

Brian's big hand went up and down over her naked thigh. It was a very sure, caressing hand, very confident, like himself. He was very sure of himself, she thought. Probably he got his own way most of the time, that was why. Or did he? Sometimes he looked tired and cross, or upset, or his mouth went down in a cynical way. Maybe he didn't get his own way always. And he must have missed his mother. She had had Maria Luisa, but Brian had had no one.

Somehow that made her feel different toward him. No one had tucked him into bed at night. No one had soothed his childish hurts; his father had bandaged him briskly and told him to act like a man, Brian had said with a laugh, but she had seen the darkening of his vivid blue eyes when he said it. Silva's hand went gently over his lean back, felt the muscular whipcord strength of it, as she thought of him as a little boy. Maybe—maybe one day she would have *his* little boy, a baby, and could give him the love Brian had not had for himself. And Brian would share in it, and his mouth would be more happy.

Brian leaned over her ardently, and brought them together. She held her breath anxiously when he entered her, but he was slow and careful, and his hands kept caressing her. He whispered precious love words to her. She put her arms about him as he directed her to do, and her hands slid over and over his back and his hard shoulders, and her lips rested against his crisp hair. She felt a hotter fire in herself, and things seemed to blur a little as he moved. She caught her breath in a gasp, then another, holding him more tightly with desperate fingers as he moved swiftly.

When it was over, he lay back, and drew her to him. He was out of breath also, as though he had been running hard. She lay with her head on his shoulder and felt him caressing her head and her shoulders. She did not want to pull away at all. Somehow she felt happy inside that he was happy. She had made him happy.

That was important, she told herself sleepily. She wanted to make Brian happy. It was very important —because—he wasn't often happy—and he was kind and good to her—and he had been unhappy as a child—

She fell asleep against him, snuggling to him with her hand on his broad chest. She could feel the hairs on his chest under her fingers. Odd—how different men were from women—

She wakened briefly when he got up in the morning. "Go back to sleepyland, Silva," he said on a breath of laughter, kissing her cheek. "I'm off to work —see you at noon. We'll go out riding, look at houses. Okay?"

"Okay," she nodded, into the pillow. Then she remembered the shots, and how Antonio always was looking around. "Be careful, Brian," she murmured.

"Hm?" But she was asleep again.

When she got up, she hummed happily in the bath, and put on a loose cotton shift and sandals. She was early; she had time to paint this morning. She ate hastily, then went to the room where she worked, and managed to put in two good hours of painting. She was working on a scene of a ghost ship that her father had told her about. It was a misty ship, wrecked on a sandbar, and all about it had grown up corals of reds and soft pinks, and barnacles had fastened themselves to it. She drew about it curious fish swimming in and out, large strange objects of brilliant hue. And the waters were greeny-blue, the deep blue of Liane's dress. It was coming along well, and she hated to stop.

But she stopped in time to dress in the green linen suit with the matching pale green blouse. With it she would wear the green linen hat and green sandals.

Brian was late again, lines about his mouth. But he kissed her, smiled, and ate a good lunch. Afterward they went out looking at houses, but not stopping to look inside them. "No hurry," said Brian. They stopped at Amy Hartman's house, and she was pleased, and fixed tea for them and talked heartily about houses.

Silva liked her more all the time. She had no pretensions about her—she showed her feelings, she showed off the pictures of her grown children, and she bragged that one would have a child soon, making her a grandmother. She was very nice.

"I do hope we can find as nice a house as yours, Mrs. Hartman," Silva told her shyly.

"Oh, Lord, Brian will never be satisfied with anything so small," she said with a cheerful laugh. "Bill is looking at something with thirty rooms and a pool as big as the ocean, Brian. He'll be calling you."

Silva was appalled. She had never thought Brian would want anything so large. Amy looked at her and patted her hand. "He will want to entertain a lot," she said comfortingly.

Brian grinned at them both. "That, and the fact that Silva must have plenty of space to display her paintings. She is a very fine artist, Amy. I think she will be famous one day, more famous than her father."

Silva stared at him. He said it as though he meant it. He nodded when she met his vivid blue eyes.

"My land, that is exciting!" gasped Amy. "Well, I do hope I can see something soon."

"You'll like her work. It is big, beautiful, romantic, with glorious colors. And her imagination is something from fantasy. I looked at your new painting,

Silva," said Brian gently. "The ship is marvelous. The water seems like something in a dream."

"I—I'm not sure of my—my technique," Silva said in a small voice. She would hate to disappoint Brian.

"Julius can say more about that. But I think he hasn't much to teach you. Oh, he can tell you something about perspective, but I don't want him to spoil your natural gifts, the way you have of seeing flowers and fish bigger and more glorious than life."

Amy said, "Now I can hardly wait. Just wait till I tell Bill!" She urged more tea on them, was disappointed when they finally left without waiting for Bill to come home.

In the car Brian said, "You like her, don't you?"

"Oh, very much, and Mr. Hartman, too. He is very nice."

"He isn't very happy with his work. I think I may get him to work with me again," said Brian thoughtfully. "I could use him in the Miami office." He was silent on the way home, thinking about business, she decided.

Finally the day came when they were to return to Desirée. Mrs. Bowles helped Silva pack, and Bowles packed for Brian. Three of the men took their suitcases out to the waiting freighter. Silva got on board, clutching a handbag of smart white linen, wearing a linen dress of green and a linen coat of white, and a linen sunhat. She felt far different from the ragged island child who had come in a motor launch to Miami with Brian on the frantic journey to aid her brother in jail.

Tyrone soon came aboard, his arms loaded with books. He gave Silva an incredulous look, then a beaming happy grin. She hurried to help him with the books.

"Hi, Silva. Guess what I'm going to be doing," he said half ruefully.

"Study hard," she replied promptly.

"Yes. You, you lucky girl, you'll be off to Europe soon. That's what Julius says."

She set down the books on a table in the lounge, and her face shadowed. She scarcely knew Tyrone; he seemed a stranger. And he stood awkwardly, instead of hugging and kissing her. They had both changed.

Julius clattered down the metal stairs, carrying more books, a roll of canvas, and a box of paints. "Hello, darling Silva," he said gaily. "We are about to sail to the island of desire! You must promise to give me two hours of every day to paint you!"

She managed a smile. Brian came down behind them. "If I can spare her," he said. "Well, Tyrone, how goes it?"

"I have an awful lot to catch up on," groaned Tyrone, with some cheer in his voice. "I took a whole ream of tests. I don't know if I'm going to become a musician, an attorney, a banker, or an engineer!"

"Well, that gives you room to choose," said Brian over the laughter. "You don't have to decide right away. Give yourself plenty of time. Julius, did you get all the books he needs?"

"Some, and the others are being ordered. The captain will bring them over."

Brian went back up on deck to make sure everything was loaded. He seemed brighter, happier, more alert today. He too was glad to be returning to Desirée, thought Silva, pleased. She soon went up on deck and hung over the white-painted railing with Tyrone, commenting on everything they had seen in Miami, what their plans were.

They chattered away, losing the faint barrier of uncertainty and strangeness that had stood between them in their absence from each other. Tyrone seemed more grown-up, Silva thought. He looked different, too, in his white linen suit and white Panama hat. The freighter pulled out, drawing away from the pier.

People waved, and Silva and Tyrone waved back enthusiastically.

"Wonder if Liane will be surprised," said Tyrone suddenly.

"Surprised?"

"Yes. You got married, and we both—look different," he said slowly. "Will she think— Will Maria Luisa— Brian expects us to live with him at Cameron Hall, you know."

"Yes." Silva leaned over to gaze down into the deepening blue of the water. She felt pierced by the thought that Brian would come between her and Maria Luisa, between her and Liane. It could not be changed. But if only Maria Luisa could have come to Silva's wedding, instead of that crowd of cold strangers . . .

She leaned against the rail silently with Tyrone beside her, each absorbed in thought. She started as a lean brown arm slipped about her waist. She lifted her head, the brim of the wide hat flipped back, and she stared up into the blue eyes of Brian.

"Hi, darling. Like it?"

She smiled shyly, yielding to his arm. "Yes, it is beautiful, and so smooth," she said.

"It's good weather today, for early November," he said. His arm tightened with a secret message for her. I desire you, said that arm, the warm body he pressed her against. And for the first time, she did not resent or fear it.

He had been kind and good. And something warm stirred in her, something became excited at his touch. She put her hand on his brown hand. He must have been working with the motor or something, for he had stripped off his coat and rolled up his shirtsleeves.

"You will be cold," she said finally. "The breeze is strong."

He looked down at her and smiled into her eyes. "Come below with me. I want a drink," he said. She went with him, and put ice in a glass while he rolled down his sleeves and fastened the cuffs, then swung into the cream jacket. He added the rum to the glass. "Want one, darling?" She shook her head.

He watched the glinting sunlight from the opened windows of the lounge play on her face. How exquisitely sensitive her smooth face could be, how the light changed in her eyes, darkening them. She was so beautiful, and did not realize it.

He tipped back his head and drank several good swallows. He had deliberately taken her away from Tyrone, testing to see whether she would come with him without hesitation, and she had. He felt exultant, and ashamed of his jealousy, all at the same time. Jealous of her brother! Yes, he was jealous of everyone who looked at her, spoke to her. Seeing her at the rail, silently companionable with her twin, he had felt such rage surging up in him that he had had to go to her and put his arm about her, marking her for his own possession.

God, he was getting it bad, he thought, setting the glass down, contemplating the long smooth legs of his wife as she stretched out in a chair. He was proud of her, the slim delicate grace of her, the way she wore the most elaborate gown in an offhand way that showed her own beauty and made one forget the dress. She had a natural rhythmic walk, a swinging stride, that made men turn and look after her. And her face, her head—no wonder Julius wanted to paint her. She was a queen, a thoroughbred from her slim feet to her silvery hair. It showed in the delicate gestures of her hands, the quiet tone of her voice, the quicksilver of her thoughts. She learned quickly; he had found her studying the newspapers intently and had subtly questioned her on what she had read. She had brains, beauty. He had not been wrong about her.

She was highstrung, yes, but already she was responding to him. He caught a quick exultant breath at the thought of the nights of their passion. He had waited before making love to her each time, wooing her with kindness, taking her to the art galleries, taking her dancing and swimming. The sight of her in a bathing suit had inflamed him so he could hardly concentrate on teaching her to jump the waves.

But his patience had been rewarded. She was no longer so terrified of him. No, she had put her hands to his neck, had stroked her fingers gently over his back, exciting him so he was close to losing control. One day soon she would give in completely, and then —then he would teach her to respond and know the full pleasure of being a woman.

Julius Payne clattered down the stairs, and Silva turned to him with a smile. Payne could scarcely keep his eyes from her, but Brian had some consolation in knowing that it was partly as a painter that the older man saw her. He would have to get accustomed to the reaction she stirred in men. He would protect her jealously, hedge her in with his care. She was naive, an innocent in every sense of the word. She had no idea of the impact of her beauty on men.

"Halfway there," cried Julius. "I can scarcely wait to see this paradise island! Tell me about it, Silva."

Her green eyes glowed as she turned further in her chair to talk to him. Brian watched her pink mouth moving, the flush in her creamy cheeks, the movements of her head in the linen hat. Oh, she was lovely, and the new clothes enhanced her loveliness.

They went back up on deck as the freighter neared the dock in a little more than five hours. They had made good time. Silva hung on the rail, Tyrone at her side, as Brian stood in the wheelhouse with the captain as he deftly edged the freighter in around the treacherous coral reefs. Then someone on shore caught the long rope a sailor flung, they were drawn to safety, and the steps went down with a clang.

Silva looked about eagerly. She waved to the men ashore, but they stared back without waving. She had known them all her days on the island. "Pablo!" she called, cupping her mouth with her hands. "Hello! Enrique! Carlos!"

They stared gravely at her, at Tyrone in the smart suit. They waved back finally—stiff, embarrassed little waves. Was she so different? Her hand fell to her side, and she turned in confusion as Brian came up to her.

"I'll send someone for the carriages," he said briskly. "We'll wait in the shade." His hard gaze was on the blackened ruins of the smelter near the docks.

The carriages arrived. Silva, Tyrone, and Julius went on ahead in the first one. Now she was becoming very self-conscious, thinking of Brian's guests, especially the blonde woman, Mrs. Larsen. What would they say? Had Brian sent word he was married?

At the first opportunity she would slip away and go to see Maria Luisa. She longed to see and hug Liane, to see her face when Silva gave her the dresses and told her of the adventures. But most of all she longed for the comfort of Maria Luisa's warm arms, to see the grave look of her compassionate dark eyes, to tell her everything and be reassured she had done right. She thought, It was the only thing I could do, to get Tyrone from jail. Brian would not agree without marriage.

The carriage drew up at the huge white house. Grooms came to help her down, and she stood awkwardly with Julius and Tyrone. Finally they went inside.

Mrs. Leoni came out, surprised, followed by Donald Keller. "Who is it? Why—why, it's Silva Armitage! My dear girl, I didn't know you," she said. Then she saw Silva's left hand, the flashing green fire of the emerald and the plain gold wedding band.

Astrid Larsen got up lazily and came out into the dim hallway. "What in the world? Fine feathers, indeed," she said disagreeably. "About time you people came back. Where is Brian?"

"He is coming with some packages from the freighter," said Silva. She lifted her hand to remove her hat. Astrid stared at her hand, stared hard, and seemed to go greenish-pale in the dimness.

"What is that? What have you done?" she whispered.

Julius gave an embarrassed cough. "In case anyone cares, I'm Julius Payne," he said brightly. "Guess we'll have to introduce ourselves."

"Did you marry her?" asked Astrid crudely, pointing to Silva as to a strange animal.

"No such luck," said Julius quickly. "I say, let's go in and have a drink."

"You have married Brian Cameron," said Mrs. Leoni slowly. "Oh, I know it. How glad I am for you!" The dark-haired woman smiled at Silva with surprise and affection.

Astrid cried out. "Married—Brian Cameron—never! He would never marry such a child!"

Tyrone thrust out his chest. "She did too marry him. I was the best man and Julius gave her away in a huge church wedding. Didn't you hear about it? Didn't Brian send word?"

Silva thought for a moment that the blonde woman would faint. She put her hand to her head and reached for a chair. She sat down quickly. Mr. Leoni clapped his hands and called for drinks, as though relieved to have something practical to do. A boy came; it was not Nathaniel.

Silva sat down on the edge of a chair. How odd to think that Cameron Hall was her home! The house of her husband. She eyed Astrid Larsen uneasily. Was the woman going to have a fit? She looked very queer indeed. Donald Keller seemed surprised, his smooth young face going questioningly from one to the other.

A strong drink seemed to help restore Astrid. She sat and glared at Silva, hatred in her big blue eyes. Silva was about to excuse herself and go away—where, she did not know—when Brian's voice boomed in the hallway.

Astrid jumped up and went to the door as Brian

came in. She flung herself at him hysterically and put her arms about his neck. "There's no truth in it, is there, Brian? You're having a joke! Oh, God, I missed you so—"

He took her hands firmly from his neck and held her away from him. "Calm down, Astrid, that's a good girl. What's going on?"

"Some fool says you're married to that—that child," she said, pointing to Silva disdainfully. "You wouldn't! You always liked older women, sophisticated girls. I mean—she is only a child, a baby—"

Brian smiled rather grimly. "We are married, yes. Let's have a drink. You may congratulate me. We've been married for over a week now."

There was a babble of talk. Mrs. Leoni kissed Silva, Mr. Leoni shook Brian's hand, and so did Mr. Keller. Only Astrid stood like a statue, her eyes glaring and hard as marbles.

Silva was relieved when Brian took her off to their rooms. He had a whole suite at one side of Cameron Hall: two bedrooms, a living room and bathroom, and an office. He showed her into her bedroom. It seemed huge to her, and dark.

"I hope you'll be happy here, darling," he said simply, and kissed her warm cheek. He left her, and she sat down limply on the edge of the massive bed.

She looked about slowly. Huge mahogany furniture, shining with polish. A massive gilt-edged mirror over the beautiful dressing table, with a little round stool covered with rose tapestry. Long drapes of sea-green over sheer white curtains. A carpet of dark green thick as grass. A mirrored wardrobe in which she would hang the clothes Brian had bought for her. Drawers in which she would set the pretty frilly undergarments he had bought for her. A jewel chest in which would repose the diamonds and emeralds and pretty beads he had bought for her.

Bought, bought, bought—and Astrid Larsen hated her for all this.

She began to open her jacket. She was warm. She was weary. She longed to rush home to Maria Luisa—but that house was home no longer. This was her home, this huge white palace with the dark rooms and elaborate furnishings.

The door opened. Silva looked up, expecting to see Brian. Astrid Larsen came in, her face ugly with jealousy and fury.

"So it's true—he did marry you! Rings on your fingers, bells on your toes," she sneered. "God, I hope you enjoy it for a few weeks or months! Because he'll get tired of you, as he did all the others!"

Silva sat stiffly on the bed, as though attached firmly to it by her stiff fingers that clung to the satin bedspread. Her wide eyes watched Astrid as the woman paced across the floor like a caged animal, and back again. Like a jaguar, thought Silva, like a terrible beast of the jungle.

"Enjoy it—yes, enjoy it, you fool!" blazed Astrid, flinging herself around to the girl, who shrank from her. "He'll get tired of you. Your marriage won't last long! He bores easily! I expect you are new to him." She looked down over the girl, searingly, her gaze contemptuous. "Oh, he thought of you as a little island princess, I expect! So new and different! He's dressed you all up, hasn't he? But wait till he tires of you! Shall I tell you of the women he has discarded? Of the model in New York City, the duchess in London, the beautiful French girl in Paris, to say nothing of the native girls of Bolivia and Peru? Shall I tell you—"

Silva found the strength to slide to her feet and face the raging woman with dignity. "No, I do not wish to listen. Leave my room," she said.

Astrid glared at her. Behind her, a native woman came in timidly, sidling past Astrid. "Mr. Cameron, he say I unpack now?" she murmured, and shrank as Astrid glared at her.

The blonde woman turned on her heel and went out, slamming the door after her.

"Whoo-ooo," breathed the woman. "She has a temper, that one. Miss Silva, I unpack for you? You got pretty things?"

"Yes—thank you, Emilie, unpack for me. Thank you. I—I have a headache."

She unfastened the suit, took it off, and put on a robe. The woman crooned over her, just as Maria Luisa would have done, turned back the satin bedspread, and helped her slip in. Then quietly she unfastened the suitcases and unpacked the pretty garments, hanging them in the cedar-lined mahogany wardrobe. Silva shut her eyes tightly, trying to shut her mind also to what the blonde woman had said. Astrid was jealous, hurt, she tried to tell herself. But what if she had spoken the truth? What if Brian wanted a woman only for a short time, then discarded her?

Wasn't that just what she had wanted? To be discarded, to return to her own free life, the carefree existence she had known before he came?

For some reason, she felt rather sick. She pressed her hand to her heart, which was beating in slow unpleasant throbs that hurt. If only she could wipe from her mind what that terrible woman had said! She thought of the way Brian touched her, how he put his arm possessively about her waist. He had married her, made her his wife. And she remembered his hard lips opening insistently against her yielding mouth. His big hands moving over her breasts, cupping them. The feel of his lean hard body on hers.

A strange desolation swept her. She had known him, and belonged to him. She would never be the same innocent child again. What if the time did come when he would discard her?

Chapter 25

Silva had fallen into a light, troubled sleep. She wakened with a jerk, turning her head. Someone sat beside her bed in a straight-backed chair. A dark-haired girl—

"Oh, Liane!" she cried, and sat up straight, holding out her arms. Liane slipped from the chair, hugged her, and sat down on the bed beside her.

Silva drew back her head after kissing Liane's cheek. There was something new about Liane, a strange intensity, a hardness. Silva gazed into the eyes that had always been gentle and dark, usually smiling, or shy. Now they were hard, wounded.

"Liane, what is it?"

Liane did not respond for a moment. Silva set her hand gently on her friend's cheek. Liane's eyelashes flickered.

"It is hard to tell you, Silva. And much has happened to you also. I hear you marry Brian Cameron."

Silva nodded. "I will tell you of that," she said simply. "Tyrone was in jail. Brian would get him out, but in return I had to marry him. I didn't know why he wished to marry me, but he would not listen to anything else I said. So—I married him. He got Tyrone from jail."

Liane studied Silva's face with something of her mother's sad, compassionate expression in her eyes. Then she looked at the green silk robe and lifted Silva's left hand to gaze at the emerald ring. "He like you. He gives you presents."

"Yes," said Silva. "Many presents, many dresses, jewels like this." She gave a great sigh. "It is all so strange."

Liane closed her eyes. "There is something I must tell you, something bad. No one else will tell you, just me, because we love her. Both so much. I will tell you. We must be brave, Silva."

"Mamacita?" whispered Silva, and clutched at Liane. "It is not—she is ill? Oh, I will go to her—"

"No, no." Liane's voice trembled, and she pressed her cheek to Silva's. She seemed to gather strength. "Mamacita—she is dead. Our Mamacita is gone. We bury her, many are possessed. It was very bad—very bad—"

Silva felt choked and sick. She clung to Liane in silence, felt tears starting from her eyes, thickness in her throat. She could not believe it. The shock had taken her breath from her body, as though she had tripped and fallen down a great cliff, and stunned herself.

Liane's voice went on in a monotone, as though she had rehearsed this. "Mamacita was attacked—by someone—stabbed—her heart opened by a knife. She died at once. Oh, Silva, how I have grieved!"

"No, no, no," whispered Silva, and began to weep, with great sobbing breaths. "No, no, no. No one would do this. All loved Mamacita."

The door opened, and Brian strode in. "What is this? Why are you crying?"

Liane drew back slightly, but Silva still clutched her. Liane turned up her face toward Brian, but it was as though she did not quite see him in the dimness. "Maria Luisa is dead." Her voice was flat.

Brian took a deep breath. "Dead? How did it happen?"

Silva felt the clutch of Liane's fingers, as though she did not know how strongly she held Silva's arms in them.

"A man attacked her, with a knife. He cut her

heart—she fell down—she gave out great blood. She die."

"No! Who did this?" he asked sharply, coming over to them, putting a hand on Silva's shoulder, as though to protect her.

"It will be known," said Liane. "Mamacita will be avenged."

"Doesn't anyone know who did it?" he bit out savagely. "We'll scour the island. Ask questions. Someone must know!"

"The gods know," said Liane. "They will avenge her." There was a weary certainty to the words.

Brian was silent. Silva wiped her hands with the sheet; they were damp and cold. She was shaking. Mamacita—to die in such a manner! It was impossible—everyone had loved her.

Brian bent over and snapped on the light. Silva started, and turned her head from it. She was accustomed to the gentle blooming of the oil lamps, not the suddenness of the electric lights. There was an electric generator behind the Cameron house, and from it they drew the power for the lights, the kitchen stove, and other items. How could she ever become accustomed to this great place? She longed for home, for Maria Luisa, for the campfire and the laughter and singing about it.

No more. It would come no more. Maria Luisa was dead.

"I'll inquire," said Brian. "Someone will talk. We'll find out what happened, and she shall be avenged, as you say." The promise was grim.

"You do not live at the house alone, Liane?" asked Silva anxiously, thinking that Nathaniel was no longer about. Had he returned to Liane in her sorrow?

"No, two women live with me there. They keep the fire going—it will go on," she said gently. She rose. "I must return, while the light remains. I heard you had come, and I wished to tell you with my lips about Maria Luisa, for you loved her as I did." Her hand lingered on Silva's hair, then fell to her side. It was as though Maria Luisa had touched her.

"But you can't go back there," Brian said briskly, as though relieved to have something practical to plan. "You must stay here. Of course! You will come—there are many bedrooms. Silva, urge her to stay here. She shall have her own room, be company for you. She must not stay at that house."

Liane hesitated. She seemed older, worn, dark smudges under her immense dark eyes, her brown skin sharp under her chin, her body thin as though she did not eat much.

Silva slid from the bed. "Oh, Liane, you will stay? There is much to say and tell you. So many plans are being made—oh, please remain. Unless—Nathaniel—?"

"He does not come," Liane said.

Brian rubbed his hand over his face. "I'll speak to the maid about it. You'll have a room nearby, Liane. That's final. We'll go over tomorrow in the carriage and get your things. After all, you are like a sister to Silva. She will want you here."

Liane raised her great eyes to his face and studied him gravely. Then she nodded. "I stay—for a time. Thank you, Mr. Cameron."

"Brian," he said. "I'll go see about your room. When you have time, we'll talk—about your mother. We'll find out what happened."

She was gentle, but aloof, watching him leave Silva's room, closing the door after him. Silva took her friend's arms in her hands.

"Liane—you know," she said in a low tone. "You know!"

Liane nodded. "I tell you," she said finally. "You too must be careful, very careful. I tell you, but no one else must know. You agree?"

Silva said solemnly, "On the memory of Maria Luisa, I agree. I will say nothing."

"The gods will avenge her, they have promised this

to me." Liane sat down on the floor, naturally. Silva sat down beside her on the rug, close, so they could speak in whispers.

"Pedro Ortega came to me," murmured Liane. "I walked the beach alone, my mind was not alert. He came, he took me. Cruelly, as he is. I bleed. I run home."

She told the rest of the story, in sparse economical words, with gestures. Silva listened, burning with rage for her, weeping with her weeping, agonized with her agony. When she came to the part about Pedro's stabbing of Maria Luisa, the way the woman fell, Silva put her hand to her face and rocked back and forth.

"Oh, the gods must avenge," she cried softly. "Oh, they must avenge her!"

Liane took Silva's hand in both of hers and told her about the ceremony when the gods had come, how Erzulie had appeared, then Damballa in the form of a snake. "Many were moved," she whispered intensely. "Papa Henri said he felt the presence of Mamacita. She was there—she was there, Silva. She will come again, and advise us."

"And it was Pedro Ortega! And he dared to come to her ceremony! Oh, they will strike him dead!"

"They will do it, in their time. It is promised," said Liane with solemn finality. They sat, discussing it for a time.

They wept a little, held each other, and took comfort from their closeness. Liane finally stood. "I must go back to my house, to bring other dresses—"

Silva jumped up. "Oh, but I have dresses for you—dress lengths for Maria Luisa—" she began eagerly, then remembered and put her hand to her mouth. In desolation, like a child, she said, "Already I forget that the gods have taken her away! Oh, how can I bear it?"

Emilie came in, tapping gently first. "Mr. Cameron, he say I show Miss Liane her room," she said with sweet familiarity. She had known both girls all their lives. Her look at them was full of motherly compassion. "You talk no more about the dead, it is bad. You come, Liane, I help you. Mr. Cameron, he say there are dresses for you."

Silva took out the dresses from her own wardrobe, where they had been placed. Liane fingered the blue silk solemnly, her face wanting to light up, her eyes beginning to sparkle a little. But something grave and somber in her forbade her pleasure. She kissed Silva's cheek, and went away with Emilie and the dresses.

Brian came to the door. "She say anything more about it? Can't she even guess who did it?" he said curtly.

"She does not guess," said Silva, truthfully. She turned away from his too-keen look. "What shall I wear this evening? Liane likes the blue dress. I think she will wear it."

He crossed to the wardrobe, studied its contents, and finally drew out a rose satin. "This is similar in style to Liane's. You'll both look like young princesses," he said.

She nodded, to please him. Some part of her wanted to hide away, to run free and mourn Maria Luisa. But part of her wished to please her husband.

"Thank you—for giving home to Liane," she said. "I would not wish her to mourn alone."

"No. We must think of something for her," said Brian, frowning slightly. "She will turn inward to brooding. That was a terrible thing to happen. If only Nathaniel—but no. There must be some other answer."

"He has treated her with terrible indifference in her sorrow," Silva blazed. "And he was devoted for a whole year!"

"Some men are like that," he said. "But not I, Silva. You are mine—for life, you know." And he bent and kissed her cheek gently, and held her against him.

She did not know whether to believe him or not.

Better not to, she thought drearily. Nathaniel had probably said the same thing to Liane, but had tired of her within a year. Men were easily swayed from those they loved when another beautiful face took their attentions.

After she had put on the rose silk, with the V neck and graceful full skirt, she went along to Liane's room, to see and approve the pretty blue-green hangings, the wide bed, the gracious furniture. Liane seemed lost in it, but looked quite lovely in the blue silk, which made her blue-black hair shine with more lights and set off the exquisite dark arms and throat. They went together to the drawing room. Brian was there, in a cream tropical suit, and went to greet them.

"Two beautiful flowers of the island of desire," he drawled to tease them. Silva flushed shyly, and Liane looked enigmatic. They had their arms entwined, holding to each other for comfort. Tyrone came over and kissed Liane's cheek.

"How I hated to hear the news," he whispered. He had wept, Silva knew by the redness about his eyes. "If I knew—"

Brian said, "No more of that now. We'll talk tomorrow. Liane, let me introduce you to our other guests." He took her by the arm and led her about.

Julius was staring at her with those penetrating artist's eyes of his, as though dazed. In the blue silk, with a pair of Silva's silver sandals on her narrow feet, her blue-black hair brushed into a low loose coil at her neck, she was suddenly more mature, in her sorrow, and more beautiful than ever before, Silva thought.

All were gracious to her but Astrid Larsen. The woman looked at her from head to feet, sneering, as though repeating her words of a while ago, Silva decided. *Fine feathers, indeed.*

Astrid wore a stunning white satin dress, cut low at her magnificent breasts. She wore sparkling sapphires at her throat and in her ears and on her arms, which were bare from the halter neck of the gown. Yet somehow she looked older against the youth and beauty of the younger girls, looked jaded and weary and faintly blowsy. She downed three drinks before dinner, and the new houseboy was busy at the table refilling her wineglass.

"Tell us all about the hasty wedding," she said viciously, but Brian turned the conversation to another subject.

Mrs. Leoni was gracious to Silva, almost anxiously so, as though wishing to ingratiate herself with Brian Cameron's wife. She spoke of life in New York City, of concerts and art exhibitions that Silva would enjoy. It was then Liane learned that Silva and Brian would be leaving soon to go to Europe for a long honeymoon.

"What is this—a honeymoon?" asked Liane.

Astrid laughed. No one else did. Mrs. Leoni said hastily that it was a time for the newly married couple to spend alone, to enjoy their own company without bothering about other people. Silva wondered if Liane would be insulted, but the other girl only looked thoughtful.

Brian was paying little attention to the conversation. He was thinking how beautiful Silva looked tonight, faintly sad, as though she had not yet fully realized Maria Luisa was gone. He had gone to question Mickey McCoy and get a report on the burned-out smelter. Mickey was cursing his broken leg and the natives who had disappeared.

He turned his thoughts to organizing the next weeks, to get his work on the island over with as quickly as possible. He wanted to be away from Desirée soon after Christmas. Silva would probably want to spend Christmas here, with her twin and Liane. Then they could be off in the New Year, a new year for them both. Impatiently he thought over all he had to do yet: get the natives back to work, investigate who had caused the explosion, who had murdered Maria Luisa. He wondered if the two incidents were related, decided there was only a faint chance.

Julius Payne was rather silent during dinner and later. He kept glancing at the beautiful Liane. When she had entered, arm in arm with Silva, he had been struck dumb by her beauty. The two girls were such a contrast, one so light blonde, the other so darkly lovely. Their profiles against a cream wall—stunning! It was then he thought of a double portrait of Silva and Liane.

He became more and more excited at the thought of the potential. It could be the best work he had done so far. The blonde girl, so youthfully innocent, naive, wondering, and the other, more mature, gentle, yet somehow hardened in the fierce fires of some terrible experience. Was it her mother's death that had tempered Liane? Could be.

After dinner, in the drawing room, seeing them together on the sofa, Julius decided. He spoke to Brian, who nodded.

"Julius wants to do your portrait, Silva," said Brian. "With Liane. The two of you. Would you pose together?" It might solve a problem of his. He was jealous again, jealous thinking of her wandering about the island without him, drawing away from him, with Tyrone, with her native friends. If she had to be still in the house or garden for a couple of hours a day, he would know where she was! He had gone pretty far, he thought wretchedly, but some part of her was shut off from him, and he could not long endure that. He wanted to be part of her, to know her thoughts, to feel them draw closer in spirit as well as physically.

Silva's eyes widened and she looked at Liane, who seemed impassive, her slim brown hands clenched on the blue fabric of her skirt. Silva put her hand over them and squeezed. "I think it would be lovely.

Could we—could we work outdoors? I have missed being outdoors," she said.

"Why not? In the patio outside, where the hibiscus hedges are? Or against the golden allamanda? I'll have a look around tomorrow morning," promised Julius, glowing already. He took a long stare at Liane, surprising a slight flush in her cheeks, an uneasiness. She wasn't used to being stared at like that.

"Oh, you are a painter?" asked Astrid with some slight interest. "I was painted in New York. Why didn't you say? Are you famous? I might commission something." She hated being left out of conversations.

Julius scratched his graying head and drank of his rum before trying to reply. "Well—actually I don't accept commissions. I've reached the stage where I can paint to please myself," he said rather apologetically. "Brian already wants to buy Silva's portrait, but I could probably get a high price for it—"

"I'll match any price," said Brian crisply. "You'll paint nothing of Silva unless you let me buy it."

It was a flat-out statement. Mrs. Leoni smiled—she adored romances. Donald Keller stared thoughtfully at Astrid, then dropped his gaze to his glass of lime juice. Tyrone seemed not to hear. Silva stirred uneasily.

"It could be my masterpiece," said Julius, and stared at Silva and Liane for the remainder of the evening. It fascinated him, the contrast.

He made the opportunity to talk to Liane later. Her slow soft speech intrigued him.

"You have lived here all your life, Liane?" he asked.

"Yes, all my life."

"And you are—what?—Twenty?"

"Seventeen," she said.

He stared at her, feeling older than his forty-five years. She looked early twenty, mature, blossoming, her bosom full, her mouth a red flower, her eyes wise.

Even the huskiness of her voice spoke of experience. But—seventeen!

She smiled faintly at his amazement. "It is not the years that give us age, but the life that quickens in us, Mr. Payne. The passions that touch us, the sorrows that make us weep," she said gently.

"You are wiser than your years, that is true. But I am sorry for your sorrow," he said softly. He touched her hand to show his sympathy, and was stunned to find he wanted to bring that slim brown hand to his lips. There was something so sweet and melancholy about her, he wished he could hold her close and tell her she would know no more sorrow.

Faintly embarrassed by his own emotions, he released her hand. She was studying his face, as though she saw beyond the lines, the grayness at his temples.

Silva moved over to them and put her arm naturally around Liane's waist, as though she would defend her.

"We are as sisters," she answered Julius's questioning look. "The mother of Liane has died. She was like my own mother, for I do not recall my own mother very well."

Liane swallowed; he saw the graceful throat move convulsively. The dark eyes closed for a moment.

"I am sorry, deeply sorry." His voice sounded strange to himself. He wondered about Liane. Someone so beautiful must have attracted a man's attention, yet none spoke of a fiancé, no one hovered protectively near her. Was she too young for a lover or husband? Or was the tragedy in her eyes partly because a lover had deserted her? Impatiently, he wanted to know all about her, to learn her, as one does a fascinating flower not yet ripened by the sun, its petals closed to him.

Silva murmured something to Liane, gesturing to the tray of coffee. Liane nodded, and the girls went together to the tray. With cups in hand, they stood speaking to each other. Julius stared at them frankly, unable to look away, his emotions caught as well as his artist's eyes.

How lovely they were—that was his recurring thought. Then he was aware of more than beauty. The silvery-haired girl so close to the girl of the blue-black hair. The creamy tanned face next to the darkly golden one. They were about the same height, though Liane was more ripely mature in the breasts and thighs.

It was not just the difference in their coloring, which was striking enough. It was the difference in their expressions: the shy diffidence of Silva, the weary maturity of Liane. Both were at the stage in life when adulthood was being forced onto them, when the budding of girlhood was changing to the flowering of womanhood, the sadness and sorrowing, the love and passion and frenzy and grief were all combining to confuse and mystify them. There was something of the ancient feminine mysteries in their faces, something of allurement in their grace and movements. If he could only capture that on canvas!

He reached for a sketch pad, never far from him, and began outlining what he wanted, drawing quick black lines on the pad. The two girls were talking together, murmuring so even Brian on Silva's other side could not hear clearly. Hand clasped hand, empathy went from one to the other. The love and attachment was clear, the years of shared experiences, the common love of Liane's mother. Even the lines of their faces, that taut look of their young shoulders, were alike.

Yes, yes, it would be a good portrait, Julius was certain.

Silva retired late. It had been a long evening. With a sigh of relief she slid between the sheets. She looked about the large dark bedroom before slipping out a hand to turn out the single light. Brian came to the doorway in his crimson robe, saw her hand at the light. She left it on, gazing back at him.

"Are you very tired?" he asked gently.

She knew that if she said she was, he would go. Yet—somehow she did not want to send him away. He might be hurt. And he had been kind and gracious to Liane, her friend.

She shook her head dumbly. He came over to the bed, took off his robe, lay down with her, and snapped out the light. Darkness was complete in the room, before her eyes adjusted to the dimness of the night between the open curtains, the purple of the sky, the brilliant blaze of the stars, never so bright as on Desirée.

He took her in his arms and drew her to him. She snuggled her head down on his chest, wondering at herself. She was beginning to like the scent of his male lotion, the faint lingering of tobacco smell, the hard sureness of his arms and hands. He stroked his hand down her back.

"You are tired, I think. Go to sleep, darling," he whispered against her ear, and kissed the small lobe.

She pressed her head against him. "Listen. You can hear the sound of the ocean waves. Pounding, pounding. Like drums," she murmured sleepily.

He listened and he could hear the faint sure pounding of the ocean against the island—as it had been for thousands of years. Brian felt as though he had never noticed such things before, not until he had held a small, slim, silky body in his arms and heard what she said to him and thought about her as he caressed her. Something eternal, ceaseless, everlasting.

Chapter 26

The next day Silva and Liane went out for a time together to talk. They walked slowly through the beautiful gardens, away from everyone, and conversed earnestly.

Liane told Silva more of what had happened. "Pedro Ortega is making big trouble," she added. She seemed more rested today, a little less tense, as though confiding the trouble had made it less. Silva wound her arm comfortingly about her friend's waist. "I think Nathaniel is in it. He does not come near me."

"He is a wicked man," blazed Silva in sympathy. "Not to come and mourn with you, not to tell of his grief."

Liane's great dark eyes gazed into the distance, as though she did not see the huge scarlet hibiscus near her cheek or smell the perfume of the white jasmine. "There is something else," she said finally. "He is under the spell of another woman. I might tell you of that one day, perhaps not. It is bitter, Silva, it is bitter in my mouth."

Another woman? Oona? Surely not, she was so coarse. Who, having once had Liane, could want such a one as Oona? Silva mused on the fickleness of men. Liane went on speaking.

"Others are being drawn into the plans of Pedro Ortega. I listen, and pretend to be passive about them. He thinks little of the mind of a woman," Liane said with bitter irony. "You must be secret about this, but somehow there must be a way to warn Brian Cameron."

Silva started violently. Her heart began to beat more rapidly. "How is Brian involved?" she whispered.

"It is stupid talk, but natives believe it, for they do not have the education your father gave to me," said Liane. "Pedro say that white men take money from them, that Desirée belong to them, that they must drive all whites away. I think they do not mean you and Tyrone, but maybe so. This I will find out."

Silva drew a deep, painful breath. "What—will they do? What does he plan?"

"I wait and find out. I think it was Pedro who blew up the smelter. He not mind if Mickey McCoy die. He not mind if all whites die. He hate the copper mine. He tell men that the sacred mountain will be stripped to bare earth, that the gods will be angry. But Pedro Ortega cares nothing for our gentle gods. He has only his god of war. He wears the red shirt all the time."

"The sacred mountain. I was afraid of this," murmured Silva, pressing her hand to her forehead. "Oh, Maria Luisa feared this, that the sacred mountain would be desecrated. The jaguar gods will be so angry. I hear their roars at night."

Liane nodded. "I also. I think Pedro will ruin the mine, and he will do it soon. Can you talk to Brian, ask him to take his men and equipment from the mine, and close it?" Her troubled eyes surveyed Silva.

"We do not talk seriously of such matters. I do not know if he will listen to me," said Silva simply. "It hurts me, but he is not close to me. I think he has only desire for me."

"Ah," said Liane, nodding her head. The girls walked in silence, arm in arm, through the garden, not seeing the roses and the golden allamanda, the scarlet trees of the flamboyant.

"But I will speak to him," said Silva presently, with a sigh. They were so close they had no need to elaborate on what they said to each other. Their minds were in tune. Liane pressed her arm.

"Do not hurt yourself on the sharp edge of his temper," she warned gently. "He is a hard man, from many years. Maria Luisa say so. But maybe he likes you well. He gives you many presents."

"I do not know," said Silva. "It is a puzzle to me."

Brian came out late that morning, and came over to them in the garden. "Julius is looking for you, Liane. He wants to start his sketching," he said.

"I also?" asked Silva as Liane gave him a faint smile and nod and began to move away.

Brian shook his head. "Not now. I want to speak to you, Silva." He looked baffled, almost angry.

Liane went to the other part of the garden, where Julius greeted her warmly. He had set up a table, with sketch pads, charcoal, a straw-seated chair. He placed Liane against the hibiscus hedge, sitting in the chair, and walked back and forth before her, staring at her. Silva turned from watching, to her husband.

"What do you talk of so much with Liane?" he demanded.

She started a little, gazing up at him. His tanned face was dark, the vivid blue eyes blazing.

"Why—we speak of her mother, and the island," she said cautiously.

"Has she told you of her mother's death, the truth about it?"

Silva looked away. "She is grieved," she said. "She wishes revenge. But she is not so strong. She cannot use a knife so well."

"Does she know who did it?"

Silva groped for words to turn away his questions. "She spoke to me about another matter," she said. "I—I wish to ask you about it."

"Well?"

The harsh word was not promising. She bit her full lips. "Brian—must you—mine the sacred mountain?" she began. "There is much talk and unease.

You see, the mountain is sacred to the jaguar god, who is powerful—"

"Damn it, I wish you would forget that nonsense!" he burst out angrily. "I asked you to confide in me about Liane, not come up with this damn foolishness about sacred mountains! You know better than that! You had a Christian upbringing!"

She shrank from his anger and his biting words, her hand pressed involuntarily to her breast. "Please —listen to me," she begged anxiously. "There are those who are angry about the mine. They will make trouble—"

"Not if they are well paid," he said harshly. "I know the language they speak—it is money! They will take my money, all right! Don't worry about that."

"You do not understand. They are troubled in their minds—" Again she tried to tell him. She could not warn him about the revolt, not yet, not until Liane released her from her promise. She gazed up at him anxiously, willing him to listen.

"You are a silly little girl. I thought you were growing up!" he said grimly. "As soon as you came back to the island you started reverting to island ways. Well, I'll soon put a stop to that. You'll come away with me, and I'll make you grow up. You have to understand I don't listen to such nonsense. Sacred mountain! The gods will revenge! You don't know one damn thing about living! It's embarrassing to me that you can't or won't learn civilized ways!"

She shrank as though struck in the face. Her head drooped. He hesitated, then strode away angrily. She could scarcely believe it, that he had so insulted her. He was ashamed of her! She embarrassed him!

She turned and walked away blindly, behind the hedges, into a corner of the garden where she could not be seen. She sat on the grass for a time, catching her breath, her hand pressed to her heart.

"How he must despise me," she murmured to a

small lizard flicking its tail smartly before her. She watched it run up a tree, flick its tail at an insect. "Oh, if only he had not married me!"

The pain seemed to be rending her heart. He was ashamed of her. She embarrassed him! She closed her eyes tightly against the tears that wanted to flow. She did not know what to do. She longed to tell him frankly about the revolt, so he could protect himself. She did not want him injured like Mickey McCoy. That would be horrible! Suppose Pedro Ortega set off an explosion in the mine when Brian was there, and he was buried in the sacred mountain! Oh, that would be—too awful for words—too horrible—under that mountain of dirt, buried alive— Silva shut her eyes, but could not shut out the picture of him lying bloody and injured, his leg broken, his handsome face shattered—

She jumped up and walked quickly toward the house. She must find him, tell him the truth. He must be warned! In spite of her word to Liane, she must warn him.

She walked into the cool, dark house through the French doors, softly into the large drawing room. At first in the dimness, before her eyes adjusted, she saw only shadowy forms. Then, standing just inside the softly blowing curtains, she saw the blonde-haired woman, her arms about Brian's neck, her face pressed to his throat, her voice murmuring languidly in his ears.

"Oh, how could you have married that foolish child?" said the sultry voice of Astrid Larsen. "You broke my heart!"

"Nonsense, your heart is as hard as a diamond," said Brian, his hands on her waist. "Come on, now, give over. Don't be silly. Astrid, you know what we had—"

Silva shrank back into the door, back into the garden. On the terrace she stood dazed, a little faint. Her husband, holding that woman in his arms! A great anger rose in her as the faintness went away. She felt fury against him. He was no better than Nathaniel, using her briefly, then turning to another woman!

She pressed her hand to her face. Where could she turn? What could she do? She felt completely helpless. He had forced her to marry him—now he shamed her in his own house with the presence of that woman.

Even a native man would not bring his mistress to his house and force his wife to entertain her. Of course, Brian thought little of Silva, and she had no duties in the house. Perhaps he did not think of her as a wife. Perhaps marriage was only a form to him, and divorce would be easy. He would discard her. He thought her a foolish child, with island ways.

Well, it would serve him right if the natives of Desirée did revolt and throw him off the island, she thought in a burst of anger. She would not warn him! He would not listen to her! Let the worst happen!

She went around the back way and entered the house through the kitchen, startling the chef and his helpers. She gave them a faint smile and padded through the hallway on her soft slippers, to her bedroom. It was so dark, though cool. She longed for the simple white-walled house of her youth . . . and Maria Luisa to hold her in her arms and comfort her. But this hurt went too deep for comfort. She had let Brian come to her, she had not refused him, but still he went to that woman for kisses, and more—she was certain.

She wondered if he was now in that woman's bedroom. If they embraced, if he lay naked with her. She slid to the floor and leaned her head against the silk bedspread. How could he? How could he? Why were men so fickle?

She heard sounds in the next bedroom. Brian had returned. Hastily she rose, took a book in her hands, and sat down in a chair near the window. When he tapped and entered, she pretended to be reading.

"Oh, here you are, Silva," he said, his voice controlled once more. "It is time for lunch."

"Shall I change my dress?" she inquired evenly, indicating the simple green cotton she wore.

"No, that's all right. For dinner in the evening I want you to dress up." He crossed to the wardrobe and flipped over the gowns critically. "The silver sheath tonight," he said.

"Very well." She did not rise or look at him.

He stood looking at her. "I suppose you are angry with me," he said finally. "I can't help being angry that you feel more for your sacred mountain than you do for—for me or anyone. You'll have to cut out those stupid superstitions."

"Shall I cut out my brain? My heart?" she flashed.

He gave an impatient sigh. He came over to her, put his hand on her cheek caressingly. She flinched from him. She could still smell on him the heavy musky scent of Astrid Larsen's perfume. He had come directly from that woman to her.

His hand fell to his side. "No, I just want you to start using your brain, learn from books, learn from those around you. When we get to Europe, I'll get you some more books, talk to you about what you should know. Until then, try to restrain your urge to act like an island girl," he said.

She felt insulted all over again. "I *am* an island girl," she said swiftly, her eyes flashing. "You are the stupid one, to have married me! You should have chosen someone more to your liking!"

"Don't say that! Never say that," he said, as quickly, his eyes flashing. "I wanted to marry you. One day, I want you to be happy with me." He hesitated, then added more gently, "Come to lunch now. You look lovely."

She rose obediently, and he indicated she should

lead the way. She was conscious of his following her closely—she could feel the warmth of his body behind her, could still smell the fragrance of Astrid's perfume. She felt sick with it, as though she could not eat or drink.

She barely touched her lunch. She was conscious of Brian's frown of concern. Liane kept glancing at her questioningly as she sat silently at the foot of the table. The servants needed little direction. Silva felt resentment in waves of bitterness sweeping through her as she saw Astrid's laughter, her secret satisfaction, the way she managed to touch Brian's hand, direct his attention to her constantly. No wonder she looked like a great satisfied cat!

After luncheon Brian went to visit Mickey McCoy, an unwilling invalid cooped up in his room. Later still she heard him riding out, calling to someone. Then she felt free to walk in the garden, restlessly, up and down.

Liane came to her there. Silva thought her friend would speak of Brian, and she could not bear it. Instead the girl said, "You noticed Tyrone at luncheon?"

"Tyrone? No, why?" Silva was surprised, ashamed of herself for scarcely noticing her twin.

"He is most silent, troubled in mind. He did not know when one spoke to him. And last night he stole from the house very late, and did not return until dawn."

"He must have gone to Oona," said Silva. Even her twin, a grown man now, must turn to the women, she thought reproachfully.

Liane shook her lovely dark head. Her face was grave and brooding. "No, he goes not to a woman. There is no smell of woman on him," she said decidedly.

"What, then?"

"I wonder."

Silva thought. "He—he might be involved with

Pedro Ortega? Do you think so? He was involved in the rumrunning with him, though we begged him not to."

"Would he turn against the other white men?"

"I don't know. I don't know Tyrone anymore."

Silva mused that she did not know men anymore at all. Had she ever? Or had she merely leaned on the wisdom and breast of Maria Luisa? Now she felt very alone, and bereft.

"I wonder if he will go out tonight," she said aloud.

"Maybe he will."

The two girls strolled along the path, their sandals making no sound. The heat of the afternoon had dispelled the dew that had lain on the flowers that morning, and the hibiscus had curled their petals against the hot sun.

"If he goes, I will follow him," Silva said.

"Your man will not like it," Liane chided her gently.

"He is not my man," Silva told her bitterly, thinking of the blonde woman with her arms twined about Brian's neck, the sight of Brian's tanned hands against the wasp-like waist of the woman. He was no better than Pedro Ortega, turning from one woman to another.

They sought out Tyrone to try to talk to him, but they did not find him. Emilie told them presently that the young man slept in his room, the sleep of the dead.

"It is the heat," she said cheerfully. "It is most hot today."

Liane looked at Silva, and they went away. Silva told her, "I'll take a siesta today also, then. Tonight I'll follow Tyrone."

"I come with you," Liane assured her.

Silva slept that afternoon, quite hard, and wakened in a daze as Emilie drew aside the curtains late in the afternoon. "It is past six, Miss Silva," said the maid. "You get up now?"

Silva had to lie there for a few minutes to bring her mind back from the far places where it had gone in sleep. She had dreamed, of jaguars in green jungles, of green eyes peering at her—eyes that changed to a hard blue, the mocking eyes of Astrid Larsen.

Finally she got up, took a long cool bath in the tub, and dressed in the flimsy silky things Brian liked her to wear. She could not endure stockings on her legs, however, and put the silver sandals on her slim bare feet. Finally she drew on the silver sheath, and Emilie buttoned it up the back to close in a sleek line on her tanned shoulders. The neckline was a square, and she wondered what to put there—she felt naked. Brian came in as she pondered over her scarves.

"Ah, you are finally awake," he said cheerfully. "I wondered about you. When I looked in this afternoon, you were sleeping hard. What is the problem?" he added as she pawed through the scarves.

"Something for my throat," she said absently. "It is so—so bare—"

He put a caressing hand on her throat—a strong hand that could have choked the life from her, she thought. "You look lovely like that," he said. "Wear just the chain and diamond pendant." He opened the boxes, found it for her, and fastened it at the back of her neck as she held her silver hair up.

She brushed her hair hastily, leaving it cascading about her shoulders, aware of his stare over her. She felt full of resentment, as she had earlier. The sleep had done nothing to dim that. Finally she was ready. Emilie beamed affectionately at her and said something in the native patois about how pretty she looked.

"Speak English!" Brian said sharply. Emilie looked hurt, her lip drooping.

"She said merely that I looked pretty," said Silva,

cold with fury. "You do not need to speak so to her."

Brian set his mouth. He took her arm and led her out of the room. He looked cross and furious again. "I was able to get a couple of men to work at repairing the smelter," he said abruptly. "The others seemed to have disappeared. Is it some holiday, some god's day?"

"In mid-November?" asked Silva. "No, none." She thought again of Pedro and his influence. He must have warned the men against building the smelter.

"I'll see if I can round up some more men tomorrow. I'm anxious to get things moving again. I wish we could get away before Christmas, but I suppose you want to stay here until after that," he said gloomily.

She was silent. Did her wishes mean anything? Her heart seemed to fail her at the thought of leaving Tyrone, Liane, all the loved people she knew, to be alone for months with Brian Cameron, who made no attempt to understand her, who did not want to listen to anything she said.

Tyrone was very silent at dinner. She noticed it this time. Liane looked at her significantly, her eyes narrowed. Silva nodded. Julius was telling a funny story about an experience with a French model, but the story went over their heads. Mrs. Leoni choked with laughter, Mr. Leoni gave great guffaws, and even Brian smiled. But Silva did not even hear Julius, for she was busily thinking about Tyrone and the trouble he must be in. Why did he follow that man Pedro? Could he not see that the man was evil? If he knew about Maria Luisa, he would not follow Pedro!

After an excellent dinner of turtle soup, baked fish, and sweet potatoes, with a fruit cup of melon and mango and tiny sweet bananas for dessert, they went to the drawing room for coffee and brandy. Silva poured out the coffee for them, glad to have something to occupy her hands and her mind briefly.

The evening turned cool, as it did in November.

Brian shut the French doors and a fire was lit in the great stone fireplace. The Leonis seemed relaxed, telling of life in New York City, advising Silva what she would like to see there. Astrid pouted, interrupting when she could, which was often. Brian watched the play of firelight on Silva's face. Julius seemed to be absorbed in his sketch pad, glancing up now and then to gaze at Liane or Silva.

Only Donald Keller was at ease, his legs crossed, his coffee cup nearby, a slight smile on his face as he listened. He seemed such a—a nonperson, thought Silva. He said little, he was easily amused, he did not seem to feel any undercurrents. What was behind that bland gaze?

Tyrone was restlessly moving about in his chair. Finally he excused himself at about eleven o'clock. Liane glanced at Silva, her face blank. Silva nodded slightly. Presently she yawned, apologized, then said, "I am very sleepy. Will you all excuse me, please?"

Brian and the other men stood up. Brian accompanied her to the door, squeezed her hand and said gently in a low tone, "I hope I didn't hurt your feelings today. You have been very quiet."

Hoped he had not hurt her feelings! With insulting her, and amusing himself with Astrid Larsen! She withdrew her hand, avoided his look, and said, "Good night," in a cool tone to the company.

In her bedroom she dismissed Emilie after the woman had gotten her out of the tight sheath. She changed rapidly to a dark blue dress, put on her grass sandals, and set a black stole about her shoulders. She could draw it over her head to conceal the brightness of her hair. Then she crept out to the back hallway.

As she passed Liane's room, the girl came out, similarly dressed. They exchanged quick smiles. Again they had thought alike. Liane led the way to the back, out to the courtyard near the stables.

"He go this way often," whispered Liane.

Presently, as they waited, they saw a dark figure steal from the back of the house. Only the brightness of the hair in the half-light of the moon revealed who he was.

They waited. He walked past the stables and rapidly out toward the south, toward the cane fields.

Liane and Silva followed, drawing their scarves and wool stoles tightly about them. Liane went first, moving surely on her light feet, and Silva went in her footsteps. They moved as silently as Tyrone, accustomed to the irregular clods of earth, the cane fields, the tall grasses. The smell of burnt cane came to Silva's nostrils. They had burned the cane again this week, she realized. Harvesting? Brian had said nothing of it. Perhaps Rodrigues was continuing the work in the sugar-cane fields.

Liane's arm shot out, halting Silva. The two girls poised, like birds ready to flee, staring ahead. At the foot of the hill ahead of them, under the shelter of some trees, a campfire burned, and dark figures stirred and stood and walked about.

The girls knelt down, watching, then crawled as close as they dared. Silva, peering from under her dark stole, discerned the head of her twin brother, bright silver in the firelight. And there was the scarred dark face of Pedro Ortega, the bulky form of Rodrigues, and the slender, nervous form of Auguste. She recognized several of the others, restless young men of the island.

They waited, growing cold, but unwilling to leave. They could hear only the murmur of voices. Pedro pointed to Tyrone, and Tyrone nodded. Silva's mouth tightened. Tyrone, conspiring with those men? It could not be! She would tell him herself, if Liane would only permit it!

But what then? Tyrone had adored Maria Luisa as she had; he would try to avenge her death. And Pedro, older, experienced, cunning, brutal, would kill him.

She put her hand to her throat. No, she would not tell Tyrone. She could not. It would be to put a knife in her twin's throat.

Liane finally moved, nudged her, and they crept backward until it was safe to stand. Liane whispered when they were far enough that their voices would not carry, "It will be dawn soon. We must get back, and not be seen. They would kill us, you know. You must tell Brian nothing of this. His life will be in danger. Have you asked him about the sacred mountain?"

"He was angry—he mocked me," said Silva, in desolation.

"Ah," said Liane, that was all.

They got back to Cameron Hall as the sun crept up over the horizon, turning to red the fields and white walls, the hedges, the grass. Pink and crimson streamed across the dark purple sky.

They opened the gates and came inside, to the kitchen door, and into the hallway, softly on their sandals. But Silva, leading the way now, bumped into a hard, warm object—

Brian Cameron!

Her husband stood there, his eyes red-rimmed from lack of sleep, his mouth heavy with white lines beside it. He glared at her with wild fury.

"And where have you been—all this night?" he demanded in a biting voice.

Chapter 27

Silva put her hand to her wildly pulsing throat. Brian was in a white-hot rage. She had seen him angry, but never like this. His vivid eyes burned with fury.

Liane stood silently behind her, protectively, like the dark bulk of Maria Luisa. But she could do nothing, thought Silva.

"We—we went out—for air—" began Silva.

"You lie!" he raged. "You went to be with men! Tell me—where did you go? Did you go to Nathaniel? To whom?"

Liane stirred. "We followed Tyrone," she said quietly. "That is all. We worry about him."

He scarcely gave her a glance. "Go to bed," he told her curtly. "Silva, come with me!"

Liane sighed but finally went away quietly, giving Silva a thoughtful look from her enigmatic dark eyes. In it was some pity, but she would not interfere between husband and wife. Silva went with Brian, impelled by the hard clasp of his hand on her slim arm.

They went to her drawing room, and he shut the door quietly. The house was hushed and silent in the dawn; even the birds had not yet begun to chirp.

He faced her, his hand still tightly on her arm. There would be bruises later, she thought. He did not seem to realize how cruelly tight his fingers were closed about her.

"Now tell me. Where did you go? Why were you out all night?" he blazed.

"Liane has said it. We followed Tyrone. He has been troubled and quiet, and we worried about him." She faced him defiantly, her pointed chin up. He brushed back the dark scarf from her hair and it fell to the floor, ignored by them both.

"Why did you go? Why not tell me of it?"

"You do not listen to me!" she flared in turn. "You call me a silly girl!"

He bit his lip, but his fury still raged. "It was your place to tell me!" he said. "You are a married woman. You can't go running around at night. I'll have a talk with Tyrone. That brother of yours is too irresponsible!"

"No!" she said swiftly. "No, do not. It may mean much trouble. Please—Brian—"

She caught at his arm with her free hand, pleadingly. He stared down at it, at her. "All right, the whole truth," he said, more quietly. "Where did he go, and what did he do?"

"He—he went to meet some men. They are—are angry at you about the mine. We could not hear their talk, but they talked all night, many of the men. It means bad trouble. Oh, please, close up the mine, Brian. It means much grief."

"Of all the damn-fool stories—" he muttered.

He did not believe her! She felt a chill stealing over her. Her head drooped. How could she protect him when he acted like this? He did not believe her when she told him the truth. Her hand went to her throat, where the pulse beat frantically. He would die; she could not convince him of the trouble Pedro Ortega would make.

She must get Liane to release her from her promise. Brian must know the whole truth, and then he would believe—

Brian caught at her arms with both hands and shook

her a little. "Tell me the truth this time! What is going on? Whom did you meet?"

"We met no one. We followed and watched," she said dully. There was no urgency in her words, for she realized he would not believe her.

"Silva! You must tell me—is there some man you want, some man you love here? Is that why you wanted to return to Desirée? Tell me!"

"There is no man," she said flatly.

He cursed softly. His vivid blue eyes still flared with anger, with worry. "God, if I could believe you! Damn it all—"

"Why did you marry me?" she asked with weary bitterness. She was so tired, she thought she would fall down at his feet. "Why did you marry me? You could have had any woman—" She thought of the greedy mouth of Astrid Larsen, the sensuous movement of the woman's body.

"Because I wanted you," he said thickly. "Because I wanted your slim golden body, the softness and silkiness of you—because—" He halted, picked her up, and carried her to his bedroom, kicking shut the door after them.

Fear rose up like gall in her throat. He dumped her unceremoniously on his wide dark bed. Only a thin stream of sunlight came through the closed draperies, slanting a golden thread on the dark satin of the bedspread that had lain smoothly on it. So he had not slept last night. Had he paced back and forth between their rooms, like a black jaguar, menacingly, waiting for her return? His anger growing until it was a fury? Waiting to tear with his claws and his furious words at the fabric of her being?

His hands were not gentle now. Furiously he took the dress from her, the silky underthings. He flung the sandals away, and she lay on his white sheets of silk like a white scarf faintly tinted with gold. He gazed at her intently as he stood again, to fling off his own clothes with hasty hands.

He was still furious as he joined her on the bed. She had not moved, paralyzed with fright and the knowledge that no fighting, no running would evade. She trembled as he touched her with his lean dark hands, his possessive hands, and his mouth pressed to her pulsing throat.

"You are mine, mine," he whispered in a frenzy. "You shall not look at any other man."

She was infinitely sad at his words. He understood her so little. Her own virginity had withdrawn from the touch of any man; they had frightened her with their passions and their needs. Brian frightened her too much. How could she turn to any other man? She wanted no man—she wanted to be left alone, to bathe alone, to keep her young body to herself.

Brian understood her not at all. There was no meeting of minds as there was of bodies. When he caressed her, it was in a possessive way as one would touch a book, a flower, a statuette which one had plucked or bought. Was this all she meant to him?

In the dimness of the room she gazed at the crisp dark hair that brushed her chin and her cheeks. She was outflung, like a sacrifice to the gods, as he had tossed her. His one hand went slowly over her slim young breast, down to her waist, to her creamy golden thigh, and she shivered at the skill of his touch. Yes, he could rouse feelings in her—briefly.

"You belong to me!" he whispered against her breast. "Belong," what was that? On the island, one gave and received and gave again. She knew that much. One did not "belong," like a piece of land, like a house, like a pet dog.

His touch had gentled a little, but he was still fierce in his kisses, the pressure of his hands on her body. He moved on her slimness, as though searching restlessly for some token of meaning.

She lay limply as he caressed her, trying not to feel any response at all. But he was a skillful lover, she thought bitterly. He knew how to arouse a woman. He had known many women, probably Astrid Larsen among them. Yes, certainly, that woman. She had clasped him with her fingers red-tipped like claws, and known the frenzied possession of his hard lean body on her voluptuous white one.

Silva tried to turn from him, revolted by her own mind. She hated the thought of him with other women. He wanted her to belong only to him, but what of his own self? Did he consider himself free to turn to other women? And if so, why should she mind? Was she not relieved that he would use up his masculine energies on other women, and leave her alone?

No, something else burned in her. Was it jealousy? How could she feel like that? She remembered the woman who had tried to give her the snake present at her wedding. Somehow she had felt the significance of that present. Brian must have had her one day also. He was an older sophisticated man; surely he had known many women. Why, oh, why, had he insisted on marrying her?

Brian lay against Silva, feeling the slim tightness in her body, feeling the rage draining away as he caught the quiver of her breath. He had been so angry with her, he had frightened her, he knew. All that night he had paced, raging, unable to find out where she had gone. No one had known.

He had been unable to keep from himself images of his slim beautiful wife with another man, smiling at him, responding to him as she rarely did to Brian. How few were the times he had felt the slim hand on his head, on his neck; how seldom had she trembled in his grasp and responded physically. He knew she never had responded with her emotions.

But he knew also that she was young, untried, that she was virginal when he had taken her. Why was he so ragingly jealous of her? He resented it when he saw her with Liane, whispering secrets. He hated it when she smiled gently at Tyrone, and coaxed him to eat. Every look, every smile she gave to Julius, to Donald, to anyone at all, would eat into him like acid.

This was contemptible, he thought, trying to turn his thoughts from it. He had never felt like this before. He was jealous of her every move, of her mind, of her body, of her emotions, of her love. He wanted all of her, first, for himself.

He had thought it would not be difficult to woo her. She was young, innocent, and he was skilled in pleasing a woman. He had known many women, discarded them lightly. He had known when he enjoyed them, and they enjoyed him. Why, then, did he fail with the one woman he wanted most to please?

He had been brutal with Silva tonight. Already the marks of his fingers were showing dark bruises on her soft flesh. Gently he moved his hand over those marks, sorry for them. Broodingly he hung over her, watched her closed white lids, the flutter of her dark lashes.

A sigh murmured through her soft pink lips. He pressed his mouth lightly to her mouth, teasingly, trying to coax a response. At first she did not answer, then finally, when he had almost despaired, the soft mouth moved, the full underlip parted from its mate, and he felt the softness of her kiss on his mouth. He caught his breath, coaxed more kisses from her.

He took one of her golden arms and wound it around his neck. At first the hand was passive on his back, then convulsively she touched him, her fingertips tentative. "That is right, darling," he murmured encouragingly. "Touch me—I adore touching you. You are soft as silk, sweet as flowers in the night—"

The lashes fluttered open, the green eyes searched his eyes for a bewildering moment, then shyly she looked away. He brushed his mouth against the peach of her cheek, over to the earlobe, and he nibbled on the silken flesh below her ear. She shivered, and he stroked his hand skillfully down over her back, and to her thigh.

He drew her closer to his body, let her feel the hardness of himself against her skin. Her other hand came up slowly and wound against his neck, the fingertips feeling him lightly. He rolled over on his side, pulling her with him, and began to teach her more about lovemaking, encouraging her slightest movements, rewarding with a kiss when she responded to his gestures.

Oh, how lovely she was, how honey-sweet when she wanted to be! He felt himself intoxicated by her, his brain spinning as she finally began shyly to give him what he wanted. Her palm stroked over his chest, tentatively, over the thick hairs down to his waist. He watched her face with half-closed eyes, noting sharply any change of expression, the quiver of her lip, the relaxing of her taut jaw. He wooed her with all the cleverness he had ever used, and did not think of it as clever, anxiously absorbed in giving her pleasure, teaching her to love.

He took her hand and put it to his male nipples, and felt pleasure sharply through him as she touched him. He ran his hand again and again through the satin of her hair, which rippled down over her golden-tan shoulders. He bent over her and kissed her from her head to her heels, making her tremble with his caresses, yet not startling her into wary withdrawal.

And finally he took her, slowly, gently, thoroughly, making her feel the stabs of pleasure as he felt them. Slowly, joining them until they were breathlessly close, hands slipping on the slippery wet flesh, her soft cries music to him as she writhed helplessly in the golden mesh of erotic satisfaction. For the first time she responded completely to him, and he felt her tremble from head to foot, quivering in her reactions.

Finally he was entirely satisfied, shaken from his

usual control, adoring her even as he used her to slake his thirst. He lay back, his body limp, his breathing coming hard, before drawing her close to him. They were cool in the early dawn, wet from their efforts. He drew up a sheet to cover them both, his hand tender on her breast.

She pressed down against him, shyly, silently. She had said not a word during their embrace. That was the next step, he vowed happily. He would get her to speak to him, to say the love words he wanted to hear.

For now—he was so sleepy, so satisfied— He slept against her, holding her possessively.

Silva lay awake for a time, drowsily aware of his closeness in his bed. His was wider than hers, and the room was utterly masculine, as he was. Her half-closed eyes studied the tall wardrobe, severe mahogany carvings, the neat dresser, the table next to the bed filled with a clock, a pad of paper, and a pencil. Some scribbled drawings lay in a pile nearby. Did he waken and work sometimes? she wondered.

She turned a little and studied his face in sleep. She rarely saw him like this. Usually she slept, and he wakened early and left her. Now she could study him unawares. The hard lines were smoothed from his tanned face, his sensuous mouth was gentle, relaxed. The dark lashes fanned his cheeks. Would his son have such long lashes? she wondered, and flushed. Did he want a son? He had never said. The islanders all wanted sons, but Brian was different from them.

How strange men were. She studied his face as he slept. He could be ruthless to the point of brutality. Her shoulders ached from his shaking, and there were bruises on her arms. Yet he had turned tender and gentle, wooing her at length. He treated her like a child, stormed at her because she was not a woman yet, would not listen to her when she spoke seriously, then raged that she told him nothing.

Men. Her father had been vague, dreamy. She

wondered how her mother had felt about him as he lost himself in his paintings. Perhaps like this. Tolerant, smiling, pleased that he had found forgetfulness. Brian worked too hard; he drove himself from morning to night. And if he wakened from sleep, sat up to draw again, then he obtained even less sleep. She mused about that, about his work.

If only she could make him see the danger of continuing to work the copper mine. Her thoughts wandered to the secret meeting of Tyrone with Pedro Ortega and the others. Was Tyrone involved in their planning? What did they plan? Liane thought they would revolt against Brian Cameron, perhaps kill him. Kill—the hard face relaxed in death . . . "No, no, no," she whispered, her hand reaching out to touch the rough unshaven cheek of the man who had just taken her.

He was hard where she was soft. He was brutal where she was gentle. Yet he needed her in some curious fashion, perhaps the way men needed women. He sought her out, came to her, caressed her, as though he were hungry and thirsty for her.

What was it in men that drove them to seek a woman, some particular woman? Why had Brian married her? She did not know the answer yet, only that her skin pleased him, he enjoyed gazing at her and touching her, and dressing her in pretty garments, and having her in his bed.

She had been old enough to know that her mother had loved her father with an all-consuming love. She had seen the looks that passed between them in the days they had been happy together in England. Her fragile silver-haired mother had patiently carried easels and canvases, paints and picnic baskets out on the sands, had sat for hours for him to study and model, had played for him when he was weary. She had cooked for him on the temperamental wood stove, struggled with the housework when she could have had a glamorous life as a pianist. Oh, not in concert halls, but in nightclubs, wearing beautiful gowns. Silva had seen pictures of her mother, in low-cut gossamer dresses, seated at a piano, smiling at an audience. She could have had that—but she had left it all for the painter she had married.

And her death had left *him* hollow inside, Silva knew that. He had had little left to give his children, only a vague attention, a distant gaze, as though he had already left them to rejoin her in some radiant heavenly field.

Shyly Silva put out her hand and touched Brian's crisp curly hair. It was vital, alive, curling about her fingers. He seemed rather boyish this early morning, resting against her breast, his arm curled about her as though she were a pet stuffed animal he hugged in his sleep.

She had given in to him completely this time. Nothing had been held back. She had held him to her with a sort of despairing rapture, yielding to his fierce demands. Why had she? After he had held Astrid Larsen in his arms— After her hate of him—her fear of him—

Why had she wanted to please him? Why had she wound her arms about his neck, taken pleasure in caressing his strong neck, his smooth shoulders, the muscles of his back? Why had she wanted to touch the crisp hairs on his chest, run her palm over his nipples, touch his male body, press herself to him?

Half awake, she mused, and the truth came to her, as it often does when the guard is down and barriers weakened by drowsiness. She loved him.

She loved Brian Cameron, who had forced her to marry him, who had taken her innocence and used her virginity and looked at her with eyes of blazing desire. She loved him.

She clenched her fists against it, but it was there, curled up in her heart as he was curled against her body. She loved him, with the all-consuming love that forgave without effort. As her mother had loved her father, though their families had cast them off, though they were alone so much, though she lacked for the glories she had known. He had taken her away with him, and she had adored him. As Silva now loved her husband.

The knowledge was a shock that startled her into alert wakefulness. She had not wanted to love or trust him. But she loved him. She loved him, and her fingers stroked lightly over his smooth shoulders, stilling only when he stirred and muttered sleepily against her breast.

She did not want him hurt. That was why she had been so troubled, she realized. Pedro Ortega was a threat to his life, to his safety. How could she protect him? She must force him to listen to her. Pedro Ortega must not be allowed to wreck him, to cripple him as Mickey McCoy was crippled, trussed up in bed with a broken leg and scars on his face and shoulders.

She shuddered, tracing a line on Brian's shoulders. No, no scars there, please God, she prayed. No scars, no wounds, no horrible death for him. Let him live—oh, God, let him live.

Would Pedro try to kill him as he had killed Maria Luisa? A great knife plunged into his hard chest, reaching the great heart which had pounded so recklessly against her own minutes ago? No, no, no—

She had thought she hated Brian for forcing her, for insulting her, for going to Astrid. But she could not hate him. She loved him too much. He had been kind in his way. He had taken in Liane, and he had rescued Tyrone. The price had been high, but she had paid it. And he had been generous to her in turn.

But what would happen now? How could she protect him if he would not listen to her? The green eyes opened wide, she stared into space with a troubled gaze. How could she help him, if he did not listen and believe her?

She must find a way to protect him. Maria Luisa

would help. Surely she would hear her, and help her, and aid as she had in her lifetime. Maria Luisa must have gone straight to heaven, and her spirit would linger nearby to protect those she loved, with the help of Erzulie.

That was it. She must beg the help of Erzulie, of the gods that Maria Luisa had counted upon. Liane would help her. Together they would implore the gods, and make sacrifices to them. Pedro Ortega was bad, wicked. The gods must destroy him, and save Brian Cameron.

Her arm closed protectively about her lover as she lay with him. And in those hours as she thought, she seemed to grow up, as Brian had begged her to do. She must be strong, she must be wise, she must beg help of the gods and do as they advised—and Brian could then be saved. Her love would remain safe for her, the man she loved, however reluctantly she had come to love him.

Chapter 28

A brown boy had brought a message to Liane. She knew him little, only that he was related to Oona. She listened quietly.

"Pedro, he wants you to meet him on the beach tonight. You come, huh?" The boy was insolent, his great dark gaze on her, his mouth curling.

In the old days, when Maria Luisa was alive, all had been respectful to Liane. Those days were dead, as her mother was dead.

"Tonight?" she asked, to gain time. Silva must not know of this. She was in enough trouble with her husband. Outside the kitchen, Liane stood facing the boy, questioning him with her somber gaze.

"Yes, tonight. He come when the moon rise. You come, he say." The boy swaggered away, important, his hand jingling coins in his ragged pants.

Liane's mouth compressed. The moon rose late tonight. Pedro had his nerve. But she must go, must play her part. She had not met him since Silva had returned.

During dinner she was silent, thinking. Silva was quiet also, yet Brian did not seem angry with her. Indeed, he seemed pleased and his gaze went often, proudly, to the softly flushed face of his wife, the Nile-green dress that showed off her golden shoulders, the emeralds about her throat and on her hand. Yes, he dressed her well. What were relations between them? Better now? Liane wondered.

Tyrone was more quiet than ever, depressed, his

young face downturned. He contributed little to the conversation. Brian's sharp stare went over him, then he ignored the boy. Julius was talking mostly. He seemed a kind man, his silver-swept hair gleaming in the candlelight, his tanned face turned pleasantly from one to the other.

When he drew Liane, he seemed to study her with a look that went right through her to the bones, as Maria Luisa's gaze had done. In his conversation, tolerant and kind, he seemed like her also. Liane glanced at him, then down again to her glass of wine. She had not touched the gleaming white wine—she needed her wits about her tonight.

Julius was watching her, though she did not suspect it. What a beautiful face she had, so full of character and sadness. What thoughts stirred her, that the mobile mouth moved with unspoken words in her? Her dark hair gleamed blue-black in the candlelight. Her eyes were shadowy, great dark blazing fires at times. When he drew her, he tried to be very quiet, not speaking, so that she would dream, forget he was there, and her face would contain the expressions that fascinated him. Tomorrow he would try again to capture that look—the sad, haunted, tragic look—that mature look that set her apart from her dear friend Silva. Their joint portrait was even more of a challenge than he had thought it would be.

Liane drew a deep breath, almost a groan. Julius stirred, and leaned to her.

"You are weary?" he murmured.

"No—no—I was thinking—"

"Sad thoughts. I am sorry. A woman like you should always be happy. You should be cherished. You have gentleness and tenderness, and you should know no sorrow," he said quietly.

No one else heard them. They were engaged in listening to Mrs. Leoni. Julius studied Liane's dark eyes.

"You are—kind. But no one is entirely free of sorrow," she said softly, thinking of her lover who had deserted her . . . and her mother, departed too quickly from this world.

"What troubles you tonight?"

She did not answer, thinking of those she loved who were gone, the dark lashes shadowy on her dusky cheeks, a pink flush coming into her face.

"Brian has spoken of taking Silva to Europe. Later I will take Tyrone to join them. Should you like to come also?"

"I? You would take me—with you? Why?" She stirred in her chair, as though disturbed, suddenly for the first time really noticing this kind silver-haired man.

"Why? Because you should see beautiful places, hear music, laugh and be happy. Would you go? I would take the best of care of you, I promise." Julius looked at her earnestly.

He and Brian had discussed it briefly, tentatively. Brian had thought Liane would not come. But Julius sensed a hunger in her, a wish for other than the life she knew.

Her full mouth trembled and the dark eyes glistened. "Thank you for your kindness. I must—consider it." She looked at Silva, then down at her full wineglass.

They moved to the drawing room for coffee. The men drank brandy. Liane had a few sips of coffee, then watched for an opportunity to slip from the room. Only Silva saw her go, she thought, but Julius saw her depart also, and for him the lights in the room seemed to flicker and go down, losing their brightness. Where did she go? Out? Or to her room to brood over the death of her mother?

Liane went to her room, changed to a dark simple dress and sandals. With a dark scarf over her head, she went out the back corridor, past the kitchen, into the night. She made her way slowly, then more quickly as the route became familiar. Past the swimming pool, the stables, the fields of cane, over the hills.

She was a little afraid in the darkness. The jaguar had been seen again in these hills, far north of its usual lair. She started and looked upward at a movement in the trees, but it was only a sleepy bird, as startled as she was.

Rapidly now she moved down the hill, into the gentle slope to the beach. She stood in the darkness under the trees and waited for the rising of the moon.

It came, and with it came Pedro Ortega. She saw him, striding confidently on the sand, and her heart lurched. She felt a little sick with what she must do. She moved out from the shadows of the trees and stood silently for him to see her. She drew her scarf from her hair and settled it about her shoulders.

He saw her, and strode up to her, glancing beyond her suspiciously, searching the trees.

"No one followed," she said, her voice hard and cutting. "What you want, Pedro Ortega?" She flung her head back defiantly.

He grasped her wrists and drew her to him, grinning. "You come. You want to ask questions?" He pulled her roughly to him. "A kiss first."

She submitted to his rough embrace, to the hard caress of his mouth. He smelled of liquor—he had been drinking. She suppressed her keen distaste of him, her fear. She must do this. She submitted, but held her body slim and taut when he would have pulled her closer.

He drew back, staring down at her hungrily. "You come. You are my woman."

"I am the woman of no man. I am free. I am Liane."

He grunted, laughed. "No, not no more. You are my woman. Or you would not come to me like this."

His vanity was his weakness, she sensed. But she must move cautiously. He was clever and sharp, knowing people much as her mother had. She must draw on her mother's sensitivity, her ability to hide her feelings and get people to confide in her.

She shrugged, and the scarf dropped from her shoulders. "I am curious, that is all. Why do you send for me? What do you want to say?"

"You not come to me for too long." His voice softened as he stroked his hands deliberately over her bare arms. "Why you not come?"

"I am busy."

"You have moved into the house of that fellow Cameron. Is he your man now?"

She knew he knew better. "No, he marries with Silva, with my friend. He knows I have no mother, no home. He tells me I must live there, for safety."

"Huh." He listened keenly to her words, her tone. "You tell him about Maria Luisa, huh? You tell how she die?" His hands tightened about her arms, ominously.

"No."

She made it brief, with no protestations. She must move warily here.

"Why not?"

"You say not to tell," she said, her voice toneless.

"You afraid of Pedro?" he whispered, against her ear. He kissed her ear, like a bite. She shivered, and he laughed, pleased. He liked his women a little afraid of him. Thy were better that way.

"I am not afraid of any man."

Yet she was afraid of him, and her fear was like a choking in her throat, and he knew it. He laughed again, and put his arm about her, hugging her to him.

He grunted in his throat and fell to kissing her again, his grip brutally tight. He pulled her with him over the sand to the shadows of some palms near the edge of the ocean that swept up in white foam that moonlit night. He pushed her down onto the sand and went down with her, holding her passionately to him.

"Mm, you smell good. You got perfume?"

"Yes, from Miami. They give it to me," she murmured. She knew he liked perfume, softness, a woman's skin. She closed her eyes tight and thought of Maria Luisa, the blood gushing from her.

Pedro nuzzled his head into her throat, breathing of the perfume and of her own scent. She felt the welling up of passion in him, the animal need in him. His big hand pawed at the hem of her skirt. He swept the skirt up to her knees, rubbed his hand roughly over her. She pressed her hands up to push him away, in vain. He only growled and laughed at her futile efforts.

She lay still then, and he had his pleasure of her. He grunted and pushed, like an animal, she thought. She closed her eyes and tried not to think. But she remembered Nathaniel, and his gentleness, his sweetness with her. Her body softened, and Pedro enjoyed it.

"Hah, you like Pedro now, I bet," he muttered against her bared breast. He had opened the dress, pawed over her, defiled her, but she endured it. She must. She had her purposes.

He was skillful in a rough way. He made her respond to him, and he exulted in it, laughing, bragging, telling her she would enjoy being Pedro's woman. "I am a man, Liane. I take care of you!"

To please him, she put one hand on his face, pushing back his rough thick hair. He lay back happily on the sand, and she sat up.

She gazed out at the peaceful sea, where the waves lapped so gently on the sand. How many moons had come and gone since she had lain here in this place with Nathaniel? A lifetime ago, a bitter hate ago.

He put his big hand on her thigh. "Ah, you can please a man, Liane. Now you got a big man. You be the woman for me. I will make you queen of Desirée. I gonna be king soon, you bet!"

"How soon?" she asked, as though idly, yawning.

"Soon you bet," he said, more cautiously. "You

come. I have to meet men tonight." He got up, and hauled her to her feet. She straightened her dress. He got her scarf and put it about her with some gentleness, pressing his hand to her breast. "You good woman. You have more beauty than the others. You smart too. You be my queen."

He paused to pick up a large jug of rum, and took a long draught from it. He offered it to her, but she shook her head. "Later on, you drink with me. We seal our marriage with rum," he said, laughing. "You forget all about other men. You belong me." There was a threat in his voice.

"With you," she said slowly, "a woman would not want another man."

He laughed, pleased, and hugged her to him. They went off over the hill, and she saw in the distance a fire built up, and dark forms about it. They went to meet the other men who waited.

And among them was Nathaniel. But not Tyrone, she was quick to see. Nathaniel saw them coming, and he stood taut and tall, watching incredulously as Liane came into the firelight, Pedro's arm still about her waist possessively. Her hair had come loose and hung about her shoulders, down to her waist, mussed, like a woman's when she has known her man that night. She met his eyes gravely, then looked away with indifference.

Nathaniel hung his head. Pedro noticed, his lips curling with silent laughter, his eyes gleaming.

"So, we make the plans," said Pedro. "Here is my woman—she knows it, I know it. Liane is my woman —no one else touch. You see this?"

There was a murmur among the men. Only Nathaniel was silent, hurt, his gentle face incredulous. Pedro gave him a sharp look. Liane remained at Pedro's side as he stood and talked to them.

Mostly brag talk, she thought. He would do this, he would do that. Nothing planned yet. Maybe he was working up to something.

"One day the white men all gone from this island," said Pedro, leaving her briefly to lift a fresh jug of rum to his mouth. He drank deeply, passed the bottle on. "We make cane grow tall, we burn it, we make the rum, we sell it in Miami. All for us. The island of Desirée will be ours again."

Liane thought, But it was never yours, Pedro! It belonged to us, not to you. You came from outside; you are the outsider. Even Brian Cameron is here longer than you, much longer. She said nothing, her dark eyes watching.

"The sacred mountain rumbles," said one man, turning nervously toward the southeast, where the mountain stood darkly against the purple-black sky. "I hear it moan at night. Bad."

"Yes, and the jaguar howls at night, baying at the moon. It mad with us," said Auguste. He wiped his wet face with his hand. "What will we do, if the man continues to order us to rebuild the smelter? That is a bad thing. For he makes us dig in the sacred mountain, and load the precious earth of it into the little cars, and take it down to the smelter, where it melts to nothing. I have seen this. Nathaniel also, and everyone here."

"It will be ended," said Pedro with quiet conviction, his bragging tone stopped for a time. "I say this, it will be stopped. The sacred mountain must stand, though all whites say no. The whites will be driven from the island. They cannot remain, for the gods are angry with them."

"What can we do? Brian Cameron, he is rich, he pays much money, he find men to do what he say." Auguste was worried, his dark eyes darting from Pedro's face to Liane's.

She stood there, warm in the firelight but cold in her heart. She had the feeling that behind her stood Maris Luisa, urging her to listen, to remember. The gods were whispering to her, through the voice of Maria Luisa:

"Listen, my daughter! Remember! The white men have been kind to you. The father of Silva taught you to read and write; he gave you and your mother a home! The husband of Silva gives you another home, dresses, a place at his table with his honored guests! He does not act ashamed of you. He gives you no side glances of desire! With respect, he treats you! *Who is your friend now, Liane?"*

Pedro's voice cried out over the strong silent voice behind her. "That white man must go! That Cameron! He does not belong here! When the time is right, we will rise up and strike him from the island! He must go! He will destroy the island! And he marries with Silva. So she must go also!"

There was a hush, a little gasp of protest from Auguste. Pedro's burning look went to him harshly.

"Silva has done no wrong. She honors our gods," said Auguste bravely. There was a murmur of agreement.

"She marries with the white man. She wears the silk dresses earned by our hard work!" Pedro roughly told them. "And her brother, Tyrone, he pretends to be one of us, but he is silent, hiding his wicked thoughts! He must go also! He is not brown of skin, like us. He is white, all through. He must go!"

Anger shook Liane. He was turning them against Silva and Tyrone! And they had done no harm! Indeed, Silva would do good, gently influencing her husband to do better by them. She kept silent, but it was hard.

She had seen how it was with Brian Cameron. When he turned his look on Silva, Liane with the wisdom of her mother saw the desire of his eyes, the gentleness of his face. She had changed him, little silver-haired girl, so that he was more gentle. Even when he was angry with Silva he touched her with hands of love. Surely Silva would one day be able to turn his thoughts from the money to be earned by wrecking the sacred mountain.

Still Liane said nothing. It was not time to speak. Only her heart seemed to burn in her, for the desire for revenge for her mother was hot in her. Only more was involved than revenge. She must be quiet, and wait for the gods to tell her to speak.

She stood there and listened while Pedro urged them to drink, and talk against the white men, and retell old stories of the wrongs white men had done against them on the islands. He told them a long, involved story of how white men had turned against him on another island, taken his beautiful girl from him, and made her a whore. They gasped and nodded. "Yes, the white men were bad all through," they agreed, and drank until their voices were thick and they could not stand erect.

Only Nathaniel had his head down, not drinking, and presently he walked away into the darkness. He was followed by the fierce gaze of Pedro, and Liane feared for Nathaniel. That gaze meant no good. Nathaniel was foolish to show his feelings so.

She wondered if he saw Oona, or if he went only to the white woman, the yellow-haired woman with the hard features and the eyes like blue stones whose presence she endured at Brian Cameron's table. She would do him no good, that one.

She had no emotion left for him. Nothing was in her but the urge to hate, to have revenge. So she remained, and pretended to drink, merely touching her mouth to the jug of rum that went around and around. She listened to the drunken bragging of Pedro, endured his hold of her, evaded the gazes of other men as he showed his possession of her by kisses on her neck and pinches on her arms.

Near dawn Pedro fell asleep, and others did also. Liane crept away from the dying fire and stumbled on her way home, back to the large white Cameron Hall. She went to her room, stripped off the dress, and went to the bathroom to wash in the great white tub.

She scrubbed and scrubbed, but could not entirely wash off the feel of the hands of Pedro, of his hot, sweaty body, the lust he had felt for her. She used what her mother had taught her, so she would not have his child. That would be the final curse, she thought, drinking deeply of the herbs.

Nathaniel had gone away to the beach. He sat alone, his head on his hands. He had lost all, he thought with desolation. He had lost the beautiful Liane. She stood, her gaze remote, not quivering with desire for him, allowing that tough Pedro to hold her. He felt sick as he thought of the way the dark man had touched his beautiful Liane, stroking his thick paws over her belly and breasts. And Liane had stood still, and let him do it! Truly, she had become the woman of Pedro.

He felt vaguely sorry, for himself. Everything had gone wrong in the past two months. Even the yellow-haired woman had turned from him when Brian Cameron had come home. His mouth tightened in anger. Well, she would not discard him so lightly! She had welcomed him into her bed, and they had known each other on the beaches. He had known the pleasure of her white flesh against his dark body, and her squeals of delight at his caresses. She would want him again!

He watched and waited, and that afternoon she came down to the beach. She had formed the habit of coming to walk on the sand, restlessly striding up and down, cursing the air and Brian Cameron. He knew it, for he had been watching her. Then she would return, all smiles and bright eyes, to Cameron Hall once more. But he, Nathaniel, knew what went on in her jealous heart.

This afternoon he waited until her light sandals came near him. She wore today a light blue dress to her ankles, and carried a parasol against the sun, to protect her glowing white skin. Her golden hair shone with light, coiled neatly about her head, but her blue eyes were sullen like the sky when a storm comes.

He stepped out from the bushes and faced her. She started back, and her eyes flashed at him.

"What are you doing?" she blazed at him. "Why do you come here?"

"Why do you come here?" he asked sullenly.

"That is my concern!" Her red mouth pouted. There was paint on it—he had kissed her at times until the red paint was all gone. He looked hungrily at her white flesh, at the soft throat revealed by the low-cut blue dress.

She turned about to leave him again. He strode forward, barefoot, desperate. Liane had left him, but he did not consider how that had come about, that he had left her waiting too many times. He had lost Liane, but he had this woman, and she must do! His loins were hungry for a soft woman.

He caught her by the waist. She flung about, dropping the parasol. "How dare you touch me!" she flared.

"You did not object before!" he told her, holding her fast. He ducked his head and pressed his mouth to her neck. She struck out at him, scratching him with her red fingernails.

"You fool! Someone will see us!" She was cold today, striking out at him until he caught her arms and held them behind her. A frenzy was boiling in him. He had to have her. He had to forget himself and his frantic worries in a woman's arms.

"Let them!"

"No, no, no—" He crushed her mouth under his. She softened. "Oh, you are a beast today," she whispered, her blue eyes gentling.

"It is the only way with you," he growled, caressing her breasts roughly.

"No, let me go—you'll muss my dress."

"Take it off, then," he whispered huskily.

"No, I'm returning to the hall—don't do that!" She tried to pull away, but he dragged her toward the deep shelter of the thick bushes.

"You beast—stop it—you'll tear my dress!"

"Take it off—or I will do it for you—"

She did not submit, threshing about in his arms wildly. He finally flung her down into the sand and fell on her brutally. She writhed about, then his passion finally began to awaken a response. He took her brutally, as he had been wanting to do, all gentleness forgotten. He tore her undergarments, the silk ripping in his strong fingers, and she sobbed, ripping at his shirt as he bent over her.

But finally he had her subdued, and she lay quietly for him, gasping with shock again and again, until he made her respond, and she wanted him also, as she had at first.

When it was over and he moaned against her breast, with pleasure this time, she said again, "You beast," but it was a soft epithet against his ear, and she kissed his lobe, nuzzling her mouth against his throat.

"It is the only way to be with you," he said darkly, and drew back to look at her peaceful features. "You come again tomorrow, huh?"

"Maybe," Astrid said and laughed teasingly.

Desolately he thought she would not. She would be afraid to come again. Not afraid of him, but afraid of being seen. She was angry about Silva and Brian, he knew that, for she had cursed them both. But she still hoped to lure the man to her bed. Poor little Silva, she had little chance against this practiced temptress.

She dressed again, and went away, her parasol erect and arrogant over her golden hair. Nathaniel watched her go, feeling empty and lost. What had gone wrong with him and Liane? What had gone wrong with Desirée?

It was all the fault of the white man, he thought. The fault of Brian Cameron. With his coming, all had gone wrong, just as Pedro Ortega had said.

Chapter 29

Brian found he needed to go back to Miami for parts for the smelter. The freighter captain had brought the wrong size. And, Brian decided with resignation, he really should go and see how his business went. He might be held on Desirée for some weeks, and with the syndicate trying to get into his mining interests he had best find out firsthand how things went.

He offered to take Astrid Larsen back with him. She gazed up at him with languid blue eyes and shook her head. "No, darling, I'm enjoying the sunshine here, and the peace and quiet."

He was dubious about that. Astrid enjoyed trouble, not peace and quiet. But since the Leonis were staying a little longer, there was not much he could do, as a host. Donald Keller seemed satisfied to stay also, and Brian had his own thoughts about that. He could tell him it was a futile trip for Donald, but the man could rest peacefully in his dreams. Brian had had him checked upon by Antonio and Marco, and the report had made him thoughtful.

Brian left Silva and Liane in Julius's care. "Take care of my girl," he said in the garden where the two girls were posing for Julius. Silva looked at him with an enigmatic green gaze, and Liane looked with great dark eyes at nothing.

Julius said, his paintbrush poised over the palette, "I'll take good care of them both, don't you worry. I'm going to get some good sessions of painting in while you are away. You're too much of a distraction!"

The men laughed, and Silva blushed a little, her head lowered. Brian went over to her, took the gentle pointed chin in his hand, and dropped a kiss on her cheek. He had said good-bye to her last night, in her bed, silently, with all the passion in his body. He hated leaving her even for a few days. He had never thought to see himself tied firmly in the silken net of a woman's presence, and love it. He stroked his thumb over her pink cheek.

"Be a good girl," he said. "Mrs. Leoni will talk to you about New York, and housekeeping, she promised. And in Miami I'll see about a traveling wardrobe for you. We'll be taking off for Europe after Christmas."

She nodded, her gaze resting briefly on his. "Yes. Have a—a good trip, Brian."

He left then, not looking back. If he did, he might not go, he decided with resignation. He had it bad, not wanting to leave her. The honeymoon would help. He could have her with him, night and day, forgetting about business and the outside world, except as an enchanted setting for themselves.

The garden was silent then, but for the buzzing of bees and the quick call of a bird in the hibiscus bushes. Silva and Liane sat, with their own thoughts elsewhere. Julius gazed at them, then back at his canvas.

The two of them looked like goddesses, poised against the hibiscus hedge, the one head glossy-dark, the other so silver-bright. The two faces were turned to the south, sun striking across them, one golden-dark, one golden-light. Liane's hand rested gently on the shoulder of Silva, from behind her, and Silva's hands held a spray of white jasmine. As Julius made the picture take shape on his canvas, he thought he could see various meanings attached to his portrait of them:

Experience hovering behind innocence.

The dark inheritance of our ancestors, advising the present.

The *loa* which whispered in the ear of the devoted girl.

Simply, they were two friends, but other meanings tinged their relationship. They had grown up together, with the wisdom of the same woman guiding them. They were close in spirit and action. They were both gentle, womanly, sweet, yet so different.

He worked all morning, absorbed, allowing them to move about the garden now and then, sitting back to relax his hand. He felt impelled by some drive to keep working, while the images were fixed in his mind.

At noon the girls went indoors, and Julius reluctantly gathered up his canvas and went inside also. The hot sun of afternoon was too much. His paints would melt. He set the canvas carefully in the large room allotted to him. With satisfaction he stood back to study it. He would add an immense blue-green butterfly to that corner, another spray of allamanda above their hair. Then just the hibiscus behind them, and their dresses lightly suggested, Liane in shimmering blue, Silva in silvery-green.

He went to lunch, distracted, and noted how much more poised Silva was. She had gone to confer with the chef about the evening meal, accompanied by Mrs. Leoni. The older woman was pleased with her new advisory role and was eager to give Silva suggestions whenever she asked.

Astrid was feeling much out of it, thought Julius, noting the pouting mouth, the glazed blue eyes. Trouble in that direction, he predicted, listening to the sugary-sweet voice as she addressed her hostess. But nothing happened that day, or the next. Julius relaxed, and worked on his painting.

Silva was happier these days. Brian had been gentler, more considerate, treating her like an adult. When he had left, he had told her seriously that he wanted her to learn about housekeeping, for she would have the care of his various homes. She wanted to learn about the foods he enjoyed, the wines he wanted, how he liked things done.

Silva felt now that she had a definite place in his life. She was not just a harem girl awaiting his pleasure. She was a woman, a wife, his woman, who could keep his house swept and ready for him, as the islanders did.

Translated into his sophisticated and complex life, that meant making a home for him wherever they were, seeing that meals were served when he wished, guests were taken care of, his work was not interfered with. He was a very busy and important man, and he could not be troubled with little details. So she conferred with the chef, studied menus, talked with Mrs. Leoni about the Miami and New York apartments. Mrs. Leoni and her husband both told her about the best wines to serve with various dishes, how cocktail parties were managed, even how to contact rum dealers in New York in these Prohibition times.

She was busy and happy now, with something special to do, to make life more comfortable for Brian Cameron. She did not know what the future would bring, but somehow he had made a place in his life for her, and he made her feel important. She would try her best to make her man comfortable.

Astrid watched her with steady, silent insolence. Finally, on the fourth day of Brian's absence, she approached her. Silva was in the dining room, studying table arrangements.

"Poor child, you have so much to learn," said Astrid, coming in from the terrace, where she had been sunning herself.

"Yes. However, Mrs. Leoni is most helpful," Silva said with polite reserve. She had noted Astrid lying out on a lounger, her short blue dress to her knees, her sapphires incongruously decorating her tanned arms and throat.

"Brian has always been a strange man," said Astrid, leaning against the tall mahogany buffet on the side of the room, watching as Silva studied the arrangement of silverware. Silva gently arranged another flower in its place in the silver epergne, and Astrid's mouth curled. "Don't you think so?"

"Strange? No, I don't think so," said Silva, coldly.

"Ah, you don't know him very well yet," yawned Astrid, patting her scarlet mouth in a gesture that implied she had tasted his strange, forbidden fruit. "I have known him for years, and believe me, he makes sudden moves you cannot figure ahead. That is why he is so clever in the business world. No one knows what he is going to do next. Who would have thought he would marry a little island nobody like you? He could have had his choice of any woman he wanted."

Silva clasped her hands before her to still the quivering. She knew that. She had asked herself the question over and over.

"I figured it out," said Astrid idly. "He wants a son, probably. And no man wants to be made a fool of. He figured an innocent young girl like you would have his son, and his only."

Silva thought violently, I should hope so! Her young mouth quivered with indignation at the daring of the older woman, but she merely moved a spoon carefully, cocking her head to one side to study the place setting.

"He pays well, of course," said Astrid callously, her eyes narrowed to slits. She held out her arm, glittering with the sapphire bracelet. "He gave me this a couple of years ago, when he was with me in New York. A very generous man. That's why women keep coming around, and will continue to do so, even though he is married. No one woman could hope to hold him forever. Don't you agree?"

Silva had to look at the gleaming stones thrust under her nose. Then she turned and walked away, Astrid's laughter cutting sharply through the silence. Silva would carry on no such conversation! She went out to the kitchen, sat down at the table, and turned the pages of the French cookbook. She could not see a single word, and her hands were shaking.

It was all bad enough to think that Brian had known many women. But to know he continued to know them, to give them gifts, that Astrid had been his mistress and been paid well for it—it made her sick.

Tyrone came into the kitchen and sat down with her. He attempted a smile. The girl who worked there silently brought him a cup of coffee and a sweet cake. He nibbled at the cake. Silva patted his hand. "How are you, Tyrone? I scarcely speak to you," she said, in the island patois.

"You have work to do. It is good," he said morosely. His face was dark and brooding. The silver hair, so like hers, fell forward on his forehead, rough, as though he had not bothered to wash or brush it for a time.

"You do not read your books?" she asked, turning the pages of the cookbook.

"What use? Where do I go?"

"Brian will direct—"

"He knows little of what will happen," Tyrone interrupted bitterly. "All the world explodes, and he knows nothing."

"What do you mean?" She felt cold at heart, and grasped his wrist as he would have risen. "Tell me."

"You cannot help. It is written what will happen."

He rushed away, and the island girl stared at Silva with wide-open dark eyes. The chef, not understanding their words, blinked after him.

Silva went to Liane's room and found her sitting at the window, watching the late-afternoon sky. Liane turned to smile at her, and Silva sat down on the divan with her. With a sigh, Silva said, "Tyrone is troubled. So am I."

"And I. I do not know what to do."

"What happens?"

"Pedro sends for me again. I cannot go," said Liane simply. "He makes me sick. I cannot submit to him again. I have the feeling that things explode soon. Oh, why are my people so blind?"

"Tyrone says this also. Ah, what can we do?"

Liane drew her gently to lay her head on her breast. It was as though Maria Luisa were there, holding her, and Silva felt vaguely comforted.

"We must consult the gods," said Liane presently. "Tonight Auguste will hold a meeting. I have sent word. We will meet on the sacred mountain. Many will come, for many are troubled."

"We must go, then."

"I will go." Liane hesitated, stroking Silva's hair. "I am not sure you should go, my dear."

"Why? I would speak with the gods. I would help in the meeting," Silva protested.

"Your man will not like it."

"He is not here."

Liane shook her head. "You must obey him whether he is here or not."

Silence. Silva sighed heavily. "I think he is in danger, Liane. What will they do?"

"They talk of blowing up the mine on the Mountain of the Cat," said Liane. "I go with Pedro and I listen. It is the only way to know. Pedro leads them cleverly along his paths of wickedness. He is a very bad man. He comes from outside, and talks big about how he will lead them. He wants only his own power, his own importance."

"How can we stop him? Brian will not listen to me."

"You must talk to him again. But the gods have been advising me," said Liane, sounding strangely like Maria Luisa, with a deeper, more certain voice. "I will consult them again tonight. Papa Henri will be there. He promises his help, though he is old and frail. Auguste is uncertain—he must hear the gods. All of us will consult the gods, and learn of their will."

"Then I must go also," said Silva firmly.

Liane finally nodded in agreement.

That evening they ate little at dinner, drinking nothing. Tyrone watched them suspiciously, then looked down at his plate. He had heard of the meeting, and he knew what they would do. Silva did not speak to him of the meeting, but after dinner she sat on the couch in the drawing room with him and put her hand on his. His hand was icy cold. She warmed it gently with hers, and hoped he would be comforted. It was dangerous for Tyrone to come to the meeting. He was a man. If they turned on him, he might be killed. He was a white man.

Silva left the company when she could. Liane had already gone to her room, pleading weariness. Julius said he would entertain the company, and he did, with his worldly-wise stories, his jokes, his gentle wisdom. She felt safe leaving them to him.

In her room she put on a simple white cotton dress, the white of Erzulie, sacred to her. She fastened back her hair with a white scarf and wore white sandals. Over this, she put on a dark full-length cloak, and a dark scarf over her hair. Stealing out, she met Liane outside the kitchen, and clasping cold hands, they went out into the darkness. It was a long walk, to the south, to the sacred mountain.

Brian had been uneasy. He hated leaving Silva for so long. He had hastened his work in Miami, and now the freighter drew into port. Rather than wait for a carriage, he walked home, the long distance, arriving at about midnight. He was weary, but happy to be back. Business had gone well, and he had the parts he needed to repair the smelter. Now work could proceed.

He entered a silent house, only the servant there to unlock the large front door and let him in. He had insisted on having all doors locked by the time all were indoors at night.

He went to his room, but he hungered to see Silva. Quietly he went to her bedroom, just to gaze upon her and make sure she was all right.

Once there, he stared incredulously at the bed. It had not been lain upon; the pillows were smooth and white in the moonlight. Her evening dress was lying over a chair, and high-heeled shoes were tumbled about. His mouth tightened.

He went to Liane's room, to find the door unlocked, and she was not there either. He went to Tyrone's room, fear in his heart. He found the boy lying awake on his bed, his hands under his head.

The boy shot up at seeing him, the green-gray eyes opening wide in the lamplight. "You—you're back early—" he stammered. There was fear in his face.

Brian asked crisply, "Where is Silva?"

The boy swallowed. Brian watched the Adam's apple move up and down. "Why—isn't she in her room—or the garden?"

"No. She isn't. She's gone, and so is Liane! Where did they go? Tell me or I'll . . ." His voice was cold and deadly. Could Silva have gone off to meet a man? Were Astrid's sugary lies really true? Astrid had told him no island girl was really innocent, that Silva surely had a lover of her own. She had hinted she had seen the girl with a man. But she must have lied—she must have!

Tyrone slid off the bed. He hitched up his pants nervously. He had not undressed for bed, Brian noted grimly. "Why—I could guess—"

"No guessing, Tyrone. You know where they went. Tell me at once."

Tyrone bent his head, then nodded. "They went out, I think, to the sacred mountain, to a meeting.

I heard about it. Auguste is planning it. They will invoke the gods," he added simply. "Silva and Liane are troubled. So are others."

Brian felt both relief and a wild impatience. That paganistic nonsense again! The sooner he got Silva away from here, the better.

"Where are they meeting? Do you know?"

Tyrone nodded. "There is a *hounfor*—a place—on the mountain, a large place. Many are coming."

"Take me there."

Tyrone stared. "But you— They won't let— I mean—you are white—"

"So is Silva," said Brian curtly. "Come along—you're dressed."

"Wait!" Tyrone took a step forward. "You can't go like that. I mean—in dark clothes."

"Why not?"

"They will invoke Erzulie. You must wear white, or it is an insult," Tyrone explained worriedly. "You have a white shirt, white pants?"

Brian was ready to hit out in his wild impatience. But he controlled himself. He would have to go along respectfully with the customs if he wished to make sure of Silva.

"All right. Meet me in ten minutes at the kitchen door," he said and strode out. In his room he changed rapidly, grimacing at himself as he put on a white shirt and cream trousers. He added a white coat, thinking they would probably be covered with dust and mud by the time he returned. But he *had* to go. He had a strange impulse that impelled him: He had to go where Silva was.

Tyrone met him at the kitchen door. In his hand was a live white chicken, trussed and squawking. "An offering," Tyrone explained simply.

"Should I take something?" Brian asked grimly.

"No, this is from both of us. We go together. This way."

Tyrone strode off into the star-studded night. Brian

followed him, mocking himself for this impulsive venture. It would be a long walk, and he was weary from the trip, from staying up half the night to get his business completed quickly in Miami. And now this!

They walked south, in silence. They walked past can fields, which smelled of smoke. Brian sniffed. Rodrigues had been burning the cane, he thought. So, they were harvesting in spite of his orders! Making rum, most likely. Rodrigues was due to be fired, no matter what happened, he promised. Things had been out of control here for quite long enough!

It was past two in the morning when they arrived at a firelit opening in the trees. Brian saw a large hut, which was composed of a roof of leaves and boughs supported by posts. About it were more walls of boughs, but a space was left between the tops of the walls and the roofs—for air, he thought. Actually it was a place for the spirits to enter, but Brian did not know that.

Tyrone's thin hand clasped his wrist urgently as Brian would have strode in. "They have started," he said swiftly. "Go in quietly. I will kill the chicken, then sit down. You sit on a mat, quietly, or stand near the door. Whatever happens, do not interfere! If Silva dances, do not go near her! Any movement of yours will be taken as insult. You are a guest only. Do you understand?"

Brian hesitated, but he had not come so far to ruin everything. He nodded grimly. Tyrone let him go in. Brian stood in the wide doorway, glancing about. Silva sat on a mat beside Liane, her gaze turned raptly toward the wizened figure of a man sitting on a chair near the center post.

Brian stared at Silva. She wore her hair loose, and in the simple white dress she looked younger than ever. Liane wore white also. Then he noticed that all the women wore white dresses, and the men white shirts and light trousers. Something drew Silva's gaze as Brian moved. She glanced up, her green eyes widening as they focused on him.

He moved inside the hut and sank down beside her. He grasped her wrist, and her fingers moved to curl inside his fingers. She gave him a surprised wide smile that reached her eyes. A smile of gladness, of pleasure. It warmed his cold heart. Liane glanced at him absently, then back at the center post.

The drums hesitated, then began again, faster than ever. There was a rhythmic pounding to them that stirred the blood. Even Brian felt it, the insistent rhythm of the great drum, and counterpoint of the little one, the rolling timbre of the middle drum. There was sweat on the dark faces of the drummers, intent on their music. Tyrone came forward, and the chicken was slashed, blood poured near the center post. Ceremoniously he offered the chicken to Papa Henri, who nodded and indicated a woman, who took the chicken and carried it out.

Tyrone sank down near them, watching intently. Brian felt someone staring at him. He glanced about, found that most of the islanders were gazing at the post. Only one stared at him—a man in the shadows. A scarred man, with a red shirt!

A red shirt! It must have some significance. He noted the man did not come forward and participate as some jumped up and began dancing. A thin wailing cry began, from Papa Henri, lifting his head and singing out. The cry made a shiver go down Brian's spine, it was so primitive, so fraught with entreaty and need.

Silva had withdrawn her hand from his. Intently she listened to the drums, her face somber. Liane was staring intently ahead of her, swaying slightly back and forth, back and forth. The drums beat faster. Auguste sprang into the center and began to dance around and around the pole in a frenzy. Someone caught him, held him, and he paused, wiping his face with his scarf. He streamed with sweat in the cool evening air.

Now Brian noticed the drawings about the mud floor. Outside was thick jungle, inside a fire and crude patterns on the floor, the smell of sweat and rum, the insistent pounding of the drums. He felt a little mesmerized himself, swaying as the drums pounded. Tyrone was intent, sober, watching his sister.

Pedro Ortega glared from outside in the shadows. He was furious. This meeting had been held against his wishes. Auguste and Nathaniel had insisted on listening to Liane. He would pay them for that.

Liane was listening, listening for the inner voice.

Silva waited, caught up in her trance.

Then the drums paused for a heartbeat, and started again in a different rhythm, the rhythm of Erzulie. Liane sprang up. Silva followed her instinctively, and both girls sprang into the center of the floor and began to dance, gracefully throwing up their arms, bowing to the center post, crying out to Erzulie to come to them, come to them.

Silence fell in the little hut, silence but for the heavy breathing and the insistent beat of the drums. The drums seemed to follow the girls as they danced. Brian was stunned. One moment Silva had been quietly beside him, so close he could have touched her. The next moment she was gone from him, physically and mentally, out there in the circle of dark-faced sweating natives. Her bare feet pounded on the earth as she followed Liane about the pole, weaving around and around, again and again.

Liane groaned, cried out, and slumped over as though a huge burden had fallen on her. Silva, behind her, clutched at her, held her upright. Auguste, young and sturdy, sprang to help. They held her upright. She struggled from them, attempted to dance once more, then cried out in a familiar voice—but not her own.

Brian started. If his eyes had been closed, he would

have sworn the voice was the husky deep voice of Maria Luisa!

But it came from Liane!

Petrified, he sat there, unable to move, staring as his wife held Liane, stroking the hair back from her wet forehead. "Speak, speak, oh, Maria Luisa, oh, Mamacita!" cried Silva, and her voice also was deep and husky in tone.

There was a low murmur of excitement, then hushed silence. Papa Henri had raised his thin long arm for silence. His wrinkled face, like a withered walnut, was turned intently to the two girls.

"Oh, Maria Luisa," he said in patois, "oh, guide us with your wisdom. Tell us, *loa* of Maria Luisa, tell us what we must do. What of your death? Oh, what of our lives? Oh, Maria Luisa—"

Liane cried out then, half in English, half in the patois, as her mother had spoken. "Oh, I come to warn you, my people, my loved ones!" She writhed convulsively as the spirit held her in its grasp. "I warn you—evil has come to Desirée!"

A low murmur swept the men and women. Liane gasped, choked, and was given something to drink by Auguste. Silva tenderly wiped her forehead with her scarf.

Liane went on: "Evil has come to our island. Pedro Ortega comes, and makes evil! You have done wrong to listen to him! He comes and kills, and makes all bad! Rodrigues and Pedro, do not follow them!"

Brian glanced quickly at the red shirt of Pedro Ortega, saw the scarred face of hate above it. His eyes sought Rodrigues, saw him staring in horror at Liane, his hand to his breast.

"They will lead you to the devil!" said Maria Luisa's husky voice. "To the devil only! Death and destruction on Desirée! I have spoken to my children, to my Liane and my Silva."

Then, to Brian's horror and shock, Silva stiffened

and flung back her bright head. "Oh, my friends," she said, in the husky voice of her beloved Mamacita. "Listen to me, listen to me. Follow not the evil ways of Pedro and Rodrigues! Who would follow the stranger who comes from the other islands, who does not know and respect our ways? Drive Pedro Ortega from the island! He brings only grief to you!"

Liane echoed her words. Both girls had their arms upraised imploringly to the gods. Auguste was holding them, his face dripping with sweat, tormented. Papa Henri listened in impassive silence. Others stared with wide eyes, breath caught in their throats. The girls cried out warnings in unison, and the islanders listened in respect.

The red-shirted man flung back his head. Evil gleamed in his eyes. He glared at the company. Brian took his gaze from him to look at Silva, then returned to Pedro. But the man was gone, slipping away into the darkness.

Liane sank to the ground; Auguste could not hold her as she writhed. Silva, eyes wild, knelt beside her sister, crying out, "Oh, Liane, Liane, Mamacita was here! I heard her voice, I spoke as she commanded!"

Brian could endure no more. He sprang up, in spite of Tyrone's urgent hand on his arm. He strode into the center of the circle and picked up the light, weak form of his wife. He nodded to Tyrone, who had dared to follow him. "Bring Liane. We'll go home," he said soberly, and glared at the company to defy them.

Papa Henri stared at him with enigmatic brown eyes. He waved his thin arms, and the crowd parted for them silently. Liane staggered along, held upright by Tyrone. Brian carried Silva, for she seemed half-conscious, moaning a little.

A woman followed them out and handed their cloaks to Brian in silence. He tucked Silva in hers and picked her up again. Liane was shuddering, exhausted.

It was a long, stumbling, nightmare walk back to Cameron Hall, the darkness filled with the sound of drums, diminishing the farther they went. Dawn was crimsoning the eastern sky as they finally stumbled wearily into the courtyard at the back of the hall.

Liane roused finally as they entered the hall. "We should have stayed. The work is not yet done," she said in a weary voice.

"You have done enough," said Brian curtly. "You must not go out again."

She gave him a tired, enigmatic look, and Tyrone escorted her to her room. Brian carried Silva's light form to her bedroom and laid her on the bed.

She half opened her eyes. "I am glad—you came," she said weakly. "You came—back—"

"Yes, I came back—just in time, it seems."

She closed her eyes and a half-smile curled her mouth. "It is in time. The trouble comes now," she murmured, and slept.

He stood, frowning down at her, not understanding, not yet. But he was awed and shaken. Something had happened tonight that could not be explained in cool, familiar scientific language. With his own eyes he had seen the frenzied dancing, the invocation of the gods. Their sincerity had touched him. Then with his own ears he had heard a dead woman speak through Liane and through Silva.

He had to believe what he himself had witnessed.

Chapter 30

Silva wakened with a jolt and sat upright. She stared about her, trying to remember what had happened. It was day, the sun blazed into her room. She was wearing a dusty, sweat-stained white dress; someone had removed her dusty white sandals from her feet.

Brian—Brian had come back last night. He had come to the meeting. He had carried her away.

Then she heard the sound, and the blood in her veins went icy. The sound of conch shells, blowing clear across the island.

The call of the conch shells!

She slid from the bed and dashed barefoot out into the hallway. She collided with Tyrone, who was coming to her. She put her hand on his chest.

"What is it? What is it?"

"Uprising," he said tersely. "Brian is breaking out the rifles and handguns. Come along." He had his hand on her wrist, drawing her to Brian's study.

She was only half awake, stumbling as Tyrone drew her along. Liane was there in the shadows, her dark eyes dazed, her hand moving as if brushing cobwebs from before her face. Julius, Donald Keller, the Leonis, and Astrid Larsen were huddled together, waiting fearfully for—they knew not what . . .

Near the mine entrance on the Mountain of the Cat, Pedro Ortega was shouting his orders. He was pleased. Things had gone well after all. Brian Cameron had broken into the meeting, and it had been taken as a bad omen. Now the men were drinking heavily. They would follow him.

"Bring the explosives up here! The long twine—yes, that is what I wish." He knew how to handle explosives. Auguste brought the sticks of dynamite to him silently, handing them to Pedro humbly, his head bowed, his face troubled.

Nathaniel came up. "This is wrong," he said, in a low tone, his face contorted with worry. "We must consult again—"

"The time for consulting is gone!" Pedro berated him and the other men. "The time for action is here! The gods are furious with us for not acting! Did you not hear the jaguar crying out last night?"

They nodded, for they had all heard the cats. Nervously they peered about. Even in the bright daylight, with men all about, they feared the giant yellow cats that lived in the branches of trees and hid in caves all about the sacred mountain.

"Nathaniel, you will go into the tunnel and set the explosives with me," Pedro commanded. He pushed the man before him, but Nathaniel dared not protest again.

Pedro swiftly set the sticks of dynamite where he wished, then drew out the lines. Near the entrance to the mine, he said, "Now go back and make sure all are connected."

Nathaniel looked as though he would protest. Pedro gave him a rough shove, which sent the younger man down again into the copper mine. Then Pedro came out, carefully dangling the lines of the explosive from his hand. He scratched a match.

Auguste called, "Wait! Nathaniel has not yet come out!"

Damn the man. Interfering—

"He chose to remain," said Pedro shortly, and lit the end of the white strands. He stood back as the fire raced swiftly along the lines.

In a minute it went up—one explosion, then

another, then another. The earth rumbled, the mountain roared, and dirt began to fly. Pedro ran and so did the others, before the massive explosion.

Auguste caught his shoulder, his young face anguished. "Nathaniel—in there. You have killed him!"

"He has killed himself. He went back of his own will. The gods were angry—he is the sacrifice," said Pedro smoothly, giving a quick look at the other men. "Anyway, it is too late to persuade him otherwise!"

Auguste stared at the blocked mine entrance, the piles of dirt and stones and huge rocks that still tumbled down, roaring over the cliffs and down the sides of the mountain. He passed his hand over his eyes in horror and disbelief.

Pedro did not wait. He sent the bottles of rum around again, ordering the men to blow again on the conch shells. The menacing warning signals were blown again, echoing across the small island.

Pedro exulted. His moment had come. He lifted his rifle high in his hand and waved it. His blood-red shirt was dusty, his face dirty, his tongue full of dirt. But he was beginning their revolution!

"Come, follow me!" he cried. "Now we drive out the white man from the island. The island belongs to us! We shall rule again, as our forefathers ruled themselves! Come, follow me to the great hall of the white man! We will throw them all into the sea!"

He set out at a run. His words caught fire, and they followed him, shouting, some with guns, most with long sticks and conch shells, which they paused to blow at intervals. Some two dozen men ran with them. Pedro promised himself to get rid of Auguste also, very soon. He was an intelligent man, and protested too much. He must be killed.

They ran, walked, paused to drink and blow the shells, then ran again, across the island, past the cane fields. Yes, those also should belong to Pedro Ortega, he promised himself gleefully. They would be planted again, harvested, and rum made from it. He would be wealthy. He would have his own women, and his power would be absolute! They would have a great feast to Ogun, his own god, by tonight!

Donald Keller called down from the red-tiled roof, where he had perched himself. "They're coming, Cameron! Across the cane fields!"

It was close to dusk, but he could see the dark figures, with the red-clad figure in the lead, and they were waving rifles and sticks.

"Come on down!" called Brian. Keller slid down, jumping the last few feet easily. His usually calm face was alive with excitement.

They closed and locked the last of the great doors, and opened the smaller windows, so that they could shoot out into the night if the men would not listen to reason. Brian had armed them all. Julius, Giovanni Leoni and his wife, who unexpectedly knew how to use a rifle. Donald Keller had his own revolver with him. Astrid's hand had shaken when he pressed a small revolver in it, and Brian had thought grimly that she was probably wishing she had returned to Miami with him.

He had questioned Tyrone and Silva and Liane. They all knew how to use weapons, and he gave each a revolver, plus a rifle to Tyrone. Then he made Silva promise to remain inside in the inner hallway, where no stray shots could reach her. Liane had disappeared; he thought she had gone toward the kitchen. The chef, disclaiming any love for violence, had gone down into his cool pantry, where he waited with a meat cleaver, his face pasty-white.

The house servants had all disappeared. The stable boys, brought over from Miami, were in the stables with the doors locked, promising to guard the horses with their lives. Brian hoped they had sense enough to keep quiet.

They waited, but not long. Pedro broke into the open ground about Cameron Hall, shouting.

"You white man! You give up to us! We belong this island. You don't belong! You must leave!"

"You don't belong here, either!" called Brian grimly. "I hear you got thrown off more islands than any other man I ever knew! What did they tell you on Haiti? Never come back, evil one? What did they tell you on Jamaica? Never come back to molest their women again?" Antonio had told him plenty, with details.

There was a brief silence. Silva, her eyes shining with pride, listened to her husband. Where had he heard about Pedro Ortega?

"This is our island!" Pedro called again. "Tell him, men of Desirée! This is our island. He does not belong here! He must go! All white men must go!"

"My people have lived here for many years," called Brian clearly. "They have worked the land, they have paid fairly, they have given medical help, and they have even allowed strangers such as Pedro Ortega to find sanctuary here! Is this our reward? I think he does not speak for all of you!"

"That man is crazy fool! He is a lying white man! Kill him, kill all whites!" cried Pedro in a wild fury. He shot off his rifle toward the house.

Silva cringed, even in the hallway, at the blast of rifle fire and revolvers. Brian shouted, "Hold your fire! Wait till they come closer! Get a man for every bullet!"

"Oh, God," moaned Silva. What she had feared had come to pass. She longed for Liane to come and wait with her. Where had Liane gone?

The noise was deafening. Rifles flared, revolvers blazed, a fire was set in the bushes of the garden where Silva had sat quietly only yesterday. She peered around the corner into the dark drawing room, where Brian stood with his rifle, poised alertly, waiting grimly. He had not yet fired; he waited, watching.

He might be killed! The man she loved! She realized suddenly that he did not know she loved him. She watched in an agony of apprehension. Brian saw her reflection in the glass of the window.

He did not turn. "Go back, Silva! Do not show yourself!" he snapped brusquely. "Sit down in the hallway."

She moved back, hurt by his abruptness. She sat down slowly in the hallway, hugging herself, for she was cold and chilled. She wondered briefly about the huge explosions they had heard earlier. Had the mine blown up? The smelter had not yet been rebuilt, so it was probably the mine.

Mickey McCoy, in his bed, hugged his pet shotgun to him, thinking also about the explosion. It had been the mine, he thought mournfully. All that work gone up in smoke. All to be done again.

Liane huddled in her dark cloak, lying on the flat red-tiled roof of Cameron Hall. She had found a small inner stairway one day, and tonight it had proved useful. Up on the roof, she could watch and wait, and commune silently with the spirit of her mother. She had been deeply troubled, and she knew more trouble was coming.

Full darkness came. Occasionally someone shouted tauntingly and fired at the hall. Judging from the thickness of the voices, the men were drinking again. Brian watched and waited with deadly patience in the shadow of the velvet curtains of the drawing room. He did not want to kill—unless he had to.

The firing died down. By midnight the natives outside had settled down at some distance, with a fire to warm them and jugs to pass around. Pedro paced about impatiently. He urged them to attack the hall, but they would not until morning.

Brian reached the same conclusion. He and Donald Keller conferred in low tones. The man knew what he was doing, and Brian smiled slightly to himself in the darkness. Yes, he was experienced at this! But Keller seemed careful not to reveal how much experience he had.

They brought out mattresses from several bedrooms, and Brian insisted that half the group sleep while the rest watched. At about four he lay down for a few hours. Donald Keller promised to waken him when dawn broke.

Silva lay near him, sleeping heavily, her drawn face turned to the wall. Brian made sure she was covered with her cloak, gently tucked it about her throat, and lay down beside her. Astrid's eyes gleamed at him like a cat's in the darkness. She was frightened and angry.

On the roof, Liane was chilled, but she was kept awake by the coolness and was grateful for that. She watched and waited, her loaded revolver at her hand. Her spine prickled with warnings, and she heard her mother speak to her in the night wind.

Dawn came. Brian got up, and the others roused when rifles began to bang at the building. "They'll try to rush us," said Brian to Silva crisply. "Stay here in the hallway. Don't show yourself at all!"

She nodded, rubbing sleep from her eyes, looking about in a daze. Astrid stumbled up to her as Brian went into the drawing room.

"This is all your fault, you—you primitive fool!" Astrid cursed her. "If it hadn't been for you, we should have been gone long ago! It's all your fault!"

She seemed haggard, older than her years. Silva simply stared at her, then turned away, brushing out her crumpled dress.

Mrs. Leoni said, "We'll go to the dining room, Giovanni and I. We can watch there."

Silva nodded, her lips unable to form a smile. She felt forlorn. Was it truly her fault? Would Brian also blame her?

The firing went on. The natives tried a halfhearted rush at the great white hall, well bolted and barred.

They were sobered by the night, and they had run out of rum. Many rubbed their heads and wondered why they had come at all. Pedro cursed them heartily, and tried to shove them into another attack.

Silva heard Brian say, "I think they are about out of ammunition. Keller, can you see beyond the wall?"

"Right," said Keller's cool tones. "They are standing there, arguing with the man in the red shirt."

Silva could not stay hidden any longer. She slipped into the front hallway and peered out the windows of the dining room near the Leonis. She could see from there, beyond the swimming pool, a small group of men gathered about Pedro Ortega. He was arguing with them, his arms waving passionately, his face contorted with rage.

Maybe this was the moment.

She saw Auguste, shaking his head, shrugging his shoulders, his rifle pointed to the ground. On a desperate impulse she opened the window slightly and called.

"Auguste! Hear me! Leave off from following that evil man, Pedro Ortega! He brings nothing but trouble!"

Silence. The men turned toward the hall, startled by her clear tones, staring in her direction. Giovanni Leoni tried to urge her away from the window. She shook her head swiftly.

"No, no, let me speak to them. Auguste!" she called again. "Emile! Enrique! Do not follow that man! He causes much trouble wherever he goes. Do you wish your wives to be without husbands? Do you wish your children to weep over your dead bodies? Do not follow him!"

There was no answer, but the men were muttering to each other uneasily. Brian strode from the drawing room, found Silva, and tried to urge her away.

"My God, Silva, they could shoot you! Come away from that window!" He had his heavy hands on her shoulders. She put one slim hand on his.

"No, no, they are listening to me. Let me talk to them," she urged.

Keller, behind him, said, "Yes, she is right. They are listening. Go on, little girl—"

Brian's hands tightened so they were painful on her. But she felt his warmth and comfort as he stood behind her, ready to fling her away from the window should a man raise his weapon.

"Where is Nathaniel? He does not follow Pedro Ortega!" she shouted.

Auguste shouted back, "Nathaniel is dead! He died in the explosion of the mine!"

Silva put her hand to her mouth. "Oh—no—no—" she whispered.

Liane, on the roof, put her fist to her mouth. Another score against Pedro, she thought in desolation. Somehow she knew that Nathaniel had not died of his own hand. It must have been Pedro. Nathaniel, her first love, the man who had held her so gently, with such sweet passion . . .

"It was the rum in you," called Silva again. "It must have been the rum, and the evil words of Pedro, who follows Ogun and twists all to his evil ways. Do not listen to him! Or you too shall die with no hope of heaven! The Camerons have been good to you also. They have been easy with you; they have given you much good. How can you forget so soon?"

Silence from the natives, who hung their heads unhappily. Pedro stared in futile anger at the great white hall. Again Silva's voice came clearly.

"Go away, my friends! Talk to Papa Henri, consult the gods! See what they tell you, what is evil and what is good! I beg you, do not follow Ortega! Have I ever said wrong to you? You know who raised me—it was the good Maria Luisa, who raised me and my twin brother. With wisdom she caused me to grow and to learn of your ways. I beg you, my friends, to listen to me!"

Pedro roared out, "Not that white woman! She

marry with the white man! She wears the jewels of the white man, the wealth of the whites hangs about her neck! What does she know of us?"

"I have lived here for thirteen years, Pedro Ortega! How long have you lived here?" called her clear, bell-like voice.

Auguste stared at Pedro, then turned from him and addressed the men rapidly. And they began to drift away, first the men on the fringes, then the others, and Auguste, leaving only Pedro and Rodrigues standing there just beyond the swimming pool.

Pedro lifted his rifle and pointed it at the windows. Brian yanked Silva away from the window and pressed her against the wall, his face dark with fury. But, watching, he saw that Rodrigues had turned away, and finally Pedro Ortega, raging, went away also, beyond the hedges, out of sight.

"Are they—gone?" whispered Mrs. Leoni. "Oh, you brave girl, Silva!" she sighed when Brian nodded. "Oh, that turned the tide of it. I've never been so frightened!"

But she had stood there, courageously, with a rifle in her hands, while Astrid cringed on the floor of the hallway, Silva realized. She smiled at the woman, patting her shoulder.

"I think they have gone now," she sighed. "Once the rum is gone from them, and they have time to consult with each other and Papa Henri, they will see the foolishness of their ways."

"I wish I shared your faith," said Brian dryly. "And, Silva, if you ever—if you ever put yourself in danger like that again—" He could not finish the threat. He caught her up in his arms so her small feet dangled helplessly above the floor, hugged her tightly, and pressed a kiss against her neck. She felt the weariness of him, the long strain, in the rare unsteadiness of his voice.

"You've got yourself a woman there," approved

Giovanni Leoni, his red face grinning with relief, as he set down the rifle.

Astrid leaned against the door. "Quite the little heroine," she mocked tonelessly. "Well, is it over? Can we breathe? Is it too much to ask for some coffee?"

"I think we had best be careful," said Donald Keller quietly. "I'll go out and scout around. We'd better be sure they did leave before we take too much for granted."

"Good idea. We'll give them an hour, then go out." Brian set the rifle on a chair and wiped his hand across his face. "I'll see if the chef is up to coffee."

Silva started out, but he told her brusquely to wait in the hallway. "The danger isn't over. Where is Tyrone?"

"At the back, overlooking the gates and the stables."

"Good lad. Keller, you might see that he is all right. Where is Liane?" Brian was looking about, mentally counting everyone.

Tyrone was found, and was glad of some coffee when Donald took it to him. But Liane had disappeared. Silva was concerned, but knowing Liane, she thought she had slipped out to see what was going on, perhaps to try to use her influence. She would return.

The chef came up from the pantry. He was the only one who had had any sleep to speak of that night. He put down his meat cleaver thankfully, and put on the water to boil.

The men watched and waited. Silva took coffee to them, then some ham and eggs, but still there was no sound from outdoors. The natives seemed to have melted away.

After more than an hour, Brian decided to go out and scout around. He reloaded his rifle, checked the loads in his revolver, and put a knife in his pocket. Donald Keller was already doing the same, with a professional ease that made Silva stare curiously.

Tyrone offered to go along, but Brian said, "You stay here, look after your sister. Leoni, keep the doors locked after us. We'll give a shout when we come back. Don't open to anyone but us, or Liane, if she returns."

"Right you are." Giovanni swelled with importance at the task. He seemed to have changed in the night, lost his nervousness and slightly fawning air, to gain in stature, thought Silva. And Mrs. Leoni had showed them all her courage. Only Astrid had remained sullenly in the hallway, afraid to venture out, her haggard face streaked with ruined makeup, her hair every which way, her dress crumpled.

The men watched, listened, then finally unlocked one door, toward the pool, and went out. Leoni locked the door after them, and remained on guard. Tyrone had gone back to his own post at the other side of the house. So they waited again.

Julius walked from one bedroom to the other, along the outside walls, meditating.

Chapter 31

Silva felt ready to collapse. She had been nerved up to anything, but now that Brian had gone out, she wanted to sleep and sleep. And have him come back safely. She said little prayers rapidly to herself as she went about the house, making sure Tyrone was all right. He gave her a grin and a wave from the window where he crouched.

She returned finally to the drawing room, to find Astrid smoking one cigarette after another, perched on the arm of a chair, looking out nervously at the garden. The hard blue eyes stared at Silva as she entered.

"You would like some coffee later, Mrs. Larsen?" asked Silva politely.

The woman just stared. She had a wild look to her, the streaked makeup looking clownish, the thick blonde hair streaming untidily about her shoulders. The blue silk dress would never look beautiful again, torn at the hem and streaked with dirt. She made no answer. Silva hesitated, then went out again.

Mrs. Leoni sat down with Silva at the dining-room table. They drank more coffee. Silva talked to her absently, half of her attention on the outdoors, where Brian might come.

"I wonder where your friend Liane went to," said Mrs. Leoni curiously.

Silva shook her head. "She must have gone to talk to them," she said. "I have not seen her since yesterday. She will return." She wished she could feel more confident. She thought of Nathaniel, dying in the mine explosion. Poor Liane, did she have any more feeling for him?

"Does this often happen?" asked Mrs. Leoni.

"No, never. The islanders are contented. It is Pedro Ortega who does this," Silva explained. "He is a man who wishes power and money."

"Well, no offense meant, but I'll be glad to be back in New York City," Mrs. Leoni sighed, her look going to her husband.

"I am sorry you have had such a bad time of it," said Silva.

They were talking idly, both listening to the sounds from outside. They heard the low murmur of a man's voice. Silva stiffened. "Is that Brian?" she murmured.

Then, shockingly, into the room from the hallway stepped Rodrigues, a rifle in his hands. He wore a dusty red shirt and dirty gray pants. He stared at Silva, sitting there. He came over to her, jerked her to her feet, and held her with one great hand. Behind him lounged Astrid, smirking.

"Where did you come from? How did you get in?" gasped Silva.

"I let him in," bragged Astrid, an unholy light in her hard blue eyes. "He just wants you, Silva. He promised to let the rest of us go!"

"You devil of a woman," gasped Giovanni furiously. He started to lift his rifle. Rodrigues pointed his gun.

"Drop it, or the girl dies!" he snapped. Giovanni Leoni looked at him longingly, then slowly set down his rifle, his red face angry.

Behind Astrid came Pedro Ortega, stepping so softly he startled the woman when he shoved her aside. "Got the woman? Good. Take her out. Where is Brian Cameron?"

Silva swallowed. She must protect Brian. "He went out—he is looking for you, with a rifle in his hands!" she said defiantly.

"I look around. Where is Liane?"

"She went away yesterday," said Mrs. Leoni quickly.

"You take the girl to the boat," said Pedro to Rodrigues. "I kill Brian Cameron. Then I come."

Silva did not understand it all. How could Astrid Larsen, deep as her hate was, let Rodrigues and Pedro into the locked Hall? Didn't she understand her own danger?

But Silva had no time to ponder this. Rodrigues took her with him, out through the drawing room, through the unlocked French doors, shoving her onto the terrace. They had two horses tied out there. She wondered what had happened to the stable boys, though they had probably hidden themselves away when they saw Pedro coming.

Liane, from her perch up on the red-tiled roof, watched, and her eyes narrowed in fury. She had heard the low-toned conversation of Rodrigues and Astrid, had seen the men enter. But she could do nothing alone. She was not sure of her ability to shoot with deadly accuracy. She knew where Brian had gone, for she had watched, and she would tell him as soon as he returned. Now she watched as Rodrigues slung Silva up on the horse and mounted bareback behind her.

He slapped the horse with his hand, and they set off across the garden, past the hedges, to the cane fields. He rode swiftly, cursing, laughing, hugging Silva.

"Now I have you! We take you with us, huh?" he bragged. "Me and Pedro Ortega, we run the island. We take the money. Soon all the white men gone! You be my woman—for a time!"

She shuddered in his tight hold. But she knew enough to keep quiet. She closed her eyes and prayed for Brian to find her in time, or for a swift death if he did not. Then she opened her eyes, and observed where they went.

They were soon at the hidden boat dock where Pedro kept his swift motor launch. Rodrigues shoved Silva aboard and looked nervously about, muttering. "You get below," he decided finally. "We wait." He shoved her down into the narrow passageway to the hold.

She saw in the hold the huge jugs of rum. They were going to Miami, or to the Florida Keys with the load of rum, she guessed. Then what? But by that time Brian might be dead!

She closed her eyes, brushing her hand over them. Oh, that evil Astrid Larsen! Pedro would kill Brian—would kill him!

She sat on a crude chair and waited, her hands clasped. She heard voices, then a commotion, and someone was pushed down into the hold with her. She shot up from the chair, then staggered at the weight of the young man pushed toward her.

"Tyrone!" she cried, holding him. His head was bloody from a cut, and he seemed to be unsteady on his feet.

Rodrigues, behind him, lifted his gun and pistol-whipped Tyrone on the back of the head. He went down like a log. Silva cried out again, and knelt beside him.

Rodrigues grabbed her, dropped his pistol, caught up a length of rope, and tied Silva. Then he tied the unconscious Tyrone with his hands behind his back, leaving him on the floor.

"Let me loose—let me bathe his head—" Silva begged frantically.

"He all right. Just asleep," said Rodrigues callously. "He no matter." He went up again, slamming the door to the hold after him.

Silva heard stamping about overhead, but no voices. Rodrigues seemed nervous, pacing back and forth. Finally he came below, where Tyrone was stirring. Rodrigues gave him a sharp look and tried the bonds.

"Oh, please let me go, so I can help Tyrone," begged Silva.

"No. We go to Miami, then come back to Desirée, rule this island," said Rodrigues. He opened one of the jugs, took a long drink of the contents, sighed, and wiped his mouth. "We go now. Pedro not come yet. He come in another boat. We start out."

"Why have you done this?" she sighed. "Oh, the white men were good to you. Brian Cameron was good—"

"All is ours now," said Rodrigues. "You my woman. Nothing belong to Cameron. And the sacred mountain is safe. Pedro Ortega blow up the mine, he kill Cameron. Now we own all."

"After Pedro Ortega has your help, he will take all," said Silva deliberately. "Do you think he will share anything with you? He wants all the money, all the rum, all the women, all the power. He is not a man to give. He only takes."

A frown wrinkled the big man's forehead. He grumbled, glared at her, and stamped away. He slammed shut the door once more, and in the semi-darkness Silva saw her twin stirring, blood trickling down his face. She was tied so tightly she could not even wriggle over to him.

She heard the motor start, felt the throbbing of the small motor launch as Rodrigues started out of the harbor. In despair, she leaned helplessly back against the small narrow bunk and drew a sobbing breath. Could anyone help her now?

At Cameron Hall, Brian had returned with Donald Keller. Giovanni Leoni let him in, his usually red face pale.

"She's gone," he said at once.

Brian stared at him, then glanced about the room. "Silva?"

He could not believe it. All was in order. But Astrid

sat on a chair, grinning, and Mrs. Leoni was pacing up and down.

"The house was locked. How—?"

"Mrs. Larsen let Rodrigues and Pedro Ortega in. Rodrigues took Silva away."

Brian turned on Astrid, and she shrank from him. He yanked her from the chair. "For what reason! Why the hell— What did you do, woman?"

"He said he would let us all go—he wanted only Silva. Why not? She's only an island brat—"

Brian lifted his fist to her, and struck her to the floor. She slid down, unconscious. Mrs. Leoni gasped. The other two men only looked at Astrid, dispassionately. Brian turned from the woman.

"Where did they go? Where did they take her?" he asked, wild with despair.

"I don't know—" Giovanni said. He hung his head. "I would have killed him—but he had the rifle on us—"

Brian cut him off with a gesture.

"I'll go. The island isn't large—I'll find her if I have to turn it upside down!"

He ran out the door. Keller ran after him. "I'm coming also," he said briskly.

Liane met them inside the garden, standing there with three horses and a stable boy. "I saw you come in," she said.

"Where did Silva go?"

"They took her to the boats," said Liane. "I watch —from the roof. They go south. They will go to the motor launch. Rodrigues take Silva with him. Pedro search for you, then he take other horse and go."

"Good girl." He took the horse's reins from her, and swung up. Keller took the second horse. Liane accepted help from the stable boy and swung awkwardly into the saddle of the third. "You had best not come, Liane."

"I will come. I know where they keep the rum boats. I must come with you."

Keller gave her a sharp look, then they followed Brian. Keller remained beside her.

Presently, in the fast pace, they drew abreast of Brian again. Liane said, "Tyrone follow them. I see him go."

"Tyrone!" said Brian sharply. "What can he do?"

"He knows where they go," she said thoughtfully. "But he is not sly. They may hurt him. They may use him to force Silva to submit to them. They want her as their woman, both of them."

Brian shuddered, his face grim, his mind confused. He had thought all was well when he set out to survey the grounds and see if they had left. He had thought Silva was safe, his silver-haired love, and instead he had left her to terrible danger.

The horses pounded on the hard earth, just beyond the cane fields. Brian lifted his gaze to where smoke still rose from the sacred mountain, where the mine shaft had been dynamited. All that work to do again! All that work—or would he? Somehow he was beginning to believe that all the trouble had started when he sank the mine shaft and tried to take out the copper. Perhaps Silva was right, that the sacred Mountain of the Cat must be left in peace.

"Did anyone know where you were?" Keller asked Liane.

She gave him a slight smile. "Julius see me. He say nothing. He lift his hand to me, that is all. He guards near Tyrone, so he sees the stables. He knows that we go."

"Julius likes you very much. I'm surprised he let you go." Keller was thoughtful as they rode along.

Liane looked enigmatic. In the night Julius had crept up the stairs, had brought her a hot cup of coffee and a thick sandwich of ham. They had talked in whispers, then he had gone down again. He had not touched her, yet she had felt his closeness and warmth and concern.

He was an older man, yet young in his outlook, a

skillful artist, who stared at her sometimes as though he would see through her to the bones. He liked her. She wondered what he wanted of her. He had asked nothing but that she pose for him. Yet somehow she knew he wanted more of her. What did he want? What all men wanted, her body? Or did he like also the mind of her, the dreaming, the softness, some wisdom, all that made her a woman?

Then her mind cleared of all those thoughts. She must think of Nathaniel, dead in the mine shaft. Of Maria Luisa, dead and under the earth, with the blood streaming from her when Pedro had struck her down in senseless anger. She must avenge them! She needed a clear, cool head to get her revenge. The gods must allow this!

She prayed silently for revenge to come on Pedro, who had done so much evil. And she prayed that her hand would help in this revenge, that she might sleep again in ease.

The paths parted, one going to the secret place where the rum motor launches were kept, the other to the dock. Liane motioned to the first path. Brian shook his head, and pointed.

"Out there—they have gone out on the open waters," he said curtly, a white line about his mouth. They followed his gaze and saw the motor launch cutting a white path through the blue-green waves.

He turned the horse toward the docks, and they followed him to where his own motor launch was tied up. He dismounted, slung the reins over the horse's sweaty head, and ran to the boat. Keller paused only to help Liane down, and they followed.

Brian was already at the wheel, studying the fuel gauge. "Full, thank God," he said tersely, and started the engine. The launch rocked deeply. Keller helped Liane get her balance, and she sat down on the deck. Keller remained near the wheel, watching narrowly as Brian skimmed the boat out to sea, following relentlessly in the wake of the first launch.

The other boat was not going very fast. Rodrigues evidently thought time was on his side. Then he glanced over his shoulder, as the other boat's noise reached him. He opened up, and zoomed out, the boat fairly leaping in the water.

Brian's mouth tightened cruelly, and he followed, matching the speed, exceeding it. Keller noticed the boat was reaching thirty knots.

"Can you run this boat?" Brian shouted to Keller as they began to catch up with the other launch in the open waters. Keller nodded, and stepped into Brian's place before the wheel. Brian snatched up his rifle in one hand, the megaphone in the other.

"Rodrigues!" he yelled. "Rodrigues! You can't get away. Come about!"

A defiant yell was his only answer. "Faster!" Brian shouted.

Keller opened the throttle up all the way, and began skillfully edging the boat closer to the other.

"Turn about! I'm going to board you—or ram you!" Brian yelled.

"Go to hell!"

The cry drifted across the waters. The men and Liane, watching, saw no sign of bright silvery heads. No Silva, no Tyrone. Where could they be?

They were watching so intently that they did not see the man come up silently from inside Brian's boat. Pedro Ortega was on them, catching hold of Liane, pressing a revolver to her head, a wild grin wreathing his thick lips.

She screamed out, and Brian turned. Keller jerked about, then turned his attention again to the wheel of the boat. Pedro must have hidden below, in the cabin of Brian's boat.

Rodrigues, watching, let out a wild yell of triumph.

"Drop your rifle!" Pedro ordered Brian. Brian, a silent curse on his mouth, dropped it near his feet.

Just then Liane bent and bit the hand of the big

man who held her, bit it viciously, so that blood spurted where her small teeth had dug deep.

"You bitch!" He swung on her, knocking her to the deck.

Brian sprang at him, and grappled with him. The revolver wavered in the air, went up, then down, up again. Keller was fastening the wheel; he had slowed to a stop as swiftly as possible. He leaned to grab the rifle, but Pedro saw the move and shot at him.

Keller fell, a revolver bullet in his shoulder, a trail of blood spreading across his chest. He lay limply.

Pedro turned on Brian again. Brian fought him desperately, trying to knock him out. But Ortega had a revolver, and Brian had nothing but his fists. He caught at the brown arm, held it high, swung at Ortega with his other fist. Pedro was slippery as an eel, greasy with engine grease, smeared with dirt from the night in the dust of the cane fields.

They fought back and forth across the deck of the slowly circling boat. Rodrigues had throttled to a halt and was watching the battle, ready with his rifle to kill Brian should he win.

Liane shook her head, in a daze, and came up on her knees. She felt her head swimming with dizziness. The men stumbled over her, and she tried to crawl out of their way. The boots thumped around her as she crouched near the rail, too far from the rifle.

Pedro got his arm free and swung it viciously at Brian. At the end of the arm was his revolver. *Crack!* Brian's head was struck. He sagged to the deck.

Pedro flung back his head in a roar of triumph. Liane let out a shrill, wild cry of despair, a thin, wailing cry high above the roar of the engines.

She came up, fighting, as he turned on her. She struggled with him, tore at the red shirt, tried to get at his throat. She was like a wild creature, a jaguar protecting her own, scratching, clawing.

He cursed her, struck at her, but she avoided him

and came clawing again, clawing at his face with her fingernails. But he pulled back, swung his big fist, and knocked her to the deck.

"Ho, Pedro! You one big fighting man!" cried Rodrigues, in high glee.

"Come about! I'm going to board you! You got the girl, Silva?" yelled Pedro.

"Sure, I got her! And Tyrone too. They tied up like chickens down there!" Rodrigues pointed to the hold of his boat, a wide grin on his brown face.

Chapter 32

Rodrigues watched as Pedro maneuvered the other cruiser closer to his, then throttled down the engine, and tossed a rope to Rodrigues. Rodrigues caught it, tied the boats lightly together with a knot of the rope.

Pedro jumped easily to the deck of the other boat. "Get the girl up here," he ordered curtly.

Rodrigues opened his mouth to ask why, then thought better of it. He went down, came up again, shoving Silva and Tyrone before him. The two blinked in the bright light, staring at Pedro.

Pedro grinned cruelly. He stared at Silva, at the light-haired twins. Then slowly his hand came up, the revolver in it.

Rodrigues leaped between them. "No—by the Gods, no! What you do, Pedro?" he yelled, reaching for the revolver. They began to fight. Silva watched in a daze. She was blinking in the light. Where had Pedro come from? Then she saw the other boat, and the motionless figures lying on the deck. Liane—Donald Keller—Brian! All motionless, Brian with blood on his face—

He must be dead! She leaned against the railing, her arms bound, moaning aloud with grief. She scarcely noticed the two natives fighting over her.

"Let the girl live!" Rodrigues pleaded. "I want her for my woman!"

"She is white! She dies! All whites will die!" Pedro cursed him, swung at him. Rodrigues ducked, and the knives came out. The men circled each other warily, fighting grins baring their tobacco-stained teeth.

Silva noticed then that lean gray forms cut the water, circling the boat. The sharks smelled blood! Some bumped against the boat, jarring it. Rodrigues slipped, went to his knees. Pedro was over him in a flash, avoiding his knife, jamming his own into the big form of Rodrigues.

Rodrigues screamed. He screamed again as the blood spurted from his chest. Pedro swung him up, in hard arms, and lifted him over his head with maddened strength.

Then—*splash!* He flung Rodrigues into the water. In an instant the sharks had gathered around, and struck. A lean brown arm stuck up from the water, Rodrigues screamed aloud, again, then—silence.

Silva shuddered and leaned against Tyrone—sickened, afraid. Pedro was turning on them.

The shout had roused Brian. In the boat next to theirs, he raised his head, shook it to clear it. He got up, staggering. Donald Keller was getting up also, to his knees. They saw Pedro Ortega in the cruiser, approaching Silva, scooping up his revolver. His face was deadly, hard, running with sweat, the eyes dark with madness.

Brian saw the line connecting the two boats. "Pull on it," he commanded Keller, and the man nodded, still dazed. Keller pulled on the rope and the boats bumped gently together as Brian gathered his wits.

He judged his distance, leaped over the railing onto the next boat, slipped, caught himself, and climbed over the rail of the motor cruiser. Pedro swung around, glaring, the revolver in his hand. He shot. Brian was under it, and to him.

The men clinched. Brian was pushing him toward the railing. His mind had but one deadly motive: to kill, to kill. This man had caused Mickey McCoy to lie injured, he had blown up the mine, and now he would kill Silva—his Silva—

Brian's mind focused on Silva, and on Pedro Ortega. The man was slippery, terrifying in his strength. But Brian must win—he must. He grappled with him, avoiding the knife, and knocked the revolver from Pedro's right hand. It spun on the deck. Silva bent to it, but her arms were tied so tightly she could not reach it. Tears of despair filled her eyes, but she blinked them away. If she had the chance, she would help.

Brian barked at her, "Keep away—against the wheel!"

She nodded and backed to the small wheelhouse. Tyrone followed her, trying to keep out of the way of the two fighting men. Brian had a grip on the arm of Pedro, holding the knife up and out of reach. They struggled back and forth across the narrow deck.

Silva glanced once toward the blue-green waters where Rodrigues had disappeared. A red film covered the water, and foam bubbled up where the sharks fought over the body and against each other. A gray form leaped up, something red in its mouth. She shuddered violently, and looked back at Brian. She prayed desperately. He must not lose this battle—he must not!

The sharks beat against the boat in their battle with each other. The boat swayed. Pedro lurched, and Brian gave him a final push. Pedro fell over the railing, and Brian shoved him deliberately overboard. Pedro let out a wild scream and disappeared into the swirling gray mass, where the sharks waited. White teeth snapped, and the water turned more red. Brian shivered, then whirled back to Silva and Tyrone.

He knew what could happen to the boat. He grabbed Pedro's knife, which had fallen on the deck, and sawed desperately through their bonds. The sharks bumped the boat again, more fiercely. The red blood had maddened them. He got Silva free, and then tossed her to the other boat. Donald Keller grabbed her and set her down on the deck. Liane was stirring, sitting up.

Brian got Tyrone cut free, then the sharks were attacking the boat. They bumped at it, they rose high in the water, frantically, raging to be at this white thing in the water. Brian heard the crack of the wood as they struck again and again.

Tyrone was still not completely free of the ropes. Brian picked him up bodily, carried him to the rail, and handed him over to Keller. The sharks were ferociously attacking now; he saw them swimming around and around the white cruiser and the gray one.

Brian leaped to the safety of the boat he owned. He cut loose the line that bound the two boats together. Then he jumped to the wheelhouse and started the engine. He swung the wheel so they were pointed away from the other boat. He had seen in the water the desperate figure of Pedro Ortega rising above the waves, then caught and drawn under again by the gray forms. The man's mouth was open in a silent scream of fear, his eyes were gone.

Then Pedro was gone.

The throb of the engine was music to Brian. He let out the engine, roaring away from the death boat. The sharks behind them circled the silent boat again and again, attacking it with their bodies and sharp teeth until the wood cracked, and they began to tear it to pieces. Some played with the two dead bodies of the men, some tore the boat to pieces, wild with fury.

Silva had seen them; so had Liane and Tyrone. The two girls thought of how the shark god had avenged Maria Luisa, as the woman had predicted. The shark god had taken Pedro and Rodrigues, and there was nothing left of them now. Maria Luisa could be at peace now.

Liane crouched over Silva. "It is done," she said, in the island patois. "It is done, and Maria Luisa is avenged. Ah, your poor arms. When we are home, I shall rub the lotion on them, and on Tyrone also."

She looked at Tyrone's head and shook her head over it. He gave her a weak smile, but he seemed dizzy, hanging his head down, holding his arms about himself. He *was* dizzy, and sick with what had almost happened to them. They would have died, but for Brian Cameron.

Brian glanced back over his shoulder at them, worriedly. Keller staggered to the wheel. "I can take it," he said. But Brian refused. The man was still weak from the bullet wound.

"Stand by to help us dock," said Brian. "I'm a bit groggy myself. That man was deadly." He bit his lips, thinking of how close it had been. He liked to think he could handle himself in a fight, but that had been too damn close.

Liane crooned a little tune to Silva and Tyrone as she shaded them from the sun. She sounded like Maria Luisa, her voice husky, singing a song that the woman had sung to them many a time. Tears stung Silva's eyes. Maria Luisa. Her spirit seemed very close to them that day. Was she satisfied now? Her killer had been killed, and the sharks had him.

Liane seemed more calm, and quiet, losing the tenseness she had had. Silva glanced up at her questioningly.

Liane nodded. "Mamacita is satisfied," she said in the patois. "I know it. Tonight I make offerings to Erzulie, and speak with Mamacita. But it is good, and all will know. Papa Henri will be happy."

Silva thought of the blonde woman who had betrayed her, coolly opening the door to her abductor. That woman had betrayed both her and Liane. What would Brian do to her? Did he like her well enough to overlook this? The idea sobered her, made her wistful. Brian had cared enough to come after her and rescue her, at the risk of his life. She looked at him, in his torn white shirt, standing at the wheel of the boat. One hand went up occasionally and rubbed at his bloody head. Compassion and love stirred in her. She wanted to make him well again, to comfort him. But did he wish this from her?

They were all weary and half sick when they docked. The five horses were waiting patiently where they had been left. Brian gathered them together and put Silva and himself on one horse, instructing Liane and Tyrone and Donald to ride the others. Silva did not seem able to ride by herself. He turned the other horse free, to be collected later. He held her gently as they rode, her head on his shoulder. He brushed back the silvery hair gently with his hand. "Soon you will be home, darling, and safe."

She gave him a tired smile. "Yes. Safe. Home."

She closed her eyes. She was so weary. They rode slowly, past the cane fields. Brian was surprised to see that the sun was not halfway across the sky. It was not even noon.

He kept a sharp eye, rifle in the scabbard, watching for any other natives. They might still have enemies. Silva seemed to read his thoughts.

"They will not harm us. It was Pedro Ortega and the rum that drove them. Auguste must be spoken to; he will be sick and ashamed."

"Auguste. Seemed like a good man. I was disappointed that he joined the rebellion," said Brian.

She roused enough to say, "He is a good man, smart also. But he was young, and drawn unwillingly into this. Pedro, he was a smart talker, always. Slick. Now Nathaniel is dead, and Auguste will know who it was who made him die. They were friends."

"Wonder if he could manage the estate here," mused Brian.

"Oh, he could!" said Silva eagerly. "I know he could. He is a good man, and he has had some schooling. He knows sums, and reading and writing."

Brian was silent then, thinking. He had revised his plans completely that day. He had no more thought of digging for copper in that Mountain of the Cat. Somehow he thought that had been the worst venture he had ever tried. And he knew what would have happened: The smoke and grit from the copper smelter and the mine would have drifted over the green island, gradually killing all the vegetation. Silva's island paradise would have died with it. He had seen other mines, and how the diseased earth had spread out over the miles, until nothing would grow.

And somehow he did not want that to happen to Desirée. It was a beautiful island, until Pedro Ortega had come—and until he himself had come, he admitted. When Brian had come, and decided to build the copper smelter and mine the earth, the island had begun to die. With the care of love, it could be restored again.

The cane would grow again, waving greenly in the sunlight, with yellow tassels on the top. They would burn the cane, with laughter and festivities, and harvest it for the sugar—not the rum which had brought more trouble to Desirée. Yes, he would give strict orders to his new foreman—Auguste or whoever he appointed—that no rum was to be made from this, except maybe a little for special occasions, he thought ruefully. He liked his own wine and rum, so why should they not have enough for themselves, just for celebrations?

They finally arrived back at the hall. The stable boys ran out to take the horses, their faces shining with great relief and grinning smiles for the boss. They chattered among themselves, exclaiming at what a day this had been. The weary horses were taken to the nearest pasture, tended carefully, rubbed down, and given water.

Brian took Silva inside. Donald was supporting Liane and Tyrone. Julius hastened out to take Liane gently by the arms and help her, his face drawn and anxious.

"You are—all right? Not hurt?" he asked. "I should not have let you go."

She was a little surprised. Did he think he could have stopped her? But she was glad for his tender concern, his support. She was shaking with delayed reaction. He took her into the drawing room, and brought a tall glass of lime at her request.

Astrid came out sullenly as Brian helped Silva into the hallway. "You—back!" She glared at Silva. "I thought you had gone with your lover!"

Silva gasped at her insolence. Brian eyed her levelly.

Mr. and Mrs. Leoni had come out, exclaiming, but on Astrid's words they were silent, watching with hard faces.

"I should like to kill you," said Brian to Astrid. "You have done such evil—you are a truly evil woman. I had not realized how much I despised you until today. If you remain here, I will kill you. So go to your room. Pack. I'm sending you away with the freighter. Go!"

She was rash enough to try to touch him. "But, Brian, darling, it was in your interest. The girl is no good. She is—"

She shrank from the wild glare of his eyes. "God, woman, don't you know how I feel? I love Silva. If you don't go—" He choked over his words.

Donald Keller took her arm, forcing her back into the hallway. "Get to your room, and stay there," he said sternly. "You've caused enough trouble. He has killed a man today. Stay out of his way, or he'll add you to his list!"

She stared at the stern-faced man, and finally believed. Her face ghastly, she ran to her room, shut and locked the door. Feverishly she began to pack. She could not get away soon enough from this horrible island!

Silva went to her room, with Brian's help. He sent for her maid. Emilie and the other servants had returned, and the woman came at once, to help her bathe and lie down. Silva was shaking, sick with all that had happened.

She could not sleep, her mind going over and over the ghastly events. She heard Brian moving around in his room, then a long silence. She thought he slept. It was late afternoon before she rose. Emilie brought her some hot tea. She drank it, and felt better.

"Sure, everyone is talking," murmured Emilie, curiosity in her stare. "What happen? That Pedro, he die?"

Silva nodded. "He tried to kill me and Tyrone. He thought he had killed Brian. Rodrigues tried to stop him from—from killing me. Pedro knifed him—threw him to the sharks. Then Brian—Brian threw Pedro to the sharks—" She swallowed over a wave of nausea, remembering.

Emilie murmured, "That is best. They bad men, they gone now. Desirée will be happy now. The gods will be happy. Papa Henri, he send word. We have the celebration tonight."

Silva nodded wearily. "Liane will go. Maybe I will go. And Tyrone."

As it turned out, Brian came also, and sat with Silva on the rush mat, watching in silence as Papa Henri conducted the service. Auguste sang and danced, and there was much singing and laughter, and prayers of thankfulness to Erzulie. Papa Henri made a long speech in his trembling voice about how Maria Luisa was pleased, and would now rest in peace. He blessed Liane and Silva and Tyrone, and was grateful to the shark god for what he had done this day. And he admonished the young, restless men who had foolishly followed an evil man.

This time Brian waited, solemnly, until the end of the ceremony, at about two in the morning, before he took Silva home. The natives had been pleased by his attendance, and shook his hand as he left. There had been no drinking that night, only reverence, and eating of sacred foods, and long draughts of cool water to quench their thirst.

"Now I can sleep," said Liane with a great sigh as they reached Cameron Hall, gleaming white in the moonlight. "Mamacita is at peace." And her face seemed relaxed and more gentle than it had been for a time.

In her bedroom, Silva thought the same thing. The tension was gone. Brian seemed to understand how they felt now, and maybe soon she could talk to him about the sacred mountain, how the people felt about it, begging him not to mine it for copper. Her heart felt lighter. In time, he might truly love her, and come to understand her also, and not think of her as a crude native girl.

Brian came to her bedroom as she lay in the dimness. She saw him, and stirred. He came on in and bent over her on the bed.

"I want to sleep with you, darling," he said tenderly.

She smiled up at him shyly and held out her arms. He bent to her, and held her to him, with a great rush of thankfulness. She had been so close to death that day, and so had he.

He got into bed with her and held her gently, not trying to make love to her. It was enough just to feel her close, and warm, her weary body relaxed against his. Tomorrow he would have a talk with Tyrone, and send for Auguste, and get things moving again. He had only a few weeks now until Christmas, and he was determined nothing would stop him from leaving with Silva after Christmas.

He had almost wrecked things, but by some great stroke of fate, all was going well again. He lay awake for a time, thinking. He had come to Desirée, with his company, contemptuous of the islanders, wishing only to get the mine working and then be away. Astrid had been an amusing interlude, though he had not made love to her on the island, not after seeing

Silva, but he might have come to that. She had appeal as a mistress.

How differently he felt now! She was a vile bitch, he thought with a shudder as he contemplated how she had almost succeeded in having Silva killed. If she remained, he would not guarantee his actions. He wanted to kill Astrid. He had never felt such blind hate in his life as when he had come home to the Hall and she had informed him with a smirk that Silva was gone, through her conniving! She must leave on the freighter, and after that he didn't care what happened to her, just so he never saw her again.

He was so fortunate; he had blundered into the happiest event of his life, he thought, holding Silva tenderly to him. This gentle, innocent girl had become his wife. She was so lovely, so good. She would have his children. She had already changed his life, so that he thought with pleasure of settling down and enjoying life with his children and her. The house in Miami—he must see about buying a fine big home for them. She would never be happy long in New York City or Europe. But they would have a beautiful honeymoon abroad, and he would show her the lovely sights he had seen alone.

Beautiful life shared—it would be more than double his pleasure, he thought. To see Venice with Silva, to ride on a gondola with her in his arms. To walk the streets of Florence, and contemplate the lovely paintings, the rusty-red walls and sienna-brown roofs. To see the grandeurs of Rome, to stand at the top of the Spanish Steps, and imagine themselves in the Rome of a thousand, two thousand years ago.

He drew a happy breath, picturing them in those places, the expression on Silva's face as she saw the beauty of them for the first time. She would want to draw and paint; he must make sure to find her canvases and sketch pads, arrange for things to be sent home. He wanted her to be comfortable with him, to be happy and content, so she would never want to leave him.

He half smiled, ruefully. In his arrogance, all his life he had thought of what he wanted, of how women could please him, of how he would work and make money and spend it as he chose. Now he could think only of the pleasure of Silva, how he could bind her to himself with silken threads, so that she never wanted to leave. That was what love did to a man. He wondered if she would ever love him, if she knew what love was. Well, he would teach her, if he could. He knew himself what love was now.

Chapter 33

Brian decided to keep the freighter there two more days, so he could clear up matters. In the afternoon he sent for Tyrone and for Donald Keller, asking them to come to his study.

A maid brought in cold drinks. After they were all served, and alone again, Brian began the conversation.

"Tyrone, you were mixed up in the rumrunning with Pedro Ortega. I want you to tell me about it: what he did, where he went. Oh—before you start, Donald Keller had best introduce himself to you."

He gave Keller a wry grin in answer to the man's surprise.

"What do you know?" asked Keller cautiously, fingering the wet glass. He drank very little, Brian had noted.

"That you're not in the stockmarket, for one thing. That you are involved in some way with the Coast Guard. Treasury Department agent, I would guess?" He knew, but he thought the man had best say it himself.

Tyrone was staring, openmouthed. Keller nodded. "Yes, but this is just for your own information. I hope you'll keep it to yourselves."

"Why did you come here?" asked Brian.

"Well—odd, actually. When you invited the Leonis to the island—and we had information that Desirée was being used as a base for rumrunning operations —I thought you must have gone into business with

Leoni. He is a known rumrunner in New York," added Donald with a slight smile. He looked more grave and professional this afternoon.

"And you thought I was involved?" asked Brian, amused. "No, thanks, I have no time to make the stuff and run it. I only drink it!" He raised his glass half mockingly to the federal agent.

"That was what I finally concluded," said Keller. "But rumrunning was going on. I tracked it to Pedro Ortega, about the time Tyrone got picked up in Miami."

"How did you get separated from Pedro?" asked Brian, turning curiously to Tyrone. "Oh, you might as well tell the whole story now."

Tyrone rubbed his sore head. "Guess I might as well. It started about a year ago. Rodrigues got me involved—he saw me looking at Oona, got her on me. She was always wanting jewelry, presents." He grimaced. "I was a fool. When Rodrigues had loaned me some money, and I had no way to repay, he got me into the rumrunning trips. Then Pedro Ortega took them over, and the business got big, and serious."

Tyrone told them the whole story, confessing frankly that he felt like a fool. He seemed sincere in vowing he would never get so involved again. Brian thought he meant it.

The next day he sent for Auguste, and had a long talk with the man. He was finally satisfied that young Auguste was intelligent and reliable, and knew about sugar-cane harvesting and planting. They discussed plans.

And the following day, Mickey McCoy, the Leonis, Donald Keller, and Astrid Larsen left the island on the freighter. Mickey McCoy would recover in Miami, and then look into some other mining interests for Brian. Brian let them all know he had no intention of continuing to mine copper on Desirée. He had told Mickey the truth, but for the others he said, "It isn't worth mining."

He meant psychologically for him and for Silva, and also for the destruction it would bring to Desirée. But he hoped word would go out to the other mining interests, and they would not attempt to come here and mine the copper when Brian's back was turned.

Silva lit up with joy. "You will not mine the copper? The sacred mountain is safe?" Her face was shining, her green eyes glowing. He looked at her with keen pleasure at her beauty, her gentleness.

"That's right, Silva. Desirée and the mountain are safe. Auguste will finish the sugar-cane harvest, and then planting will start again. He will be foreman here."

The visitors left, and then it was just Tyrone and Silva, Liane and Julius, Brian and the islanders. Julius went on with his painting, finishing it to his great satisfaction. Brian studied it, then said, "How much?"

"I want to exhibit it!" protested Julius.

Brian grinned at his friend. "You can exhibit it all you please, but you don't sell it to anyone but me."

They both stared at the picture intently. Silva came, her arm linked with Liane's, and timidly watched them. "You like it, Brian?" she asked.

He nodded. The girls were shown together, dark head and light, against the background of the island flowers, and somehow the more one looked, the more beautiful was the painting, and the more meanings one could find. "When Julius is finished exhibiting it, we'll hang it in our new home in Miami," he said.

Her face shadowed, presently she slipped away again. Julius was absorbed in persuading Liane to pose for him again. Brian followed Silva out to the gardens, and beyond, to where they could watch the brown forms in white clothing as they worked in the sugar-cane fields, singing. The melodies drifted up to them.

He put his arm about her when he came. She turned slightly and rested her head against his broad chest. He slid his hand under her thick silvery hair and gently caressed the back of her neck.

"You are not happy?" he asked softly.

"We—we will leave the island," she said, in a muffled voice.

"I want to show you the world, Silva. But we'll come back again. Don't you want to see the art, and hear the music? I told you about it—"

"Where will—Tyrone be?"

He repressed his impatience. "Julius will guide his work. I want him to pass his exams, and enter college in a year or less. And Julius will keep an eye on Liane, too. They are all three coming to join us in Italy in the spring."

"Liane also? She will come?"

"I think Julius will persuade her to come."

"He likes her, I think," said Silva slowly, thinking of the glances that had passed between them, the way his gaze lingered on her dark oval face.

"Yes, very much," said Brian, in whom Julius had confided. One day Julius might persuade Liane to marry him, when she was over the sadness that gripped her now.

An odd marriage it would be, to some ways of thinking. But Julius, though years older than she, was young at heart, and a lover of beauty. And Liane was mature for her years, and yet longing for stability and security. She needed to be loved and cared for. And Julius, for the first time in his roving life, thought Brian, had found a woman to adore.

"Desirée will still be here when we return," said Brian. "The mine will not be built, and your island will remain green and unspoiled, waiting here. And when we come, you may swim again in the lagoon—though I do not promise to let you alone to swim!"

He laughed down at her, and she blushed as she thought of how he had sought her out. He turned her gently back to the great white Cameron Hall, and they walked slowly, not speaking, just thinking.

Brian took her to the library, to show her some books about the places they would visit. He drew out volumes on England, France, Italy, Spain, and Switzerland, showing her on a map where they would travel. Her cheeks glowed with color and her eyes gleamed with excitement as she opened books and saw the beautiful art there.

"Will we see this? And this painting? And this view—and the tower there?" He laughed and drew her down to his lap, pressing a kiss to her golden-tanned throat.

"Absolutely, my sweet. Wherever you want to go, whatever you want to see."

He took the book out of her fingers and tossed it aside. They were completely alone for practically the first time since the attack on the hall.

"Silva, darling." He drew her closer and pressed a kiss on her ear. "I want to tell you something. You remember the day I came, when I rode down the hill and saw you swimming in the lagoon?"

She nodded, looking down at his pocket instead of his face.

He put a finger under her chin, lifting her face. "Look at me, darling. I want to tell you—since that day I have loved you. I thought of nothing but how to protect you, how to have the right to look after you. I was jealous of everyone who seemed to come between us."

"Ohhhh," she breathed, watching his lips move, instead of seeing his eyes. Her cheeks were pink and her lashes fluttered against his lips as he kissed the lids gently. "You—love—me?"

"Yes. And you drove me crazy! Spitting like an angry cat, pushing me away when I tried to kiss you—"

She bit her full lips. He watched them, enchanted, as she struggled to say something. She rubbed her cheek against his shoulder. He teased at the soft curls on her neck. "Silva, aren't you going to tell me—Do you like me very much?"

"Ummmm," she said, nodding her head.

He controlled his exasperation. He did not want to frighten her off. He persisted: "And how much? How much do you like me?"

She gave him a shy, wary look. "Well, I—I think I—I think I love you—"

He stared at her serious face. "You *think* you love me?" He was going to explode with frustration soon!

"Yes," she said. "You see—I know so little of the world—I mean, how people are outside—and I never did love a man before—I'm not sure."

His face flushed with fury. "Silva—you devil! You will drive me out of my mind! What kind of answer is that? You think you love me!"

She stiffened and held herself back in alarm. His arms gripped her more tightly.

"But—truly—I don't know, Brian. I mean—you have probably loved many times, and I have not. I don't know if what I feel is love—and I don't know how long you will love me . . ." Her low voice was so soft he had to bend his head to hear.

He could not decide if she spoke innocently, or if she was rebuking him for loving lightly and too often. He himself knew that never before in his life had he loved like this.

"Silva, my love! I have never felt like this in my life! Oh, I have—have known other women—" All too well, some of them, he thought grimly, known enough to be repelled by their greed. "I love you. I have made you my wife, and it is for our lifetime. I want to keep you with me forever. I want you to have my children, and make my home happy for me." He spelled it out clearly, watching her face anxiously.

"Ohhhh—is that what you mean? You love me like

a woman to have in your house?" she asked eagerly.

"Yes, of course!"

"I did not understand that," she said, and rested her head again against his shoulder. "I thought you only wanted me for a time. And often you did not treat me like a woman. Only a girl whom you kissed and put aside from more serious things."

Brian could scarcely suppress his wrath. And then, strangely, he began to laugh. He hugged her tightly. "So—you don't know if you love me or not? And you aren't sure of me! Just you wait, darling—you will be! I'm going to convince you of my feelings! You shall be left in no doubt at all!"

They sat in the big chair and talked, exploring each other's thoughts openly for a long time, and sometimes were silent to kiss, and caress.

Her small hand moved on his arm shyly, up to his shoulder, and then her fingers touched his bronzed throat. He bent his head, and she lifted her face. His mouth caught hers passionately, a little roughly, as he kissed her with desire, and adoration. He could not get enough of her sweetness. He drank thirstily of her lips, like a man in a desert with cool water offered.

And her lips moved under his, shyly beginning to respond. He could not quite believe it, and kissed her again. Her lips pressed against his as she learned how to reply to him.

"Oh, darling, darling," he whispered against her throat. He felt her lips against his cheeks. He lifted his head, and she put her slim hands on his face, and studied his deep blue eyes. Her own were misty and glowing with happiness, the expression open to him, tender and wistfully sweet.

"You do—love me—and no one else?" she whispered.

"You may be very sure of that, darling," he reassured her. He pressed his hand to her shoulder, and caressed down to the soft curve of her breast.

The next weeks were very happy ones. Auguste worked out well as foreman. Brian spent much of the time with him, showing him how to keep the accounts, how to pay the men, how to run a company store fairly. He found another man to help in the store, a crippled older man who was glad of the work, and Papa Henri vouched for his honesty.

Julius was happy, painting Liane in a variety of settings, coaching Tyrone in his schoolwork. He would stay on in Miami with Tyrone and Liane, visit the island if necessary.

Their Christmas was an extravagant one, and a strange one for Brian and Julius. They attended a religious ceremony conducted by Papa Henri and Auguste, an odd combination of a Christian ceremony and voodoo. The islanders brought flowers to the great hall, and Silva decorated the house with great vines of bougainvillea, huge crimson poinsettias, and a pine tree for Christmas.

Brian and Julius had both sent for presents. Liane was overcome with the strangeness of a mink coat, and Silva received white ermine with a mink collar. Both girls received so many dresses, suits, blouses, pins, necklaces, bracelets, and rings that they were overwhelmed. Tyrone was gleeful over his new suits and shirts, but dubious over his tight thick shoes after the ease of sandals. But Brian told him he had best get accustomed to wearing shoes.

Julius gave Brian the painting of the two girls. In return, Brian gave Julius the keys to an apartment in Miami, one with a skylight and huge rooms for books and for painting. "You'll need a big place to have Tyrone and Liane with you," said Brian, waving away Julius's thanks.

By the New Year, Brian and Silva left Desirée on the freighter. She hung over the railing, a little frightened, though Brian kept his arm about her. She was seeing the last of Desirée for many months.

"In Miami, we'll stop only long enough to pack our

suitcases. Then we're on our honeymoon at last, darling!" Brian exulted in her ear, kissing her hair quickly.

And from there, they would take a boat up to New York City, stay for a month or so in Brian's plush Fifth Avenue apartment, visit with the Leonis, see the wonders of New York City.

Then on to Europe on another ship, a great liner this time. To England, on to Holland and France—wherever they wished to wander. Silva's eyes were wide with wonder.

She waved again to Liane, to Tyrone, to Julius, to the islanders who had come out to see their silver-haired girl depart. She carried an armload of flowers, and now, on impulse, she leaned over the rail and dropped the flowers one by one, so that they floated, great crimson and yellow and pink blooms, on the white wake of their departure.

The flowers floated back slowly to the island. Silva waved again, but she could see little for the tears in her eyes. The figures waving to her grew dimmer. They were gone now. She would not see them again for a long time.

Brian's arm tightened on her waist. "You'll come back, darling," he comforted, understanding.

"We'll both come back," she whispered, and wiped the tears from her eyes.

"But first we will see the beauties of the world, my love. Though none will be so beautiful as you—" And he kissed her more passionately, though the sailors were busy on deck.

She clasped his hard arm in her hand, feeling the security of it, and gazed back toward Desirée. It was fading also now, but still she could see it in the bright morning sunlight.

They would return, she and the man she loved. But for now she must imprint on her mind, to save and bring out for moments of homesickness, the picture of Desirée.

Island of Desire

It lay like a green jewel on a bed of sapphire velvet, the island she loved. As it receded, she saw it becoming misty, soft emerald-green against the deep, vivid blue of the ocean. Her island. Desirée. Island of Desire.